P9-BZU-731

REBORN

also by F. Paul Wilson

HEALER (1976)
WHEELS WITHIN WHEELS (1978)
AN ENEMY OF THE STATE (1980)
THE KEEP (1981)
THE TOMB (1984)
THE TOUCH (1986)
BLACK WIND (1988)
SOFT & OTHERS (1989)
DYDEETOWN WORLD (1989)
THE TERY (1990)

REBORN

a novel by

F. PAUL WILSON

Illustrated by Stephen Gervais

Arlington Hts., Illinois · 1990

Trade Hardcover Edition ISBN 0-913165-52-2

Manufactured in the United States of America

FIRST EDITION

Dark Harvest / P.O. Box 941 / Arlington Heights, IL / 60006

The publishers would like to express their gratitude to the following people. Thank You: Stan and Phyllis Mikol, Kathy Jo Camacho, Dr. Stan Gurnick PhD, Wayne Sommers, Gary Fronk, Linda Solar, the people of the All American Print Center, Raymond, Teresa and Mark Stadalsky, Tom Pas, Tony Hodes, Ken and Lynda Fotos, Richard, Barb and Amy at Type Plus, and Ann Cameron Williams.

And special thanks to both F. Paul Wilson and Stephen Gervais.

for William Sloane
the early brewer of science with the supernatural

PROLOGUE

Sunday

February 11, 1968

He was calling himself Mr. Veilleur these days — Gaston Veilleur — and tonight he found it difficult to sleep. A remote uneasiness made him restless, a vague malaise nettled his mind, stirring up old memories and ancient nightmares. But he refused to give up the chase. He measured his breathing and soon found the elusive prey within his grasp. But just as he was slipping off, something dragged him back to full wakefulness.

Light. From somewhere down the hall. He lifted his head to see. The glow was coming from the linen closet. Blue-white radiance was streaming out along the edges of the closed door.

Moving carefully so as not to awaken his wife, Mr. Veilleur slipped out of bed and padded down the hall. His joints creaked in protest at the change in position. Old injuries, old wounds, reminders of each hung on, sounding little echoes from the past. He knew he was developing arthritis. No surprise there. His body looked sixty years old and had decided to begin acting accordingly.

He hesitated a moment with his hand on the knob of the closet door, then yanked it open. The very air within seemed to glow; it flowed and swirled and eddied, like burning liquid. But cold. He felt a chill as it splashed over him.

The source — what was causing this? The light seemed most intense in the rear corner of the bottom shelf, under the blankets. He reached down and pulled them away.

Mr. Veilleur bit back a cry of pain and threw an arm across his eyes as the naked brilliance lanced into his brain.

Then the glow began to fade.

When his eyes could see again, when he dared to look again, he found the source of the glow. Tucked back among the towels and sheets and blankets was what appeared to be a huge iron cross. He smiled. She'd saved it. After all these years, she'd still hung on to it.

The cross still pulsed with a cold blue radiance as he lifted it. He gripped the lower section of the upright with two hands and hefted it with an easy familiarity. Not a cross — a sword hilt. Once it had been gold and silver. After serving its purpose, it had changed. Now it was iron. *Glowing* iron.

Why? What did this mean?

Suddenly the glow faded away completely, leaving him staring at the dull gray surface of the metal. And then the metal itself began to change. He felt its surface grow coarse, saw tiny cracks appear, and then it began to crumble. In seconds it was reduced to a coarse powder that sifted and ran through his fingers like grains of sand.

Something has happened. Something has gone wrong! But what?

Slightly unnerved, Mr. Veilleur stood empty-handed in the dark and realized how quiet the world had become. All except for the sound of a jet passing high overhead.

* * *

Roderick Hanley twisted in his seat as he tried to stretch his cramped muscles and aching back. It had been a long flight from L.A., and even the extra width in first class was snug on his big frame.

"We'll be landing shortly, Dr. Hanley," the stewardess said, leaning close to him. "Can I get you anything before we close the bar?"

Hanley winked at her. "You could, but it's not stocked in the bar."

Her laugh seemed genuine. "Seriously, though . . ."

"How about another gimlet?"

"Let's see." She touched a fingertip to her chin. " 'Four- to-one vodka-to-lime with a dash of Cointreau,' right?"

"Perfect."

She touched his shoulder. "Be right back."

Pushing seventy and I can still charm them.

He smoothed back his silvery hair and squared his shoulders inside the custom-made British tweed shooting jacket. He often wondered if it was the aura of money he exuded or the burly, weathered good looks that belied his years. He was proud of both, never underestimating the power of the former and long since giving up any false modesty about the latter.

Being a Nobel prizewinner had never hurt, either.

He accepted the drink from her and took a healthy gulp, hoping the ethanol would calm his jangled nerves. The flight had seemed interminable. But at last they were approaching Idlewilde. No, it was called Kennedy Airport now, wasn't it. He hadn't been able to get used to the name change. But no matter what the place was called, they'd be safely down on terra firma shortly.

And not a moment too soon.

Commercial flights were a pain. Like being trapped at a cocktail party in you own house. If you didn't like the company you couldn't just up and leave. He much preferred the comfort and convenience of his private Learjet, where he could call all the shots. But yesterday morning he had learned that the plane would be grounded for three days, possibly five, waiting for a part. Another five days in California among those Los Angeleans who were all starting to look like hippies or Hindus or both was more than he could tolerate, so he had bitten the bullet and bought a ticket on this Boeing behemoth.

For once — just this once — he and Ed were traveling together.

He glanced at his traveling companion, dozing peacefully beside him. Edward Derr, M.D., two years younger but looking older, was used to this sort of travel. Hanley nudged him once, then again. Derr's eyes fluttered open.

"Wh-what's wrong?" he said, straightening up in his seat.

"Landing soon. Want something before we touch down?"

Derr rubbed a hand over his craggy face. "No." He closed his eyes again. "Just wake me when it's over."

"How the hell can you sleep in these seats?"

"Practice." Thirty years of regular attendance together at biological and genetic research conferences all over the world, and never once had they traveled on the same plane. Until today.

It would not do to have the pair of them die together.

There were records and journals in the Long Island house that were not yet ready for the light of day. He couldn't imagine any time in the near future when the world would be ready for them. Sometimes he wondered why he didn't simply burn them and have done with the whole affair. Sentimental reasons, he guessed. Or ego. Or both. Whatever the reason, he couldn't seem to bring himself to part with them.

A shame, really. He and Derr had made biological history and they couldn't tell anybody. That had been part of the pact they had made that day in the first week of 1942. That and the promise that when one of them died, the other would immediately destroy the sensitive records.

After a more than a quarter century of living with that pact, he should have been accustomed to it. But no. He had been in a state of constant anxiety since taking off from Los Angeles. But at last, the trip was over. All they had to do was land. They'd made it.

Suddenly came a violent jolt, a scream of agonized metal, and the 707 tilted to a crazy angle. Someone behind them in coach screamed something about a wing tearing off, and then the plane plummeted, spinning wildly.

The thought of his own death was no more than a fleeting presence in Hanley's mind. The knowledge that there would be no one left to destroy the records crowded out everything else.

"The boy!" he cried, clutching Derr's arm. "They'll find out about the boy! He'll find out about *himself!*"

And then the plane came apart around him.

Tuesday
February 20, 1968

1.

A form was taking shape out of the darkness, shadows were merging, coalescing into an unholy shape. And it moved. In utter silence, the night became flesh and glided toward her.

Jim Stevens leaned back in his chair and stared at the paper in the typewriter. This wasn't going the way he wanted. He knew what he wanted to say but the words weren't capturing it. It was almost as if he needed new words, a new language, to express himself.

He was tempted to pull one of those Hollywood scenes. Rip the paper out of the platen, ball it up, and toss it at the waste basket. But in four straight years of writing every day, Jim had learned never to throw anything away. Somewhere in the mishmash of all the unpublished words he had committed to paper might lurk a scene, an image, a turn of phrase that could prove valuable later on.

No shortage of unpublished material, unfortunately. Hundreds of pages. Two novels' worth neatly stacked in their cardboard boxes on the top shelf of the closet. He had submitted them everywhere, to every publishing house in New York that did fiction, but no one was interested.

Not that he was completely unpublished. He glanced over to where THE TREE, a modern ghost story, sat alone on the otherwise bare ego-shelf in the bookcase. Doubleday had acquired that two years ago and had published it last summer with the publicity budget accorded most first novels: zero. What few reviews it received had been as indifferent as its sales and it sank without a trace. None of the paperback houses had picked it up.

The manuscript of a fourth novel sat at the far left corner of his desk, the Doubleday rejection letter resting atop it. He had hoped the astonishing success of ROSEMARY'S BABY would open doors for this one, but no dice.

Jim reached over and picked up the letter. It was from Tim Bradford, his editor on THE TREE. Although he knew it by heart, he read it again.

> Dear Jim —
>
> Sorry, but I'm going to have to pass on ANGELICA. I like its style and I like the characters. But there's no market for the subject matter. No one will be interested in a modern day succubus. I'll repeat what I said over lunch last year: You've got talent, and you've got a good, maybe great, future ahead of you as a novelist if you'll just drop this horror stuff. There's no future in horror fiction. If you've got to do weird stuff, try sci-fi. I know you're thinking of how ROSEMARY'S BABY is still on the bestseller list, but it doesn't matter. The Levin book is an aberration. Horror is a dead end, killed by the A-bomb and Sputnik and other realities that are scary enough.

Maybe he's right, Jim thought, flipping the letter onto the desk and shaking off echoes of the crushing disappointment that had accompanied its arrival in the mail on Saturday.

But what was he to do? This "weird stuff" was all he wanted to write. He'd read science fiction as a kid and had liked it, but he didn't want to write it. Hell, he wanted to *scare* people! He remembered the ripples of fear and jolts of shock he'd received from writers like Bloch and Bradbury and Matheson and Lovecraft when he'd read them in the fifties and early sixties. He wanted to leave his own readers gasping, to do to them what the masters had done to him.

He was determined to keep at it. There was an audience for his writing, he was sure of it. All it took was a publisher with the guts to go find it. Until then he'd live with the rejection. He had known it was an integral part of a writer's life when he started; what he hadn't known was that it could hurt so much.

He closed his research books on Satanism and witchcraft and got up from the desk. Time for a break. Maybe a shave and a shower would help. He got some of his best ideas in the shower.

As he rose he heard the mail slot clank and detoured toward the front door. He turned on the hi-fi on his way through the living room. *The Rolling Stones Now!* was on the turntable; "Down the Road Apiece" began to cook through the room. The furniture was all leftovers from when Carol's folks had owned the place: austere sofas, slim-legged chairs, asymmetrical tables, lots of plastic — the "modern look" from the fifties. When they got some money, he promised himself to buy furniture designed for human beings. Or maybe a stereo, instead. But all his records were mono. So maybe the furniture would be first.

He scooped the mail off the floor. Not much there except for his paycheck from the Monroe *Express* — a fair sum this week because the paper had finally paid him for his series of feature articles on the "God Is Dead" controversy.

Great. He could buy Carol dinner tonight.

Finally to the bathroom. "Hello, Wolfman," he said to the mirror.

With his dark brown hair hanging over his thick eyebrows, his bushy muttonchop sideburns reaching almost to his jawline, and tufts of wiry hair springing from the collar of his undershirt, all framing a stubble that would have taken the average guy three days to grow, his old nickname from the Monroe High football team seemed as apt as ever. Of course, the hair on his palms had been the real clincher. *Wolfman* Stevens — the team's beast of burden, viciously ramming through the opponent's defensive line in play after play. Except for a few unfortunate accidents — to others — his football years had been good ones. Great ones.

He was adopting the new long-haired look. It hid his ears, which had always stuck out a little farther than he liked.

As he lathered up the heavy stubble on his face, he wished someone would invent a cream or something that would stop beard growth for a week or more. He'd pay just about anything for a product like that. Anything so he wouldn't have to go through this torturous ritual every day, sometimes twice a day.

He scraped the Gillette Blue Blade in various directions along his face and neck until they were reasonably smooth, then gave his palms a quick once-over. As he was reaching for the hot water knob in the shower, he heard a familiar voice from the direction of the living room.

"Jimmy? Are you here, Jimmy?"

The thick Georgia accent made it sound like "Jimmeh? Are you heah, Jimmeh?"

"Yeah, Ma. I'm here."

"Just stopped by to make a delivery."

Jim met her in the kitchen where he found her placing a fresh apple pie on the counter.

"What's that awful music?" she said. "Dear me, it boggles the ears."

"The Stones, Ma."

"You'll be thirty in four years. Aren't you just a little old for that sort of thing?"

"Nah! Brian Jones and I are the same age. And I'm younger than Watts and Wyman."

"Who are they?"

"Never mind."

He ducked into the living room and turned off the hi-fi. When he returned to the kitchen, she had taken off her heavy cloth coat and laid it across the back of one of the dinette chairs. She was wearing a red sweater and gray wool slacks underneath. Emma Stevens was a short, trim, shapely woman in her late forties. Despite the faint touches of gray in her brown hair, she could still draw stares from much younger men. She wore a bit more make-up and tended to wear clothes that were a bit tighter than Jim liked to see on the woman he called Mother, but at heart he knew she was a homebody who seemed happiest when cleaning her house and baking. She was a bundle of energy who volunteered for all the charitable functions in town, no matter whether the beneficiary was Our Lady of Perpetual Sorrow or the Monroe High School band.

"I had extra apples left over after I made Dad's pie, so I made one for you and Carol. Apple was always your favorite."

"Still is, Ma." He bent to kiss her on the cheek. "Thanks."

"I brought some Paladec, too. For Carol. She's looking a bit poorly lately. Some vitamins every day will make her feel better."

"Carol's just fine, Ma."

"She doesn't look it. Looks peaked. I don't know what to contribute it to, do you?"

"'*At*tribute it to,' Ma. *At*."

"*At*? I don't know what to contribute it *at*? That doesn't sound right."

Jim bit his lip. "Well, at least we both agree on that."

"So!" she said, brushing imaginary crumbs off her hands and looking around the kitchen. Jim knew she was inspecting the countertops and the floors to see if Carol was still measuring up to the standards of spotlessness Ma had adhered to all of Jim's life. "How are things?"

"Fine, Ma. How about you and Dad?"

"Fine. Dad's at work."

"So's Carol. She's at work, too."

"Were you writing when I came in?"

"Uh-huh."

It wasn't exactly the truth, but what the hell. Ma didn't consider freelance writing Real Work anyway. When Jim rode the night desk part time on the Monroe *Express*, that was Real Work because he got paid for it. He might sit there for hours, doing nothing more than twiddling his thumbs as he waited for something newsworthy to happen in the Incorporated Village of Monroe, Long Island, but Ma considered that Real Work. Hunching over a typewriter and dragging sentences kicking and squealing from his brain to put on paper was something else.

Jim waited patiently. Finally, she said it.

"Any news?"

"No, Ma. There's no 'news.' Why do you keep bugging me about that?"

"Because it's a mother's parenteral obligation —"

"'Parental,' Ma. 'Par*en*tal.'"

"That's what I said: Parenteral obligation to keep checking as to if and when she's going to become a grandmother."

"Believe me, Ma. When *we* know, *you'll* know. I promise."

"Okay." She smiled. "But remember, if Carol should drop by some day and say, 'Oh, by the way, I'm three months' pregnant,' I'll never forgive you."

"Sure you will." He kissed her forehead. "Now, if you don't mind, I've got to —"

The doorbell rang.

"Are you expecting company?" his mother said.

"No. Not even you."

Jim went to the front door and found the mailman standing on the front step holding a letter.

"Special delivery, Jim. Almost forgot it."

Jim's heart began to race as he signed the return receipt. "Thanks, Carl." Maybe they'd had a change of heart at Doubleday.

"Special delivery?" Ma was saying as Jim closed the door. "Who would —?"

His heart sank as he read the return address.

"It's from some law firm. In the city."

He tore it open and read the brief message. Twice. It still didn't make sense.

"Well?" Ma said, her fingers visibly twitching to get at the letter, her curiosity giving the word a second syllable: *Way-ell?*

"I don't get it," Jim said. He handed her the letter. "It says I'm supposed to be present at the reading of Dr. Hanley's will next week. I'm listed as one of his heirs."

This was crazy. Dr. Roderick Hanley was one of the richest men in Monroe. Or had been until he died in that air crash last Sunday. He'd been a local celebrity of sorts. Moved here to the Village of Monroe — then truly little more than a village — shortly after World War II and lived in one of the big mansions along the waterfront. A world renowned geneticist who had made a fortune from analytical lab procedures he had developed and patented; a Nobel prizewinner for his work in genetics.

Jim knew all about Hanley because he had been assigned the guy's obit for the Monroe *Express*. The doc's death had been big news in Monroe. Jim's research had revealed that the Hanley estate was worth something like ten million dollars.

But Jim had never even met the man. Why would he name him in his will?

Unless —

In a dizzying flash of insight, it all suddenly became very clear to Jim.

"God, Ma, you don't think —"

One look at her stricken face told him that she had already come to the same conclusion.

"Aw, Ma, don't —"

"I have to go see your father . . . uh, Jonah," she said quickly, handing the letter back to him and turning away. She picked up her coat and slipped into it as she headed for the door.

"Hey, Ma, you know it doesn't matter. You know it won't change a thing."

She stopped at the door, her eyes glistening. She looked upset . . . and frightened.

"That's what you've always said. Now we'll find out for sure, won't we?"

"Ma . . ." He took a step toward her.

"I'll talk to you later, Jimmy."

And then she was out the door and hurrying down the walk toward her car. Jim stood at the storm door and watched her until his rapid breaths fogged up the glass. He hated to see her upset.

When she was gone, he turned away and read the letter again.

No doubt about it. He was an heir to the Hanley estate. Wonder bloomed in him. Dr. Roderick Hanley — genius. His hand shook as it held the letter. The money that might be coming his way meant nothing compared to what the letter didn't — couldn't — say.

He rushed to the phone to call Carol. She'd be as excited as he was. After all these years, after all the searching — he had to tell her now!

2.

"When am I going home?"

Carol Stevens looked at the old man who had spoken. *Calvin Dodd, 72-year-old Caucasian male. Transient cerebral ischemia.*

He looked a lot better than he had a week ago when he had been admitted through the emergency room. He had sported a seven week growth of beard then, and had been dressed in a frayed, food encrusted bathrobe that smelled of old urine. Now he lay in a clean bed and wore a starched hospital gown; he was clean-shaven — by the nurses — and smelled of Keri Lotion.

She didn't have the heart to tell him the truth.

"You'll be out of here as soon as we can get you out, Mr. Dodd, I promise you."

That didn't answer the old fellow's question, but at least it wasn't a lie.

"What's the hold-up?"

"We're trying to find some help for you."

Just then Bobby from Food Service strolled in and picked up Mr. Dodd's breakfast tray. He gave Carol the up-and-down with his eyes and winked.

"Lookin' good!" he said with a smile. He was all of twenty, and desperately trying to grow sideburns. He came on to anything in a skirt, even an "older woman," as he had once referred to her.

Carol laughed and jerked a thumb over her shoulder toward the door. "Beat it, Bobby."

"Like your hair," he said, and was gone.

Carol smoothed her long, sandy blond hair. She had been wearing it it a gentle flip for a couple of years but had been letting it grow lately. She had the slim figure and oval face to carry off the long, straight look, but wondered if it was worth the trouble. It was such a bother at times to keep it smooth and tangle free.

Mr. Dodd was pulling at the nylon mesh vest that enclosed his chest and was strapped to the bed frame. "If you really want to help me, you can get this thing offa me."

"Sorry, Mr. Dodd. The restraints are your doctor's orders. He's afraid you'll get out of bed and fall again."

"I never fell! Who tol' you that crock?"

According to his chart, Mr. Dodd had crawled over his bed's side rails three times and tried to walk. Each time he had fallen after one or two steps. But Carol didn't correct him. In her brief time here at Monroe Community Hospital, she had learned not to argue with patients, especially the older ones. In Mr. Dodd's case she was sure he truly did not remember falling.

"Anyway, I don't have the authority to discontinue your restraints."

"And where's my family?" he said, already on to another subject. "Haven't you been lettin' 'em up to see me?"

Carol's heart broke for the old man. "I . . . I'll check on that for you, okay?"

She turned and started for the door.

"You'd think at least one of my girls'd come an' see me more than once or twice in the whole time I been here."

"I'm sure they'll be in soon. I'll stop by tomorrow."

Carol stepped into the hall and sagged against the wall. She hadn't expected a bed of roses when she had taken the position in the hospital's Social Services department, but in no way had she been prepared for the daily heartaches she'd encountered.

She wondered if she was cut out for this sort of work. One thing they never taught her in all the courses she had taken toward her degree in social work was how to distance yourself emotionally from the client. She was either going to have to learn how to do that, and do it automatically, or risk becoming a basket case.

She'd learn. It was a good job, and there weren't many like it around. Decent pay and good benefits. She and Jim didn't need much to live on — after all, she had inherited the house from her parents and it was free and clear — but until his writing career clicked, she would have to bring home the bacon, as it were. But sometimes . . .

A passing nurse gave her a questioning look. Carol put on a smile and straightened up.

She was just tired, that was all. She hadn't been sleeping well the past few nights . . . restless . . . vaguely remembered dreams. Bad dreams.

I can handle it.

She headed for the tiny Social Services office on the first floor.

Kay Allen, was there. A beefy brunette in her forties who chain-smoked unashamedly, Kay was head of the department, a veteran of nearly twenty years at Monroe Community Hospital. As Carol entered, she looked up from the clutter of case reports on her desk.

"What can we do about Mr. Dodd?" Carol said.

"The dump job on Three North?"

Carol winced. "Must you, Kay?"

"That's what he is, ain't he?" Kay said around the fresh cigarette she was lighting. "His family found him on the floor in his apartment, called an ambulance, dumped him here, then went home."

"I know, but there's got to be a better way to put it. He's a sick old man."

"Not as sick as he was."

True. Doctor Betz had stabilized him as much as possible and so now he was Social Services' problem. Another limbo case: not sick enough for a hospital, but not well enough to live alone. He'd *never* be well enough to live alone. He couldn't go back to his apartment and his daughters wouldn't take him into their homes. The hospital couldn't very well kick him out on the street, so they were stuck with him.

"Let's call a spade a spade, Carol: Mr. Dodd was dumped on us."

Carol didn't want to admit to the truth of that. At least not verbally. That would seem like taking her first step down the road to where Kay was. Hard and cynical. Yet she sensed that Kay's hard shell was just that — a shell, a protective chitinous carapace, the inevitable result of dealing with a steady stream of Mr. Dodds year after year.

"I'll never get used to daughters abandoning their father like that. They don't even visit him."

She understood their reasons for staying away, though: Guilt. The daughters lived in small houses where there was no room for Pop. They'd have to babysit him all the time in case he passed out again. They didn't have the heart to tell him that he couldn't stay with them, so they avoided him. She saw it all too often. But understanding it didn't make it any easier to accept.

God, if I had my parents around, I'd never neglect them, she thought.

Did you have to lose your folks to really appreciate them?

Maybe. But that was beside the point. It was left to Kay and Carol to find a nursing home bed for Mr. Dodd. The problem was, he couldn't afford one, so they had to get him on welfare first and wait for one of the limited number of welfare beds to open up somewhere.

It was a merry-go-round: The paperwork, the persistent assaults against the bureaucracy. Medicare was only three years old and already it was a mass of red tape. Meanwhile, Mr. Dodd was occupying a bed that could be used by someone with an acute illness who really needed it.

"I wish I could take him home. He just needs someone to look after him."

Kay laughed. "Carol, honey, you're a riot!" She held out a handful of papers. "Here. Since you're in a nurturing mood, see about arranging transport for this one."

Carol's heart wrenched when she saw that the patient was a child. "Where's he going?"

"Sloan-Kettering. He's got leukemia."

"Oh."

Steeling herself, Carol headed for the Pediatrics wing.

Twenty minutes later she was sitting on the edge of Danny Jacobi's bed, watching him out of the corner of her eye as she spoke to his mother.

I wonder if he knows he's dying?

He was squatting on the floor shooting suction-tipped darts at a mechanical dinosaur called King Zor. Danny was seven years old, tow-headed, and painfully thin. His two top front teeth were missing and the new ones hadn't moved in yet, so he tended to lisp. Dark circles hung under blue eyes sunk deep in his deathly pale face; large, equally dark bruises ran along his arms and skinny little legs.

He hadn't been beaten, she knew. It was the leukemia. His white blood cells were multiplying like mad in his bone marrow, crowding out the red cells along with the platelets that helped the blood to clot. The slightest bump, even squatting on the floor like he was now, caused bruising.

"Can't they give him the treatments here?" Mrs. Jacobi was saying. "Sloan-Kettering is in the city."

"Dr. Martin thinks his best chance is there."

Mrs. Jacobi glanced at her son. "Whatever's best for Danny," she said.

Carol showed her where to sign for the medical transport and the direct admission to Sloane-Kettering, then they sat together and watched the boy play, moving from the adventure of an imaginary dinosaur hunt to a Mickey Mouse jigsaw puzzle.

Carol wondered which was worse: Never to have had a child, or to have a child and lose him to something so vicious and insidious and so damned *capricious* as leukemia. She wondered only briefly, for she knew in her heart what her answer would be. Better to have the child. Oh, definitely better.

She prayed that she *could* have one. And soon.

She and Jim wanted a family. She just hoped she could fulfill her part in the process.

Her mother had had fertility problems. It had taken her a long time to conceive Carol, and although she had tried for years after Carol was born, there had never been a second child. It seemed like it had been pure luck that Carol was conceived.

According to Dr. Gallen, Carol was following in her mother's footsteps. Her periods had been irregular all her life, and although she and Jim had been following his directions — charting her basal body temperature and such — for almost a year now, nothing had happened.

Maybe nothing would ever happen. That was the dread that followed her like a shadow.

Please let us have one of our own, God. Just one. We won't be greedy. After that we'll adopt kids who need a home. But just give us one of our own.

Danny had the puzzle all together except for part of Mickey's left ear. He looked up at them.

"Piethe mithing," he said, pointing to the gap.

I know the feeling, Carol thought.

"Mrs. Stevens?" said Danny's mother, breaking in on Carol's reverie. "I think that nurse over there wants you."

Carol looked up to see the charge nurse holding up a telephone receiver and alternately pointing to it and Carol.

It was Jim and he sounded excited.

"Carol! I've got great news! We're rich!"

"Jim, what are you talking about?"

"I've found my real father! Come home and I'll tell you all about it!"

Real father?

"Jim, I can't. What's this all —?"

"Forget work. Come home! We've got things to do! Come on!"

And then the line was dead. He wasn't giving her a chance to argue. And then some of his words cut through her confusion.

I've found my real father!

Why didn't that thrill her? She knew of the desperate searches Jim had made to uncover his biological parents, all to no avail. She should have felt happy for him.

Instead she felt a faint trickle of dread down her spine.

3.

As Carol drove home, her thoughts bounced between the past, present, and future. She thought of how excited Jim must be. He had been searching for his natural parents for so long. What had happened at home today? How had he found out? The subject of parents made her think of her own, dead now almost ten years. She wondered for the millionth time how they would have felt about their only daughter marrying Jim Stevens. She knew they had never cared much for Jonah and Emma Stevens, although they hadn't known them well. Her folks would have much preferred Bill Ryan, she was sure, but he had wound up entering the priesthood.

Who'd have ever thought Carol Nevins, Miss Mary Catholic-school herself, would wind up married to the Wolfman, the football crazy? Not Carol.

Oh, but he had been something to see back then. Only occasionally did he carry the ball. Mostly he cleared the way for those who did. And he seemed to relish the job, leaving a trail of battered and broken defensive players in his wake, some seriously hurt.

But there was a gentle side to Jim, too. That was Jim she had loved since that dreadful time in 1959 when both her parents had been killed on a rainy, foggy night in a head-on crash with a semi-trailer on the L.I.E. In an instant of smashing glass and screaming steel she had become an orphan. The grief had been crushing, numbing in its intensity, but the terror of being an only child suddenly alone in the world had made it even worse.

Jim had saved her. Until that time, he had been a high school friend, a football hero she had dated occasionally. Nothing serious. She hadn't been going with anyone special then. She and Bill Ryan had drifted apart a few months before. There had been lots of sparks between Bill and her but his shyness and reticence had dampened any fires before they got started. When her whole world seemed to be collapsing around her, Jim had been there for her. Plenty of friends had expressed their sympathy and tried to comfort her, and her Aunt Grace, her father's only sister, had taken a leave of absence from her nursing job in the city to stay with her, but only Jim seemed to understand, to *feel* what she was feeling.

That was when Carol got the first inkling that this was the man she wanted to marry. That wouldn't happen for a while, however. Not until after four years of college together at the brand new State University at Stony Brook. And it wasn't until their junior year as they lay in bed together in a motel room that he told her he was adopted. He had held off for years, thinking it would make a difference. She remembered being amazed. What did she care who his forebears were? None of them lay curled against her in bed that night.

Graduation flashed before her — Stony Brook class of '64, Jim with his journalism degree, Carol's in social work, starting careers, growing closer until finally the wedding in 1966 — a small affair, with Jim squeezed into a tux and suffering through a nuptial mass. An uncommon man doing such a common thing, an irreligious man taking vows before a priest just to make Carol and her Aunt Grace happy, an anti-ritualistic man partaking in one of the most primitive of rituals.

"It's okay," he had said to her before the ceremony. "It's all the years that follow the voodoo that really matter."

She never forgot those words. The laconic blend of cynicism and sincerity typified everything she loved about Jim Stevens.

She pulled into the driveway and stared at their home. She had grown up in this house. A tiny ranch on a tiny lot, white asbestos shingle siding with black shutters and trim. She didn't like the way it looked in winter with the trees and the rose bushes bare, the rhododendrons drooping from the cold.

Spring, spring, you can't come too soon for me.

But it was warm inside and Jim was fairly bouncing off the walls. He was like a kid at Christmas. Dressed in an oxford shirt, straight-legged jeans, smelling of Old Spice, his hair still wet from the shower, he hugged her and whirled her around as she stepped in the door.

"Can you believe it?" he cried. "Old Doc Hanley fathered me! You're married to a guy with Nobel Prize genes in him!"

"Slow down, Jim," she said. "Just cool it a little. What are you talking about?"

He put her down, and in a rush he told her about the letter and the "obvious" conclusion he had drawn.

"You sure you're not getting carried away?"

"What do you mean?"

"I don't want to be a wet blanket," she said, smoothing down his wet hair, "but no one's calling you Young Mr. Hanley yet, are they?"

His smile faded. "And no one ever will. I'll be James Jonah Stevens until the day I die. I don't know what Hanley's reasons were for dumping me in an orphanage, and I don't care how rich or famous he was. Jonah and Emma Stevens took me in and raised me. As far as I'm concerned, *they* are my parents."

Then why did you search so long and hard for your biological parents? Carol wanted to say. For years it had been an obsession with Jim. Now he seemed to be to be saying that it really didn't matter.

"Fine. But I just don't want you to get your hopes up again and then get hurt. You had a lot of false leads before when you were looking, and it always got you down when they didn't pan out."

She remembered many days through their college years and after, combing through the tangle of old records at the St. Francis Home for Boys. Jim had finally given up the search after their marriage. She had thought he'd put the question of his natural parents' identities behind him for good.

And now this.

"But this is different, don't you see? This came to *me*, I didn't go after it. Look at the whole picture, Carol. I was a foundling, less than two weeks old when the Jebbies literally *found* me on the steps of the orphanage. All the scene needed was a snowstorm howling around me to make it a perfect cliché. No trace of my biological parents. Now, twenty-six years later, a man I never knew, never even met in my entire life, names me in his will. A famous man. One who may not have wanted his name touched by scandal back in the forties, which is a long ways away in time and temper from the hippies and free love we've got today." He stopped and stared at her a moment. "Got the picture?"

She nodded.

"Good. Now tell me, hon. Given those facts, what is the first explanation that comes to your mind when you try to figure out why the rich old man names a foundling in his will?"

Carol shrugged. "Okay. Score one for you."

He smiled brightly. "So! I'm not crazy!"

His smile always warmed her. "No, you're not."

The phone rang.

"That's probably for me," Jim said. "I called that law firm earlier and they said they'd get back to me."

"About what?"

He gave her a sheepish look. "About who my real . . . uh, biological father is."

She listened to his end of the conversation and sensed his frustration when he couldn't get any information out of the lawyer on the other end. Finally he hung up and turned to her.

"I know what you're going to say," he told her. "Why is this so damned important to me? What does it really matter?"

Her sympathy for him was mixed with confusion. She wanted to say, *You're you. Who you came from doesn't change that.*

"It wouldn't be the first time I've asked," she said.

"Yeah, well, I wish I could drop it, but I can't."

"You let it eat at you."

"How do I explain it? It's like having amnesia and being alone on a ship drifting over the Marianas Trench; you drop anchor but it never hits bottom, so you go on drifting and drifting. You believe that if you knew where you came from, maybe you could get some idea where you were going. But you look behind you and it's all empty sea. You feel cut off from your past. It's a form of social and genetic amnesia."

"Jim, I understand. I felt that way when my folks were killed."

"It's not the same. That was tragic. They were gone, but at least you had known them. And even if they had died the day after you were born, it would still be different. Because you could go back and look at pictures of them, talk to people who knew them. They would exist for you, consciously and subconsciously. You'd have roots you could trace back to England or France or wherever. You'd feel part of a flow, part of a process; you'd have a history behind you, pushing you toward someplace far ahead."

"But Jim," she said, "I never think of those things. Nobody does."

"That's because you've got them. You take them for granted. You don't think about your right hand much, do you? But if you'd been born without one, you'd find yourself wishing for a right hand every day."

Carol moved close and slipped her arms around him. As he hugged her, she felt the tension that had been rising begin to recede. Jim could do that. Make her feel whole, complete.

"I'll be your right hand," she said softly.

"You always have been," he whispered back. "But I've got a feeling that this is it. Soon I'm going to know for sure."

"I guess you won't need me any more then," she said, putting on an exaggerated pout.

"That'll be the day! I'll always need you."

She broke away. "You'd better. Otherwise I'm sending you back to St. Francis!"

"Christ!" he said. "The orphanage! Why didn't I think of that! Maybe we won't have to wait till the reading. Maybe we can find a connection there now!"

"Oh, Jim, we've been through those records a thousand times at least!"

"Yeah, but we never looked for any mention of Dr. Roderick Hanley, did we?"

"No, but —"

"Come on!" He handed her her coat and went to the front closet for his own. "We're going to Queens!"

4.

Emma Stevens waited impatiently inside the employee entrance to the slaughterhouse. It was a small, chilly foyer, silent but for the ticking of the time clock. She rubbed her hands together, one over the other in a continuous circular motion. It helped to generate warmth, but she felt she would have been doing the same even if it were July. The anxiety jittering through her seemed to have given her hands a life of their own.

What was taking Jonah so long? She had sent word that she was here. She hadn't wanted to disturb him at work, but had been unable to restrain herself any longer. She had to talk about this. Jonah was the only one who would understand. Why wasn't he coming out?

Emma glanced at her watch and saw that it had been only a couple of minutes. She took a deep breath.

Calm yourself, Emma.

She stared out through the small, chicken-wired window in the outer door. The employee parking lot looked almost deserted compared to how it had been before the layoffs. And now there was talk of the slaughterhouse closing down for good by the end of the year. What were they going to do then?

Finally she could wait no longer. She pushed through the door, went down the short hall, then through the door that opened into the slaughterhouse proper. She stood transfixed as a freshly skinned side of beef, steaming in the cold, dripping red, sped by her, wobbling and twisting on its chain as it rolled along the overhead track. Another followed not far behind. The smell of blood, some old and clotted, some still warm from the throat, filled the air. And faintly, in the background, the uneasy lowing of the cows waiting their turn in the pens outside.

Suddenly Emma looked up and Jonah was there, dressed in a big rubber apron, gray overalls, black rubber gloves, and snow boots, all splattered with blood and hair and bits of gore. He stared down at her. He had just turned fifty but he had the lean, tautly muscular frame of a much younger man. Clear blue eyes and rock-hard features. Even after thirty years of marriage, the sight of him still excited her. Except for the black felt patch over his left eye, he could have been an older version of that American actor they had seen last year in one of those Italian made Westerns.

"What is it, Emma?" His voice was as rough hewn as his face, his Southern accent thicker than hers.

She felt a flash of annoyance. " 'Hello, Emma,' " she said. " 'It's so good to see you. Is anything wrong?' I'm fine, Jonah."

"I've only got a few minutes, Emma."

She realized how he must be fearing for his job, and her annoyance faded. Luckily it was hard to find anyone who wanted to take over Jonah's duties in the slaughterhouse, otherwise he might have been out of work for months now like so many others.

"Sorry. It's just that I thought this was too important to wait. Jimmy heard from some lawyers today. He's named in the will of that Dr. Hanley who died in that plane crash last week."

Jonah stepped to a nearby window and stared through the grimy glass for what seemed like a long time. Finally he turned and gave her one of his small, rare smiles.

"He's comin'."

"Who? Who's coming?"

"The One."

Emma felt suddenly weak. Was Jonah going to start talking crazy again? He was a strange one, Jonah. Even after all these years, Emma really didn't understand him. But she loved him.

"What are you saying?"

"I've sensed it for more than a week now, but it was so faint, I wasn't sure. Now I am."

Over the years, Emma had learned to rely on Jonah's premonitions. He seemed to have an extra sense about things. It was uncanny at times. Sometimes he even seemed to see things with that dead left eye of his. The most memorable instance was when he had sensed that the baby they were to adopt had arrived in the St. Francis orphanage back in 1942.

It came back to her in a flash. A windy January morning only a month or so after the Japanese had attacked Pearl Harbor. The sun had been blinding, pouring from the sky and reflecting off pavements wet with melting snow. Jonah had been frantic. He'd had another of his visions during the night then, too. It was the one he had been waiting for, the moment he said they had been preparing for by moving to New York City.

Queens! The vision had showed him where he had to go in Queens. They had to be there first thing in the morning.

How Jonah trusted those visions! He guided his life by them — *both* their lives. Years earlier a vision had prompted him to move them both from Missouri to New York City, to start new lives there pretending to be Catholics. Emma hadn't understood any of that — rarely understood much of what Jonah was about — but she had gone along, as always. He was her man, she was his woman. If he wanted her to forsake her Baptist faith, well, fine. She'd never practiced it anyway.

But why become Catholic?

Jonah had never shown the least bit of interest in any religion since she had met him, but he had insisted that they register in a Catholic parish, go to church every Sunday, and make sure they were well known to the priest.

She found out why on that January day in 1942. When they pulled up to the St. Francis Home for Boys, Jonah told her the child they had been waiting for lay within. And when they went inside to apply to adopt an infant boy, they stated they were lifelong Roman Catholics.

No one could prove different.

The child he wanted had been left there the day before. Jonah had carefully inspected the infant boy, especially his hands. He seemed satisfied that he was the one he had been waiting for.

They suffered through the home inspections, the background checks, and all that rigmarole, but it paid off. Finally they were the proud parents of the child they named James. That boy was the best thing that ever happened to Emma Stevens. Better even than Jonah, though she loved her husband dearly.

And so she trusted those visions as much as Jonah. Because she never would have had Jim without them.

"So, the famous Dr. Hanley was his father," Jonah said, mostly to himself. "Interesting." Then he turned to Emma. "It's a sign. It has begun. Our time is coming. The One is beginning to accrue wealth and power to his name. It's a sign, Emma. A good sign."

Emma wanted to hug him but refrained because of the gore that covered him. A *good* sign, that was what he had said. As long as it was good for Jimmy. A welter of varying emotions swirled around her. She began to cry.

"What's wrong?" Jonah said.

Emma shook her head. "I don't know. After all these years of wondering when . . . or if . . . to finally have him know who his real parents are . . ." She sobbed again. "I don't want to lose him."

Jonah removed a glove and laid a gentle hand on her shoulder.

"I know how you feel. It won't be too long now. Our reward is coming."

There he went again, talking in circles.

She clutched his hand with both of hers and prayed that nothing would take her Jimmy away from her.

Two

1.

"Father Bill! Father Bill!"

Father William Ryan, Society of Jesus, recognized the voice. It was Kevin Flaherty, St. Francis' six-year old town crier and tattletale. He looked up from reading his daily office to see the little redheaded fellow running down the hall at top speed.

"They're fighting again, Father Bill!"

"Who?"

"Nicky and Freddy! And Freddy says he's going to kill Nicky this time!"

"Just tell them I said to stop fighting immediately or it will mean the Bat for both of them."

"There's *blood*, Father!"

Bill sighed and snapped his Breviary closed. He'd have to deal with this personally. Freddy had two years and about forty pounds on Nicky, with a bully's temperment to boot. It sounded like Nicky's mouth had brought him a pack of trouble again.

As he strode from his office, he picked up the dreaded red whiffle bat from its place in the corner by the door. Kevin ran ahead, Bill walked quickly after him, hurrying but trying his best not to appear so.

He found them in the hall outside the dormitory section, encircled by the rest of the boys in a shouting, jeering group. One of the onlookers glanced up and saw him approaching.

"It's Big Bad Bill! Beat it!"

The circle evaporated, leaving the two combatants wrestling on the floor. Freddy was atop Nicky, raising his fist for another blow at the younger boy's already bloody face. When they saw Father Bill, they suddenly forgot their differences and joined the others in flight, leaving Nicky's glasses behind on the floor.

"Nicholas! Frederick!" Bill shouted.

They skidded to a halt and turned.

"Yes, Father?" they said as one.

He pointed to a spot on the floor directly in front of him.

"Get over here! *Now!*"

They approached and stood before him, looking at their shoes. Bill lifted Nicky's chin. The ten-year old's normally misshapen face was bruised and scraped. Blood was smeared over his left cheek and chin and still trickled slowly from his left nostril.

Bill felt the anger rise in him. It flared higher when he lifted Freddy's chin and saw that the older boy's round, freckled, blue-eyed face was unmarked. He had an urge to give Freddy a taste of his own medicine. Instead, he forced himself to speak calmly through his tightly clenched teeth.

"What have I told you about bullying people?" he said to Freddy.

"He called me a dirty name!" Freddy said, his lower lip quivering in fear.

"He knocked my books out of my hand!" Nicky said.

Bill said, "Now wait a —"

"He called me a *scrofulous!*"

Bill was struck dumb for a second. Then he turned to face the smaller boy.

"You called him *what*?" he said, biting his cheek. It was all he could do to keep from laughing. This kid was too much! "Where did you hear that word?"

"I read it in a book once," Nicky said as he wiped the blood from his nose onto the sleeve of his white shirt.

Once. Nicky never forgot anything. *Anything*.

"Do you have any idea what it means?"

"Of course," he said offhandedly. "It's a tuberculous condition characterized by chronically swollen glands."

Bill nodded vaguely. "Right."

He had known little more than that it was some sort of disease, but he couldn't allow Nicky the slightest hint that he might be one up on him. The kid could be a terror if he sensed that.

Bill lifted the red whiffle bat and slapped it softly against his left palm.

"All right. You guys know what's next. Frederick, you call out the troops while Nicholas retrieves his glasses."

Freddy blanched and ran toward the dorm doors. Nicholas turned and picked up his thick, black-rimmed glasses.

"Aw, they broke again," Nicholas said, holding up the left temple piece.

Bill held out his hand. "Give it to me. We'll fix it later." He slipped them into the side pocket of his cassock. "For now, get over by the wall and wait for Freddy."

Nicky gave him a look, as if to say, *You're not really going to do this to me, are you?*

Speaking in a low voice, Bill said, "Don't expect special treatment, Nicholas. You know the rules, so you take your lumps just like everybody else."

Nicky shrugged and turned away.

Is this why I joined the Jesuits? Bill thought as he stood in the middle of the hall and fought to keep his personal frustration from turning into anger at the boys. Playing nursemaid to a bunch of wild kids was not the future he had envisioned for himself.

No way.

The writings of Pierre Teilhard de Chardin, S.J. had directed him to the Society. Bill had already known he had a vocation for the priesthood, but he found de Chardin's work of such staggering intellectual scope that he knew he had to join the order that had produced such a mind — the Society of Jesus. The Jesuits were giants in both the religious and secular spheres, striving for — and achieving — excellence in all their endeavors. He had wanted to be a part of that tradition, and now he was.

Sort of.

The Society was changing as rapidly as the Church itself and the world around them all. But he was cut off from most of that here. Well, this wouldn't last forever. Repeating that thought over and over in his mind was the personal litany that got him through each day here at St. F.'s

"Prefect of Discipline." That was his title. What it really meant was that he played nursemaid and father-figure to the residents of one of the last Catholic boys' orphanages in New York.

Me, a father figure! That was a laugh.

Bill looked up and saw the residents of St. Francis', two-and-a-half dozen boys between the ages of six and thirteen, arrayed before him in the hall. Freddy had already taken his place next to Nicky near the window. All were silent.

Showtime.

This was an aspect of his position as Prefect of Discipline that Bill particularly disliked. Wielding the Bat. But it was a tradition at St. F.'s. There were rules of conduct here, and it was his job to enforce them. If he didn't, the place would quickly degenerate into anarchy.

As much as he would have liked to try it, he knew democracy wouldn't fly here. Although most of its residents were good kids, some of them had been through a child's version of hell and were pretty tough cases. Given free rein, they would turn the home into a little corner of hell. So there were rules that needed to be strictly and evenly enforced. And someone had to do the enforcing. Every boy knew where the lines were drawn, and each one knew that if he stepped over those lines he risked a date with the Bat. And in the rule against fighting was the understanding that no matter who had started it, both combatants would be punished.

"Okay, guys," he said to Freddy and Nicky. "You both know what to do. Drop trow and assume the position."

They both reddened and began loosening their belts. With excruciating slowness, they dropped their dark blue uniform trousers to the floor, turned, bent over, and grabbed their ankles.

A small brown stain became visible on the back of Freddy's jockey shorts as they stretched over his buttocks. Somebody said, "Hey, skid marks!" and the audience laughed.

Bill glared at them. "Did I hear someone say he wanted to join them over against the wall?"

Dead silence.

Bill approached Freddy and Nicky and readied The Bat for a swing, thinking how absurd it was to punish them this way for fighting.

Not exactly Gandhian, is it?

But not totally useless, either. If the rules weren't too restrictive, if the punishments weren't too harsh, Big Bad Bill and the Bat could push the boys closer to each other without crushing their spirit. He could help bond them, make them brothers of sorts, give them a sense of community, a feeling of unity. That was good. St. F.'s was the only family they had.

He started with Freddy. The Bat was hollow, made of lightweight vinyl. He swung it across the backs of the older boy's thighs once. The slap of the plastic against flesh echoed loudly in the hall.

It stung, Bill knew, but not much. In the hands of someone with a sadistic streak, this could be a painful punishment. But physical pain was not the object here. The embarrassment of dropping and bending before their assembled peers would probably be enough, but he had to use the Bat. It was the symbol of authority at St. F.'s and couldn't be allowed to gather dust when rules were broken.

He gave Freddy a total of four shots; the same for Nicky, although he backed off his swing a little on Nicky.

"All right," Bill said as the sound of the last slap echoed away. "Show's over. Everybody back to the dorm."

The kids broke and ran for their quarters with Freddy hurrying after them, buckling up as he ran. Nicky stayed behind.

"You going to fix my glasses, Father?"

"Oh, right." He'd forgotten about that.

Nicky looked stranger than usual without his specs. He had a misshapen head that bulged above his left ear. His records showed that his mother had been unwed and had tried to flush him down the toilet as a newborn, fracturing his tiny skull and nearly drowning him. Nicky had been a ward of the state and the Catholic Church ever since. Besides the misshapen skull, he had bad skin — his face was stippled with blackheads — and poor vision that required Coke-bottle lenses for correction.

But it was his intellect that truly set Nicky apart from the other kids. He tested in the genius range and Bill had detected an increasingly scornful attitude toward lesser minds. That was what got him into fights and added to the already difficult task of finding him a home — he was far brighter than many of the prospective adoptive parents who applied to St. F.'s.

But despite the fact that Nicky acted like an insufferable pint-sized intellectual, Bill could not deny his fondness for him. Maybe it was a sense of kinship — Nicky's intellect set him apart from the other boys just as Bill's calling had set him apart from his own generation. At least once a week they played chess. Bill managed to win most of games, but he knew that was due only to his greater experience. In another year he'd be lucky to play a draw against Nicky.

Back in his office, Bill took out a small tool kit and set about trying to repair the eyeglasses. Nicky wandered away, poking into the corners of the tiny room. Bill had noticed during his time at St. F's that although Nicky seemed to have an insatiable curiosity about the world and how things worked, he had no interest whatsoever in actually *making* things work.

"How about a game?" Nicky said from over by the chessboard.

"That's 'How about a game, *Father*,' and I'm a little busy right now, as you can see."

"Spot me a knight and I'll whip you in twenty minutes!"

Bill gave him a look.

". . . Father," Nicky finally added.

It was a game Nicky played, trying to see how far he could push their familiarity. As much as Bill liked the boy, he had to keep a certain amount of distance. St. F.'s was a way station. He couldn't allow the boys to feel that leaving here was leaving home. They had to feel they were going *to* their home.

"Not a chance, kid. We play on Saturdays. And besides, you need to be spotted a piece like Cassius Clay needs to be spotted a right to the jaw."

"He calls himself Muhammed Ali now."

"Whatever. Just keep quiet while I try to fix this."

Bill concentrated on rethreading the screw that held the temple to the front of the frame. He just about had it in place when he heard Nicky say,

"So. I see Loyola turned you down."

Bill looked up and saw Nicky holding a sheet of paper. He recognized it as Loyola College stationery. Anger flared.

"Put that down! That's my personal correspondence!"

"Sorry."

Bill had requests in to the Provincial for transfer to a college campus and had queried Fordham, Georgetown, B.C., and others about positions as instructor. He was qualified in history and philosophy. As soon as something opened up, he would be out of here and on his way to the academic life he had dreamed of through all those years in the seminary.

Serving God through Man's intellect. That had been his personal motto since his second year in the seminary.

He had expected to find little at St. Francis for the intellect. Two interminable years here as Prefect of Discipline had confirmed it.

A mind-numbing job. He could feel his creative juices dripping away, evaporating. He was twenty-six years old and wasting what should have been the most productive years of his life. Momentous changes were taking place out there in the real world, especially on the college campuses. The whole society was in ferment, the very air alive with ideas, with change. He wanted to be part of that process, wanted to fight his way to the heart of it.

Stuck here as he was in this anachronism called St. Francis' Home for Boys, he could only grasp the hem of what was going on. Last weekend he had managed to get away for two days. He and some friends from his seminary days had dressed in civvies and driven all night to campaign for Eugene McCarthy up in New Hampshire. The primary was only a few weeks away and it looked as if Senator Gene might give President Johnson a real run for his money.

God, the excitement up there! All the young hippie types shaving their beards and getting their hair cut short — "Get clean for Gene" was the slogan of the day — and canvassing neighborhoods door to door. The air had rippled and vibrated with a sense of purpose, with a feeling that history was being made. He had been depressed on Sunday night when they'd had to leave.

To return to this. *This*. St. Francis Home for Boys.

Bill firmly believed that there was something to be gained, some wisdom to be gleaned from any experience. Although he wasn't exactly sure what it was, he was certain he had derived whatever wisdom St. F.'s had to offer. From here on it was just more of the same. So now he wanted to get himself out of neutral and start moving forward.

All right, Lord. I've paid my dues. I'm through with this chapter. Let's turn the page and move on to the next, okay?

But he had to wait until he was given the green light. In addition to vows of poverty and celibacy, he had also taken a vow of obedience when he had become a Jesuit. He had to go where the Society of Jesus sent him. He just hoped the Society sent him away from here soon.

"You've got no business going through my papers."

Nicky shrugged. "Yeah, but it helps to know that we kids aren't the only ones around here who get rejected. Don't feel bad. Look at me. I'm a pro at being rejected."

"We'll find you a place."

"You can be honest with me, Father. I know you've been trying to bail out since you arrived. It's okay. You're no different from anyone else under a hundred years old who comes through here."

Bill was stung. He thought he had been pretty discreet.

"How do you know?"

"Ve haf verrry interrresting vays of learning zings ve vish to know," he said in a fair immitation of Arte Johnson's German soldier.

Bill had noted that Nicky never failed to be in the first row when the boys watched *Laugh-in* on Monday nights. He couldn't be sure if the attraction was the quick humor or the bodypainted girls in bikinis.

The phone rang.

"Oh, hello, Mr. Walters," Bill said when he recognized the voice.

Immediately he wished he hadn't spoken the man's name. Nicky's head snapped around. Bill could almost see his ears pricking up with interest. Mr.

and Mrs. Walters were interested in adopting a boy, and Nicky had spent a few days with them this week.

The story Mr. Walters told was a familiar one: Yes, Nicky was a nice enough boy, but they just didn't think he'd fit in with their way of life. They now were reconsidering the whole idea of adopting. Bill tried to reason with the man as best he could with Nicky listening to every word, but finally he was forced to allow the conversation to end. The Walters would call back when they had thought it over some more.

Nicky's smile was forced. "George and Ellen don't want me either, right?"

"Nicholas . . ."

"It's okay, Father. I told you: I'm a pro at rejection."

But Bill saw the boy's lips quivering and tears welling in his lower lids. It broke his heart to see this happen time after time. Not just with Nicky, but with some of the other boys, too.

"You intimidate people, Nicky."

There was a sob hiding within Nicky's voice. "I . . . I don't mean to. It just happens."

He threw an arm over Nicky's shoulder. The gesture felt awkward, stiff, nowhere near as warm as he would have wished. "Don't worry, kid. I'll find you a place."

Nicky pulled away, his expression shifting quickly from misery to anger.

"Oh, right! Sure you will! You don't care about us! All you care about is getting out of here!"

That hurt. Bill was speechless for a moment. Forget the disrespect. That didn't matter. What did matter was that the kid was speaking from the heart and speaking the truth. Bill *had* been doing a half-assed job here. Not a *bad* job, but certainly not a good one.

That's because I don't belong here! I wasn't cut out for this type of thing!

Right. Granted. But at least he could give it his best shot. He owed the kids and the Society at least that much. But something about Nicky's extraordinary run of bad luck bothered Bill.

"Tell me, Nicky: Are you trying?"

"Of course I am!"

Bill wondered about that. Had Nicky been rejected so many times in the past that he was now deliberately sabotaging the trial visits? In effect, rejecting the prospective adoptive parents before they could reject him?

On impulse Bill said, "I'll make you a promise, Nicky. I'm going to see you adopted before I leave here."

The boy blinked. "You don't have to do that. I didn't mean what I —"

"But I've got to see you trying a little harder with people. You can't expect people to warm up to you if you go around acting like Clifton Webb playing Mr. Belvedere."

Nicky smiled. "But I *like* Mr. Belvedere!"

Bill knew that. Nicky had watched *Sitting Pretty* at least a dozen times. He scanned *TV Guide* every week to see if it was on. Lynn Belvedere was his hero.

"But that's not real life. No one wants to live with a ten-year old who's got all the answers."

"But I'm usually right!"

"That's even worse. Adults like to be right once in a while, too, you know."

"Okay. I'll try."

Bill sent up a silent prayer that he wouldn't regret his promise to Nicky. But it seemed like a safe bet. He wasn't going anywhere. Every place he had contacted so far about an instructorship had turned him down. It looked like he was going to be at St. F.'s for some time to come.

The intercom buzzed. Sister Miriam's voice said:

"A young couple is here and they want some information from the old adoption records. Father Anthony is out and I'm not sure what to do."

Bill quickly tightened the temple screw on Nicky's glasses and scooted him out of the office.

"I'll be right down."

2.

This is it, Jim thought as he and Carol stood in the foyer of St. Francis. *This is where my history begins.*

Even though he had no childhood memories of it, the place never failed to raise a lump in his throat. He owed these priests and nuns a lot. They had taken him in when his real parents had no use for him, and had found him a home where he was wanted. He tended to be suspicious of altruism, but he felt he had certainly received a lot from St. F.'s while unable to offer a thing in return. That must be what the nuns in school had meant when they talked about "good works."

The drafty foyer was as drab as the rest of the building. The whole place was pretty forbidding, actually, with its worn granite exterior and flaking paint on the wood trim around the windows and doors. The molding and trim had been painted and repainted so many times that whatever detail had been carved into the orginal wood was now blunted into vague ripples and irregular ridges.

He shivered, not just with the February cold that was still trapped within the fabric of his corduroy jacket, but also with the anticipation that he was finally going to be able to move backward in time, beyond the day he was left here. In all his previous trips to St. F.'s, that day in January of 1942 had proven an impenetrable barrier, impervious to all his assaults. But he had found a key today. Maybe it would open the door.

"It's starting to become real to me," he said to Carol.

"What?"

"The Hanley thing."

"Not to me. I still can't believe it."

"It's going to take awhile, but this is going to open all the doors for me. I'm finally going to find out where I came from. I can feel it."

There was concern in Carol's eyes. "I hope it's worth the effort."

"Maybe I can really start to concentrate on what's ahead if I can stop looking back and wondering what was there."

Carol only smiled and squeezed his hand in reply.

Maybe he could get a better grip on the novels if he could find the answers to all the *why*s that cluttered his mind.

Like *why* had he been dumped here?

If Dr. Roderick Hanley was his natural father, it stood to reason that the old boy may have felt that his reputation would be damaged by acknowledging a bastard child.

Fine. Jim could live with that.

But what about his mother? Why had *she* deserted him as a newborn? He was sure she had a good reason — she *must* have! He wouldn't hold anything against her. He just wanted to know.

Was that too much to ask?

And there were questions he had about himself that he'd never discussed with Carol, questions about certain dark areas of his psyche that he wanted answered.

Suddenly Carol was tugging at his sleeve.

"Jim, look! My God, look who it is!"

3.

Carol could hardly believe her eyes. She had been struck by the young priest's good looks — the short collegiate cut of his thick brown hair, the clear blue eyes, the broad shoulders and trim body that even the dresslike cassock couldn't hide. And then she suddenly realized she knew him.

Billy Ryan from Monroe.

Seeing him now gave her a flash of heat reminiscent of the first time she had laid eyes on him in high school, standing by himself in a corner at the year's first Friday night CYO dance at Our Lady of Perpetual Sorrow, an echo of the intense warmth that had propelled her across the floor at the start of the next ladies' choice — a slow tune, of course — to ask him to dance. She even remembered the song: the ethereal "Been So Long" by the Pastels. He turned out to be the shiest boy she had ever known.

And now he was staring right back at her.

"Carol? Carol Nevins?"

"Stevens now. Remember?" she said.

"Of course I do. Even if I couldn't make the wedding." He pumped Jim's hand. "And Jim! Is that you under all that hair? You really look like the Wolfman now. God, it's been so long!"

"Four years at least," Jim said, smiling.

Bill slapped his hand against Jim's belly. "Married life seems to be agreeing with you." He turned to her. "And you, too, Carol. You look great!"

Carol resisted an impulse to embrace him. It had been almost a decade since their last date. They had hugged and kissed a lot in the months after they had met at that CYO dance, but Billy Ryan was a priest now. *Father* Ryan. She wasn't sure how proper that would be, or how he'd react.

"What on earth are you two doing here?" he said.

As Jim gave him a quick rundown of his life story, Carol studied Bill. The even teeth, the quick smile, the sharp cut of his nose, the way his hair curled just a little at his temples, the way the unbuttoned top of his cassock hung open to reveal the white of the T-shirt underneath — God, he was still gorgeous!

What a waste!

Carol was startled by the thought. That wasn't like her. Bill was doing what was most important to him, living the life he had chosen, dedicating himself to God. Why should she put him down for that?

But she couldn't escape the realization that in a way it was indeed a shame that this big, virile man would never marry, would never father children. And she couldn't deny the stir his very presence caused deep within her.

"I'm proud of you," Carol blurted, a bit too loudly perhaps, at the end of Jim's monologue. "I mean, working here with these homeless kids. It must be very rewarding."

Bill turned his serene blue eyes on her and Carol thought she saw them cloud for an instant.

"It . . . has its moments." He turned back to Jim: "So you were abandoned as a newborn right here in the foyer of St. Francis?"

Jim nodded. "Right. January fourteenth, to be exact. They estimated I was a little over a week old, so I was assigned January sixth as a birthday."

"I never knew any of this," Bill said, shaking his head. "Never even knew you were adopted."

"Well, it's not exactly the sort of thing you discuss in the locker room."

"I guess not."

As Carol idly wondered about what boys *did* talk about in locker rooms, Bill led them inside a small room with a desk and chairs. She knew from previous trips to St. Francis with Jim to search the adoption records that this was where they conducted initial interviews with prospective adoptive parents.

"So what can St. Francis do for you now?" Bill said.

Carol watched the intense animation in her husband's eyes as he filled Bill in on his invitation to the reading of the Hanley will and the conclusions he had drawn from that.

"So I guess what I need now is a chance to go through your old financial records and see if Dr. Hanley was ever a contributor to St. Francis'."

"We don't allow anyone to go through those," Bill said.

Carol couldn't help noting the *we* — Bill was really part of something else now, something that excluded her and Jim and the rest of the world.

"It would mean a lot to me."

"I know. I'll make a quick search for you myself if you'd like."

"I'd really appreciate that, Bill."

Bill smiled. "What are old friends for? What year was that again?"

"Forty-two. I arrived here January of Forty-two."

"I'll see what I can find. Sit down. This shouldn't take too long."

4.

"Imagine . . . Bill Ryan," Jim heard Carol say when they were alone.

He gave her a sidelong glance and put on a lecherous stage whisper: "Still got the hots for him?"

Carol swatted him on the arm. Hard. It stung. She meant that one.

"That's not even funny! He's a priest!"

"Still a good-looking guy."

"You can say that again," Carol said with a wink, smiling.

"I'll pass. Once was enough, thank you."

Jim closed his eyes and listened to the old building around him. St. Francis Home for Boys. The last of its kind, as far as he knew. He'd been here many times since his teenage years, but had no memories of the place as a child. Why should he? He'd spent only the first few weeks of his life here before Jonah and Emma Stevens adopted him. Quite a coincidence. Within hours of his being found on the doorstep, the Stevenses were there, looking to adopt a male infant. The U.S. had entered World War II only six weeks before but already applications for adoption had fallen way off. The foundling found a home and became James Stevens before he was two months old.

Lucky.

Even luckier now that he was a rich man's heir.

What about all the other not so lucky ones? What about all the other homeless kids, parentless by fate or design, who had to spend *years* here, shuttled in and out of strange homes until they finally clicked somewhere or got old enough to move out into lives of their own? He ached for them.

What a rotten life.

Granted, a kid could do a lot worse. The nuns from Our Lady of Lourdes next door taught the kids in the parish school, changed their sheets, and did their laundry, while the priests provided father figures. It was a stable, structured environment with a roof overhead, a clean bed, and three squares a day. But it wasn't a home.

Somehow Jim had lucked out in 1942. He wondered how lucky he'd be at the reading of the will next week.

If I get a couple of those millions, I'll adopt every kid in St. F.'s, every one of the poor little bastards.

He couldn't resist a smile.

Yeah. Bastards. Like me.

"What are you grinning at?" Carol asked.

"Just thinking," he said. "Wondering how much I'll get from the Hanley estate. Maybe it'll be enough to allow us to get away for a while and do some serious work on starting some little feet to patter around the house."

Carol's face was troubled for an instant as she slipped her hand into his. "Maybe."

He knew how worried she was about her ability to conceive. They'd been over the territory hundreds of time. The fact that her mother had had fertility problems didn't mean Carol would follow. Every doctor she'd been to had told her she had no reason to worry. Yet he knew it haunted her.

And so it haunted him. Anything that bothered Carol bothered him more. He loved her so much it hurt at times. A cliche, he knew, but sometimes he's stare at her as she read or worked in the kitchen, unaware of the scrutiny, and he'd feel an actual pain deep inside. All he wanted to do was someday be able to make her feel as fortunate to have him as he felt about having her.

Money wouldn't do it, but at least with this inheritance he could buy her everything, give her the kind of life she deserved. For himself, he had everything he needed, corny as that sounded. But Carol . . . money couldn't buy her what she needed and wanted most.

"And even if we don't get our own," he told her, "there's plenty of kids available right here."

She only nodded absently.

"Anyway," he said, "if that job at the hospital is getting you down, you'll be able to quit. No sweat."

She smiled crookedly. "Don't get your hopes up too high. With our luck there'll be a thousand other 'sons' of his waiting in line at the reading."

Jim laughed. That was the Irish in Carol: For every silver lining there had to be a cloud, invariably dark and rumbling.

"Nice of Bill to search the records for you," she said after a while. "Especially after we missed his ordination and all."

"You had appendicitis, for Christ sake!"

"You know that and I know that, but does he? I mean, knowing the way you feel about religion, maybe he thinks we just made it up as an excuse not to come see him made a priest. Maybe he's hurt. After all, we haven't seen him in years."

"He knows better. It's just your Irish guilt projecting."

"Don't be silly!"

Jim smiled. "It's true. Even though you were hospitalized, you feel guilty as hell about missing his ordination."

"Swell choice of words, Jim."

5.

Bill hurried back to the interview room, wondering why he was in such a rush. He didn't have anything to tell them. It had taken him only an hour or so, but he was sure he had found all there was to be found.

Was it Carol?

She looked good, didn't she? Her hair was longer, straighter, but her face was the same, that same sharp, upturned nose, thin lips, fine sandy hair, the same natural high coloring in her cheeks.

Was he in a hurry to see her again?

Not likely. She had been a teenage infatuation, a stage in his adolescence. That was all over and done with.

So why this sense of urgency to get back to where she was waiting?

As he entered the little room, he pushed the question away. He'd think about it later.

"Sorry," he said, dropping into a chair. "Couldn't find a thing."

Jim slammed his fist against his thigh. "Damn! Are you sure?"

"I started the search somewhere around three years before your drop-off date and went through every year since. The name Hanley doesn't crop up a single time."

Jim obviously wasn't satisfied. Bill could guess what was on his mind. He was probably looking for a delicate way to question how thoroughly anyone could have combed through three decades of records in a little over an hour.

"That's an awful lot of years, Bill. I'm just wondering . . ."

Bill smiled. "A lot of years, yes, but not a lot of contributions, I'm afraid. And the name Hanley doesn't appear in any of our index files or on our mailing list." As he saw Jim's shoulders slump, he added, "But —"

"But what?"

"But just ten days after you were left here, St. F.'s received an anonymous contribution of ten thousand dollars. One whale of a sum in those days."

"It's nothing to sniff at these days, either, let me tell you!" Jim said, animated again. "Anonymous, huh? How unusual is that?"

"Are you kidding? Even today we occasionally get twenty-five or fifty, or rarely, a hundred bucks anonymously. But the rest of the time everyone wants a receipt for tax purposes. A five-figure donation that won't be written off is unheard of."

"Guilt money," Jim said.

He nodded. "Heavy guilt."

Bill glanced over at Carol. She was staring at him. Why was she looking at him that way? It made him uncomfortable.

At that moment a mailman stopped in the hall at the door. He held up an envelope. "Care to sign for this, Father? It's certified."

Bill took the envelope and dropped it on the table as he signed the receipt. When he turned back, Jim was on his feet, clutching the envelope in his hand.

"Look at the return address! Fletcher, Cornwall & Boothby! That's the same law firm that contacted me!" He shoved it toward Bill. "Open it!"

Propelled by the infectious urgency in Jim's voice, Bill tore open the envelope.

After skimming the astonishing contents, he handed the letter to Jim.

"They want St. F.'s to send someone to the reading of the Hanley will!"

Jim glanced at the letter and grinned.

"Same letter I got! I *knew* it! This clinches it! Let's celebrate! Dinner's on me! What do you say, Bill?"

Bill took back the letter and shook his head.

"Sorry. I can't get away just now. Maybe some other time."

Partly true. With Father Anthony out, he couldn't simply walk off and leave the boys without supervision. Of course, if he really worked at it, he could probably find somebody to cover for him, but in a strange way he was glad to get out of it. He was finding it difficult to keep his eyes off Carol. And every time he looked her way, she was looking back.

Like now. Carol was staring at him again.

She said, "A raincheck, then. We'll owe you one."

"Sure. That'll be nice."

The good-byes were protracted, with much handshaking and promises of keeping in touch this time and getting together soon. Bill breathed a quiet sigh of relief when he finally closed the door behind them, figuring his insides would begin to quiet down now.

But they didn't.

6.

Carol waited for Jim to start the car but he just sat behind the wheel, staring straight ahead.

She shivered with the cold.

"If we're not going anywhere, Jim, how about just starting the car and getting the heater going?"

He shook himself and smiled. "Sorry. Just thinking."

He turned the ignition and the ten-year old Nash Rambler shuddered to life. He steered it toward Queens Boulevard.

"Thinking what?"

"How pieces are starting to fit together. Won't be long before I know who I am."

Carol leaned over and kissed him on the cheek. "*I* know who you are. Why don't you ask me?"

"Okay. Who am I?"

"The man I love. A great guy, a talented writer, and the best lover on the East Coast." And she meant every word of it.

He kissed her too. "Thanks. But just the East Coast? What about the West Coast?"

"I've never been to the West Coast."

"Oh." He braked at a stop sign. "Well, where do we eat?"

"Can we really afford it?"

"Sure. I got paid for the God Is Dead series today. We're 'in Fat City,' as our president is wont to say."

"About time they paid up."

That explained the dinner invitation. Jim was about as modern as could be, but he remained mired in the fifties when it came to spending her salary on luxuries.

"We can go that way —" he pointed east toward home — "and catch some seafood at Memison's, or we can try someplace in the city." He pointed toward the setting sun.

Carol wasn't really hungry — hadn't been hungry for days, in fact. She couldn't think of any food that would appeal to her, but she knew that Jim was a pasta freak.

"Let's try Little Italy. I feel like Italian tonight."

"Funny . . . you don't look Italian."

"Corny. Drive" she said.

As they approached the ever graceful Queensborough Bridge, an idea struck Carol.

"You know, it's a bit on the early side to eat, don't you think? So as long as we're heading into the city, let's stop at Aunt Grace's."

Jim groaned. "Anyplace but Grace's. I'll even hang around Saks with you."

"Come on. She's a sweetheart, and she's special to me."

Carol loved her spinster aunt who had acted as a sort of stand-in mother during Carol's college years, giving her a family to come "home" to over the holidays and to live with during summer break. Carol had always got along well with her. The same could not be said for Jim, however.

"Yeah, but that apartment of hers gives me the creeps."

"Nothing gives you the creeps. Besides, I don't feel right going into town with this much time to kill and not stopping in to say hello."

"Okay," he said as they crossed the East River and headed down the ramp into Manhattan. "To Gramercy Park we go. But promise me: As soon as she starts trying to save my soul, we leave."

"Promise."

INTERLUDE ON CENTRAL PARK WEST - I

Mr. Veilleur wasn't sure what it was at first.

It came as he was half sitting, half reclining, half dozing on the living room sofa while a news special on the effects of the Tet offensive in Vietnam filled the nineteen-inch screen of their brand new color television. A feeling, a sensation, a prickling in his hindbrain. He couldn't identify it, but there was an ominous feel to it.

A warning?

As it grew stronger, it seemed in some way familiar. Like something from the past, something he'd known before but had not encountered for many years.

A *presence?*

Suddenly alarmed, he shook himself awake and sat up.

No. It couldn't be.

He rose from the couch and went to the window where he stared out at the naked trees of Central Park below. The park was bathed in an orange glow from the setting sun except where it was blocked by the buildings rising along Central Park West. His own apartment building cut a thick swath of shadow into the light.

The feeling was growing, getting stronger, more defined, flowing from the east, from straight across town.

It can't be!

He saw his ghostly reflection in the window glass: a large framed man with gray hair and a lined face; he looked sixtyish but at this moment he felt much older.

There was no doubting the feeling, yet how could it be? It wasn't possible!

"What is it, dear?" his wife said in her thickly accented English as she entered the room from the kitchen.

"It's *him!* He's alive! He's here!"

THREE

1.

Grace Nevins munched a Ry-Krisp as she dusted the largest of her Infant of Prague statues. It wasn't really an infant; actually, the twelve-inch porcelain figure looked more like a young boy wearing a golden crown and holding a globe before him. A cross jutted up from atop the globe. There were four such statues in the front room of her apartment, one at each point of the compass. All were still garbed in their Christmas raiments, but soon it would be changing time. Lent was fast approaching. Ash Wednesday was next week. That called for somber purple robes on each of the statues.

She moved on to the crucifixes. All told, she had twenty-two of them, and some of the more ornate ones were real dust collectors. After that she worked on the eight statues of the Blessed Mother, from the little six-inch one she had picked up in the National Cathedral in Washington D.C., to the three-foot marble beauty in its own miniature grotto in the corner opposite the door. There were six pictures of the Sacred Heart, each with a blessed palm frond behind the frame. The fronds were brittle and brown with age, each being almost a year old. That was all right. Their time was almost up, anyway. When Palm Sunday came again in early April, she'd get fresh fronds for all the pictures.

She was about to start on her praying hands and relics when the buzzer rang. Someone was down at the front entrance. When Grace recognized

Carol's voice on the intercom, her heart gave a little extra beat of joy as she buzzed her in.

Always nice to see her only niece.

As she waited for Carol to climb the three flights of stairs, Grace became aware of a vague uneasiness within her, a gradually mounting tension, with no object, no identifiable cause. She tried to shake it off.

"Carol!" she said at the door when her niece arrived, reaching up to give her a kiss and a hug. "So good to see you!"

She was a good quarter of a century older and three inches shorter than her niece, but probably weighed twice as much. Sometimes Grace fretted about her weight, and had even gone so far as to join that new group, Weight Watchers, but then decided it wasn't worth the trouble. Who was she trying to impress? There was no man in her life, and certainly the Lord didn't care how much you weighed when you came to Final Judgment. She told herself, *The color of your soul is more important than the size of your waist*. It was far more important to watch the shape your soul was in. Say, that was a great idea for a religion group discussion — Soul Watchers. Catchy.

"How are you, Aunt Grace?" Carol said. "I hope you don't mind. We were in town and —"

"'We'?"

"Yes. Jim came along."

Grace's enthusiasm for this surprise visit dropped a few notches at the sight of Jim's face peeking out from behind her niece, but nothing could dampen it completely.

Except perhaps the nameless uneasiness growing within her.

She pushed it down.

"Hiya, Aunt Grace," he said, putting his hand out.

Grace gave it a quick shake. "Hello, Jim. I'm surprised the . . . both of you came."

"Oh, Jim's the reason we're in town," Carol said brightly.

Grace ushered them into the apartment. As she took their coats she held her breath, waiting for Jim to make one of his comments about her religious articles. It took a moment, but then he started.

"Have you added to your collection, Aunt Grace?"

"A few items, yes."

"That's nice."

She waited for a skeptical remark, but he merely stood there with his hands clasped behind his back, smiling blandly.

This was not the usual Jim. Perhaps Carol had warned him to be on his

best behavior. Carol was such a dear. Yes, that was probably it. Otherwise her husband would be behaving as he had the last time he was here, commenting on the Infant of Prague's taste in clothes or citing the fire hazards of keeping old, dried palm fronds around the apartment.

She took a deep breath. The tension was beginning to stifle her. She needed help. She went to her curved glass china cabinet and took out her latest treasure: a tiny fragment of dark brown wood on a bed of satin in a clear plastic box. She prayed that holding it would ward off the strangling uneasiness, but it did nothing. She handed it to Carol.

"Look. It's a relic. A fragment of the True Cross."

Carol nodded. "Very nice." Then she handed it to Jim.

Grace saw that Jim's face was bright red and that he was biting his upper lip. She saw Carol hurl him a warning look. Finally he let out a sigh and nodded.

"Yes. Very nice."

"I know what you're thinking," Grace said as he handed it back to her. "That if all the wood that's been sold as splinters of the True Cross were assembled in one place, the amount of lumber would probably equal the Black Forest in Germany." She replaced the relic within the cabinet. "Many religious authorities are skeptical, too. Perhaps they're right. But I like to compare it to one of Jesus' miracles. You remember the Loaves and the Fishes, don't you?"

"Of course," Jim said.

"Same principle."

And that was enough on the subject. She offered them tea but they refused. After they all found seats she said,

"What brings you here to the city from the wilds of Long Island?"

Grace saw Carol glance questioningly at Jim.

He shrugged and said, "Tell her. It'll be public knowledge next week."

And so Grace listened distractedly as her niece told her about Dr. Roderick Hanley's death, Jim's invitation to the reading of his will, and why they had good reason to believe that Jim might be Hanley's son.

Grace was having difficulty concentrating on Carol's words. The tension — she could barely stand it. Its intensity had nothing to do with what Carol was saying. It was simply *there!* And it was growing stronger by the minute.

She didn't want Carol to know anything was wrong, but she had to get away, had to leave the room, even if for only a few minutes.

"How interesting," she said, rising from her seat. "Excuse me for a moment, won't you?"

It took every ounce of Grace's will to keep from running as she headed for the bathroom. She forced herself to latch the door gently, and then she leaned against the sink. The glaring white tile and porcelain of the confined, cell-like space only seemed to intensify the sensation. In the mirror her face was pale and beaded with sweat.

Grace clutched her Miraculous medal in one fist and her scapular medal in the other. She felt as if she were about to explode. She pressed her fists tightly over her mouth. She wanted to scream! Nothing like this had ever happened before. Was she going crazy?

She couldn't let Carol and Jim see her like this. She had to get them out of here. But how?

Suddenly she knew a way.

She forced herself to return to the front room.

"I'd love to discuss this some more, dear," she said, praying her voice wouldn't break, "but this is the time I set aside each day in the weeks before Lent to say the Rosary. Won't you join me? I'm doing the Fifth Glorious Mystery today."

Jim shot to his feet and looked at his watch.

"Whoa! Time to get to dinner!"

Carol was not far behind.

"We really must be going, Aunt Grace," Carol said. "Why don't you come to dinner with us? We're going down to Mullberry Street."

"Thank you, dear," she said as she pulled their coats from the closet, "but I've got choir practice tonight and then I'm on the eleven-to-seven at Lenox Hill."

"Still nursing?" Carol said with a smile.

"Until the day I die." She pushed their coats at them, wanting to scream, *Get out! Get out before I go crazy right here in front of you!* "Sorry you have to run."

Carol seemed to hesitate. As she opened her mouth to speak, Grace quickly pulled her favorite Rosary beads — the clear crystal ones, blessed by the Holy Father himself — from the pocket of her housecoat.

"Yes," Carol said quickly. "So are we. I'll call you soon. We'll give you a raincheck on dinner."

"That will be lovely."

Carol paused at the door. "Are you all right?"

"Yes-yes. Jesus is with me."

She kissed Carol, waved a quick good-bye to Jim, then sagged against the door after she had closed it behind them. What would happen now?

Would she have a convulsion or go into some sort of screaming fit? What was happening to her?

Whatever it was, she couldn't let anyone be here. She knew that was foolhardy from a medical standpoint, but what if she said some things she didn't want to, things she wanted no one else to hear? She couldn't risk that, no matter what the danger . . .

Wait . . .

The feeling . . . the dread, the tension. It was lessening. As mysteriously as it had come, it was leaving. By slow degrees, it was oozing out of her.

Quickly, fervently, Grace began her rosary.

2.

"Do you think she's all right?" Carol asked Jim as they stepped out onto cold, wintry East Twentieth Street. "Her face looked kind of strained to me."

She dearly loved that pudgy little woman with her twinkling blue eyes and apple cheeks. Grace was the only family she had left.

Jim shrugged. "Maybe it was me. Or maybe living with that decor is affecting her."

"Oh, Jim."

"Really, Carol. Even though she doesn't like me, I think Grace is a sweet old lady. However, she's a paradigm of religiosity, and maybe it's getting to her. Look at that place! It's loaded with guys nailed to crosses! Disembodied hands folded in prayer rising out of the counters. And not one but *six* pictures of bleeding hearts on the wall."

"You know very well that's the Sacred Heart." She fought a smile away from her lips. She couldn't let Jim get rolling. Once he got started, there was no stopping him. "Now cut it out! Seriously, Jim. I'm worried about her. She didn't look well."

He looked at her more closely. "You really are worried, aren't you? Come to think of it, she did look ready to jump out of her skin. Maybe we should go back up."

"No. I don't think she wanted company today. Maybe I'll give her a call tomorrow to see how she's doing."

"Good idea. Maybe we should have insisted on taking her out for a drink at least."

"You know she doesn't drink."

"Yeah, but I do, and right now I could use a drink. *Two* drinks. *Many* drinks!"

"Don't overdo it tonight," she warned, sensing that he was in the mood for some serious celebrating.

"I won't."

"I mean it, Jim. One word about warts later on and we're on our way home."

"Warts?" he said, all shock and wounded dignity. "I never talk about warts!"

"You know you do — when you've had one too many."

"Well, maybe. But drinking has nothing to do with it."

"You never mention them when you're sober."

"The subject never comes up!"

"Let's eat," she sighed, hiding a smile.

3.

Later, when she was calmer, Grace sat on the edge of her bed and thought about what Carol had told her about Jim being an heir to the Hanley estate.

She felt good now. The Rosary, a bowl of hot cream of mushroom soup, and it was as if nothing had ever happened. Within minutes of Carol and Jim's departure, she had felt fine.

An anxiety attack, that's what it had been. She had seen so many of them back in her days as an emergency room nurse but had never imagined that she would ever fall victim to one. A little phenobarbital, a little reassurance, and the patient, usually a thin young woman who smoked too much — *I certainly don't fit that picture* — would be sent on her way in much improved condition.

But what could have triggered it?

Guilt?

Very likely. She had read articles in her nursing journals about guilt being at the root of most anxiety.

Well, I've certainly got plenty to be guilty about, haven't I?

But Grace didn't want to think about the past, nor even about her anxiety attack. She turned her thoughts to what Carol had said. Astonishing things, such as Jim being an orphan — Grace hadn't had the slightest notion about that — and about his being named in a will . . .

Dr. Roderick Hanley's will.

Grace vaguely remembered doing private duty for a Dr. Hanley, shortly before World War II. She had cared for a newborn boy in a town house about twenty blocks uptown in Turtle Bay. It had been a live-in job. The child's mother, whoever she was, was nowhere to be seen. The doctor never mentioned her. It was as if she had never been.

Could that have been the same Dr. Hanley?

Could that infant have been Jim Stevens?

It didn't seem probable, but the timing was right. Jim would have been an infant at that time. Jim Stevens could very well have been that child.

Oh, I hope not, Grace thought.

Because there had been something wrong with that child, with that whole house. Grace hadn't been able to identify exactly what it was that had made her so uncomfortable there, but she remembered being grateful that the job had lasted only a few days.

Shortly thereafter, she changed her evil ways and returned to the Church.

She wished Carol would return to the Church. It saddened her to think of her only niece as a fallen away Catholic. She blamed that on Jim. Carol said he wasn't to blame. She said the Church just didn't seem "relevant" anymore. Everyone seemed to talk about "relevance" these days. But didn't she see that the Church, as God's instrument in the world, was above and beyond something as transient as "relevance"?

No, the relevance angle sounded like Jim talking. The man was an incurable skeptic. The Church taught that no one was beyond hope of redemption, but Grace was quite certain that Jim was testing the limits of that teaching. She hoped he hadn't permanently endangered Carol's soul.

But he seemed to make Carol happy — happier than she had ever been since her parents died. And there was much to be said for making another person happy.

Maybe there was hope for Jim yet. Grace vowed to pray for both their souls.

Grace worried about souls. Especially her own. She knew that before she returned to the Church in her late twenties, she had blackened her soul almost beyond repair. Since then she had worked at cleansing it by doing penance, doing good works, and seeking absolution.

Absolution was the hardest for her. She had received a plenary indulgence on a number of occasions from various visiting bishops, but she wondered if it had worked for her, wondered if it had really had the effect she'd prayed for: to wipe her soul clean of all her past sins. There were so many! She had committed the worst of sins in her younger days, terrible sins she was afraid to think about, hideous sins that so shamed her that she had never been able to speak them to a priest, even in the confessional. The lives she had taken! She was sure — *knew* — that if anyone in the Church learned of the things she had done in her youth, she certainly would be excommunicated.

And excommunication would kill her. The Church was her only source of peace now.

Grace glanced at the clock next to her bed — the dial was set into a pair of hands folded in prayer — and saw that she would be late for choir practice if she didn't hurry. She didn't want to miss that. She felt so good when she was praising the Lord in song.

4.

"They outdid themselves with the garlic tonight," Jim said as he twirled his linguini in the thick golden clam sauce.

They had discovered Amalia's last year, a tiny restaurant on Hester Street, right off Mulberry, where the waiters were unperturbed by Jim's habit of eating his meat course before the pasta. Everyone at Amalia's ate together at long tables covered with red-and-white-checkered cloths. Tonight, though, they had a corner all to themselves.

"This is *so* good!" he said. "Sure you don't want to try even a bite?"

Carol shook her head. "You finish it."

His eyes were a little bloodshot and she could guess why. They had each had a cocktail before dinner, and wine with. Carol had only had one glass of Soave with what little she had eaten of her pasta, but now, as the meal drew to an end, they had an empty Soave plus a near empty Chianti.

"Hard to believe that I've finally found my father," he said. "And by next week I'll probably know who my mother is, too. Is that great, or what?"

Carol reached over with her napkin and wiped a bit of the butter sauce off Jim's chin, thinking how she loved this grown man, but loved equally the little lost boy inside him who was still looking for his Mommy and Daddy.

He took her hand and kissed her fingers.

"What was that for?" she asked, touched.

"For putting up with me."

"Don't be silly."

"No, I mean it. I know I get pretty wrapped up in myself when it comes to finding my parents. It's got to be a drag for you. So thanks for the support — as always."

"Whatever's important to you is important to me."

"That's easy to say. I mean anybody can mouth the words, but you really mean it."

"That's because it *is* easy when you love someone."

"I'm not so sure. You've encouraged me to go on writing novels that no one wants to publish —"

"It's only a matter of time." She never wanted him to stop writing, no matter how many rejections he got.

"Let's hope so. But the important thing is you never made me feel I should give it up or that you were impatient with me. You never once used it to put me down, even when we fight."

She winked at him. "It's an investment. I know you're going to be a rich and famous author before long and I want you to feel you owe it all to me."

"So there's a financial motive, ay? Well, I think I'd better — wait a minute!"

He suddenly dropped her hand and poked through the remains of his clam sauce with his fork. He lifted a small, round piece of garlic and put it on her plate.

"Doesn't that look like a wart to you?"

"That's it!" she said, beating him to the Chianti bottle as he reached for it.

"What?" He looked baffled. "What I say?"

"Time for coffee."

His eyes lit. "With Sambucca?"

"Straight and black. Espresso, even!"

"Aaaawww!"

5.

Grace was in good voice tonight. She listened to her voice mix with the deep chords from the organ as they reverberated through the vaulted spaces of St. Patrick's Cathedral. She was hitting the highs with a richness of tone that was exceptional even for her. "Ave Maria" was her favorite hymn. She had begged for the solo and had been granted it. Now she was doing it justice.

She was aware that the other members of the choir had remained in their seats behind her, listening. This added personal pride to her usual joy of praising the Lord in song, for it was common during a soloist's practice for the choral singers to step outside for a cigarette or retreat to a distant corner for quiet conversation. Not this time. They sat in rapt attention as she sang.

A meaty voice, her choir director had said. Grace liked that expression. She did have a full, rich, meaty voice. It went with her solid, meaty body. She had given over most of her spare time to singing for the last two decades of her fifty-three years, and all those years of practice were finally coming to fruition. Her "Ave Maria" would be the highpoint of the Easter Mass.

Grace lost herself in the rapture of the song, giving it her all . . . until she noticed that the organist had stopped his accompaniment. She glanced back and saw the horrified expressions on the faces of her fellow choir members.

And then she heard it, the one, high, clear voice ringing though the otherwise silent church, singing a simple repetitive melody, almost a chant. A quarter note, followed by two eighths, then another quarter. She could pick out the melody in her head: *Fa-re-fa-mi . . . fa-re-fa-mi . . .*

Then she heard the words: "Satan is here . . . Satan is here . . . " Over and over.

Who was —?

And then Grace realized that it was her own voice singing so high and sweet, and she couldn't stop it. The rapture was still there but horror mingled with it as her voice sang on, faster and faster.

"Satan is here . . . Satan is here . . . Satan is here . . ."

6.

It was warm in the car. As Jim dozed beside her, Carol blinked to stay awake as she guided the old Rambler up Third Avenue through the Fifties toward the Queensborough Bridge.

She wondered how Aunt Grace was doing. Right now she was probably at choir practice just a few blocks west of here in St. Pat's. She hadn't looked well. Carol hoped it was nothing serious. She loved that chubby little spinster.

She found the on ramp for the bridge and headed across the East River, looking for the signs that would direct them toward the Long Island Expressway. Behind them the city gleamed brightly in the crystalline night.

The car swerved as a particularly strong gust ripped across the span.

"You okay?" Jim said thickly, straightening up in the seat and looking at her.

"Sure," she said, keeping her eyes ahead. "I'm fine. Just a little tired is all."

She didn't say so, but she too was sleepy from the wine she had had with dinner.

"Me, too. Want me to drive?"

"No thank you, Mr. Goodtime Charlie."

"Smart girl."

Jim did like to celebrate, and when he celebrated, Carol drove.

To help keep them awake, Carol turned on the radio. She wished they could get F.M. like some of the new cars. She liked the music on that new station, WNEW-FM. But she gladly settled for the WMCA Good Guys. The psychedelic bubblegum sound of "Green Tambourine" filled the car.

"Some meal," Jim said.

"One of the best."

He slipped an arm around her shoulder and nuzzled her ear.

"Love you, Carol."

"Love you, too, hon."

He snuggled closer to her in the warmth of the car as the Lemon Pipers faded out and Paul McCartney began the vocal to "Hello Goodbye."

INTERLUDE ON CENTRAL PARK WEST - II

"Are you going to stand at that window all night?"

"Just a moment longer, my dear," Mr. Veilleur told his wife.

The feeling was gone — or almost gone. He wasn't sure. He stared down at the dark blotch of the park below, its blackness cut by the illuminated ribbons of its traverses, mostly empty now on this wintry night. The same with the street directly below, and Columbus Circle off to the right.

The prickling alarm in the most primitive regions of his brain had finally quieted, but that gave him scant comfort. Its cause could be out there still, its aura attenuated by distance. It could be growing stronger beyond the limits of his perception.

Or maybe it was just a bad dream. Maybe he had fallen asleep in front of the TV and had had a nightmare that carried over briefly into consciousness.

Yes, that had to be it. A nightmare. That was what he had told his wife.

He couldn't be back. It was impossible.

But for a moment there . . .

No. A bad dream. Nothing more.

But what if I'm wrong?

He shuddered. If he was wrong, untold horrors lay ahead. Not only for him, but for all those living and yet to be born.

He turned to his wife and forced a smile.

"What's on the boob tube tonight?"

FOUR

Saturday
February 24

You watch with glee as the Judean infants are torn from the arms of their screaming mothers. Those who protest in a more physical manner are brutally and efficiently subdued by the Roman soldiers in your command. The fathers who run to their families' aid are threatened with swords, and those who will not be cowed are hacked down. The cries of the parents and children alike are music to you, their pain and anguish an exquisite ambrosia.

Only infants of one month or younger may be taken, and only in and around this little town south of Jerusalem. You wish it could be all the children for miles around, but your limits have been set.

Finally all the helpless, squalling infants have been piled in a clearing in a nearby field. The soldiers hesitate in their duty. You scream at them to follow their orders. You pull a sword from the nearest and wade into the tangle of tiny arms and legs. You swing the short, broad blade back and forth in a scything motion, feeling it slice through smooth skin and soft bones as easily as a heated knife through ripe cheese. Tiny crimson geysers shoot up, spraying you. The spilling insides steam in the cold air.

You laugh. You don't care if the soldiers hang back. You'll gladly finish the job yourself. And why not? It's your right, isn't it? After all, weren't you the one who told that doddering old fool, Herod, that the King of the Jews was rumored to have been born in this very area within the last week or two? Weren't you the one who convinced him that this was the only sure way to guarantee that his little corner of the world would pass on to his sons as he has planned?

Finally the bloodlust grips the soldiers and they join you in the slaughter. You step back now, watching them do the work, for it is so much better when you allow others to sink to new depths.

You watch them slashing . . . slashing . . . slashing . . .

Carol awoke screaming.

"Carol! Carol!" Jim was saying, holding her. "What on earth's wrong?"

She lay there drenched in sweat, wanting to be sick.

"Oh, Jim, it was awful!"

"It was only a dream, only a dream," he whispered, trying to soothe her.

But the horror wouldn't go away. So real. So *real!* Almost as if she were right there. The Slaughter of the Innocents. She only vaguely remembered it as a passing reference in one of the Gospels. What had injected it into her subconscious tonight?

"You okay?" Jim said after a while.

"Yeah. Okay now," she said, lying. "Must have been the pepperoni pizza."

"Pepperoni never gave you nightmares before."

"It did this time."

"Here. Cuddle up and get warm."

She fit herself against him. That was better, but she couldn't forget —

. . . slashing . . . slashing . . .

"You're shaking. Next time, we get plain — no pepperoni."

But it wasn't the pepperoni pizza. It was something else, but she didn't know what. She'd been having so many nightmares lately. Mostly they had been vague, formless, ill-remembered experiences, leaving her frightened and unsettled.

But *this . . .*

Jim was soon dozing again. But Carol lay awake the rest of the night, afraid to sleep.

Monday
February 26

1.

Jim checked out the paintings on the walls as they were led down a hall to the conference room. They were all country scenes, full of dark, muted greens and inhabited by dogs and horsemen.

"Somehow I don't think we'll be seeing any Peter Max on the walls here," he said out of the corner of his mouth.

Carol gave a warning squeeze to his hand that made him wince.

The Park Avenue offices of Fletcher, Cornwall & Boothby were staid and hushed, reeking of the Establishment with their high ceilings, solid oak paneling, and thick carpets the color of money. It was late afternoon and most of the staff looked as if they were readying to call it a day.

"There's Bill!" he heard Carol say as they entered the conference room.

Sure enough, Bill was already seated at the long mahogany table, his cassock fully buttoned to the throat this time, trim brown hair neatly combed, looking every bit like a Father William Ryan, S.J., representing St. Francis Home for Boys at the reading of the will should look.

There was an elderly couple at one end of the table and a group of four lawyer types in quiet conversation at the other. One of the latter, a short, dark, intense fellow Jim gauged to be about thirty, broke away as soon as they entered. He approached with an outstretched hand.

"Mr. Stevens? I'm Joe Ketterle. We spoke on the phone last week."

"Right," Jim said, shaking his hand. "This is my wife, Carol."

"How do you do? Well, you're the last one. We're ready to get down to business. Please take a seat." He pulled two chairs from the table and eased Jim and Carol into them.

They sat next to Bill. He looked around the table again. Besides himself and one or two of the attorneys, there was no one in the room young enough to be another of Hanley's offspring.

"I don't see any potential brothers and sisters here," he whispered to Carol.

She nodded. "Looks like you're it."

Excitement expanded within him as an older attorney who introduced himself as Harold Boothby put on a pair of half-lens glasses and began the reading of the will. There was a lot of legalese, but finally they got down to the good stuff — the bequests. A cool million went to Hanley's longtime associate Dr. Edward Derr. An attorney who seemed to be apart from the others made notes and said something about the bequest passing via Derr's will to his wife. Jim guessed he represented Mrs. Derr. The elderly couple — Hanley's longtime housekeeper and groundsman — each got a quarter million. The old woman broke into tears. St. Francis Home for Boys got a quarter million, as well.

Bill seemed shocked at the amount. "Can we ever use it!" he said in a hoarse voice.

Jim's palms were slick with sweat. *There's nobody left but me!*

"'And finally,'" Mr. Boothby intoned, "'I leave the remainder of my estate, all property and financial assets, to James Jonah Stevens.'"

Jim's throat was suddenly dry. "Wha-what are we talking about when we talk about 'remainder'?"

"We haven't worked out the value of the estate to the penny as yet," Mr. Boothby said, gazing at Jim over the top of his reading glasses, "but we estimate your share to be worth something in the neighborhood of eight million dollars."

Jim felt as if all the air had suddenly been sucked from the room. Beside him he heard Carol give out a short, high-pitched cry, then clap a hand over her mouth. Bill was on his feet, slapping Jim on the shoulder.

"That's *some* neighborhood!" Bill cried.

The next few minutes were a blur of smiles and handshakes and congratulations. Jim wandered through them in a daze. He should have been jubilant, should have been dancing on the table, but he couldn't help feeling disappointed, cheated. Something was missing.

Eventually, he and Carol were alone in the conference room with Joe Ketterle who was talking at breakneck speed.

"— so if you feel the need for any legal advice on how to manage your share of the estate, any advice at all, please don't hesitate to call me."

He pressed his card into Jim's hand. Jim suddenly realized why he had been receiving the red carpet treatment: He was now a wealthy potential client.

"You're pretty familiar with the Hanley estate?" Jim said, staring down at the card.

"Very."

"Was there any mention at all in his papers about *why* he left so much of his estate to me?"

"No," Ketterle said with a shake of his head. "No reason given at all. You mean you don't know?"

Jim wanted out of here. He wanted a quiet place where he could huddle with Carol and the two of them could talk this whole thing out. *Eight million dollars!* Suddenly he was filthy rich and it scared the hell out of him. Life would never be the same and that was what was frightening him. He didn't want the money to change what he and Carol had together.

"Can I have a copy of the will?"

"Of course!"

"Thanks. And the house — it's mine?"

"Yes." He handed Jim an envelope. "Here's a set of keys. We'll have to have you back here to sign some papers for legal transfer of ownership, of course, but —"

He took the envelope. "Great. We'll be in touch."

Jim pulled Carol out into the hall. He spotted Bill standing in the atrium by the elevators and was glad to see he hadn't left yet, but he cursed under his breath when he saw who was talking to him.

2.

"Damn!"

Carol glanced at Jim. He seemed more tense now than he had before the reading of the will. She had expected him to return to his laconic, wisecracking self, but if anything, he had become grim.

Maybe he was in shock. God knew *she* was. Eight million dollars! It was an unimaginable sum. Her mind couldn't get a grip on it. What she did know for sure was that their lives were going to be changed by the inheritance. For the better, she prayed.

"What's wrong, Jim?"

He gestured ahead. "Look who's with Bill."

Carol recognized the tall, slovenly fellow with the long black hair and blotchy skin.

"Gerry Becker? What's he doing here?"

Before Jim could answer, Becker turned toward them and threw his arms wide.

"Jim Stevens! Heir to the Hanley fortune! Far *out!* Hold it right there!"

He raised the Nikon slung from his neck and flashed a photo of them as they approached. Carol had met Gerry Becker only twice before — both times at Monroe *Express* Christmas parties — and had disliked him immediately. He attached himself talked into your face, backed you into a corner, and talked about himself, always about himself. People at the parties took turns scraping him off on each other. He was overweight but that didn't stop him from wearing fitted shirts. A roll of fat was squeezed above his three-inch wide leather belt. Despite the fact that he was nudging thirty, he seemed to have bought the whole hippie look in a package — beard, long hair, fringed suede jacket, tie-dyed shirt, bellbottoms, and an aversion to soap. All he needed was a couple of strands of love beads to complete the picture. Carol didn't mind the hippie look itself, so she could not put her finger on just why she disliked him, other than the fact that he epitomized what her mother used to call "skeevy." She knew Jim liked him even less.

"Hi, Gerry," she said, trying to be polite.

Just then the elevator door opened next to Bill. Jim pulled her toward it and they crowded in behind him.

"Bye, Gerry," Jim said.

But they weren't quick enough. Becker darted between the doors before they slid closed.

"Hey, man. You weren't trying to duck an interview with me, were you, Stevens?"

"What are you doing here, Gerry?"

"You kidding? Monroe's richest resident gets killed and one of my fellow journalists on the *Express* is named in the will — that's *news*, man!"

Up close, Carol could see large flakes of dandruff salted through Becker's oily hair. The skin along his hairline and his eyebrows was reddened, irritated, and flaky as well. She wondered when he had last brushed his teeth.

She slipped to the back of the elevator car.

"I was just talking to the good father here," he said, nodding toward Bill, "telling him about my days at the *Trib*. He says his orphanage made out pretty well. How'd you do?"

Carol glanced at Bill, saw him smile and roll his eyes as if to say, *Where'd you find this guy?* She realized with a start that this was the first time he had looked directly at her since they had arrived. His gaze had been either avoiding her or sliding off her all morning.

"I did okay," Jim said in a guarded tone.

Becker pulled out a note pad. "Far out! How about some details?"

"Look, Gerry," Jim said. Carol could sense his growing annoyance. "I don't want to discuss it now. In fact, this whole scene here is pretty intrusive."

Becker's face twisted into a grimace that managed at once to look nasty and offended.

"Oh, I get it, Stevens. Inherit a little money and first thing you do is turn your back on your friends?"

She felt Jim stiffen, so she laid a hand on his arm. As he hesitated, the elevator stopped at the ground floor and the doors opened. Stepping out into the lobby, Jim said,

"Not now, Gerry. Meet me tomorrow around noon at the Hanley mansion and I'll give you an exclusive."

"The Hanley mansion? That's cool. Why there?"

"I own it now."

Becker seemed too dazed to follow them as they fled the building.

"I think a celebration is in order," Carol said once they were outside and around a corner and were sure he wasn't going to catch up. The sun was low and Park Avenue was in deep, chilled shadows. She tugged Bill's sleeve. "And this time you're coming along. No excuses."

Bill seemed flustered. "I really can't. I should get back. And besides," he opened his overcoat to expose his cassock, "you don't want a priest along to throw a wet blanket over wherever it is you plan to celebrate."

"Well, let's see," she said. "We're half way between Xavier and Regis. Surely there's got to be a Jebbie at one of those two places who's your size and who'll lend you some civvies."

"Well, yeah. I know a guy at Xavier who's about my size, but —"

"Then it's settled." She looked at Jim. "Right?"

He smiled crookedly and pulled out the car keys. "Downtown it is. J. Carroll will take us."

"John Carroll?"

"No. *J*. Carroll. It's a car, not a Jesuit."

Bill's face took on a pained look. "It wouldn't happen to be a Nash would it?"

"Of course."

"That's awful!" He grinned. "Okay. As long as you're sure I won't be in the way when you're accosted by other future Pulitzer prizewinning journalists like the last."

They all laughed as they headed for the garage, and for the first time, their new found millions notwithstanding, Carol felt really good about the day.

3.

Amalia's Clam House, Little Italy:

"Remember Jerry Shauer?" Jim said as he twirled spaghetti onto his fork.

He was finally beginning to relax. The three of them had this end of the long table to themselves. A black couple was deep in whispered conversation at the other. The chianti was good, his spaghetti *aglio et olio* was *al dente*, just the way he liked it.

"Sure," Bill said around a mouthful of *scungilli Fra Diavolo*. Dressed in a borrowed crew neck sweater and a pair of wide wale cords, he now looked like a graduate student. "Our old quarterback."

"Right. Married Mary Ellen Kovach. They had a kid last year."

"Really?"

"Yeah. Named her April."

"That's nice," Bill said, then he almost choked. "Oh, no! April Shauer?" He looked to Carol for confirmation. "That's got to be a joke!"

Carol shook her head, then began to laugh. Soon they were all laughing. Jim wondered why it was so funny tonight. Maybe it was the wine. They broke up three times before order was restored.

This was like the old days. Jim thought about the Bill Ryan he used to know. The long-armed kid who had all the speed on their high school football team, the Hawks from Our Lady of Perpetual Sorrow — or "Perpetual Motion," as the guys called it. Bill had been a wide receiver; Jim had been an iron man, playing running back on offense and linebacker on defense. Bill dazzled their opponents with his speed and footwork while Jim frightened them with the crushing force of his blocking and the howling ferocity of his tackling. He couldn't repress a twinge of guilt, even after all these years, as he remembered the dark pleasure he had taken from ramming into members of the other team, hearing them grunt in pain as he butted them aside or hurled them to the turf. He hit them harder than he had to, hit them with everything he had. And he had hurt quite a few of them. Some seriously. He was glad now that Stony Brook hadn't had a football team. Otherwise he might well have joined and the carnage would have continued. As he matured, he had learned how to bottle his violent urges. Marriage to Carol had helped.

But he wondered: Had Dr. Hanley possessed a seething core of violence like his own? Had he managed to lock it away as Jim had?

He turned his thoughts back to Bill who had been a valued member of the team, as well, but had never really been one of the gang. When locker room talk turned away from school and sports and got into who had been the latest to feel up Mary Jo Munsey, Bill faded away. Still, he had been somewhat of a regular guy. He could work miracles with carburetors and would go to the parties and CYO dances and dance with the girls, had even dated Carol fairly steadily for a few years. But he had always seemed one step removed from the crowd, always slightly out of tune with everybody else. One of those guys who heard a different drummer.

Some of the guys would tease him for being such a square, but Jim could never get into that. He had always liked Bill. He had been able to discuss things with Bill that he could not even approach with the other guys. Heavy stuff. Ideas. They both were voracious readers and so they often discussed books. He still remembered the long arguments they'd had over *Atlas Shrugged* when it first came out. They rarely agreed on anything, that was what made the conversations so stimulating. Bill was always on the up side. "Idealman," Jim had called him. And Bill had dubbed him "Cynicalman" in return.

Initially, Jim had been stunned to learn that Bill Ryan had joined the Jesuit seminary after high school. "I thought you were going to be a mechanic!" he remembered telling him, jokingly. But after thinking about it for awhile, he had concluded that he should have seen it coming all along. He knew that Bill believed in God and Man and in Virtue and Decency being their own rewards. Believed it then and believed it now, apparently. There was something refreshing about that in the God Is Dead age.

And now he was at St. F.'s.

Funny how things ran in circles.

"Good to see you laugh, old buddy," Bill said, finally.

"What do you mean?"

"You've been pretty glum for a guy who's just become filthy rich."

"Sorry about that," Jim said, knowing it was true and regretting it. He hated being a wet blanket. "Yeah, Hanley attached a lot of money to my name in that will. Just wished he'd attached a couple of extra words along with the dough."

"Like 'my son'?" Bill said.

Jim nodded, glad that Bill was tuned into him. That old rapport, that static-free FM wavelength they used to groove on was still working.

"Yeah. Those would do just fine."

"I don't think anyone will doubt you're his son."

"But that's not enough. I need to know it all. What's my nationality? When do I salute or puddle up? Do I stand for the "Marseillaise" or weep at "Danny Boy"? Should I have a swastika hidden in the bedroom and do secret *Sieg Heil*s every night, or should I be trying a few years in a kibbutz? If I came from Hanley, where the hell did *he* come from?"

"Judging from your dietary preferences," Carol said, "you *must* be part Italian."

Bill said, "At least you know who your father is. Was. Obviously he never forgot you."

"Yeah, but he could have legitimized me in print."

He felt Carol's hand slip over his. "You're legitimate to me," she said.

"I think you're pretty legit, too," Bill said. "What else do you need?"

"Nothing." Jim couldn't help smiling. "Except maybe figuring out who Mom is."

Bill glanced heavenward. "Lord, teach this man to let things lie . . . at least for tonight." Then he looked straight at Jim. "After that, I'll do anything I can to help."

"Great! What say we blow this place and head for the Village. It's amateur night at the *Wha?*"

4.

Cafe *Wha?*, Greenwich Village

Bill shook his head to clear his buzzing ears. The *Wha?* was a long, narrow room; the stage was set in the center of the left wall. A Lovin' Spoonful-type quartet that billed itself as Harold's Purple Crayon was carting its equipment off the stage to make room for the next act.

"Loud, but not bad," he said to Jim and Carol. "The harmony was pretty good. And I liked that washboard jugband number."

"They're not going anywhere," Jim said, quaffing the rest of his bottle of Schaeffer. "Some Stones, some Spoonful, a little Beatles, a touch of the Byrds. *I* liked them, but they're not commercial. No definite sound. A mishmash. But better than that first group putting Kahlil Gibran to acid rock. Whoa!"

Bill couldn't help laughing. "Jim Stevens: World's Toughest Critic! Gibran's not so bad."

Carol touched his arm. "Let's get back to what you were saying before the band drowned us out. About going up to New Hampshire. Do you really think McCarthy's got a chance in the primary?"

"I think so."

He reached for his beer, not because he had to have a sip at that moment, but to remove his arm from contact with Carol's hand. It felt so nice there, so soft and warm, awakening feelings better left asleep. He glanced at her.

Carol Nevins-now-Stevens: Girl, did I ever have it bad for you. Movies, holding hands, an arm over your shoulder or around your waist, good-night kissing. No further. Puppy love. Now you're a woman and your hair is longer and your figure fuller, but your smile is as dazzling and your eyes are as bright and as blue as ever.

Bill knew she was going to be a problem. Already was. For a couple of nights now, increasingly erotic thoughts of Carol had kept him awake way past his usual bedtime.

Through his years in the seminary he had struggled to condition himself into automatic observance of his vow of chastity. To become, in a sense, asexual. It hadn't been as difficult as he had thought. At first he had taught himself to approach it as a form of daily *Spannungsboden*, a self-imposed delay between the desire for something and the act of reaching out for that something. Day after day, he would put off today's sexual desires until tomorrow. But tomorrow never came. The *Spannungsboden* was interminable.

Over the years, it became easier. It had taken time, but now he could reflexively wrap up temptations or potentially troublesome urges and channel them off into oblivion before they could find purchase in his consciousness or his libido.

So why wasn't it working with Carol? Why hadn't he been able to keep her from wandering in and out of his mind since he had seen her last week?

Perhaps because Carol was from *before*. No woman could find a place in his feelings today, but Carol had lived in that private interior garden before he had erected the walls. He had thought his feelings for her long dead and gone, but apparently it wasn't so. There was still life in those old roots.

Isn't it all foolishness, this celibacy thing?

How many times had he heard that question, from others, from himself? A hostile someone had even quoted Marx to the effect that it was easy to become a saint if one did not want to be a man. Bill's answer was a shrug. Celibacy was part of the package, part of the commitment he had made to God — you give up power, wealth, sexual involvement, and other distractions in order to focus your energies on God. The self-denial tempers the faith.

Bill knew the depth of his faith. It infused his heart and soul and mind. He prided himself on being neither a heavenward-gazing acetic nor an overgrown altar boy. Both his feet were planted firmly in the real world. His was a mature, intellectualized belief that cut through the fairy tales and myths and Bible stories. He had read the lives and works of the saints, and de Chardin, of course, but he had studied Heidegger, Kierkegaard, Camus, and Sartre as well.

He had handled them with ease. But could he handle Carol?

"I don't trust McCarthy," Jim was saying.

Bill had to laugh. "The return of Cynicalman!"

"He was never gone," Carol said.

"Seriously, though," Jim said, leaning forward, "I just don't trust one-issue candidates. In fact, I don't trust candidates, *period*. The political process seems to corrupt everyone who gets involved. The people who'd make the best candidates lack sufficient bad taste to run for office."

"I believe Eugene McCarthy's an exception," Bill said. "And I believe he's got a damn good chance of winning in New Hampshire. The Tet offensive turned a lot of the country against the war."

Jim shook his head. "We should clean up our own yards and tend to our own neighborhoods first, *then* worry about the rest of the world. If we all did that, maybe there wouldn't be so much in the world to worry about. Want another beer?"

Bill said, "I'd love one."

"Okay. We'll see what the next band sounds like. If they're awful, I know a quieter place we can go.

5.

Monroe

Emma Stevens was roughly yanked out of sleep by the sudden movement beside her. Jonah had bolted upright in bed.

"What's wrong?"

"I have to go out!"

His voice sounded strained, upset. And that frightened her. Jonah never made an abrupt movement, never showed alarm. Everything he did seemed calculated. He seemed to have nerves of insulated copper wire.

But he was tense now. She could see him sitting there in the dark, his hand cupped over his good right eye, staring into the night with his blind eye, as if he were seeing something with it.

"You've had a vision?"

He nodded.

"What's it about?"

"You wouldn't understand!"

He leapt from the bed and began to pull on his clothes.

"Where are you going?"

"Out. I've got to hurry."

Emma threw the covers back. "I'll come with you."

"*No!*" The word cracked like a whip. "You'll only get in the way! Stay here and wait."

And then he hurried from the room.

Emma pulled the covers back over her and shivered. She could not remember the last time she had seen her husband hurry. Yes, she could. It had been back in the winter of '42 . . . rushing to the orphanage.

6.

Jonah raced down Glen Cove Road toward the LIE.

Something terrible is going to happen!

He wasn't sure how exactly, but the One would soon be in deadly danger. Whether through pure earthly happenstance or through the machinations of the other side, he could not say. He had to hurry, or all his life until now would be made meaningless.

He pressed a hand over his right eye. Yes, there, to the west, a red glow of danger in his left eye.

All my life made meaningless . . .

It seemed as if he had been preparing for this, for what was happening these days, forever. But it hadn't been forever. Only since he was nine. It was then that he had learned that he was different from others.

He remembered that day in 1927 when the flood waters had come roaring through their town in what the history books would later call the Great Lower Mississippi Valley Flood Disaster. Up until then he had thought of himself, when he thought of himself at all, as just another normal everyday farm boy. He had burned alive his share of beetles, torn the wings off his share of butterflies, tortured and killed his share of kittens, and enjoyed it all. His folks had been upset with him, and maybe even a little scared of him, but wasn't that what childhood was all about — learning, testing? He assumed all kids experimented as he did, but he didn't know for sure, because he had no brothers and sisters, and no real friends.

The Great Flood changed all his perceptions and preconceptions.

Luckily for him, he had been out by the barn when the water hit. The yard had been a sea of mud after days of heavy rain. He heard a roar like a great train rolling on a downgrade, looked up, and across the field he saw the onrushing wall of dirty brown water, swirling madly with debris as it raced toward him.

He had been able to make it just in time to the giant oak tree that stood in the center of the yard. With the water surging and lapping at his heels, he scrambled up through the lower branches. The thick trunk swayed and groaned at the onslaught of the churning water, but its roots held.

He heard an explosive crack and turned toward the house. As he watched from his high perch he heard one sharp, high scream from his mother and nothing from his father as his home was flattened and broken into kindling by the wall of water. The barn collapsed and was swept away along with the livestock and the splintered remnants of his house.

He did not escape unscathed, however. A particularly powerful wave caught his legs and knocked them from the branch that supported him. As he fell, clutching frantically at another branch, a protruding twig pierced his left eye. The pain was a jab of lightning into his brain. He howled in agony but held on, finding new footing and pulling himself beyond the water's reach.

He reached a high branch and straddled it, cupping the socket of his bloodied, ruined eye, rocking back and forth and retching with the pain that throbbed like a white hot coal.

The water rose higher but the tree held firm. As the day faded toward night, so the pain in his eye faded to a dull ache. The torrent slowed to a steady southward current.

Things, living and otherwise, began to float by: a child screaming in lonely terror as it clung to a rooftop, a woman wailing from a log, drowning cattle, bellowing and gurgling, a man leaping from some floating debris and swimming for Jonah's tree, only to miss it and be carried away out of sight.

Young Jonah, high and dry, watched them all with his good eye from the safety of his perch in the oak. By all rights he should have been terrified, should have been racked with grief and horror at the loss of his home and parents, should have been speechless and near catatonic with his own injury and the scope of the death and destruction around him.

But he was not. If anything, he was just the opposite. He found himself energized by the disaster. He clung to the branches and avidly watched as each corpse, each struggling survivor passed by. And when dark had fallen completely, he hung on to the sounds of the night, each cry of misery and pain, each howl of terror, drawing strength from them.

The hurt and fear of others was like a balm to his own pain, draining it away. Never had he felt so strong, so *alive!*

He wanted more.

To his dismay, the waters receded too rapidly. Soon a boat came by and the soldiers upon it picked him from his branch like a stranded kitten. They took him to a church in the highlands that had been converted to a makeshift hospital where they patched his left eye and laid him down to rest.

But he couldn't rest! He had to be up and about, had to roam, had to drink in all the destruction, the loss, the death. He wandered the ruins along the edge of the slowly receding waters. He found children crying for their parents, for their brothers and sisters, grown-ups weeping for their mates, for their children. He found hundreds of dead animals — dogs, cats, cows, goats, chickens — and occasionally a dead person. If no one was in sight, he'd poke the dead folks with a stick to see if he could puncture their bloated remains.

The air was so heavy, so *oppressive* with misery, it was all he could do to keep from screeching with ecstatic laughter.

But he knew he had to keep quiet, had to look glum and lost like everyone else. Because he knew then that he was different from the people around him.

Different from everyone.

After that it took him years of trial and error, but he learned to hide his differentness from the world. Eventually he found legal, even productive ways to keep his hungers in check. And over the years he came to learn that he had traded one sort of sight in his left eye for another. It was that sight that had wrenched him from his sleep tonight.

His good eye blazing, he pushed the accelerator to the floor.

7.

The Back Fence, Greenwich Village

Carol watched with relief as Jim returned from a quick trip to the restroom. She and Bill had had the table to themselves for a few moments and the atmosphere had become strained. Bill seemed so uptight when he was alone with her.

"How about another round?" Jim said.

Carol didn't want another drink — she had switched to Pepsi a while ago — and she didn't want Jim to have another, either. She wanted to say something, but not in front of Bill — anything not to sound like a nagging wife in front of Bill. So she held off.

Besides, he hadn't mentioned warts yet.

"One more," Bill said. "Then it's time to go."

They've both got hollow legs! she thought. Where were they putting it all?

"Carol?" Jim said, pointing at her glass.

She glanced down at the flat brown liquid that was nearing room temperature now, at the thin oily scum on its surface — *Who's their dishwasher?* — and decided to stick with what she had.

"I'm fine. And so are the two of you, I'd think."

"Nah!" Jim said with a laugh. "We're just getting started!"

He ordered two more beers, then turned back to Bill, pointing a finger at him.

"Quick! 'Theology is anthropology.'"

"Uuhh." Bill squeezed his eyes shut. "Feuerbach, I think."

"Right. How about, 'We are proceeding toward a time of no religion at all.'"

"Bonhoeffer."

"I'm impressed!" Jim said.

"Do I detect a common thread in those quotes? Is the Village Atheist trying to make a point?"

Carol let her mind drift off. She might as well have been home in Monroe for all the attention they were paying her. It was quieter here in the Back Fence, at the corner of Bleecker and something. No live music, just records. "Boogaloo Down Broadway" was thumping softly in the background at the moment. The relative quiet had got Bill and Jim to talking and they'd been going at it like two college freshmen debating the meaning of life, of *everything!*

Maybe it was a male thing. Male bonding — wasn't that what they called it?

Bill looked at her and smiled beatifically, obviously more comfortable with her now that Jim was here. He seemed to be at peace with himself. A man who knew himself, an idealist who was sure that he was doing exactly what he wanted with his life. She was certain there were ambitions and dissatisfactions bubbling under the surface there, but she detected none of the wild turmoil she knew to be raging within her husband, James the Skeptic, skewerer — was there such a word? — of Current Wisdom and Common Knowledge.

Oddly enough, she found both extremes appealing.

She said, "I'm just glad to hear the two of you stop arguing for ten consecutive seconds."

"Didn't you know, Carol?" Bill said, poising the mouth of his Budweiser an inch from his lips. "Jim and I agreed long ago to disagree on everything."

"The hell we did!" Jim cried, and the two of them cracked up like schoolboys.

Jim suddenly stopped laughing. His face grew stern.

"Wart's so funny about that?"

"Wart?" Carol said, immediately alert. "Did he say 'wart'?"

"Of course," Bill said. "Haven't you been listening? We've been talking about the wart in Vietnam all night."

"I'm thinking of going to business school," Jim said. "I wonder if *Wart*on will accept me?"

"A good place to make love, not wart," Bill replied, nodding vigorously.

"That does it!" Carol said. *Two of them!* "No more for either of you. The bar is closed as far as you two are concerned. It's late and we're going home as soon as you finish those! And *I'm* driving!"

8.

Carol clutched Jim's arm as they walked into the icy wind on their way to the car, which he had parked somewhere east of Washington Square. Suddenly he broke away and left her with Bill as he darted into an all-night deli. In a moment he was out again, carrying three oranges.

He began juggling them as he returned to the sidewalk. From there he led them along like a circus act, pausing under each streetlamp to show off in its cone of light, then moving on. He dropped them at least once between each lamp.

"Where'd you learn to do that?" she asked, amazed that he could juggle.

"In the living room," Jim said as he somehow managed to keep the oranges aloft in the dark.

"When?"

"I practice while I'm writing."

"How can you do that?"

"Not all writing is done at the typewriter. A lot of it's done in the head before you start hitting the keys."

Carol was suddenly uneasy. She didn't remember it being so dark and deserted-looking along this stretch earlier in the evening. It had seemed safer then.

"You know something, Jim?" Bill said. "I've always wanted to juggle. In fact, I'd give my right arm to juggle like that."

Jim burst out laughing and the oranges went rolling into the street. Carol began to laugh, too.

A strange, whiny voice cut her off.

"Hey, you laughin' a' me, man?"

She looked around and saw a half dozen or more figures huddled at the edge of a vacant lot to their left.

"No," Jim said, good-naturedly. He pointed at Bill. "I'm laughing at him. He's crazy."

"Yeah, man? Well, I don' tink so. I tink you wuz laughin a' me!"

Carol felt Bill grip her upper arm as he said:

"Let's head for the car, Jim," he said.

"Right."

Jim fell in on her other side and the three of them started up the street. But they didn't get far before they were surrounded by the gang. If that's what they were. All were a little underdressed for the weather, Carol noted, all on the thin side, all smaller than Jim or Bill, the ex-football players. But there were six of them.

"Look," Jim said, "we don't want any trouble."

She heard a tremor in his voice. She knew someone else might mistake it for fear, but Carol recognized it as anger. Jim had good control over his temper, but when he lost it, he *lost* it.

"Yeah?" said that same whiny voice. "Well maybe we do!"

Carol watched the speaker. His hair was long and matted, a a wispy attempt at a beard dirtied his cheeks. He couldn't seem to stand still. His arms were jerking, his body twitching this way and that, his feet scuffing back and forth. She glanced around. They were all alike.

They're on speed!

Carol's mind suddenly flashed to an article she had read in *Time* about mainlining methamphetamine as the latest thing in the Village. She hadn't given it much thought then. Now she was facing the result.

"All right," Jim said, stepping away from her. "If you've got a problem with me, we'll talk about it. Just let them go on their way."

Carol opened her mouth to say something but was cut off by a sudden tightening of Bill's grip on her arm.

"No way," the lead speedfreak said, smiling as he stepped forward and pointed at Carol. "She's what we want."

Carol felt her stomach constrict around the flat Pepsi. And then, as if watching in slow motion, she saw Jim smile back at the leader and kick him full force in the groin. As the speedfreak screamed in agony, all hell broke loose.

9.

The effects of the night's beers had been evaporating steadily in the tension of his encounter with these punks. As he punted their grinning spokesman in the balls, Jim's head cleared completely. He had expected to get some of the old pleasure out of that kick, but it wasn't there. Concern for Carol overrode everything.

In the darkness he dimly saw the guy to his left pull something from his pocket. When it snapped out to a slim, silvery length of about three feet, he knew it was a car antenna, one hell of a wicked weapon with the knob pulled off the end. Had to get in close now, no hesitation or he'd whip that thing across his eyes.

Jim ducked and charged forward, driving his shoulder into the creep's solar plexus, ramming him up against the front of a building. It was almost like footall. But these guys were playing for keeps.

Behind him, Carol screamed.

He called out to Bill. "Get her to the car!"

That was the all-important thing: get Carol to safety.

Then somebody or something slammed hard against the side of his head and he saw lights flash for an instant but he held on to consciousness, drove a fist at the source, and heard somebody grunt. Somebody else jumped on his back and he went down on one knee. Screaming in the back of his mind was a white-hot mortal fear that he was going to get kicked to death here on this dark nameless street, but he could barely hear it. He was pissed and he was pumped and he knew that despite how badly he'd let his body go since his football days in high school, he was in better shape than any of these shitheads and he was going to make some of them very sorry they'd messed with him.

He shook the guy off his back and rolled over just in time to see somebody start to swing a short length of heavy chain at his head.

10.

Bill stood paralyzed for an instant at the sudden chaos around him. He and Carol seemed to have been forgotten for an instant as the gang converged on Jim. Carol screamed and started forward to help him but Bill grabbed her and steered her toward the street instead, toward the car.

He was torn between seeing her to safety and helping Jim. He didn't want to leave her side, but he knew Jim wouldn't last long in the center of that melee.

"Get to the car and get it running!" he told her, pushing her down the street. "I'll get Jim."

This is not what I'm about, he thought as he turned toward the fight. He was a man of God, a man of peace. He didn't fight in the streets. March in them, yes. But he didn't fight in them.

Then he saw the gleaming links of a doubled length of nickel-plated chain rise up over the squirming tangle of bodies. He charged. He grabbed the chain as it started to swing down, jerked its wielder around, and rammed a fist into his face.

God forgive me, but that felt good!

Then Jim was on his feet and they were back to back. There was an instant's respite in which he heard Jim's whisper.

"Carol's safe?"

"On her way."

I hope!

Then the gang charged again.

11.

What am I going to do? Carol thought as she fumbled in her purse for her keys.

What was better? Go for help or back the car up to the fight and shine J. Carroll's headlamps on the scene. Maybe the bright lights and her leaning on the horn would scatter the rats.

The purse was suddenly snatched from her hands.

"I'll take that, babe."

Carol cried out in fright and turned to see a scraggly-haired youth standing beside her. There was enough light at this end of the block to make out the leer on his face beneath his dirty wool cap. She reached for the purse.

"Give that back to me!"

He dropped the purse on the hood of the car and grabbed her. In one rough move he twisted her around, swung an arm across her throat, and pulled her back against him. Through the coat she felt his hands slide over her breasts.

"This is gonna be fun!" he said. "Gonna fuck you three ways from Sunday, babe, and you're gonna *love* it!"

Carol struggled frantically against him, trying to kick back at his shins and twist free, but he was strong despite his frail appearance. He started to pull her between two of the cars.

"Babe, when I'm through with you you're gonna beg for more. You're gonna —"

Carol heard a dull *thunk!*, felt her captor jerk, then stiffen, then release her. She broke away and glanced back in time to see him topple face first to the pavement. In the faint light she could see that the top of his skull was caved in, and blood was beginning to soak through the cap.

Over the tops of the parked cars she saw a tall, dark figure gliding away toward the fight.

12.

Jim struggled for air. He was pinned on his side. Someone had the chain wrapped around his throat and was pulling it tight while somebody else was kicking him in the gut.

He knew he was going to die. He didn't have it anymore. The old black ferocity from his football days that would have sent punks like these running for their mothers was gone. When he needed it most, it was gone.

Where was Bill? Was he down, too? He just hoped Carol got away. Maybe she could flag a black-and-white and get some help. Maybe . . .

He twisted violently. If only he could get some air! One breath and he could hold on a little longer. Just a puff —

Suddenly the chain around his throat went slack. He gulped air and looked up. The one who had been kicking him paused and looked past Jim. Just then something blurred in from the left and caught the punk on the side of the head with enough force to lift him clear off his feet.

Something warm and wet and lumpy splattered Jim. He didn't have to look to know it was brain tissue.

He twisted around and saw two more of the gang sprawled on the sidewalk behind him. One lay still; a length of chain rattled softly in the twitching grasp of the other.

He heard a meaty *thunk!* and saw a tall, dark figure swing something against the head of one of the guys over Bill. The guy dropped into a boneless heap.

The last creep took off with the dark man chasing him.

Jim got up and staggered over to Bill.

"You okay?"

"My God!" Bill gasped. "What happened?"

"*Jim!*" Carol ran up and threw her arms around him. "Are you all right?"

"I think so. Bill? You there?"

Bill was on his feet, swaying. Jim couldn't make out his expression, but his voice shook as he spoke.

"I . . . I don't know. My stomach . . ."

He turned and staggered a few steps away, retching in the darkness. A moment later he returned.

"Sorry."

"It's okay, Bill. I may join you in a moment."

"Let's get moving before these guys come to and —"

"I think they're dead," Jim said.

He knelt and checked for a pulse in the throat of the nearest. He had no experience with this sort of thing, but he'd seen it done on TV. He found no pulse but he did get a close look at the ruin of the guy's skull and his open, staring eyes.

He leapt to his feet.

"Let's get out of here!"

"Shouldn't we call the police?" Carol said.

"We will. From a pay phone somewhere. But I'm not hanging around to get blamed for this."

"But who did it? Who *was* that?"

Jim wasn't sure what it was, but there had been something disturbingly familiar about that dark figure.

"He helped me, too," Carol said.

Jim felt spicules of ice run through his blood. "*You?*"

"One of them grabbed me by the car. If the guy with the club hadn't —"

Jim pulled her close against him. If anything ever happened to Carol, he knew he'd go mad.

"Maybe one of us has a guardian angel, Carol."

"That was no angel," Bill said.

Jim was not inclined to argue.

"Let's get to the car.

13.

Carol had managed to hold it in while Jim drove the three of them around in aimless circles, hold it through the violent shakes that had started as soon as she slipped into the front seat, through the cold chills that tremored through her despite the heater going full blast. But when Bill got out to call 911 at a phone booth they found at Houston and the Bowery, leaving her alone in the car with Jim, it all came out. Loud, deep, racking sobs burst from the deepest part of her.

"It's okay," Jim said, hugging her tight. "We're safe now."

"But we could have been killed!"

"I know. I'll never forgive myself for endangering you like that."

"It wasn't your fault!"

"Next time we pay for a garage or a lot space near a main drag. No more penny-pinching where safety's concerned."

His arms around her seemed to absorb her fear. The sobs began to fade.

She felt more herself by the time Bill returned to the back seat.

"Done," he said.

"You didn't mention names, did you?"

"I told you I wouldn't. But I don't like it."

"So you said. But just remember: If anyone asks why you look bruised, just say you slipped on the ice. I'll do the same."

They had argued about making a police report — Bill for, Jim against. Both were adamant, but Jim had finally put the problem into chilling focus.

"For all our sakes, Bill, you can't go to the police."

"What's that supposed to mean?" Bill had said from the back seat.

"For all we know, they may be only a part of a bigger gang. If they are, what about their buddies?"

"What *about* them?"

"What if they blame us? What if they feel embarrassed and humiliated by half a dozen of their number being so easily laid to rest? What if they figure they've got to even the score to regain their honor? Our names and addresses will be on the police report. What if they retaliate against us?"

Bill had been silent as Carol shuddered at the thought.

Jim went on: "I don't know about you, but I don't want them breaking into my home to finish off what their friends started with Carol back there. You want them lobbing a Molotov cocktail into St. F.'s dorm some night?"

"Maybe you're right," Bill had said softly after a long pause. "But at least let me make an anonymous report. We can do that much, can't we?"

Jim had nodded. "Of course. As long as you don't mention any names."

Now the call had been made and they were moving again. Jim turned the car east on Fourteenth.

Bill said, "Somebody killed five people —"

"Five *killers*, you mean," Jim said. "Five guys who would have killed us and raped Carol if that somebody hadn't stepped in!"

"Probably six dead if he caught up with the last one."

"Be that as it may," Jim said, "I'm not sure I want to put him behind bars. I owe him."

"That was cold-blooded murder, Jim!" Bill said.

"Granted. But what could I add to an investigation? That he reminded me of my father?"

Carol gasped. That tall dark figure she'd seen had resembled Jonah Stevens. But that was impossible.

"Oh, Jim," she said lightly, actually managing a smile. "Your dad's not exactly Mr. Warmth, but he's not a killer. And he certainly doesn't hang around the East Village!"

Bill said, "I don't remember your father too well, Jim, but you've got to be kidding. This guy was efficient — *brutally* efficient. I mean, he dispatched those guys one after the other. One swing apiece."

"Do you know what my father does for a living?"

"He's a butcher or something, isn't he?"

Carol heard Jim's voice drop into a monotone.

"He works at the slaughterhouse, but he's not a butcher. He does one thing all day long, and I guess he's pretty good at it. As each cow is led inside, it's his job to brain it with a sledgehammer before its throat is cut."

14.

Emma heard Jonah's car pull into the driveway. She tried to suppress her excitement as she wondered what he'd be like this time. Sometimes he went out late at night and came back and just sat in the living room with the lights off, drinking beer.

Other times . . .

She wondered where he went on these little jaunts. What did he do, what was he looking for? Like so many other things with Jonah, you learned not to ask. It got you nowhere.

At the moment, she didn't particularly care what he had gone out for; she just hoped he'd found it. Because on certain nights he didn't sit up in the living room when he came home. Instead he came directly to the bedroom. And when that happened, he always wanted her. Wanted her badly.

And when that mood was upon him, he drove her to ecstasy beyond imagining.

Emma heard him enter through the kitchen from the garage.

"Is everything all right?"

"Fine, Emma. Just fine."

She felt her heart begin to race as she heard Jonah's footsteps bypass the living room and come down the hall, felt herself grow moist between her legs as he stepped into the room and began stripping off his clothes. She could hear his rapid breathing, sense his arousal like a throbbing heat in the room.

He slipped into bed and pressed himself against her back. He was stiff and hard, like oak, like iron. She turned toward him and felt his arms go around her, felt his hands slide down her flanks and lift her nightgown.

This was going to be one of those nights. Maybe the best ever.

Ash Wednesday
February 28

1.

"Remember, man, you are dust, and to dust you will return."

Grace dwelled on the priest's words as he dipped his thumb in the ashes of last year's palms and dabbed them on her forehead in the form of a tiny cross. She crossed herself and walked down the center aisle of St. John's toward the front entrance.

Outside, she jumped at the touch on her arm as she stood atop the stone steps.

"You're Grace Nevins, aren't you?"

She turned and saw a thin, intense looking young man perhaps half her age. His face was very pale; his blond hair was so thin and wispy she could see his scalp right through it; his pallor was accentuated by the dark smudge of ash in the center of his forehead. His mouth seemed too large for his face, his nose seemed too small. Two of him could have fit inside the stadium coat he clutched around him. It was of good quality, but he was too thin for it.

"Who are you?"

"I'm Martin Spano. We've been looking for you."

Grace was immediately uneasy. Why should anyone be looking for her?

"You've found me."

"It wasn't easy. I waited outside every Mass at St. Pat's last Sunday. You weren't there. The Holy Spirit led me back downtown. This happens to be my parish."

"What do you want?"

"Brother Robert heard about what happened at choir practice at St. Patrick's last week."

Grace turned away and started down the steps.

"I don't want to talk about it!"

She had not been back to St. Patrick's since that awful night. She now attended Mass at St. John's instead. It was closer to her apartment. And besides, what was there to go back for? The choir director obviously could not trust her with the solo. She had pleaded with him that she didn't know what had come over her, that she hadn't meant to sing those horrid words, but that only seemed to bolster his decision: If she could not help it, how could she guarantee it wouldn't happen on Easter?

He was right, of course. She had rushed out of the cathedral in shame.

The young man followed her down the steps to Thirty-first Street.

"It wasn't easy to find you, Grace. You've got to listen to me. You're one of us!"

That stopped her.

"I don't even know who you are, Mr. Spano —"

"Martin, please."

"— so how can I be one of you?"

"Brother Robert says that what happened to you at choir practice is proof. You've felt the presence of the Evil One. You know that he is among us!"

Grace tensed. "Are you a Devil worshipper? I want nothing to do with —"

"No-no! I'm just the opposite! I'm one of the Chosen."

The Chosen? Hadn't she seen that title in bookstores on the cover of a bestseller?

"Chosen by whom?"

"By the Lord, of course. By the Holy Spirit. We have received the knowledge that the Antichrist is coming. We are to spread the warning among the nations of the earth. We are to expose the Evil One when he appears!"

This was crazy!

"I'm not interested."

Martin gently took her hand. "You're afraid. I myself was afraid when I first realized the responsibility God was placing on my shoulders. But it's a responsibility neither of us can shirk. Brother Robert will explain it to you."

"Who is this Brother Robert you keep talking about? I've never heard of him."

Martin's eyes glowed. "A wise and holy man. He wants to meet you. Come."

Something about the younger man's intensity frightened her.

"I . . . I don't know."

He gripped her arm insistently. "Please. It will only take a minute."

Grace wanted to run from this man, yet he was offering her answers to the questions that had plagued her since that awful night in St. Patrick's when she had begun singing about Satan instead of the Blessed Virgin. She had not had a good night's sleep since.

"All right. But only for a minute."

"Good! It's this way."

He led her up Fifth Avenue past the Art Deco splendor of the Empire State Building, then east on Thirty-seventh Street into the Murray Hill district with its procession of stately row houses in various states of repair. Half way between Lexington and Park they stopped before a three-story brownstone.

"This is it," Martin said.

Brownstone steps ran up to the front door on the first floor. A shorter flight curved down to the right to the basement. A hand printed sign on the basement door read "Chapter House." A slim, leafless tree stood to the left. Naked vines clung to the stucco front.

"Which floor is your apartment?"

"All of them — this is my house."

It occurred to Grace then that if she was getting involved with a crazy man, at least he was a well-to-do crazy man.

He led her up to the heavy glass-and-oak front door and into the blessed warmth of the foyer, then down a narrow hall to a sitting room. Their footsteps echoed on the highly polished bare hardwood floor; the walls and ceilings were painted a stark, flat white. Grace followed him into a brightly lit sitting room — as stark and white and bare as the hallway except for some sparse ultramodern furniture and abstract paintings on the walls.

And a man standing at the window, looking out at the street.

She recognized him immediately as a Cistercian monk by his beige habit, wide leather belt, and long, brown, cowled scapula. The cowl was down. He stood bareheaded and tonsured, a striking anachronism amid the glass-and-chrome and abstractions, yet he appeared to be perfectly at home. His graying hair was on the long side, falling from the glistening bareness of his tonsure over the tops of his ears and trailing to the base of his neck. He was of average height but very lean. As he turned to face her, Grace saw that he had a neat, full, dark beard, salted with gray. For all his leanness, he had a round, cherubic face. His eyes were deep brown and kind; the weathered skin around his eyes crinkled with his smile as he stepped toward her.

"Miss Nevins," he said. His voice was deep, chocolate smooth, and French accented. "How good of you to come. I'm Brother Robert."

He pronounced it *Robair*.

"I can only stay a minute," Grace said.

"Of course. I simply wanted an opportunity to personally invite you into our little circle. And to impress upon you how special you are."

His eyes . . . so wise . . . so gentle and kind . . .

"Special? I don't understand."

"God chose you to announce the warning in His own house. You must be destined to play an important part in His plan to defeat the Antichrist."

Me? Why would God choose me?

"The Antichrist?"

"Yes. Your words in that song were a warning for all of us from the Lord. The Spirit touched you and made you aware — as He has Martin and myself and a few select others — that the devil has been made flesh and dwells among us."

Grace didn't think she knew any such thing.

"Why me?"

Brother Robert shrugged inside his robes. "Who would be so bold as to explain why the Lord moves in the ways He does?"

"Won't you come to the service tonight?" Martin said, his pale face eager.

Grace hesitated. Then, in a burst of revelation, she realized that this might be the chance she had been praying for, the chance to atone for her past, to make right all the sins of her youth. All those lives. Was God offering her salvation?

This would explain the horrid corruption of that lovely hymn, and the malaise she had felt lately. Satan had entered the world and God had chosen her as a soldier in His army to battle him.

Yet still she hung back. She wasn't worthy!

"I . . . I don't know."

"If not tonight," Brother Robert said, "then Sunday afternoons, here, at three o'clock."

"Here?"

"Martin has given us the use of his basement for our prayer meetings."

"I'll try," Grace said, turning and heading down the hall. She had to get away, be by herself, think this over. She needed time. "Not tonight. Maybe Sunday. Not tonight."

"You can't stay away," she heard Martin say behind her. "You have been called. Like it or not, you are one of us now!"

2.

Brother Robert went to the window and watched the plump little woman hurry down the sidewalk.

At his elbow, Martin said, "She's afraid."

"And well she should be," he replied.

"I'm not afraid. This is the Lord's fight, and I am ready to die for His cause!"

Brother Robert glanced at the younger man. Martin was a useful ally, dedicated and eager — sometimes too eager. His militancy could be a bit much at times.

"I'm going to my room to pray that she does not turn away from us."

"Will you be having lunch later?"

He shook his head. "I am fasting today."

"Then I will fast as well."

"As you wish."

Brother Robert went up to the second floor to the bare four walls and single window that served as his quarters. In the corner, straw had been spread on the floor and covered with a blanket. This was his bed. He lifted his habit and kneeled bare-kneed on the uncooked rice he had sprinkled over the hardwood floor upon his arrival. He stared out the window at the cold blue of the sky. Before beginning his prayers, he thought about the abbey in Aiguebelle, and his cell there, and how he wished he could return. He missed the two a.m. rising for matins, the daily routine, the simple common labors, the time for meditation, the nearness to God, the *silence*.

No weakness of the flesh had drawn him away, but rather a weakness of the spirit. The discipline, the celibacy, the fasting, these had not been burdens. He had reveled in them. No, it was another appetite that had called to him, an insatiable lust — for knowledge. He had wanted to *know*, he had hungered for answers. The hunger had driven him to the farthest, darkest corners of the world, where he had learned too much.

It had finally brought him here, to this small group of Catholic pentacostals who met in this brownstone. For some reason, the people who gathered here had been touched by the Spirit and made aware that the Antichrist had slunk into the world like a thief in the night. These people, and Grace Nevins, as well, had been recruited, just as he had been recruited. He could not return to the abbey now. He had to stay with them and wait until the Spirit moved them all toward God's will, toward Armageddon.

He prayed they would be strong enough for the terrible tests that lay ahead.

3.

"Oh, I can hardly wait!" Emma said.

Jim stood in his parents' small living room and smiled at his mother's childlike excitement over the prospect of a guided tour of the Hanley mansion.

"It's quite a place," he told her.

And it was. He had explored the old Victorian monstrosity with Carol yesterday. She was a longtime admirer of Victorian homes, and he had taken real pleasure in her delight over the place.

"Dad's not home yet?" he said.

"No." She glanced at her watch. "It's almost four. Maybe he was held up at the plant."

Jim nodded absently as memories of Monday night strobed across his mind. He and Carol had explained away their bruises with the story of a slip on the ice, each one pulling the other down. That had stopped other people's questions, but it hadn't stopped the questions roiling in Jim's mind.

Who had saved them two nights ago? And why?

He couldn't escape the insistent impression that it had been Jonah Stevens wielding that club or whatever it was. But that was absurd! How would he have known where they were, let alone that they were in trouble? How would he have arrived in time? It was a crazy thought.

And yet . . .

"So what have you and Dad been up to lately?" he asked. "Been to the city?"

She looked at him strangely. "Of course not. You know how your father hates to go out."

"Just been hanging around the house, huh?"

"Why are you asking?"

"Oh, I don't know. When we were downtown Monday night, I thought I saw Dad — or someone who looks an awful lot like him."

Jim thought he saw her stiffen, but he couldn't be sure.

"Why, that's silly, Jim. Your father was with me all night. By the way . . . what was this man doing?"

"Just walking by, Ma."

"Oh. Well, we stayed at home Monday night. Watched *Felony Squad* and *Peyton Place*." She sighed. "Just like most other Monday nights."

That should have settled it, but it didn't. The questions wouldn't let go. And that was when the idea hit him.

"Is the door to the garage unlocked?"

"I think so," she said. "Why?"

"I wonder if I could borrow a" — Jim's mind searched for something to borrow: *what?* — "a tape measure. I want to get the dimensions of some of the rooms in the mansion."

"Sure. Take a look. I'll wait out in the car with Carol."

"Great!"

As Emma went out the front door, Jim hurried through the kitchen to the door that opened into the garage. He searched along the wall where Jonah kept all his tools hung on nails and hooks. There were hammers and axes and even a rubber mallet, but they were too small. Their savior Monday night had wielded a longer, heavier weapon, using only one hand, and he had put some real power behind it. Jim picked up a tire iron and hefted it. This baby could have done it, but it still didn't look right.

What am I thinking?

His father — Jonah — had nothing to do with Monday night's madness. Sure, he was a strange guy; cool, aloof, impossible to get close to — hadn't Jim tried often enough through the years? — but he wasn't a crazed killer.

Actually, Jonah was more than remote. He was damn near *unknowable.* Maybe Ma had some idea of what bubbled beneath that impenetrable granite exterior, but Jim didn't have the faintest. He wasn't really sure he wanted to know, either. Because there was a damn good possibility he wouldn't like what he'd find there. Although he had never witnessed a single overt act, he sensed a core of cruelty within his adoptive father. The closest thing he had to evidence had surfaced during his sophomore year in high school after he had tackled Glen Cove's quarterback and broken his arm. Jonah had been barely interested in the sport until then. But when Jim had ashamedly confessed to him how good it had felt to hear that breaking bone, Jonah had metamorphosed into an avid listener, questioning him closely on the details of the incident.

Jonah never missed a game after that. But what he lacked in everyday human warmth and compassion he made up for in reliability. He had always been around. A hard worker, a good provider. He did not steer his adopted son in any particular direction, but he did not discourage him from anything, either. More like a guardian than a father. Jim could not say he loved the man, but he certainly felt indebted to him.

Jim was about to head back inside when he spotted the steelcrowbar leaning in the corner. As soon as he lifted it and swung it, he knew this had been the weapon. Not this particular one, but something just like it. He was certain he wouldn't find anything, but he examined the leading edge of the bar's curve anyway. He smiled to himself.

What will I do if I find dried blood and bits of scalp?

"Be kind of hard to measure a room with one of those," said a deep voice behind him.

Jim whirled, his heart thudding. The tall, lean figure silhouetted in the doorway looked almost exactly like the man who had helped them Monday night.

"Dad! Don't scare me like that!"

Jonah's half smile was humorless and his eyes bored into Jim as he stepped down into the garage.

"What're you so jumpy about?"

"Nothing." Jim quickly set the crowbar back in the corner, hoping he didn't look as guilty as he felt. "Where do you hide your tape measure?"

Jonah reached into the toolbox and pulled out a Stamey fifty-footer. "Right where it's always been." He motioned toward the door. "We'd better go. The women are waiting."

"Sure."

Jim led the way to the front door, thinking of what a jerk he was for still feeling uneasy. His mother had told him Jonah had been home all night, and the crowbar was clean. What more did he want?

Nothing. Except that the crowbar had been *too* clean. Every other tool in the garage was layered with a fine winter's coat of dust . . . except the crowbar. Its hexagonal shaft had been dirt and oil free, as if someone had taken a Brillo pad to it within the last couple of days.

He decided not to think about it.

4.

Carol sat in the front seat and watched the Hanley mansion peek over the high stone wall as Jim unlocked the wrought iron front gate. Its pickets were eight feet high, with an ornate torsade along the bottom and wickedly pointed atop. Beyond the gate was the house, and it was beautiful. She had never dreamed that she would someday live in a place like this. As Jim got back in and pulled into the driveway, she saw the whole house in all its splendor and it took her breath away again, just as it had yesterday.

"Oh, it's beautiful!" Emma cried from the back seat.

Jonah sat next to Emma and said nothing, but then Carol never expected to hear much from Jonah. She drank in the sight of the big, three-storied mix of Italianate and Second Empire features nestled amid its pines and willows, the Long Island Sound gleaming behind it.

The shingles were cream colored, the wood trim and the mansard roof a deep brown. A square, five-story tower rose over the center of the front porch. There were ornate dormer windows on the third floor and bay windows on the sides, all leaded with fruit and flower designs. A fanlight window arched over the front door.

Carol led them up the three steps to the front porch. To the right was a wicker swing settee, hung on chains, and wicker chairs to the left. The slim glass sidelights on either side of the front door were etched with graceful cranes and delicately arched reeds.

Emma stood back on the driveway, staring.

"Come on, Ma," Jim said.

"Don't you worry about me. I'll be there, strangling along behind, as usual."

Carol gave Jim a look.

"I won't say a word," he whispered.

Beyond the heavy oak front door was a narrow front hall cluttered with floor lamps and plants on pedestal tables. Carol had spent a good part of yesterday watering each thirsty vine and frond. On the right, the staircase ran up and toward the rear, its flowered runner held down by a series of brass rods fastened to the base of each riser. On the left was a combination mirror-hat rack-umbrella stand of intricately carved walnut.

"Take a look at the front parlor," she said, leading them to the right.

"Oh my!" said Emma, stopping at the threshhold. It's so . . . so . . ."

"*Busy* is the word, I think," Jim said.

"A true Victorian home is *very* busy," Carol said.

She had concluded from her explorations that Hanley had spared no effort or expense in returning the mansion to its former glory. And it *was* busy. The wallpaper was striped, the carpet was flowered, the lamps were tassled, each chair was layered with lace antimacassars, and each corner supported a plant on a multitiered what-not. The bay window was a jungle of plants. The walls were festooned with paintings and old photos. On every available surface, littering the tops of the tables, the organ, the mantle over the Carrara marble fireplace, were cards and boxes and knickknacks and souvenirs. A maid's nightmare.

"I declare, this place would wear my feather duster to the nub in no time!" Emma said.

"Let me show you the downstairs library, Dad," Jim said.

"*Downstairs?* You mean there's more than one?"

"Two. The upstairs one is sort of a science library. But the downstairs is bigger."

"Who'd want more than one?" Jonah said, following Jim back into the hall.

"Wait till you see the stereo."

"And wait till *you* see the kitchen," Carol told Emma.

"Dear me, I hope it's not as, uh, authentic as the parlor," Emma said.

Carol laughed, leading her down the hall. "Not even close!"

The kitchen was large, with an electric double oven, a huge refrigerator, and a freezer. The floor here was part tile, part pine planking, and dominating its center was a massive six-foot rectangular oak table with paw feet.

Carol and Emma met up with Jim and Jonah in the living room which sported colorful stained-glass windows.

"Who'd ever thought our son would own this place!" Emma said, clutching Jonah's arm. "And this is only the first floor!"

"That's what I'd like to talk to you two about," Jim said. "I want to share my inheritance with you."

Carol watched Emma's eyes widen.

"Oh, Jim —"

"No, I mean it," Jim said, cutting her off. "I can never repay you for the life you've given me, but I want to see you two live in comfort without worrying about layoffs and property taxes and things like that. I want to give you a million dollars."

As Emma began to cry, Carol put an arm around her shoulders and gave her a squeeze. She and Jim had discussed this last night. He had wanted her approval and she had encouraged him. She only wished her own parents were alive to share some of the bounty.

Jim said, “Dad, you can quit your job and just take it easy, if you like.”

Jonah stared at them both for a moment, then spoke in his slow, South-tinted voice.

“That’s very generous, son, and it will sure be nice not having to worry about being laid off, but I believe I’ll keep working. A man’s got to work.”

“At least you can get a more sedimentary job,” Emma said.

“That’s *seden*tary, Ma.”

“That’s what I said. One where he can sit down more and not work so hard.”

“For the time being, I’ll stick with what I’m doing at the plant,” Jonah said firmly. “That is, if none of you objects.”

Carol felt a twinge of resentment at the sarcasm in his voice, but that was quickly overcome by the revulsion of knowing what Jonah’s job was, and realizing that he liked it too much even to think of quitting it.

SEVEN

Saturday
March 2

1.

Nicky's bishop and queen were laying a trap for his king, but Bill thought he saw a way out. He moved his remaining knight onto a square that posed a potential threat to Nicky's queen.

"Your move."

"Don't rush me," the ten-year old said. "This is going to take some thinking."

Five days since that ghastly incident on Monday night. A deep breath still gave Bill a stab of pain where he had been kicked in the ribs, but he was able to function, and the slip-on-the-ice story had been accepted by everyone. His body was slowly healing, but his mind, his soul — he wasn't sure they would ever recover.

"CARNAGE IN THE VILLAGE" the Daily *News* had said. Six bodies — four clustered mid-block, and two more, one at each end of the block, all killed by a single crushing blow to the skull. The police were laying it off to a "hippie drug war" because of all the speed they had found on the victims.

Victims! The irony of it! We were almost their *victims! And what they got was probably right in line with what they had planned for us!*

Still, it didn't sit right. Even though he knew he could tell the police nothing that would help them solve the case, it felt wrong to be hiding his involvement. He firmly believed that everything in life should be open, honest, and aboveboard. An impossible ideal, he knew, one the world would laugh at, but one by which he struggled to live his life.

The ideal had to start somewhere.

But another nagging question tormented him. Who was their savior? And why? Some sort of vigilante? Someone who just liked to kill? Or both?

He shook off the questions. He was too tired to wrestle with them today. They'd never be answered, anyway. At least not by him. He wasn't getting his usual amount of sleep lately. Visions of Carol, teasing, vamping, dancing across his brain, were still keeping him too excited to sleep.

This had to stop.

With an effort Bill turned his mind back to his weekly chess game with Nicky.

"There's someone I think you should meet," Bill told him.

"Who's that?"

"A new applicant who wants to adopt a boy."

Nicky didn't look up. "What's the use?"

"I think this couple is right for you. Their name's Calder. The husband is an assistant professor at Columbia. The wife's a writer. They don't want an infant. They want a bright boy under twelve. I thought of you."

"Did you tell them my head looks like a grapefruit someone left sitting on one side too long?"

"Knock it off! I don't think they'll care."

At least they had *said* they didn't care when Bill spoke to them. They were a bright, young, stable couple. They had passed their interviews, reference checks, and home inspections. And they'd said they were more interested in what was inside their child's head than the shape of his skull.

"Save us both the trouble and match them up with someone else," Nicky said and moved his queen. "Check."

Bill moved his king one square to the left.

"No way. You're it, kid. This is one couple who won't be put off by your Lynn Belvedere act."

Still Nicky did not look up. In a careless tone, he said, "You really think these folks might be the ones?"

"Never know until you try each other out."

"Okay."

One word, but Bill detected a note of hope in his tone.

He watched Nicky picking at his face as he hung over the board, studying the pieces and their positions. Suddenly his hand darted out and brought in his bishop from half the board away. He looked up and grinned.

"Checkmate! Ha!"

"Damn!" Bill said. "I hope Professor Calder's good at this game. Someone needs to teach you some humility. And stop picking your face. You'll turn that blackhead into a fullblown pimple if you don't watch it."

"It's called a comedo," Nicky said. "The little white ones are called 'closed' and the black ones are called 'open.' The plural is comedones.' "

"Really."

"Yeah. That's Latin."

"I'm vaguely familiar with the language. But I never realized you were such an expert on blackheads."

"*Comedones*, if you please, Father. Why wouldn't I be an expert? I'm covered with them. *Comedo ergo sum*, you might say."

Bill's barking laugh was cut short by a shooting pain in his ribs. But inside was a warm glow. He loved this kid, and no question about it: Nicky was going to make a great addition to the Calder family.

2.

"Oh, my *God!*"

It was Carol's voice. Jim rushed into the downstairs library.

"What's wrong?"

She was sitting in a dark green wing chair that dwarfed her. But then, Hanley's downstairs library with its high ceiling and rows and stacks of books that seemed to go on endlessly, tended to dwarf everyone.

"Take a look at this!" she said, pointing to the open book on her lap.

Jim knelt beside her. The book was obviously a college yearbook. He stared at the black and white photo under Carol's fingertip. It showed a dark-haired fellow with an old-fashioned center-parted haircut, intense eyes, a square jaw, and slightly protruding ears. Below the picture was a name:

Roderick C. Hanley

It was the first time Jim had ever seen a photo of Hanley as a young man. Other than that . . .

"So?"

"You don't see it?"

"See what?"

"Trim your hair, lop off those big sideburns, and that's *you*!"

"Get off!"

Carol took out her wallet and pulled a photo from it. This one was in color, a miniature of one that hung in their bedroom: their wedding portrait. She put it next to the old Hanley photo.

Jim gaped. The resemblance was astonishing.

"We could be twins! I wonder if he played football?" *And if he did, I wonder if he enjoyed breaking arms and legs on the other team?*

"Doesn't mention it here."

"So he probably didn't."

"Well," Carol said, "we still don't know who your mother was, but from this it looks like you're all Hanley. If there was ever any doubt that you sprang from his loins, as it were, let them now be forever put to rest."

"Far out!" said a third voice.

Jim looked up to see Gerry Becker leaning over the wing on the other side of the chair. He bit his tongue. Becker had hung around the mansion all day yesterday and had showed up this morning shortly after Jim had arrived with Carol. He wanted to tell him to take a hike, but Gerry said he was doing a "feature" on Jim for the *Express* and needed lots of background. Jim liked the idea of a feature article. Maybe it would get picked up by the wire services. Maybe his mother would see it and get in touch with him. And maybe, too, the recognition factor might tip some fence-sitting publisher toward buying his new novel.

Who knew? Maybe it would work. But if it meant putting up with Becker on a daily basis, was it worth it? He had practically moved in with them.

"Two peas in a pod, all right," Becker said. "You know, when I was at the *Trib* —"

"I thought I left you upstairs," Jim said, trying to hide his exasperation.

"You did. But I came down to see what all the excitement was about." He pointed to the yearbook photo. "Hey, you know, if we could get a copy of your yearbook from — where was it?"

"Stony Brook, class of sixty-four."

"Right. Stony Brook. We could put them both side by side in the article. The effect would be groovy. Think you could find Jim's old yearbook, Carol?"

"I'll hunt around when I get home," Carol said.

"Make sure you do, okay? Because I'm going to make this a big article. Really big."

Jim saw her eyes flash at him, silently begging to get this pushy so-and-so out of here. He knew how much she disliked Becker.

"Come on, Gerry. Let's get back to the upstairs library."

"Right on. Don't forget, Carol. I'll check with you tomorrow, okay? Or maybe later on after you guys get home."

"I'll let you know when I find it, Gerry," she said with a smile that looked so forced it would have been far better had she not tried to smile at all.

3.

Bitch! Gerry Becker thought as he followed Jim upstairs. Stevens' wife must think her shit don't stink! Where'd she get off with the high-and-mighty act? Nothing but a hick broad from a hick Long Island town who's husband suddenly got lucky. Big fucking deal!

Gerry held it all in. He had to stay on Jim Stevens' good side until he got what he wanted for this story. Yeah, a feature on James Stevens, sudden heir to Dr. Roderick Hanley's fortune, including exclusive interviews with the famous scientist's unacknowledged son — that alone might be enough to ride the wires.

But Gerry had a feeling there might be more than just another rags-to-riches story here.

"All right," Stevens said as they reentered the upstairs library. "Let's pick up where we left off."

"Sure," Gerry said. *Right.*

Where they'd left off was nowhere. Stevens was looking for Mommy and Gerry was helping him. Not out of any deep feeling for Stevens, but because it would add tremendous human-interest value to the feature.

But what Gerry was really looking for was juice. Hanley, for all his fame in the scientific community as an innovator with a commercial bent, had been pretty much of an enigma, always shunning interviews. A lifelong bachelor, always in the company of that M.D., Edward Derr. Gerry had a suspicion that maybe the guy was queer. Sure, he fathered Stevens — after seeing those two pictures a moment ago, no one could doubt that — but maybe that had been just a momentary aberration. Or maybe he liked to swing both ways. Gerry's nose for news told him that there was some pretty weird shit hiding in Roderick Hanley's private life. All he needed was to find a couple of juicy bits and his feature would be hot stuff indeed.

And a hot feature on the wires would get him off a hick rag like the

Monroe *Express* and back into the journalistic mainstream. Maybe the *Daily News*. Maybe even the *Times!*

Gerry had been in the mainstream once. Younger guys like Stevens — younger only by a few years but that was like a generation away these days — seemed satisfied to diddle around on a local rag and write the Great American Novel on the side. Not for Gerry. News was the only writing that mattered. He'd been on his way up at the *Trib*, living in a fourth floor walk-up, but slowly inching ahead, doing what he wanted. Then the *Trib* had folded, just like the *World Telegraph & Sun*. Black days, those. Only the *News*, the *Post*, and the *Times* were left, and they were up to their eyeballs in guys more experienced than Gerry. For a while he had tried *The Light*, hoping for a shot at the top spot after its editor mysteriously disappeared, but it went to someone else. A weekly didn't prove to be his style, so he had hooked up with a small-time daily and waited for his chance.

His chance was now.

He slammed a notebook back into its slot. So much for that shelf. Nothing but notes and jottings and equations and abstracts of scientific articles pasted onto the pages. No love letters or dirty pictures — not a drop of juice.

Time to go to the next shelf. Boring as hell, but something was going to turn up, and Gerry intended to be here when it did.

He went to pull a volume from the next section of bookshelves, but couldn't seem to budge it. When he took a closer look, he saw why. Suddenly excited, he squeezed his fingers in above the books, grabbed hold of the tops of their spines, and pulled.

The whole row of books pulled free in one piece.

Only they weren't books, just a facade of old spines glued to a board. He heard Stevens at his side.

"What've you got here, Gerry?"

At the rear of the shelf, a dull gray metal surface reflected the light from the window.

"Looks like a safe to me, Jim. A big one."

But where was the combination?

Eight

First Sunday in Lent
March 3

1.

"You're welcome to stay for the service, Grace."

Grace smiled at Brother Robert and looked around the room. They were in the oblong basement of Martin's brownstone in Murray Hill. This room did not seem to belong to the rest of the house. It was so much warmer. Fluorescent lights, recessed into a beige suspended ceiling, glowed through multicolored panels, giving a stained glass effect. There was wall-to-wall carpeting and the walls were deeply stained tongue-and-groove knotty pine. Rows of chairs were lined in a semicircle around a low platform at the far end. The walls were bare except for the crucifix at the far end; both it and the statue of the Blessed Virgin in the left corner were covered in purple drapes, just as they were in churches throughout the world during Lent.

But this wasn't a church.

About two dozen or so people stood around, chatting. Nothing special about them. The Chosen looked like people off the street of any middle class neighborhood in the city. Some wore suits and dresses, some wore jeans; one woman who didn't have the legs for it, sported a miniskirt. And they were all *very* friendly. They had greeted her with genuine warmth.

"Yes, do stay," Martin Spano said.

"I don't know, Marty —"

"Martin," said the pale young man grimly. "Please don't call me Marty. Nobody calls me Marty." Then he smiled quickly. "Well, what do you think of our little group?"

"They seem very nice."

"Believe me, they are."

He was called away by one of the Chosen, leaving her alone with Brother Robert.

"Are you going to have a Mass?" Grace asked.

"Oh, no," he said in his French accent. "Just some readings from the Bible, the Old and New Testaments. The Church doesn't really recognize groups such as these. They are clearly Catholic, but the monsignors and Bishops and such think they are a little, you know how you American say . . ." He pointed his index finger at his left temple and moved it in a circular motion. "Loony Tunes."

"Oh, dear!" Grace said.

She was not at all sure she wanted to get involved in this sort of thing. During the past year or so, she had heard of these groups. Catholic Pentecostals, they were called. Charismatics.

"I have not encountered this sort of thing anywhere else in the world, and I find it truly fascinating, truly extraordinary. In a way it is a return to Christianity's humble origins." He gestured to the room. "Believers gathering together in homes to pray and hear the word of God, to witness the presence of the Spirit. That's what Christianity should be about. They have accepted me as a leader of sorts, at least for the time being, but I am not here as a priest. I am here as another one of the Chosen. They don't pretend that what happens here is sacramental, or in any way a substitute for the sacraments. It is an adjunct to the sacraments."

"I don't see how the Church can object to that."

"It doesn't object, but neither does it approve. It will never say so, but I believe the Church is a little concerned about groups like this. Although they are few in number, they are growing. They go to Mass and to confession and receive Communion in the orthodox ways, as we all did earlier this morning. But every Sunday afternoon, and every Wednesday night, when they gather in meetings like this, they are on their own, with nothing between them and the Spirit. Surprising things happen."

"How surprising?"

He touched her hand gently. "Stay and see."

Grace stayed.

She sat in the last row and listened to readings from the Gospel, from various books of the Old Testament — mostly the frightening ones from *Ecclesiastes* — and to a homily from Brother Robert. His voice was mesmerizing. He was fiery and moving as he exorted the Chosen, whom he called "the Army of God," to be ever vigilant for signs as to the identity of the devil incarnate, the Antichrist.

While he was speaking, some people sat and listened quietly, but some called out Amens, others stood and held their arms aloft as they swayed back and forth in time to a music audible only to them. Grace was shocked. This was more like one of those Protestant revival meetings they put on television every so often.

Then they all began to pray. And they prayed holding hands. The woman in front of her turned and reached her hand back for Grace to take but Grace shook her head and folded her hands in front of her. She didn't want to hold hands during prayer! What kind of praying was that?

And then it happened.

A woman in a tweed suit in the front row stood up, rigid and trembling, then fell down onto the floor and began to shake. The nurse in Grace brought her out of her own chair.

"She's having a seizure!" Grace cried.

As she started forward, hands held her back, voices told her, "No, wait. She's all right" . . . "She has the Spirit" . . . "The Spirit is upon her."

Sure enough, in a moment the woman lay still, then turned over and sat up. Her eyes were unfocused. Her tongue moved strangely as she opened her mouth and began to speak. The words that came out were like no human speech Grace had ever heard.

Suddenly, directly to Grace's right, someone else, a man in a plaid flannel shirt, sprang up rigidly from his chair. He didn't convulse but started talking in a foreign language, one that sounded exactly like the first woman's. He stared blankly and his jaw continued vibrating up and down after he had finished.

"Hear them?" said a voice in her ear.

She turned and it was Brother Robert, standing at her side.

"What's happening?"

"They're speaking in tongues. Just like the Apostles did on the first Pentecost Sunday." His brown eyes sparkled. "Isn't it fascinating?"

Another woman stood up and began to babble.

"Three!" Brother Robert cried. "The Spirit is strong with us tonight! And always the same tongue! I understand that in other groups they speak in many tongues. But since I have been here, the Chosen have spoken in only one tongue!"

Grace suddenly felt flushed and weak. This wasn't the safe, sane, staid Catholicism she knew, with its comfortable rituals and regimented responses. This was like one of those crazy holy roller tent revivals. This was chaotic, frightening.

"I need some air!"

"Of course you do," Brother Robert said.

She let him take her elbow and lead her upstairs to the brownstone's front foyer where it was cool but protected from the drizzle and the March wind.

"That's better," she said, feeling her pulse begin to slow toward normal.

"These prayer meetings can be upsetting at first, I know," Brother Robert said. "I was not sure what to make of them myself when I first came here. But they prove that the Spirit is with us, on our side, urging us forward."

Grace didn't know about that, wasn't really sure of anything right now.

"Is that what He's doing?" she said. "Urging you?"

"*Yes!*" Brother Robert's eyes hardened. "This is war! Evil such as the world has never known is coming. Satan in human form, here not just to claim our lives, but our very souls as well! War, Grace Nevins! And you are part of God's chosen army. The Spirit has called *you!* You cannot say no!"

Grace could say nothing at all at that moment. Brother Robert was frightening her.

"Look," he said in a softer tone, pointing through the door glass at the street outside. "Even now we are being watched. I have seen him here a number of times this week."

Grace looked and saw a gray-haired man of about sixty standing under a tree across the street, facing their way. As she stared at him, he turned and walked away.

2.

The leafless trees offered no shelter as Mr. Veilleur walked west on Thirty-seventh Street through the rain, shaking his head, baffled at the turmoil he sensed in the world around him.

What was happening?

Not far away, to the east, he sensed a kernel of chaos, throbbing like an open, infected wound. All these years of peace, and now this. How? Why? What had triggered it?

Questions with no answers. At least none that he wanted to hear. For the news could only be bad. Worse than bad.

And yet here on East Thirty-seventh he detected a warm glow. He had sensed it faintly before, but today it had been unusually strong, calling to him in a familiar voice, drawing him here.

Something was going on in that brownstone, something playing counterpoint to the festering discord to the east. Those inside were receiving a warning. They were interpreting it in their own fashion, dressing it up in their personal myths, but at least they were responding.

That gave him some hope, but not much. The battle lines were being drawn again. For what? A skirmish, or an all-out assault? Hopefully a standard-bearer would emerge from the group clustered in the brownstone.

Not that it mattered much to him. He had served his time. Someone else could shoulder the burden this go-around. He was out of it. Out of it for good.

He stopped when he reached Lexington and raised his hand, searching for a taxi, a usually futile quest on a rainy day. But just then a battered yellow cab pulled up to the curb in front of him and discharged two elderly women. Mr. Veilleur held the door for them.

"Where y'goin', mac?" the cabbie said.

"Central Park West."

"Hopinski."

As he slipped into the back seat, Mr. Veilleur mused that if he believed in omens, he would take this near miracle as a good one.

But he had long ago stopped believing in either.

3.

"I know what this is about," said Catherine, the older, heavier sister. "And we can't take him in with us. At least *I* can't."

Carol sat before Mr. Dodd's two daughters in her office at Monroe Community Hospital. It had taken her a week and a half to get both of them together in one place. This was the only day they all could do it. Kay Allen, her supervisor, would send her for psychiatric evaluation if she found out she was in on a Sunday.

"Neither can I," said Maureen.

"He's very depressed about going to the nursing home," Carol said.

Mr. Dodd's welfare paperwork finally had gone through and she had found a bed for him at Sunny Vale in Glen Cove. He was due to be transported there on Thursday. She had seen a rapid deterioration in the old man since he had learned that he was now "on the dole," as he put it, and destined to spend his final days in a nursing home among strangers. He no longer cared about eating, shaving, or anything else.

"No more depressed than we are about sending him," said Catherine, her tone daring Carol to challenge her.

Carol sensed the guilt underlying the hostility, and empathized. The sisters saw themselves in a no-win situation.

"He can dress himself, feed himself, bathe himself, get himself up in the morning, and put himself to bed at night. He doesn't need a nursing home. He needs his meals cooked and his clothes washed and someone to keep him company. He needs a *family*," Carol said.

Catherine rose from her chair. "We've been over all of this before on the phone. Nothing has changed. My sister and I and both our husbands work. We can't leave Pop alone in the house all day. The doctor told us his memory is bad. He could start to boil some water for coffee or soup and forget about it and then one of us would come home to a roaring fire where our house used to be."

"There are ways to overcome that," Carol said. "You can hire people to stay with him during the day — we can get him an allowance for a visiting homemaker for a while. Believe me, there *are* ways, and I can help you work things out if you'll give it a try." She decided to play her ace here. "Besides, it won't be forever. He's seventy-four. How many years does he have left? You can make them good ones. You can say good-bye to him."

"What's that supposed to mean?"

"Most people don't get a chance to say good-bye to their folks," Carol said. She swallowed the sudden lump in her throat.

She thought of her own parents, as she always did in instances such as this, thought of all the things she wished she had said to them while they were alive, not the least of which was good-bye. It seemed she would live out her life with a feeling of something left forever undone. She had added sparing others that burden as an unwritten, unspoken addition to her job description.

"I mean," she went on, "one day they're here, the next day they're gone."

Maureen took out a tissue and blotted her eyes, then looked up at Catherine.

"Maybe we could —"

"Maureen!"

"I'm serious, Cathy. Let me talk to Donald. Let's think about it. There must be something we can do besides dumping him in a nursing home."

"*You* think about it, Mo. And *you* talk to Donald. I already know what Tom will say."

Carol figured this was as good a time as any to end the meeting. One of the sisters, at least, was having second thoughts.

They're weakening, Mr. Dodd! I'll have you back with your family yet!

After they were gone, she slumped into a chair. She'd have enjoyed this moment more if she felt better physically. It was those dreams. Night after night, the blood and violence, the pain and suffering. None as vivid as Monday's, but she kept waking up in cold sweats of fear, trembling and clutching Jim, unable to remember specific details, only their overall effect. Memories of the incident in Greenwich Village added to her malaise.

Her stomach was adding the coup de grace. Always sour. She'd be ravenously hungry one moment, but when she'd go to have something to eat, the sight and smell of it would nauseate her. If she didn't know better she'd almost think —

Good Lord! Am I pregnant?

She ran to the elevators. Both cars were down in the basement so she took the stairs up. At the second floor she hurried along the corridor to the lab.

"Maggie!" she said to the young woman at the lab desk, glad that someone she knew had pulled duty this weekend. Maggie had frizzy red hair and a face like a goose, but her smile was winning.

"Carol! Hi! What are you doing in on a Sunday?"

"I need a test!"

"What for?"

"Uh . . . pregnancy."

"You late?"

"I'm never on time, so how can I tell if I'm late?"

Maggie looked at her sideways. "Is this 'Oh-God-I-hope-I'm-not' or 'Please-God-say-I-am'?"

"Am! *Am!*"

"Well, it's only supposed to be done on doctor's order, but since it's Sunday, who's to know, right?" She handed Carol a plastic-wrapped cup. "Give us some pee-pee and we'll see-see."

Carol hesitated, fighting to keep her hopes from rising too far. She couldn't allow herself real hope. The test was a double-edged sword — too much hope and a negative would be crushing.

With her heart thumping in her throat, she headed for the door marked *Women*.

4.

Frustrated almost to the wall-kicking stage because he hadn't been able to open the safe, Jim turned his attention to other matters. It was after five by the time he had lugged all of Hanley's personal journals down from the upstairs library and lined them up on a separate shelf in the downstairs one. They were gray, leatherbound affairs with dates on their spines. One per year, beginning with 1920 and ending with 1967. He left a gap in the middle for the volumes they could not find.

"He must have had this year's with him when the plane went down," Jim said. "But where are the other four?"

"Beats me, man," Gerry Becker said, standing beside him. "We've combed every bookshelf in the place."

Jim nodded. He had pored through many of the journals. They contained summaries of Hanley's projects, his plans for the future, and day-by-day comments and observations on his personal life. They were a priceless peephole into his father's life.

But where were 1939, 1940, 1941, and 1942? The four most important years — the three years before and the year of his birth, the ones that might contain his mother's name — were missing.

Frustrating as all hell.

"Maybe they're in that safe," Jim said. He looked at Carol, sitting in the wing chair. "What do you think, hon?"

She was staring into space. Carol had been glum and withdrawn all night. Jim wondered what was bothering her.

"Carol?"

She shook herself. "What?"

"You all right?"

"Oh, yes. Fine, fine."

Jim didn't believe a word of it, but he couldn't go into it with Becker still hanging around. He was getting to be a fixture around here, and that was a real drag.

"Dig this," Becker said. He had been flipping through the 1943 volume. He shoved the book in front of Jim. "Read the second para on the right."

Jim squinted as he deciphered Hanley's crabbed hand:

Ed and I had a bit of a laugh over Jazzy's pitiful attempt at blackmail. I told her she had seen the last penny she would ever see from me last year and to be on her way.

"Jazzy!" Jim said. "I saw a name like that in — where was it? — 1949!" He pulled the volume out and flipped through it. Where had he seen it? "Here!"

He read aloud:

"Read in the paper today that Jazzy Cordeau is dead. Such a shame. What disparity between the woman she became and the woman she could have been. The world will never know."

Jim's mind raced. Jazzy Cordeau! French . . . New Orleans? Could she possibly be his mother? Jazzy Cordeau was the only female name he had found that was linked to the missing years.

He had to get into that safe!

"I think I'll be cuttin' out," Becker said. "I'm bushed."

"Yeah," Jim said, trying to hide his relief. "Same here. Look, why don't we give this a rest for a while? We've been beating this place to death."

Becker shrugged. "Fine with me. Maybe I'll check the morgues at a couple of papers for you, see if I can turn up anything. Buzz you in a couple of days."

"Great. I appreciate that. You know the way out."

When Jim heard the door slam, he turned to Carol and grinned. "Finally! He's gone!"

She nodded absently.

"Honey, what's wrong?"

Carol's face twisted as tears filled her eyes. She began to cry. Jim rushed over and pulled her into his arms. She felt so small and frail against him.

"I thought I was pregnant but I'm not!" she sobbed.

He held her tight and rocked her back and forth.

"Oh, Carol, Carol, Carol, don't take it so hard. We've got all the time in the world. We've got nothing better to do from now on than work on producing little feet to patter around this big old house."

"But what if it never happens?"

"It will."

He led her toward the front door. It killed him to see her so sad. All this newfound wealth didn't mean squat if Carol was unhappy.

He kissed her.

"Come on. Let's get back to our own bed in our own little place and do some homework."

She smiled through her tears.

That was better!

Monday
March 4

1.

Brother Robert knelt on the cold, rice-littered floor by the window and silently chanted the Prime. When he was through, he remained kneeling. His window faced east and he looked out at the brightening sky.

The evil was growing stronger. Every day it cast a greater pall over his spirit. And it was from there, to the east, from somewhere on Long Island, that it seemed to emanate. Martin had driven him the length of the island but he had been unable to pinpoint its source. The closer he got, the more diffuse it became until he had been engulfed in a cacophony of evil sensations.

A sign, Lord. Show me who it is. Show me your enemy.

And then what? How would he fight Satan incarnate?

Will you teach me, Lord?

He prayed so. He had no battle plan, no strategy. He was not a plotter, not a general. He was a contemplative monk who had given up the world in order to be closer to his God.

Forgive the impertinence, Lord, but perhaps you made a mistake in choosing me to lead this flock. The burden is wide and my shoulders are so narrow.

Perhaps he hadn't given up enough of the world. He had fasted and prayed and worked in the fields around the monastery, but still he had wanted to *know*. The lust for knowledge had driven him to petition his abbot and the Abbot General himself for permission to search out and catalog other monastic orders. Not the Benedictines and similar well established examples, but lesser, more obscure orders that might have something to offer the monastic life as a whole.

He had been given two years, but he had gone beyond that. His trek across the world had been endlessly fascinating. He had met with some of the Orphic brotherhood and a few Pythagoreans in Greece. He had found remnants of Therapeutae and Anchorites in the Mideast, and even a trio of Stylites, each sitting alone atop a stone pillar in the Gobi Desert. In the Far East he investigated many cenobitic Buddhist sects, and in Japan, he met with the last two surviving members of an order of self-mutilating monks.

He should have stopped then. His compendium of monastic orders and their ways of life was the most complete on earth. But it was not enough. He went further. He had been tantalized by hints he had heard of dark secrets buried in ancient ruins, in forbidden books. He had searched them out. And he had found some of them. He had dug into the fabled ruins, had read some of the ancient, mythic tomes.

And he had been changed forever.

He no longer lusted for knowledge. All he wanted now was to retreat to his abbey, to hide himself away from the world and what he had learned.

But that was not to be. The changes within had led him here, to these Catholic Pentacostals. Secrets were unraveling and he sensed that the Lord wanted him here when they were revealed.

But would he be able to rise to the challenge? Neither his boyhood on a farm in Remy, nor his adult life in a contemplative monastery had prepared him for anything like this.

2.

"Do you still like the Jefferson Airplane?" Carol called from the big wing chair in the Hanley library. Already she had started thinking of it as *her* chair.

She felt better this morning — at least emotionally. Jim had made such tender love to her last night, whispering such wonderful things in her ear that she no longer felt like such a miserable failure as a woman for not being pregnant. She had brought Laura Nyro's first couple of albums along to the mansion today and now that wonderful voice and quirky lyrics were booming from the hidden speakers of Hanley's stereo, making the big house feel a little bit more like home.

Physically though, she felt just as queasy, just as tired as she had every other morning recently. Another blood-soaked dream last night hadn't helped, either.

Something was wrong with her. She had decided this morning to make an appointment with Dr. Albert for a good general check-up. And if he didn't find anything, she'd go to a gynecologist and really go to work on getting her periods straightened out.

But for right now, she was taking it easy. She had made herself comfortable with the "Arts & Leisure" section of yesterday's Sunday *Times*. She was only now getting around to it. Jim had made her call in sick today because she'd been so tired this morning.

Actually, he wanted her to quit. After all, they no longer needed the money, he said, so why should she drag herself off to the hospital every morning? Good, logical reasons, but Carol didn't want to quit. Not just yet. Not until she had kids to stay home for. Until then, there were people at MCH who needed her. People like Mr. Dodd.

Kay had called from the hospital this morning to tell her that Maureen Dodd had agreed to take her father home. She was picking him up tomorrow. The news had made Carol's morning.

"The Airplane?" Jim said around a mouthful of food as he walked into the room. He had a well-bitten apple in one hand and one of Hanley's journals in the other. He had done little else but pore over those things since they'd arrived this morning. "Don't really care for much of their new stuff. Why?"

"Oh, just wondering. Korvette's has *After Bathing at Baxter's* on sale for two-thirty-nine."

Jim swallowed and laughed. "On sale? Honey, we don't have to worry about sales ever again! If we want it, we'll buy it at list and pay the whole four-seventy-nine! We'll buy a stereo and never buy mono records again! Don't you understand? We're rich!"

Carol thought about that a second. They were spending an awful lot of time here at the Hanley place, but still slept and ate and made love in their own little house. Maybe she should stop referring to it as the Hanley place. Legally now it was the *Stevens* place.

"I don't *feel* rich," she said. "Do you?"

"No. But I'm going to start working on it. It's scary, though."

"How do you mean?" She knew she was scared, but Jim?

"The wealth. I don't want it to change us."

"It won't," she said.

"Oh, I know it won't change you. It's me. I don't want to stop writing, but what if the money makes me too comfortable? What if I stop being hungry? What if I mellow out?"

Carol had to smile. Every so often he would do this — break out of his tough skeptic persona and become vulnerable. At times like these she loved him most.

"You? Mellow?"

"It could happen."

"Never!"

He returned her smile. "I hope you're right. But in the meantime, what say we hit Broadway this weekend?"

"A play?"

"Sure! Best seats in the house. Our penny-pinching days are over." A new cut began on the Nyro album. "Hear that? That's us. We're gettin' off the Poverty Train. You've got the section there. Pick a play, any play, and we'll go."

Carol thumbed to the front. She saw ads for *I Never Sang for My Father, How Now Dow Jones, You're a Good Man, Charlie Brown,* none of which much appealed to her. Then she came to a full-page ad quoting rave reviews for Neil Simon's latest.

"Let's see *Plaza Suite*."

"You got it. I'll call a ticket agent and see if he can dig us up a couple of good seats — price no object."

Carol hesitated. "Do you think we could make it a matinee?"

"I guess so. Why?"

"Well, after last week . . ."

"Sure," Jim said with a reassuring smile. "We'll be out of the city by dark. We'll drive back here and have dinner at Memison's. How's that sound?"

"Absolutely wonderful!"

In a burst of warmth for Jim, she opened her arms and he fell into them. She wanted to make love to him right here and now in this big old chair. She kissed him, trailing her hand into the tangle of one of his sideburns. He pulled away for a second to place the journal he had been reading on the table beside the chair. That was when Carol noticed the writing along its bottom edge.

"What do those mean?" she said, pointing.

Jim picked up the book again. "Never noticed them."

He held it closer. A series of numbers and letters had been printed in a line:

33R - 21L - 47R - 16L

"My God, Carol!" he said, leaping from the seat. "That's a safe combination! And it's written on the bottom of the 1938 journal, the one right before the gap! Got to be to the safe upstairs!"

Carol was filled with a sudden foreboding. She grabbed at Jim's arm.

"Why don't we leave it locked?"

Jim's expression was frankly puzzled. "Why?"

"Because if Hanley — your father — locked it away so securely, maybe it should stay that way. Maybe there's stuff in there he didn't want anyone to know, stuff he would have destroyed if he'd known he was going to die."

"Whatever's in that safe is the truth. And I've got to know the truth — about who my mother is, or was, and about my father's relationship with her."

"What difference does that make? It's not going to change who you are!"

"I need my past, Carol. I've got the Hanley half. Now I need the rest — my mother' side. This Jazzy Cordeau he mentions may be her. But no matter what Becker digs up on her, I'll only be guessing as to whether she's the one. But I've got a strong feeling that after we open that safe, I'll *know*."

Carol hugged him against her. "I just hope you don't regret it. I don't want you hurt."

"I can handle it. I don't know what Hanley's hiding. The truth may not be pretty, but it's got to come out of that safe." He smiled. "What's that they say — 'The truth will set you free'? That's the way I feel about what's in that safe. Besides, how bad can it be?"

He stood up and held out his hand to her.

"Come on. Let's open it together."

Carol felt her queasiness double as she rose and followed him upstairs.

3.

It took Becker most of the early afternoon to track down anything on the Jasmine Cordeau murder. After all, as the cops told him time and again until he was sick of hearing it, the case was nearly twenty years old.

Yeah, so what? he wanted to shout.

But he kept his cool, kept smiling in their faces. After all, his press card could only take him so far, especially with his long hair and all. Longhairs tended to call cops pigs and cops didn't take too kindly to that.

A desk cop took him to the basement and pointed to a jumble of filing cabinets and told him that if the file on that old murder was still around — and no one was saying it was — it would be in one of those.

Maybe.

More scut work.

Gerry had spent the morning in the New York Public Library's periodical section, spinning through an endless stream of microfilmed pages, scanning the obits and local news, determined to find Jazzy Cordeau.

Because Jazzy Cordeau was Jim Stevens' mother.

No doubt about it. Something deep inside Becker was as sure of that as he was sure of his own name. And that wasn't all. The journal's casual mention of her "pitiful attempt at blackmail" left little doubt that there was something ugly between Hanley and the Cordeau broad. Something juicy.

But what?

That was what made this search so intriguing, what had kept his burning eyes fixed on the screen all morning, fighting vertigo as the pages whirred by.

Finally, he had found it, buried in the lower right hand corner of the October 14 late edition, a single paragraph:

> **Woman stabbed in midtown alley**
> The body of a young woman, who was later identified as one Jasmine Cordeau, was discovered in an alley off 40th St. between 8th and 9th Avenues early this morning. She died of multiple stab wounds. Her purse was missing.

That was it! Jasmine — Jazzy — it had to be!

Excitement still quivered through him. *Stabbed to death.* Why had she been killed? To shut her up? To put an end to another "pitiful attempt at blackmail?"

He rubbed his sweaty hands together as he approached the filing cabinets. Despite the drudgery ahead, the thrill of the hunt began to work its spell on him. This was going to be *good!* There was something really rotten here. Even twenty years later, he could still catch a whiff of the stink.

After two hours of bending and kneeling and pulling and sifting until his hands were filthy and his back was killing him, Becker found a single sheet on Jazzy Cordeau. And that by accident. It was folded between two other files, as if it had dropped there by accident.

He held it up to the naked bulb hanging from the ceiling and cursed after he read it. This was no damn good! It was a summary face sheet from the coroner's report, saying Jasmine Cordeau had died from a deep laceration to the left carotid artery and multiple stab wounds to the anterior chest causing lacerations to the anterior wall of the myocardium.

So? She'd had her throat cut and was stabbed in the heart. That didn't tell him anything new, other than the fact that someone seemed to have wanted Jim Stevens' mother dead real bad. *Who?* That was what he wanted to know! *Who* was Jazzy Cordeau and *who* had killed her?

He took the face sheet up to the Records Department. The sergeant there wasn't too surprised that the file couldn't be found. He took one look at the sheet and grunted.

"When'd y'say dis happened?"

"October fourteenth, 1949. On West Fortieth."

"Kelly might be able to help yiz. Used to walk dat beat."

"And where do I find this Kelly?" Becker said.

"Dat's *Sergeant* Kelly. Right here. He's on d'next shift. Be here'n a coupla minutes."

Becker took a seat and wondered what kind of cop was walking a beat twenty years ago and was now only a sergeant in the Records Department. When the balding, overweight Kelly finally strolled in, Becker got a pretty good idea why: The whole department was suddenly redolent of cheap Scotch.

He gave the shifts a chance to change, gave Sergeant Kelly a chance to settle in, then approached him. He showed him his press card and the coroner's face sheet.

"I was told you might be able to help me find the rest of this file."

"You was, was you?" Kelly said, eyeing him briefly, then glancing at the sheet. He started, then laughed. "Jasmine Cordeau? It's an old one you've got here! I knew that one well! What's the likes of you doing looking up the likes of Jazzy?"

Becker decided a piece of the truth might appeal to this old rummy. "A friend of mine, an orphan, has reason to believe she might be his mother."

"You don't say? Jazzy a mother? It don't seem likely. She was one of the top whores in midtown in her day."

"Whore?" Becker felt the blood start to race through his vessels. Stevens' mother had been a prostitute! What a story! "You're sure?"

"Course I'm sure! Had a record a mile long!"

This was too good to be true. And getting better by the minute!

"Did they ever find her killer?"

Kelly shook his head. "Nah! Some john did a hit-and-run on her. Cut her up and took her roll."

Something didn't fit here.

"If she was such a high-priced piece, what was she doing in an alley of Forty-first."

"She started off high-priced, but she got on the H and began the slide. At the end she was doing b-j's in alleys. Shame. She was a beautiful woman in her prime."

"What happened to her file?"

"You wanna see it?" Kelly said, rising from behind his desk. "C'mon. I'll show you."

It was back down to the musty old cellar, but this time to a secluded corner where Kelly pulled a dust cloth off a relatively new file cabinet.

"My personal files," he said. "Any case I had anything to do with, any victim or perpetrator I knew, I keep the files here."

"Far out!" What a stroke of luck! "How come?"

"For my book. Yeah, I'm gonna write me a book about walking a beat in midtown. Think it'll sell?"

"Depends on how it's written," Becker said, sensing which way the conversation was going and dreading it.

"Say, you're a writer, right? Maybe you could help me."

"Sure. That's cool. Sounds real interesting," Becker said as sincerely as he could. "But do you have that Cordeau file?"

"Sure."

Kelly unlocked his private cabinet, flipped through the top drawer — Becker noticed a half-empty fifth of Scotch at the rear — then pulled out a manila folder. He opened it and started paging through the contents. It was all Becker could do to keep from snatching it away.

"Is it all there?"

"Looks like it. I just wanted to see if I still have that eight-by-ten glossy she had done when she was a dancer, before she found out there was more money in hooking. Yep. Here it is." He handed Becker the photo. "Wasn't she a piece?"

For a moment, Becker stared at the picture in mute shock. And then he couldn't help himself — despite the crushing disappointment, he began to laugh.

4.

Jim's palms were sweaty and his fingers trembled. It took him three tries at the combination before the tumblers clanked within the safe door.

Why am I making such a big deal of this?

He yanked the lever to the right and pulled the door open. He saw three shelves inside, two of them empty, the third nearly so.

"Looks like a crash dieter's refrigerator," he said.

He emptied the third shelf and brought everything to a nearby table. The entire contents of the safe consisted of four yearly journals, uniform with the others he had found, a small black-bound volume, and an over-size green book. The only other item was an unsealed legal-size manila envelope. Jim picked this up and found a few hundred dollars in tens and twenties within.

"Mad money," he said.

Carol had opened the big green book.

"Look at this."

Jim leaned over her shoulder. Inside the front cover was a faded black-and-white photo of a shirtless Hanley holding an infant, tiny enough to be a newborn, in his arms. It was dated, *Jan. 6, 1942*.

"I'll bet that's me!" Jim said. "I must be newborn!"

"Look at how hairy he is," Carol said. "Remind you of anyone?"

Jim smiled. "I wonder if he had hairy palms?"

Wonder filled him as he looked into Roderick Hanley's smiling face. A proud father if there ever was one. He turned the page and saw another photo of a brick fronted garden apartment. He recognized it immediately.

"That's Harbor Terrace Gardens! We lived there till I was seven!"

There followed a few blurry, long range photos of an unrecognizable child playing in front of the apartments, then a shocker. A class photo of little children, with an inscription in Hanley's now familiar hand: *Kinder-garten, 1947*.

"That's my class! That's me at the end of the second row!"

Each page had a different class picture, even an occasional portrait shot.

Carol said, "Where did he get these? Do you think Jonah and Emma —?"

"No. I'm sure they didn't know anything about Hanley. It would be easy enough for him to go to the photographer and buy prints, don't you think?"

"Sure. I guess so." Carol sounded uneasy.

Jim looked at her. "What's wrong?"

"Well, don't you feel kind of creepy knowing he was secretly watching you all the time?"

"Not at all. Makes me feel good in a way. I mean, it tells me that although he'd let go of me physically, he hadn't let go emotionally. Don't you see? He lived most of his life in a Manhattan townhouse until 1942. Then he suddenly sold it and moved to Monroe. Now I know why — to watch me grow up.

Thinking about it gave Jim a warm feeling inside. *He didn't raise me, but he never forgot about me, never completely abandoned me. He was always there, watching over me.*

"Here we go," Carol said with a little laugh that sounded forced. "The Football Years."

There followed page after page of newspaper clippings. Anyplace his name was mentioned, even if it was simply a list of the players who had seen action in a game, Hanley had cut it out, underlined Jim's name, and pasted it into the scrapbook.

Jim was struck now by the irony of those football games. Jonah and Emma were in the stands for every game. In his mind's eye he saw himself turning on the bench and waving to his parents — all three of them. For right behind them sat Dr. Hanley, enthusiastically cheering Our Lady's Hawks — and one running back in particular — to victory.

Weird. And touching, in a way.

He wondered how Hanley had reacted to the injuries his son inflicted on the field. Did he cringe at the pain he saw, or did he hunger for more?

After football came photos cut from the Stony Brook yearbooks, and later on, even Monroe *Express* articles with the James Stevens byline.

"He was really some sort of completist, wasn't he?"

"Yeah. From reading his journals, I feel I know him. He definitely wasn't the kind of guy to do anything halfway."

The doorbell rang.

Who the hell —?

Jim went to the window and looked down at the front drive. He recognized the rusty Beetle.

"Oh, no! It's Becker!"

"He's kind of late, isn't he?"

Then Jim remembered what Becker had been looking into and decided he'd better talk to him.

"Maybe he's learned something about Jazzy Cordeau."

He hurried downstairs with Carol close behind and pulled open the door as the bell rang a third time. Becker stood there on the front porch, grinning.

"What's up, Gerry?" Jim said.

Becker kept grinning as he stepped into the front hall.

"Still think Jazzy Cordeau might be your mother?"

"What did you find out?"

"This and that."

Jim felt his fists clench and his muscles tighten. *He* had wanted to be the one to uncover her identity before anybody else — especially before Gerry Becker! And now Becker was playing cute.

"*What?*"

"She was a hooker."

Jim heard Carol gasp beside him. His anger grew, fueled by Becker's taunting tone.

"Very funny."

"No. It's true. I have it on reliable authority — first from a Sergeant Kelly, NYPD, and later from an old pal of his who used to work vice — that she was midtown's finest piece of ass in the late thirties and on through the war. Except for a period of time right before the war when she dropped out of sight for almost a year. Some people say that in her final years, when she was shooting smack like I drink Pepsi, she talked about having a baby someplace, but no one ever saw the kid. The timing's right. Think that kid might be you, Stevens?"

Anger had ballooned into barely suppressed rage. Jim could see how much Becker was enjoying this. He forced himself to speak calmly.

"That's all you've got?"

"Nope. Got a picture of her when she was a stripper." He pulled a photo out of a manila envelope and handed it to Jim. "What do you say? Think this could be Mama?"

Jim stared at the photo of a shapely young woman in a rhinesone G-string. She was beautiful, but there was no way in the world she could be his mother. Because she was black — *very* black.

Becker guffawed. "Had you going there, didn't I? I really thought I'd tracked her down, and turns out she's as black as the ace of spades! Is that a riot or what?"

Something exploded in Jim. He shifted the photo to his left hand, cocked his right arm, and belted Becker in the face. His arms windmilling for balance, Becker stumbled backward out the door and landed flat on his back on the front porch. Blood began to drip from his nose as he looked up at Jim in shock.

"What —?"

"That's for being a malicious bastard!" Jim said through his clenched teeth.

"Can't you take a joke?"

"Not funny, jerk! Now get the hell out of here and don't come back!"

He slammed the door closed and turned to see Carol's shocked expression.

"Sorry," he said.

"It's okay," she said, slipping her arms around him. "That was a really rotten thing to do you. But did you have to . . . ?"

"Hit him?" Jim shook his head. "No, I suppose not." He hadn't even enjoyed it. Maybe that was a good sign. "You know what they say."

"I know. 'Violence is the first resort of the mentally inferior party.'"

"I'd like to beg an exception to that rule."

"Granted," Carol said.

"I'd also like to beg a drink."

"Also granted."

Jim looked again at the photo of Jazzy Cordeau's slim, sensuous black body and seductive smile.

"*Sheesh!* Make it a double!"

5.

"I'm back!"

Carol carried the sack of Cokes, fries, and burgers into the library and found Jim just where she had left him, slumped in the wing chair, engrossed in one of the newfound Hanley journals.

"Yoo-hoo," she said. "I'm home. And don't get too comfortable there. That's my chair."

Jim looked up but didn't smile. His expression was troubled, and his eyes had a far away look.

"Something wrong?" Carol said.

"Hmm?" he said, straightening up. "Oh, no. No, everything's fine. I'm just having a little trouble with some of this scientific stuff, is all."

He wasn't much company during dinner — if indeed the cooling, soggy cheeseburgers from Wetson's deserved to be called dinner — and she noticed that he poured his glass of Scotch into his Coke before he drank it. He

initiated no conversation, which was highly unusual for him. Jim always had something to talk about — a wild idea or a diatribe about some aspect of the current political and social scene. But he was definitely preoccupied tonight, answering her attempts at conversation with monosyllables.

As soon as he gobbled down his third and last burger, he stood up and drained his Coke.

"Look, I hope you don't mind, but I'd like to get back to those new journals."

"Sure. Go ahead. Come across any good stuff yet?"

His expression was bleak as he turned away toward the library.

"No. No good stuff."

Carol finished her second cheeseburger and swept all the wrappers and fries bags back into the sack. Then she wandered into the library. Jim didn't look up from his hunched posture over the journal. Carol wandered along the shelves, looking for something to read. There were lots of classics, from Aeschylus to Wyss, but she wasn't in the mood for anything long or heavy. She stopped by the wing chair where Jim sat and noticed a small black journal on the table next to him. She remembered seeing it in the safe when they'd opened it earlier.

She picked it up and opened the cover. A title was block-printed in capitals on the first page:

PROJECT GENESIS

"What's this about?" she asked.

Jim's head snapped up.

"What?

His eyes widened when he saw the journal in her hand and he snatched it away.

"Give me that!"

"Jim!" Carol cried, shocked.

"I'm sorry," he said, obviously flustered. "I . . . I'm just trying to put all the pieces together and I . . . I can't if . . . the pieces start wandering away. You know? Sorry I snapped. Really."

She noticed that as he was speaking he closed the journal he had been reading and slipped the black one under it. She had never seen him so distracted, so tentative, and it made her uneasy.

"Jim, what's wrong?"

"Nothing, Carol," he said, rising from the chair.

"I don't buy that. Something in those journals is upsetting you. Tell me. Share it."

"No. I'm not upset. It's just heavy going, that's all. When I get it straight in my head, I'll lay it out for you. Right now . . . I've got to concentrate. I'll take these upstairs and you take the chair and read or watch TV."

"Jim, please!"

He turned and headed for the stairs.

"It's okay, Carol. Just give me a little time alone with this stuff."

She noticed that he grabbed the Scotch decanter on his way out of the room.

Time crawled.

Carol tried to occupy herself but it wasn't easy. The disquiet over Jim's obsession with these journals and his past gnawed at her, making it impossible to read, or even to involve herself in the new color TV in the corner of the library. She spent most of the night spinning the dial. *The Avengers* seemed vapid, *The Beverly Hillbillies* and *Green Acres* were more annoying than usual, and even *The Jonathan Winters Show* couldn't wring a smile from her.

By eleven o'clock she couldn't take any more. She went upstairs to the science library to pull Jim away from those damn journals.

The door was locked.

Alarmed now, she pounded on it.

"Jim! Are you all right?"

She heard papers shuffling within, then Jim opened the door — but only part way. He stood in the opening, blocking her from entering. His eyes had a haunted look.

"What is it?" he mumbled.

She could smell the Scotch on his breath.

"It's late," she said, trying to keep her voice calm. "Let's call it a night."

He shook his head. "Can't. Gotta keep after this."

"Come back in the morning when you're fresh. You might get a whole new —"

"*No!* I can't leave this now! Not yet! You go home. Take the car and leave me here. I'll come home later."

"You're going to walk home? You can't be serious! You'll freeze!"

"It's only a mile or so. The exercise will do me good."

"Jim, this is crazy! What's wrong? Why can't you tell me what's —?"

"Please!" he said. "Just go home and leave me here. I don't want to discuss it any more right now."

With that he closed the door in her face. She heard the lock click.

"Fine," Carol said.

She went downstairs, grabbed her coat, and drove home in J. Carroll. Somewhere along the way her anger gave way to hurt. And fear.

Jim had looked frightened.

TEN

Tuesday
March 5

1.

You hear the cries from behind the walls of the sick houses as you trod Strasbourg's misty, filth-encrusted streets. Two months ago when you arrived from Genoa, the streets at this hour were clogged with people. Now you can number your fellow travelers on one hand. Unlike you, they hurry along with nosegays pressed to their faces to protect themselves from the disease and to fend off the odor of corruption that hangs over the town like a shroud.

Fear. Fear keeps the small surviving remnant of the populace indoors, hiding behind their shuttered windows and barred doors, peeping through the cracks; fear of catching the pestilence, for they know not whence or why it has come; fear that the whole world is coming to an end.

And perhaps it is. Twenty million dead in the last four years, bishop and beggar, prince and peasant alike, for the pestilence cuts across all classes. There are not enough peasants to till the fields, not enough knights to force the remainder to work. The whole fabric of Europe's social order is unraveling around you.

Fear. The very air is saturated with fear, laced with grief and tinged with the death throes of a ravaging disease. They blame God, they blame the alignment of the planets, they blame the Jews. Fear. You breathe deeply, sucking it in like a bracing tonic.

You find the house you are seeking and push your way inside. There are seven people within, two adults and five children, but no one resists your entry. Instead the survivors plead for your aid. Two more have died since you stopped by last night. Now only the father and one of the daughters remain alive, each with draining, egg-size swellings in their groins and armpits. Their eyes are feverish, their cheeks hollow, their lips and tongues swollen and cracked as they hoarsely beseech you for a sip of water.

You hover over them a moment, drinking their misery, then tear yourself away and proceed to the back room. You lift the wicker trap you baited with cheese last night and feel the squealing weight within.

Rats. A pair of them. Good! Your supply of sickly rodents is sufficient now. You can move on.

And you must move on. The pestilence is beginning to taper off, its spread is slowing. You can't allow that. This is too good. You must make this ecstasy last.

You start back toward the street. Your horse and loaded cart await you at the stable. You really must be on your way to Nurnberg where they say there is no plague.

You'll remedy that.

But you tarry in the front room over the father and daughter. Their agonies are so exquisite. You draw up a chair to sit and watch them . . .

Carol awoke cold and trembling. Another sickening nightmare. It was getting so she was afraid to go to sleep. She reached for Jim and experienced a moment of panic when she realized he wasn't beside her.

Last night she had waited up in bed alone until late, trying to distract her thoughts with Fletcher Knebel's new bestseller, but even *Vanished* couldn't keep her awake. She had fallen asleep before Jim came home.

Had he come home?

She went looking for him. It didn't take long to search the two-bedroom ranch–he wasn't here. Anxious now, she phoned the mansion, and with each unanswered ring the tension grew inside her. Finally Jim answered. He sounded groggy, his voice hoarse, his words garbled.

"How're you feeling?" she said, trying to sound bright and cheery.

"Terrible."

"Probably hung over. You were hitting the Scotch pretty heavily last night."

"Or not heavily enough."

"Did you finally get everything straightened out with those new journals?"

"I think so. If I can believe them. It ain't pretty."

"What's wrong? Did they tell you who your mother was?"

"Yeah. Nobody."

"Come on, Jim! It's me: Carol. Don't keep me in the dark. This isn't like you."

"Like me? Hon, are you sure you know what's like me? I'm not even sure *I* know what's like me."

"I know that I love you."

"I love you, too. And I'm sorry about the way I acted last night."

"Then why didn't you come home?"

"Too bushed to make the walk. I stayed up with the journals all night."

"Okay. I'll pick you up and we'll have breakfast somewhere and you can tell me all about this."

"Later. We'll talk later. Go to work, let me go through these things one more time, and I'll explain everything — if that's possible — when you get back this afternoon. Okay?"

"I can't wait until then!"

"Please don't come out here now. I've still got a few more things to work out in my head."

"What *is* it, Jim?"

"It's weird, Carol. Really weird. I'll see you later."

Carol hung up and sat there by the phone, baffled and worried by Jim's mood. When there were problems, he tended to withdraw, think them out, then return with a solution. But he was so *down* this morning. She couldn't remember him ever getting this low before.

She shook herself and stood up. Whatever it was, they could handle it together. She'd work through the day and they'd settle everything tonight. She headed for the shower. Mr. Dodd was due to go home with his daughters today.

At least something will go right this morning, Carol thought.

She called Jim again at around 10:15 on her coffee break, using the booth in the hospital lobby so she could have a little more privacy than afforded by the Social Services office. But Jim was still uncommunicative, and if anything he sounded even more strung out. She wondered if Bill could help. Maybe he'd talk to Bill.

As she pulled another dime from her wallet, she saw Catherine and Maureen, Mr. Dodd's daughters, come in through the main entrance. She dialed hurriedly.

2.

Professor Albert Calder and his wife, Jane, struck Bill as a stuffy couple, the kind of people who consider themselves the intellectual superiors of most of the human race. But that was fine. Especially if they were going to adopt Nicky. They would need to be superior to keep pace with that boy.

So far Bill had overseen two meetings of the prospective parents and child here in St. F.'s, and both had gone well. The Calders were impressed with Nicky's quick mind, and Nicky had felt free to pull his child genius routines without fear of alienating the adults. The Calders' references showed they were a stable, childless couple with a decent income and, although not terribly active in their parish, at least regular attendees at Mass.

It appeared to be a match made in heaven.

The next step was a weekend stay. The Calders were in his office now to make those arrangements.

"Okay, Father. Then it's all set," Professor Calder said. "We'll pick him up Friday afternoon after school."

He was in his mid-thirties with thick, horn-rimmed glasses, a neat Van Dyke goatee, and dark hair prematurely salted with grey that he was letting grow over his ears. There were suede elbow patches on his tweed jacket. Here was a man who reveled in being a college professor.

Jane Calder was a short, plump redhead with a generous smile.

"We can't wait to have him over," she said.

"I know Nicky's looking forward to it, too."

The intercom buzzed and Sister Margaret's voice said, *"Personal call on two, Father."*

"Tell them to hold."

Professor Calder stood up and gave him a crisp handshake.

"Father Ryan, it's been a pleasure."

"That's mutual, I can assure you, Professor." He shook hands with Mrs. Calder and ushered them into the hall. They knew their way out.

Bill's spirits were high. He had a feeling in his gut that this was it for Nicky — out of St. F's and into a home that could nurture his mind, body, and spirit. He felt good about the imminent adoption. This was what it was all about.

On top of that, he had had a call from the Maryland Provincial yesterday to clarify a few items on his curriculum vitae. That could mean that either Loyola or Georgetown were interested in him. Either way he'd be in or near the nation's capital, right in the thick of things.

Nicky, old pal, we're both getting out of here!

He picked up the phone. "Father Ryan."

"Bill, it's Carol. Carol Stevens. I need your help."

Involuntarily he flushed with pleasure at the sound of her voice, even though it sounded tight, tense.

"Something wrong?"

"It's Jim. He's been looking through Dr. Hanley's old journals, hunting for the identity of his mother. I think he's found something that's really upset him."

"What?"

"He won't tell me a thing about it. I'm worried, Bill. He sounds like he's about to explode. We're supposed to talk the whole thing out tonight, but that seems a long time away. I was wondering if maybe you could —"

"I'll call him right now," Bill said.

The relief in her voice poured through the phone. "Will you? Oh, thank you! I hate to impose but —"

"Carol, this is what friends are for. Don't give it a second thought."

After jotting down the number and saying good-bye, Bill sat there a moment with his hand on the receiver, thinking.

Carol again. There didn't seem to be any escape from her. Just when he thought he was getting a handle on his obsession with her, she says a few words to him over the phone and he's on fire again. This had to stop. He had to beat this.

But first he had to see about Jim.

He lifted the phone and hesitated. As a priest he did his share of counseling in the confessional. But those were strangers, and they had initiated the encounter by coming to him.

This was different. Jim was an old friend, and from the sound of it, Jim didn't want to talk about whatever it was that was upsetting him.

Jim . . . upset. That was hard to imagine. Jim Stevens was usually pretty unflappable.

Except about his roots.

Bill had realized from their conversations during last week's night on the town that Jim's roots were an obsession with him, and thus a vulnerable area in his psychological defenses.

Listen to me: Bill Ryan, S.J., parlor psychoanalyst!

But he had made a point of studying a lot of psychology in the seminary. He had come to see the interplay between the human mind and human emotion as the wellspring of faith. To speak to man's faith, you had to understand its mechanisms. And how better to understand faith than to study the human psyche?

What could Jim have learned to disturb him so?

He felt an unaccountable burst of sorrow for his old friend. Had the diehard, stonewall rationalist come upon something that he did not want to accept? How sad.

He dialed the number Carol had given him. When he heard Jim's gruff voice on the other end, he put on his best hale-fellow voice and said,

"Jimbo! It's Bill Ryan! How's it goin'?"

"Just great." The flat tone made no attempt to hide the lie behind his words.

"Getting used to being a rich member of the establishment?"

"Working on it."

"So what's new?"

"Not much."

This was getting nowhere. Bill decided to come straight to the point.

"Find out anything new about your natural parents?"

"*What makes you say that?*" The words sounded as if they'd been ripped out of Jim—the first sign of emotion he'd shown since he'd picked up the phone.

Bingo!

"Just wondering. When we were out to dinner last week you seemed satisfied that Hanley was your father and said you were going to comb the mansion for the identity of your mom."

Jim's voice was thick. "Yeah, well, maybe I didn't know as much as I thought I knew."

What's that supposed to mean?

"I'm sorry, Jim. I don't get it."

But Jim had leapt off the subject.

"Just a minute," he said. "Did Carol put you up to this?"

"Well, she's worried, Jim. She —"

"It's okay, Bill. I know she's worried. I haven't been playing fair with her. But I'll straighten things out today — I think."

"Can I help?"

"Bill . . . I don't think anyone can help."

A terrible, crushing sadness flowed across the line.

"Hey, surely —"

"Gotta go, Bill. Thanks. Bye."

And then the line went dead.

Bill sat there and knew with pitying certainty that his old friend had discovered the roots he had quested after for so long and was being torn apart by what he had found.

3.

Gerry Becker drove along Shore Drive to the Hanley mansion. He found the spike-topped wrought iron gates closed and no car in the driveway. But that didn't mean Stevens wasn't there. He parked at the curb but remained behind the wheel for a while, staring at the huge place as the afternoon sun warmed the inside of the car and Big Dan Ingram yakked between the records on WABC.

He sat a little longer, basking in the clear March sky's preview of spring until Big Dan started playing "Daydream Believer." The Monkees. Perfect. Four jerks grabbed off the street get fame and fortune handed to them. Just like Jim Stevens. What a bummer!

He figured he should stop putting it off and get on with what he had come to do.

It was crow-eating time.

He pushed the gates open, stepped up on the front porch, rang the bell, and held his breath.

He hated doing this. After all, the jerk had slugged him in the nose yesterday. So maybe it hadn't been in the best of taste to present the fruit of his whole day's research in that particular way. That didn't give Stevens the right to belt him. Did he think he could get away with that sort of shit because he was rich now?

But he had to stay on Stevens' good side. He wasn't going to let this story and the chance of a wire service pick-up go blooey over one misunderstanding. If he had to eat a little crow today to ensure his exclusive on the story, well then, pass the mustard.

But after all this was over and the story was in print under his byline, he'd tell Jim Stevens to fuck off.

The heavy oak door swung open and Stevens stood there, staring at him.

"What the hell do you want?" Jim said.

His tone was hostile but his eyes showed something else. Becker wasn't sure what it was.

"I came to apologize."

"It's already forgotten."

"No, really. That was a stupid thing for me to do. Incredibly bad taste."

"Don't give it a second thought." His tone had gone flat, utterly emotionless

Hey, this was going better than he had ever hoped. This was easy and damn near painless! He wished he could come in out of the cold, but Stevens kept the door almost closed and made no move to invite him inside.

"That's cool. Really big of you, Jim. So, have you turned up anything new we can put into the article?"

That strange look returned to Stevens' eyes. He said, "Don't give the article a second thought, either, Gerry."

Becker went numb. "I don't get it."

"It means I don't want you around anymore."

"We had a deal!"

"You've got your story."

"I've only got half of it!"

"You've got all you're going to get. Forget the rest."

"We were going to find out who your mother was! The story's not complete without it!"

At mention of his mother, that strange look deepened in Stevens' eyes.

"Sorry about that. You'll have to go with what you've got. Or better yet, drop the whole thing."

"Not on your life, you son of a bitch! This is my ticket off the *Express*! You're not robbing me of it!"

"Good-bye, Gerry."

He slammed the door shut. Furious, Becker gave it a kick, then hurried back through the gate to his Beetle, so angry that he could barely keep from screaming. And then he recognized Stevens' strange look for what it was.

He's afraid of me!

Becker took an immediate liking to the notion. He could not remember another time in his life when someone had been afraid of him. It gave him a good feeling, powerful.

There could only be one reason for Stevens' reaction: He had discovered something in his past he didn't want made public. That had to be it.

Gerry Becker promised himself that, one way or another, he was going to ferret out that something.

4.

"Jim?"

No answer.

The house seemed empty. Carol had sensed that the moment she stepped through the door, yet she had called out anyway.

So quiet. Dust motes glowed and swirled in the late afternoon sun slanting through the front windows. Carol looked around for a note. When she didn't find one, she went directly to the phone to call the the Hanley mansion.

She was angry. She'd had just about all she could take now. This should have been a great day. She'd sent a very happy and grateful Mr. Dodd home with his daughters today — he was going to stay with Maureen, Catherine taking him on weekends — and she would have been high as a kite if not for Jim's secretive, erratic behavior.

She was about to dial when she heard a rustle from the study. A single step, a craning of her neck, and she saw him in profile as he sat on the convertible sofa.

He was staring off into space. He looked so lost, so utterly miserable that she wanted to cry for him. As she started forward, she saw his eyes close and his head sag back against the cushion. His breathing became slow and rhythmic, the tension eased from his face. He was asleep.

Carol watched him for a few minutes. She didn't have the heart to awaken him. For the moment at least, he had escaped whatever demons were pursuing him.

And then she saw the source of those demons — the journals from the safe, lying on the cushion next to him. Her first impulse was to grab them and find out for herself what could upset him so, but she hesitated. What if he woke up and found her sneaking out of the room with them? What would he think then about her respect for his privacy?

But damn it, this affected her, too!

She tiptoed over to the sofa and gently slid the books off the cushion. There was a bad moment as she was lifting the pile away from him when the smaller black one almost slid out of her hands and onto Jim's lap, but she steadied it and slipped from the room without waking him.

She took them to the bedroom and, with trembling fingers, began flipping through one of the gray journals.

5.

Gerry Becker pulled into the curb across the street and about fifty feet up from the Stevens place. Earlier he had followed Jim on his walk back from the mansion, resisting the urge to gun the engine and run him down. That would end this whole shitty deal. He could close his exclusive article with an obituary.

But that would leave too many unanswered questions.

So he had driven around for a while after Steven's wife had come home, and now that it was good and dark, he was back. He had decided to sit here in the cold and watch the house until it looked like everyone was tucked in for the night. Then he'd be back at the crack of dawn with a thermos of coffee, watching, cruising, not letting Stevens out of his sight, waiting for a slip, waiting for him to give something away.

He lit a joint, wrapped himself in the wool blanket he had brought along, and watched the lit windows. He knew his chance would come if he hung around long enough. And he was sure it would be worth the wait.

6.

It had been hours and Jim was still sound asleep. Probably his first sleep since Monday morning. A good thing, too, because Carol wasn't getting anywhere. She shook her head in frustration as she pored over another of the gray journals. There was too much here. And with no idea of what she was looking for, she could spend all night deciphering the crabbed handwriting without learning a thing.

She opened up the black journal to the middle and gasped at the salutation on the first page of text. Instinctively she knew she had found what she sought.

She began to read.

ELEVEN

January 6, 1963

Dear Jim —

It's your 21st birthday. I'm going to spend the next few days writing this letter to you. It's a letter I pray you never get to read.

But if you have this in your hands, it means that something has gone dreadfully wrong.

I'm sorry about that.

You were never supposed to learn about yourself. You were supposed to lead a normal, happy, productive life, and then maybe — *maybe* — after I was long gone and after you had died a natural death, what you are about to learn would be made public.

But if you are indeed reading this, it means I'm dead and so is Derr, and that all my plans have gone awry.

That's why I'm writing this. To set the record straight. In the locked-away journals you will find the same story unfolding on a day-to-day basis in far greater detail but with little or no perspective. (Back then, if I'd had the perspective I have now, I can't imagine that I would have gone so far.) This letter will give you the whole story in a nutshell.

What you are about to read will strain your credulity to the breaking point. If you do not choose to believe it, that is fine with me. Take these journals and this letter and burn them now without reading any further. Your secret will be safe. But since I know you better than anyone, I'm sure you will never settle for that. I know you will search and dig and chase and harry until you have all the answers.

That, after all, is just what I would do.

* * *

It started for me in 1939.

I'm sure the government had been mulling the idea for a few years before that. You didn't have to be Jewish to be uneasy about Hitler's saber-rattling during the Thirties and his endless harangues about a Thousand Year Reich led by a pure-bred Aryan Master Race. They were upsetting to a lot of people in this country, myself included. The topic of eugenics (a term that has fallen out of usage these days, but which refers to improvement of the human race through selective breeding) was much on my mind then and, I imagine, the subject of not a few conversations at State Department cocktail parties.

Somewhere along the way, the idea of researching the possibility of breeding a perfect (or, at the very least, *superior*) American soldier began to brew. It probably never would have amounted to anything if I hadn't written a letter to President Roosevelt on the subject in the summer of 1939, and if Hitler had stayed within his own borders.

I don't want to toot my own horn too much here, Jim, but I was quite a fellow in my heyday. I was born in 1901, so that meant I was not yet forty at the time, but I'd already made a fortune (and this was in the Great Depression, mind you) off my patented diagnostic procedures for commercial labs. I also had caused quite a stir among the biologists of the time with my papers on genetic manipulation through selective breeding and my private experiments on the *in vitro* fertilization of primate ova.

Oh, I was a cocky bastard back then. And why not? The world was my oyster. I'd never been poor, but by hard work and intuition I'd become independently wealthy while other people all around me were falling into financial ruin. It was a time when one man's mind could arm itself with all (and I do mean *all*) the available knowledge in a field such as genetics and forge across the frontiers into virgin territory.

I had money, fame, and notoriety, and I lived the life of the rich bachelor to the hilt. So when I became concerned enough about Hitler cleaning Germany's genetic house (so to speak) on a national scale, I didn't contact any intermediaries. I wrote directly to the president. I told him that America could probably develop a genetically superior soldier without programs and detention camps. All it took was sufficient funds, commitment, and the right man to head the project: Roderick C. Hanley, Ph.D.

Little did I know that Albert Einstein was simultaneously writing a similar letter to Roosevelt regarding the development of an atom bomb.

As I said above, it all would have come to naught if Hitler had behaved. But his attack on Poland in September of that year spurred Roosevelt into initiating two secret research projects. The atomic project was codenamed "Manhattan" and given over to Oppenheimer, Fermi, Teller, and Bohr. The eugenics project was assigned to yours truly and a very bright young M.D. named Edward Derr. Our project was called "Genesis."

I did not receive much in the way of funding, but that didn't matter. When the government appropriations fell short, I supplemented them with my own funds. I wasn't in this for the money. I had more than I could spend! I was in it for the *doing!*

It is so very important to me that you understand that part of my persona, Jim. This was new ground, virgin territory, *terra incognita*, like Roald Amundsen leaving the first human footprints in the snow at the South Pole. I wanted to be *first*. Some might call it the pioneer spirit, some might call it monomania. Call it what you will, I wanted to do what no man had done before.

Once I get started on a project, there is no stopping me. The Genesis Project was no exception. I even infected Derr with my mania. We worked like automatons, sometimes going days without sleep, weeks without stopping. The government wasn't pushing us. Pearl Harbor was still two years away. There was no time limit. We created our own pressure.

You see, in a way, we were trying to reinvent the wheel. Early on we looked at natural selection, which is the way Nature came up with the fittest species for an ecological niche, and tried to transpose that onto a fighting man. We quickly came up with theories and possible solutions to the problem of breeding the supersoldier, all of which would take generations to prove.

So we discarded them.

I was dissatisfied with the very idea of breeding, anyway. At root no doubt in that dissatisfaction was my impatient nature. I wanted results *now*, not generations hence. But even more so, the capriciousness of genetic mixing seemed an unscalable barrier.

Let me give you a few basics.

Each human cell is *diploid*, which means it has 46 chromosomes. The combination and arrangement of genes on these chromosomes makes up the *genotype*, which in turn determines the *phenotype*, the physical expression of those genes; that is, the bodily characteristics of each individual person: sex, skin color, body type, even personality to some extent. If the presence of one gene was all that was required to make a supersoldier, there would be no problem — eugenics would give us a high success rate.

Unfortunately that is not the case. A supersoldier phenotype can only result from a highly specific and extraordinarily complex genotype providing such characteristics as a large-framed skeleton, strong musculature, agile limbs, quick reflexes, high threshhold of pain, an obedient, aggressive personality, and so on.

Here's where the whole breeding approach falls apart. You see, we mammals reproduce by joining a female gamete (an ovum) with a male gamete (a spermatozoan). Each gamete is *haploid*, meaning it has only 23 chromomsomes (half the normal complement). When they join together, they form a brand new 46-chromosome (diploid) person. The stumbling block for us would-be breeders is that when a diploid cell breaks up into two haploid gametes, we have no way of controlling which genes go into which gamete. The process is random. So anything is possible. This is a wonderful means of providing the human race with nearly endless variety within the parameters of our species, thereby allowing us to adapt to various environments and situations. But it is pure hell to someone trying to produce the same genotype and phenotype over and over.

So to give you an example, let's take Attila the Hun and mate him with Joan of Arc. We could get a strong, brave, ferocious, idealistic supersoldier. Or we could get a 98-pound anemic accountant. Attila and Joan, no matter how strong and brave and aggressive they each may be, have recessive anemic accountant genes hiding on their chromosomes. If we take from each a haploid gamete rich in recessive anemic accountant genes, and pair them, we will get an anemic accountant. The pairing of any two random gametes from each could result in *anything* between the two extremes. The odds can be skewed in your favor by rigorous investigations of the family trees, but it's still a crapshoot. And since humans don't breed like mice or rabbits, it would take lots of luck and many generations to breed a supersoldier army.

What was needed was a way to move a desirable genotype intact (the word *intact* cannot be overemphasized here) from generation to generation. In other words, we had to find a way of creating identical twins (or triplets or quints, or what have you) a generation removed from the original.

We needed to produce a series of beings genetically identical to their parent. (Note the singular, please.)

Clones, if you will.

We had to learn how to clone a human being.

Now, when you remove yourself from the fray and sit back and consider it without emotion, that is a pretty frightening concept. But Derr and I were in the thick of the fray. We were filled with the passion and fervor of discovery. Nothing frightened us. Questions of ethics or responsibility were far from our minds.

The only question that mattered was: *How?*

A tissue culture was out. A human body is a complex system of many different tissues. We could not culture out individual organs and patch them together like a modern Frankenstein. What we needed was a way to induce a human ovary to form an egg with a nucleus that was diploid instead of haploid. The result would be cloning by parthenogenesis, and only females would result, but it would be a start.

Then a chance remark by Derr set us on the right track. He said, "Too bad we can't just get hold of some ova and plop the genotype we want *into* them."

It was one of those rare moments of shared epiphany. You look at each other with wide eyes, then leap up and jump around and begin shouting ideas back and forth like a couple of madmen. That was Derr and I.

Looking back now, I think that perhaps we truly were mad.

But it was a glorious madness. I can't describe the excitement we felt. And even now, I wouldn't trade those times for anything. We shared a feeling of *masterfulness*. I'm not sure there is such a word, but if it doesn't exist, it should. We felt that we were on the verge of something epochal, that just beyond our questing fingertips lay the secret of mastering Creation.

And it was just the two of us. That was the most enthralling part of it. Only Derr and I had the Big Picture. We had technicians for the scut work, of course, but the duties of each were narrowly circumscribed. My three floor townhouse was partially converted into two labs. Some worked in the third floor lab, others worked in the basement lab. Only we knew where the sum of all the scut work was headed. The whole would truly be greater than the sum of its parts.

We started small. We looked for an aquatic, oviparous reptile with good-size eggs. We settled for an amphibian. That was Derr's idea. He had trained in Europe where frogs are frequently used for research. We obtained a supply of green frogs, and some special pure white albino frogs. We were ready to begin.

After much trial and error, we perfected a microscopic technique of removing the haploid nucleus from the egg of a green frog and replacing it with a diploid nucleus removed from a body cell of a white frog. All the genetic information from the albino frog now resided in the egg cell from the green. The egg cell, in a sense, had been fertilized. After many failures and botch-ups, we eventually got it right. Soon we were awash in white tadpoles.

This was ground breaking work that would have set the scientific community (and no doubt the religious and philosophical communities as well) on its ear. Think of it: We were reproducing without recourse to the sexual process! This was a mammoth achievement!

But we could not publish. Everything we were doing in Project Genesis was classified top secret. In a very real sense, the government *owned* our work. I won't say it made no difference to us. It most certainly did. But we felt we could wait. We could not publish now, but someday we would. At the moment, we were, quite frankly, much too busy even to consider wasting the time it would take to document our work for publication.

After perfecting our microtechnique, we moved on to mammals. I won't bore you with the details of each species we tried — it's all recounted on a day-by-day basis in the gray journals — but suffice it to say that after a seemingly endless run of daily grinding work, we felt we were ready to tackle the human ovum.

Our first problem, naturally, was where to get the raw material. One does not simply send out to a laboratory supply house and order a gross of human ova. We were entering a very sensitive area. We would have had to tread softly even if we were on our own, but with the extra burden of security from the government, we felt hamstrung.

I then came up with the bright idea of letting the government help us out. I told our contact in the War Department that we needed human ovaries. Colonel Laughlin was one of the few in the entire government who knew of the existence of Project Genesis. He paused only a moment, then said, "How many?"

It wasn't long before we began receiving regular shipments of human ovaries in iced saline solution. Some were cancerous, but many were merely cystic and provided us with a small supply of viable normal ova. These we nurtured in a nutrient solution while we practiced our microtechniques.

We came to learn that the human ovum would not tolerate too much manipulation. The double trauma of removing the original nucleus and inserting another was apparently more than the cell membrane could stand. We ruptured one test ovum after another. So we devised a method of using ultraviolet light to inactivate the original genetic material within the ovum. We could then leave the old haploid nucleus where it was and insert the new nucleus right next to it in the cytoplasm.

Finally it came time to find the human diploid nuclei to transplant into the ova. This was going to be a problem. Along the way, as Derr and I progressed through a number of mammals toward human tissue, we had learned that we could not use just any nucleus from any cell in a mammal's body. Once a mammalian cell becomes fully differentiated (i.e., becomes a functioning part of the skin or the liver or any other organ) its nucleus loses its capacity to regenerate an entire organism. We had to go to the wellspring of the gamete, the diploid cell that divides into two haploid gametes: the primary spermatocyte. And to obtain those, we would have to burrow into a healthy, functioning human testicle.

I volunteered myself.

Call it part of the madness that was upon us. Call it pragmatism, as well. Colonel Laughlin sent us what testicular specimens he could, but none of them were suitable. Undamaged, undiseased testicles were difficult to come by.

Besides, I had a number of reasons for wanting my own genotype thrust into the ovum. The first might be called ego. I admit that without apology. This whole project was my idea. I wanted to see my work result in a new generation of Roderick Hanleys. The second was more practical: I had to be certain of the race of the donor genotype. Do not rear up on your egalitarian steed at this. I had my reasons and soon you will understand them.

Through Colonel Laughlin we arranged for an army urologist to do a wedge resection on my left testicle under local anesthesia. (He tied off an annoying varicocele while he was there, so it was not a totally frivilous procedure from the surgeon's viewpoint.) Derr took the section and culled out the primary spermatocytes. With these living and thriving in their nutrient bath, we were ready to begin the next phase.

It was time to find an incubator — a woman who would host the manipulated ovum and bear the resultant child.

Derr and I had decided on a number of characteristics: She had to be young, healthy, and single, with a clockwork menstrual cycle. And she had to be Negro. As I alluded above, this final criterion was not prompted by a racist bias. It was based on solid, scientific reasoning. Our plan was to insert a diploid nucleus from one of my primary spermatocytes into a human ovum and, in turn, insert that ovum into the uterus of a human female. We had to be sure that the resultant child (if all went as hoped) had actually arisen from the manipulated cell.

My genotype is lily white. My parents came from the British Isles late in the last century and I doubt very much that anyone in my family tree had ever even *seen* a Negro, much less had sexual relations with one. Therefore, if after nine months our host mother gave birth to a male who exhibited the slightest hint of Negroid features, we could be quite sure that the child did not carry my genotype. (A female child would obviously not be ours, either.)

Although not exactly parallel, we were doing on human terms what we had done with the frogs when we started: inserting the genotype from an albino into an egg from a green. Just as a white hatchling was proof of our success with the frogs, a lily-white infant boy from a Negro womb would confirm our success with a human genotype. (Yes, I'm sure you can come up with a very rare exception, but we had to be satisfied with this level of control.)

Once we had proven we could do it, we would report our success to the government. The War Department could then begin its search for the man who would provide the genotype for the American supersoldier.

Finding the woman: that was left to me. And with good reason. Once Project Genesis started, I lived a virtually celibate life. There was no room in my life for sex, only the project, *the project!* Ah, but before that, I was quite the ladies' man, the *bon vivant*, the Man About Town. I had many friends, high and low, who knew that no matter where or when they threw a party, Rod Hanley could be counted on to appear. I was known in the poshest nightspots and the sleaziest dives. And I knew men who could supply women who would do just about anything for a price.

That is how we began our relationship with the amazing Jasmine Cordeau. I don't have any photographs of her, but if you could see her, you'd know what I mean. She was a stunning Negress. Her skin was as black as the night and her figure was something every red-blooded male dreams of. Fresh from the bayous outside New Orleans, she migrated to New York and became a popular ecdysiast — *stripteaser* seems much too common a term for what she did on the stages of the uptown after-hours clubs I once frequented. But as the Great Depression steadily deepened despite two terms of grandiose promises from FDR, she had to turn to prostitution to make ends meet.

For a while, Derr and I gave her a respite from that.

I knew her "manager" — who was acting as her procurer at the time. After a gynecological exam certified her free from venereal disease, I persuaded him to let us take and keep her for up to two years. He would be paid one thousand dollars per month for that period, no questions asked. He eagerly agreed. (If $12,000 a year seems like princely sum now, please realize that it was worth much much more at the start of 1941.)

All we had to do was convince Jazzy, as she called herself. We met with her and explained what we wanted: She was to allow herself to become impregnated by us and to bear the resultant fetus to term. During the period in question, she was to live with us in comfort and class, but under no circumstances could she leave my townhouse unless accompanied by either Derr or myself.

Jazzy was understandably reluctant at first. She was used to the fast life and, for obvious reasons, did not want to be pregnant. She was a stripper by profession and her body was her meal ticket. She was rightfully protective of it; she didn't want to get fat, and she didn't want stretch marks.

She didn't want to be a prostitute, either, but with the Depression hanging on as it was, she had no alternative. "A gal's gotta eat," she would say. We promised her she'd eat very well, that we would help her take good care of her body during the pregnancy, and that if she bore us the baby we planned, she would receive a bonus of $10,000.

She agreed.

We sent the technicians packing with a month's pay so that we would have the townhouse to ourselves.

We were ready to begin.

The procedure was relatively straightforward and simple. Derr and I would "fertilize" an inactivated ovum (see above) by extracting a diploid nucleus from one of my primary spermatocytes and inserting it into the ovum. When we had three successful transfers, we would save them until Jazzy entered the ovulatory phase of her menstrual cycle. Then she would get on the examining table and assume the lithotomy position. We would then insert a fine rubber tube through the os of her cervix and inject a solution containing the three "fertilized" ova into her uterus.

After that, it was out of our hands. All we could do was hope that the one of the ova would find its way to the endometrium — the lining of the uterus — and attach itself. There was, of course, the theoretical threat of all three ova implanting and Jazzy bearing triplets, but neither Derr nor I was concerned about that. We knew we would be extremely lucky if just one implanted.

We first inseminated her in mid-December, 1940. She menstruated on New Year's Day. We tried again in mid-January, but her period arrived right on schedule at the end of the month. And so it went, through the winter and into the spring. Each month we would hold our collective breaths as her period came due, and each month we would be disappointed by the cramps and menstrual flow.

She was due for a period in late April. By May 1st, she was late. I stopped believing in God when I was 8, but I remember saying silent prayers during that time. May 2nd and 3rd, still no show. Around midnight on May 3rd, however, she gave us a bad scare. She had been feeling tired and so she had gone to bed early. Suddenly the townhouse was shaken by her shrill, horrified screaming. We ran to her, and when we found her doubled up in her bed, clutching her abdomen, we feared the worst — a miscarriage. But physically she was fine. The commotion proved to be the result of a particularly frightening nightmare. It must have been a lollapalooza because the poor thing's tremors were shaking the whole bed. It took us a long while, but finally we quieted her down and got her off to sleep again.

Four days late became a week late became two weeks late. Jazzy complained of breast tenderness and morning sickness. A pregnancy test was positive. Jazzy had not been out of the house for a minute and neither of us had had sexual relations with her.

We had done it!

What a celebration we had! Champagne, caviar, and the three of us dancing to the radio like fools. Derr and I were acting like it was New Year's Eve because, in a way, we knew it was an eve of sorts — the eve of a new epoch for mankind. We were taking the first step toward eliminating the random factors from reproduction, toward allowing humanity a say in Creation, towardremaking humanity in our own design, in our own image.

I won't say we felt like gods, Jim, but we sure as hell felt like godlings.

The months crawled by. Jazzy grew restive, moody, became prone to temper tantrums and maniacal outbursts. We noticed personality changes. She didn't like being pregnant, and hated what was happening to her body. She threatened countless times to sneak out and have an abortion, so we kept a close watch on her; we pampered and cajoled her, telling her to hang on, that it was only until January, and after that she'd have a fat wad of money and would be free to go wherever she wanted.

I remember how, on certain nights when Jazzy was calm and would permit us, Derr and I would kneel at the sides of her bed as she lay there with her swelling abdomen exposed, and we would take turns with the foetalscope (which is like a regular stethoscope except that the cup is attached to a metal band that goes around the examiner's head, allowing him to listen via bone conduction as well as through the conventional earpieces), pressing it against her abdomen to count the faint, rapid beats of the tiny heart within.

And we would place our hands over her silky skin and feel the kicks and turns beneath it and laugh with wonder.

She had about a month to go when the Japs hit Pearl Harbor. It wasn't long afterward that we heard from Colonel Laughlin. He said that with the United States now officially at war with the Axis, strict priorities were being set for the allocation of all research funds. He informed us that if Project Genesis was to "remain viable" (he was so pleased with his little play on words) we would have to come up with something more than albino frogs; we would have to show real progress toward a supersoldier, or at least demonstrate something of military value.

(I learned later that almost all the available research money was being funneled into the Manhattan Project and that Genesis never had a chance anyway. Just as well.)

Without going into detail (I had learned through the years never to promise more than you are sure you can deliver; promise less, *then* deliver the knockout!), I told him that a major experiment was coming to fruition and that we should have the results in four to six weeks. He said that was stretching the time limit, but that he could keep the project open until the middle of January, but no longer.

That was fine with us. Jazzy was due around the first of the year.

You can't imagine our excitement, the agony of the suspense as her due date approached. We were sure we were going to be successful. Even if the child were stillborn, as long as it was male and lily white, we would consider the experiment a complete success. And what outcome could there be other than complete success? We had implanted the altered diploid ovum ourselves, she had had no opportunity to become pregnant by any other means, the viable fetus inside her uterus could be nothing other than my clone, and yet . . .

And yet we still had our doubts. No one had ever done this before, or even *attempted* to do it! The idea that we might be the first in history to take such a momentous step was mind-numbing. We were looking immortality in the eye. Our names would be known the world over. Every history book written from this day forward would include our names because what we were doing would shape history from this point on.

Something had to go wrong.

Neither of us were pessimists by nature, but we had the feeling that it was all going too smoothly. We kept waiting for a catastrophe. And it was the waiting that was killing me. Derr at least had his preceptorship in the obstetrical section at Flower Fifth Avenue to keep him busy. But while he was brushing up on the latest delivery techniques, I was home alone, babysitting Jazzy.

Finally, around dinnertime on January 3, she went into labor. Her membranes ruptured spontaneously. With a gush of warm fluid, we were on our way.

There was little drama about the delivery itself. The contractions became longer and closer together just as they should. Jasmine Cordeau had a generous pelvic structure; the child was in a normal cephalic presentation; as labor progressed at a steady pace toward delivery, we anticipated no problems. The only question hanging over us was, *What will she deliver?*

Finally, amid cries and moans, Derr delivered a head, and then an entire male infant. (*Male!* We were part of the way there!) He cut the cord, got him crying with a whack on the rump, then handed him to me for cleaning up. As I gently wiped the blood and membranes from his shivering, squalling body, my heart was thudding so hard and fast I feared it would break through my ribs. I examined him closely. His skin was red and mottled, as with all newborns, but he was *Caucasian*, as Caucasian as Derr or myself.

Myself.

I was holding myself! You were that infant, Jim, but you are me. I wasn't a new father holding a combination of himself and his wife. This child was *all me!* It *was* me!

I wrapped him up in the flannel blanket we had for him. He was a hairy little thing, hairy like me. Even had little tufts of hair on his palms. I wondered if I'd had hairy palms at birth. I thought of asking my mother, and then realized she was *his* mother, too!

I held him (you, Jim) against me and I felt an enormous surge of emotion. Until that moment you had been just another experiment; a momentous one, I'll grant, but just an experiment, the culmination of the long process we had begun with frogs and run through rats and pigs. You were an experimental subject, a thing, an *it*. First an embryo, then a fetus, but never a person.

All that changed as I cradled your red, squalling little body in my arms. I looked into your face and the enormity of what we had done hit me full force. Suddenly you were a person, a human being with a whole life ahead of you. In a flash I saw what you could expect in the years to come as the world's first human clone. A childhood under the microscope and in the spotlight; a tortured adolescence as a freak, the butt of jokes, the object of bigotry, scorn, ridicule, possibly the object of hatred by some of the world's more fanatical religious groups.

And after a youth filled with that sort of trauma, what sort of man would you turn out to be? What sort of tortured soul would you possess? I saw you hating me. I saw you wishing you had never been born. I saw you killing yourself.

I knew right then that I could not allow any of that to happen.

After Derr had delivered the placenta, I asked Jazzy if she wanted to hold you but she wanted no part of you. She seemed afraid of you. After he gave Jazzy something for pain, I handed you to Derr. As he held your squirming little body, he looked at me. There was wonder, joy, and triumph in his eyes. But there was a cloud there, too. I remember our conversation as if it were yesterday.

"We've done it," he said.

"I know. But now that we have him, what do we do with him?"

He shook his head and said, "I don't know. I don't think the world is ready for him"

"Neither do I," I said.

We fed you a sugar-and-water solution, bundled you up in your bassinet, and talked long into the night. For the first time since we had begun Project Genesis, I think we had some perspective on what we had been striving for, and what we had achieved. We had been pulp-magazine mad scientists up to now. Your cries were a dose of sanity. But we still weren't agreed on where we should go from there. I wanted to tell Laughlin that we had failed utterly and urge him to scrap the whole project. Derr thought that was too precipitous. He thought I was exaggerating the public response to a human clone.

Our argument grew heated, and Derr stormed up to the second floor to check on Jazzy. Lucky he did. Because of our argument, tragedy was narrowly avoided.

He was only gone a moment when I heard him calling Jazzy's name. I went to the bottom of the stairs and asked what was wrong. Derr told me that she wasn't in her room. He was going to check the bathroom. I went upstairs to check on you and that's where I found her. She was leaning over your bassinet. My first thought was that Jazzy's maternal instincts had finally fought their way to the surface. Then I noticed that she had a pillow in her hands and was pressing it down over your face.

With a shout, I leapt forward and yanked her away. To my immense relief, you immediately began to howl. I knew then that you were unharmed, but I had to fight to keep Jazzy off of you. She was like a wild animal, eyes wide, foaming at the mouth, screaming in her Cajun accented voice.

"Kill it! Kill it! It is a vile and hateful thing! Kill it! Kill it! Kill it!"

Derr came in and helped me pull her away, then sedated her. As we locked her bedroom door, I saw the look in Derr's eyes and knew that Jazzy's outburst was causing him to reconsider his position.

Her behavior was all the more shocking because, as far as we knew, Jazzy had no idea of what we had implanted in her uterus. I had been sure she thought us a couple of strange ducks, perhaps even a pair of pansies, who had impregnated her by artificial insemination (although I doubt very much those words were in her vocabulary). There was no explaining her bizarre, violent reaction to you, but the incident had united Derr with me in my opposition to letting the War Department know what we had accomplished.

We rented a hotel room for Jazzy and paid her her bonus. Derr visited her daily for the rest of the week until she was completely recovered from the delivery. As soon as she was out of the house, I hired a nurse to take care of you.

After long deliberation, we decided it would be best for you if we put you up for adoption. So we left you at the St. Francis Home in Queens. You know the rest of the story. You were adopted almost immediately by Jonah and Emma Stevens and taken to Long Island. We reported utter failure to Colonel Laughlin, turned in a set of phony experimental records, and were informed that Project Genesis was closed for good.

That should have been that.

But Jim, I could not let you go. You were on my mind constantly. I had to know how you were, how you were developing. You became such an obsession with me that in 1943 I sold the Manhattan townhouse and moved to Monroe where I bought this old mansion. I lurked around the apartment house where the Stevenses first lived; when Emma took you shopping with her, I'd tag along behind and do some shopping myself, always watching you to see how you were doing, assuring myself that they were treating you right — that they were treating *me* right.

And I must confess to some scientific interest. (Don't be offended. Once a scientist, always a scientist.) I had a chance to satisfy my curiosity about the nature-or-nurture question: Which shaped us more, environment or heredity? I had been raised in an intellectual environment and, although endowed with the physique for it, I never had much interest in sports. Although gentically identical to me, you were raised in a household where I doubt you ever saw anyone crack a book. As a result, you became a star football player. I thought that answered the question, but you also did extremely well academically in high school, were editor of the school paper, were accepted to college, and now I understand you are majoring in journalism. I recall my own intense interest in writing as a student.

The result of my years of observing my clone? Confusion. I have more questions now than when I began.

Does this sound cool and clinical? I hope not. But more than that, I hope you never read these pages. Derr and I have made a pact. We are the only two who know the combination to the safe where these records are hidden. We will never travel together. When one of us dies, the other will put these records into the hands of a law firm we have dealt with for many years. That firm will be instructed to keep the very existence of these records a secret until the day you die. After that, they will be published. You will be beyond hurting then. Who knows? Perhaps cloning will be commonplace by that time. If it is, all the better. Derr and I will smile in our graves knowing that the scientific world will have to recognize us as the first.

I know all this is a shock of unimaginable proportions. But I'm sure you can handle it. Just remember: You were never supposed to know. And, having watched you all these years, I know you are wise enough not to make your origin public. On the other hand, I beg you not to destroy these records. Derr and I deserve our recognition someday. We are in no hurry. If you are reading this, it means we are both dead. So we can wait. We have time.

Please do not hate me, Jim. That would be akin to hating yourself. We are one. We are the same. I am you and you are me. And neither of us can change that.

Your older twin,
Roderick C. Hanley, Ph.D.

TWELVE

1.

It's a hoax!

Carol sat at the kitchen table, drenched in sweat, gaping at the last page of the letter. She flipped back through the journal's curling pages.

It has to be a hoax!

But in the deepest recesses of her heart and mind she knew that Hanley himself had written the letter — she knew his handwriting well enough by now — and that what he said was true. The detailed experimental records, the cache of photos, the yearbooks, the scrapbooks, all the contents of the safe supported his fantastic claims. But more than anything else, it was Hanley's reputation that weighed so heavily on the side of truth — if any man could have accomplished what was described in this letter, it was the Nobel prizewinning Dr. Roderick Hanley.

Jim was a clone! *A clone!* Roderick Hanley's clone!

God, this is a nightmare!

For Jim, not for her. The shock of it was numbing, frightening, but Carol forced herself to step back from it. And when she did, she saw that it really didn't matter to her. For it didn't change how she felt about Jim.

So he was a clone. So what?

He was still the man she had married, the man she loved. So what if he had Hanley's genes? She hadn't married a bunch of chromosomes; she had married a man. Jim was still that man. The letter changed nothing for her.

But oh, how it had changed things for Jim.

Poor Jim. So eager and full of hope as he had searched for his roots, only to find that he didn't have any. He had always been insecure about where he had come from — no wonder he had been acting so strange the past twenty-four hours.

It's not fair!

Carol was suddenly angry. How had this come to be? Jim never should have learned about this! Hanley had been right in his intent to keep Jim's origin a secret from him. What had gone wrong? The letter said —

Then she remembered: Hanley and Derr had been killed together in that plane crash.

What a strange twist of fate. He'd said they never traveled together. Yet they had been together that night. Which left no one alive to put the Project Genesis files into the hands of the lawyer he had mentioned. So they had been left behind for Jim to find.

Fate could be cruel.

But Carol's anger was not solely for fate. She was furious with Hanley and Derr. She looked down at the last page of the letter in the journal, still in her hands. One line caught her eye:

. . . I beg you not to destroy these records.

Why not? They should have been destroyed the day Hanley and Derr gave up Jim for adoption. If they had really cared about the child they had created, they never would have risked these records falling into the wrong hands. But no, they had kept all the damning evidence squirreled away.

Derr and I deserve our recognition someday.

That was the key. Vanity. Ego. Glory-seeking bastards . . .

Carol pressed her palms over her eyes. Maybe she was being too hard on them. They were pioneers. They had done something unique. Was it so bad to want the history books to chronicle that?

She realized suddenly that she couldn't hate them. Without them, there would be no Jim.

But poor Jim. What was she going to do about Jim? How was she going to get him back on his emotional feet again?

And suddenly she knew. She'd do what Hanley and Derr should have done in 1942 — destroy this junk.

Jim would be furious, she knew, and justifiably so. After all, these records were a part of his legacy from Hanley. They belonged to him and she had no right to dispose of them.

But I have a right to protect my husband — even from himself.

And right now this letter and these journals were tearing him apart. They would destroy Jim if she didn't destroy them first. The longer they were around, the worse it would get. They'd be like a cancer, eating away at him day by day, hour by hour, until there was nothing left of him. Look at how he had been acting since last night! If this went on much longer, he'd be a wreck!

She looked around her. But how? If only the house had a fireplace. She'd set a match to the papers and watch them go up in smoke. That was the only safe way to go — incinerate the evidence.

Incinerate. Tomorrow was garbage day. The can was out at the curb, waiting for the pick-up. First thing tomorrow, the truck would come by, dump the can, and haul the load out to the county incinerator. That was it. Throw this stuff in the garbage where it belonged!

She got a brown grocery bag from the kitchen, dumped the journals and the letter inside, then tied it with string. Wrapping her coat around her, she hurried outside to the curb. But as she lifted the lid of the garbage can, Carol hesitated.

What if the wrapper got torn and one of the sanit men just happened to see the journals and read them? As remote as it was, the possibility chilled her.

And beyond that, this just didn't *feel* right. These were Jim's. As much as they were damaging him, he had a right to them.

What if she simply *told* him that she had thrown them away? Wouldn't that be just as good?

But she'd have to have a damn good hiding place to make that plan work. Where . . . ?

The crawlspace! It was perfect! Nothing down there but pipes, footings, cinderblocks, and dirt. No one had been in there since the plumber they'd hired two years ago to fix a pipe. And Jim would never search there because he wouldn't be searching — he'd believe they'd gone up in smoke at the county incinerator.

Carol was excited now as she hurried around to the side of the house to the access door. Thank God that Monroe had such a high water table that crawlspaces were the rule rather than cellars. She squatted and reached between a pair of rhododendrons, searching for the handle on the hinged wooden board over the crawlspace opening. The opening was small, about a yard wide and only half that in height. She grabbed the handle, lifted the board, quickly dropped the bundle inside, then eased the door back into place.

There, she thought, straightening and brushing off her hands. *No one will read those now except the bugs.*

The beauty part of this plan was that after Jim had blown his top and fumed over the loss of the records, he could get on with the task of accepting his origin and putting it behind him where it belonged. The journals would no longer be staring him in the face every day. gnawing at him, focusing his anxieties and insecurities. And when he had finally stabilized again — and Carol knew he would with her support — and put it all in proper perspective, maybe then, in a couple of years, she would return the journals to him. By that time they would be old news, and he would be better able to deal with them.

She hurried back to the front door to get out of the cold. Tomorrow was going to be rough after she told him her lie, but once the storm was over, it would be a new beginning.

Everything was going to be all right now.

2.

Gerry Becker watched Carol disappear into the house.

What the hell was that all about?

First she comes out with a package, very furtively, then she goes around to the side of the house, kneels in the bushes, then comes out without the package.

Crazy.

But something crazy might be just what Gerry was waiting for. Stevens' wife was obviously hiding something. From whom? Her husband? The IRS? Who?

Gerry waited a few more minutes and saw the lights go out. He smiled. He'd give those two in the house a chance to settle into a nice deep sleep, then he'd go looking. He was good at finding things.

It wouldn't be long now.

THIRTEEN

Wednesday
March 6

1.

Jim awoke stiff, sore, and nauseated, feeling like Charlie Watts had been using the back of his head for a bass drum. He hadn't slept a wink Monday night. He'd tried — he'd curled up on the couch under a blanket and hoped he'd doze off so he could wake up and find this was all a bad dream. But sleep hadn't come. And so he'd lain there in the dark, tense and rigid, his mind racing and his stomach twisted into a tight, heavy knot until dawn had crept in and Carol had called. Only exhaustion and a few shots of JD had let him sleep last night. But he didn't feel the least bit rested.

This was no good. He was going to have to get a grip. He loathed self pity and could sense that he was turning into some sort of woeful basket case.

But he had a right to be a basket case, dammit! He'd gone searching for the identity of his parents and discovered that he didn't have any! Worse, his *own* identity was in question now!

I'm not really me — I'm a piece of somebody else!

The knowledge was a weight in is chest, pressing down on his stomach. *Why? Why me?* Why couldn't he have had a mother and a father like everybody else? Was that asking for so much?

This was all so damn unreal!

He squinted in the bright morning sun pouring through the window. The clock read a little after eight. Almost reflexively, he reached for the journals.

They weren't there!

He could have sworn he'd left them right here by his side on the couch. He jumped up and lifted the cushions. He looked under the couch, even unfolded the hidden mattress. Gone!

His heart thudding in his throat, Jim hurried down the short hall and across the living room toward the master bedroom. The smell of fresh coffee stopped him.

"Carol?"

"In here, Jim."

What was Carol doing home? She wasn't off today. Then it struck him: She must have taken the journals! She must have read them! *No!*

He rushed into the kitchen.

"Carol, the books! Where are they?"

She put down her coffee cup and slipped her arms around his neck. Her long sandy hair trailed over the shoulders of her robe. She looked beautiful.

"I love you, Jim."

Normally this would have stirred his desire, but there was room in his mind for only one thing.

"The journals — did you take them?"

She nodded. "And I read them."

Jim felt as if the floor were giving way beneath him.

"Oh, I'm so sorry, Carol. I didn't know, really I didn't. I never would have married you if I'd known."

"Known what? That you were cloned from Hanley?"

Her eyes were so soft, so loving, her voice gentle and soothing. How could she be so calm?

"Yes! I swear I didn't know!"

"What difference does it make, Jim?"

"What difference? How can you say that? I'm a freak! A scientific experiment!"

"No you're not. You're Jim Stevens. The man I married. The man I love."

"No! I'm a piece of Roderick Hanley!"

"You're Jim Stevens — Hanley's twin."

"I *wish!* He took a piece of himself and stuck it in that whore and grew me out like a goddamned cutting from one of our forsythia bushes. You know — snip it off, stick it in the ground, water it enough, and you've got a new bush."

"Don't talk like —"

"Or maybe I'm not a cutting. I'm more like a tumor. That's what I am — a fucking *tumor*!"

"Stop it!" she cried, showing strong emotion for the first time. "I won't have you talking about yourself like that!"

"Why not? Everybody else will!"

"No they won't. I'm the only other person who knows, and I don't feel that way."

"But you're different."

"Well, I'm it. Because nobody else will ever know unless you tell them. And even then, they won't believe you."

She said it with a tone of such finality that Jim was afraid to ask the next question.

"The journals! Where are they?"

"Where they belong — in the garbage."

"Oh, *no!*"

He spun and headed for the front door.

"Don't bother," he heard Carol say behind him. "The truck came by at six-thirty."

Suddenly he was angry. More than angry. He was enraged.

"You had no right! No goddamn right! Those journals were mine!"

"I'm not going to argue that with you. They were yours but I threw them out anyway. If they haven't been fed into the incinerator yet, they soon will be."

She was so cool, so composed, so utterly remorseless. Her attitude of *fait accompli* infuriated him.

"How could you?"

"You gave me no choice, Jim. You were letting those journals eat you alive! So I got rid of them! You were going to let what they said ruin your life. I couldn't stand by and watch that happen! But now it's over and done. They're gone and so you're going to have to take what you learned from them and pick up the pieces and go on from here. You've got to admit that's going to be easier if you don't have those journals staring you in the face all the time, if you don't keep going back to them time after time looking for some sort of flaw that will prove them wrong."

She was right. The cool logic of her words was worming its way past his anger, damping it, but not dousing it. After all, those had been *his* journals. His legacy.

"Okay," he said. "They're gone. Okay . . . okay . . ."

He kept repeating the word, walking around the kitchen in small circles. His thoughts were all jumbled up with his emotions. He couldn't separate them. If this had been someone else's problem, he was sure he would be calm and cool and completely rational.

But this is me!

"I did it for you, Jim," Carol said.

He looked in her eyes and saw the love there.

"I know, Carol. I know." But what did he *really* know? What could he be sure of now? "I just . . . I need to sort this out. I need to take a walk."

"You're not going back to that mansion, are you?"

"No. Just a little walk. I won't even leave the yard. I'm not running away. I just need to be by myself a bit. I won't be long. I just —"

He opened the kitchen door and stepped out into the backyard. The air was cold outside but he barely noticed. Besides, he couldn't bring himself to go back inside to get a jacket. Not just yet. As he strode around the side of the house, he noticed that the cover on the crawlspace entry had fallen out. He fitted it back into place and kept on walking.

2.

As the door closed, Carol slumped against the stove and held back the tears. That performance had been the hardest thing she had ever done in her life.

But it's going to work. It has to!

She hadn't slept a wink last night. Hour after hour she had lain awake planning how to handle this confrontation. Should she cry, beg his forgiveness for throwing the journals out, and make a thousand promises to make it up to him? Or should she simply apologize, admit she was wrong, and leave the rest up to him — put the ball is his court, so to speak?

Her heart had pulled for the easy way, urging her, in fact, to run out to the crawlspace and bring those damn books back inside. She didn't want the confrontation she knew the morning would bring. But she had to face it. This was too important to back away from.

She had chosen the second. And it hadn't been easy. The hurt and betrayal she had seen in his eyes had required every ounce of her will to keep her from blurting out where the books were hidden. But she had held on, resisting the urge to take him in her arms and coo to him and whisper that everything was going to be fine. Instead she had kept pushing him, almost goading him to take the control of his life back into his own hands.

Would it work? She hoped so. She prayed she hadn't made the wrong choice.

3.

Carol was sitting in the living room a short while later,waiting with her nails digging into her palms, when she heard the back door open. It was Jim. He came out of the kitchen and stood there looking all around the room, anywhere but directly at her. Finally, with his hands thrust deep into the pockets of his jeans, he walked over to where she sat and plopped down next to her on the couch. She noticed how badly he needed a shave. He didn't say anything for a while, just stared straight ahead.

Carol watched his troubled profile, aching to touch him, to throw her arms around him, but holding back, waiting for him to make the first move.

Finally, when the tension within her had reached the screaming level, he spoke.

"You shouldn't have thrown out those journals," he said, still staring straight ahead.

"I had to," Carol said as softly as she could. "I had no right, but I had to."

After a pause, he said, "I thought about what you did. I think it was the right thing to do, and pretty damn brave."

She put her hand on his arm and ran it down to his hand; his fingers grabbed hers when she reached them.

"But neither of us can erase what we learned from them. That's there to stay, like a brand. It's . . ." His voice broke and he swallowed. "It's kind of funny, isn't it? I spent all those years trying to figure out who I am, now I've got to figure out *what* I am."

Carol saw a tear slide down his cheek, and her heart broke for him. She drew his head down onto her shoulder.

"You're my Jim. That's the who and what of you. That's all you have to be as far as I'm concerned."

He began to sob. She had never seen him cry and she held him close, aching with the wonder of it. Finally he straightened and pulled away.

"Sorry," he said, sniffing and wiping his eyes. "I don't know what started that."

"It's okay, really."

"It's just that it's such a shock. I'm kind of torn up inside. Don't know which way to turn. Didn't mean to go wimpy on you."

"Don't be silly! You've been through hell these past few days. You've earned it."

"Did you really mean that . . . what you said about it not mattering? I mean, it matters a hell of a lot to me, so why doesn't it matter to you?"

"It doesn't change a thing. What we had before, we have now — if you'll allow it."

His eyes searched her face. "You really mean that, don't you?"

"Of course! If I didn't, those journals would still be here and *I'd* be gone instead."

He smiled for the first time. "Yeah. I guess you're right." He grasped her hand. "Carol, if I can believe that, hold onto that, I think I can make it. The more I think about it, the more I see you were right to get rid of the evidence."

"Thank God!" she said and really meant it. "I thought you'd never forgive me!"

"Neither did I. But now I see that I've got to go on just as before. I can't let this thing own me. Only you and I know about it — I can live with that. I can adjust to being a — to being what I am."

Carol decided then that it would be a long, long time before she told him where the journals were hidden.

"Just go on being the same Jim Stevens I married," she said. "That's what's really important."

He smiled again. "You sure you don't want any changes? This is probably your only chance to put in your order."

"Just one, maybe."

"Name it."

"Next time something upsets you, don't keep it to yourself like you did this time. Share the load. We're partners in this. There shouldn't be any secrets between us."

He slipped his arms around her and squeezed, almost crushing her. Carol wanted to laugh and wanted to cry. He was back — her old Jim was back.

4.

Grace sat in the last row in the basement of the Murray Hill brownstone and listened to Brother Robert's homily. Wednesday evening seemed an unorthodox time for a prayer service, but she found herself intrigued by these people who called themselves the Chosen. Especially Brother Robert.

There was a magnetic quality about his ascetic appearance, such an air of wisdom about him, yet he was not distant. He exuded a love of God and humanity. And his speaking voice — strong, clear, wonderful, almost mesmerizing. He had been speaking for nearly an hour now, yet it seemed like no more than ten minutes.

Suddenly he stumbled over a word and stopped. He stood at the lectern and stared. For an awful moment, Grace thought he was staring at her, then realized that his gaze was directed past her. She turned and saw a gray-haired stranger standing at the rear of the room.

Martin immediately rose from his chair near the front and approached the man.

"This is not a public meeting," he said indignantly.

The stranger seemed a bit confused, a little unsure of himself.

"I will go if you wish," he said. "But surely you would allow me to listen."

Grace suddenly recognized him. He was the man who had been standing across the street from this old brownstone last Sunday, watching them. What did he want?

She watched Martin. He seemed undecided as to what to do. They both turned and looked at Brother Martin.

Grace remembered how on Sunday the monk had inferred that the man was some sort of enemy, even though he obviously didn't know him.

"Martin," Brother Robert said, "we cannot deny someone the right to listen to the word of God. Please be seated, friend."

Grace stiffened as the man seated himself at the end of the last row, her row, just two chairs to her right. She kept her eyes straight ahead and listened to Brother Robert as he resumed his homily. But the monk was clearly distracted. He stumbled over some sentences, rushed through others, and was not nearly as effective as he had been before he was interrupted.

Grace risked a glance at the newcomer.

Close up like this, she realized how big a man he was, his large frame made even bulkier by a heavy tan double-breasted raincoat. There was the slightest hint of swarthiness in his complexion and the faintest of red highlights in his silvery hair. High cheek bones, a long straight nose, and no hint of jowls despite his years. He sat straight and tall with his big, scarred hands resting in fists on his thighs. A gold band encircled his left ring finger. And all around him, an aura of faded power.

He must have sensed her scrutiny, for he turned her way and gave her a faint smile that narrowed his blue eyes. Then he returned his attention to Brother Robert.

Grace felt the tension ease out of her. That smile . . . it had been as much to reassure her as himself. This was not a man to fear.

The service ended with Brother Robert's plea:

"Give us a sign, Lord. Reveal the Antichrist to us so that we may confront him with Your holy power."

Then all twenty or so of the gathered Chosen stood and said the Apostles' Creed and a Hail Mary as they held hands. The newcomer neither stood nor prayed. As before, Grace kept her hands to herself while she prayed with them.

Suddenly she felt a tingling in her face. She turned toward the stranger and began to speak to him. To her horror, the words were not her own. The language was alien to her.

The stanger started in his seat, his eyes wide as he stared at her. She tried to stop herself, but her voice went on, uttering those strange, incomprehensible syllables.

"Stop that!" he said. "You don't know what you're saying!"

Members of the Chosen were turning to look at her. Brother Robert hurried up, beaming.

"The Spirit is with you, Grace! Don't fight it! Give praise to the Lord!"

"She's not praising anything!" the stranger said.

"You understand the tongue she's speaking?" Brother Robert said, his eyes wide.

Before he could answer, the words stopped and Grace's voice was once more her own. The stranger remained seated as the worshipers drifted out, staring at him as they passed. Soon only Grace, Brother Robert, Martin, and the newcomer remained in the room. Brother Robert approached his chair and stood over him.

"Who are you?"

"My name is Veilleur," said the gray-haired man. "And you?"

"Brother Robert from the Monastery at Aiguebelle." Neither offered to shake hands. "You understand the tongue? What was she saying?"

"You wouldn't understand."

"Don't be so sure of that," Brother Robert said.

Martin stepped forward. "Why did you come here? Why have you been lurking outside, watching us?"

Veilleur's face was troubled. "I don't know. I sense something here. I seemed to be drawn to this group."

Grace tried to place his faint accent. It sounded vaguely British, and yet not like any she had ever heard.

"You are not one of us," Martin said with a certainty that brooked no argument.

"Quite true. But who is this 'us' you refer to? Why do you come together here?"

Brother Robert said, "We come to praise the Lord and to prepare ourselves to do battle with His enemy. The Antichrist is amongst us. We await a sign."

"The Antichrist?"

"Yes. The Evil One has taken on flesh."

Mr. Veilleur stared at Brother Robert, then at Grace who felt the weight of his gaze like a blow.

"So. You know."

Brother Robert nodded. "Satan has come to try to claim this world for his own."

"I don't know about Satan. But something is coming. What I don't understand is why you people have been touched."

Martin stiffened. "What do you mean, 'touched'? We are as sane as anyone else — *saner,* in fact!"

"I meant sensitized, alerted, made aware. Why you people in particular?"

"Why not?"

"Because you make a pitiful defense force."

"And I suppose you think *you* should lead us?" Martin said.

Mr. Veilleur's smile was sour as he shook his head. "No, I want no part of this. I'm out of it. In fact, I thought it was all over."

"It's *never* over," said Brother Robert.

"Perhaps you're right. I suppose I should have known that. But I'd hoped it might be."

"What are you talking about?"

"You wouldn't understand."

Brother Robert's eyes narrowed as he spoke in a low voice. "I have traveled far. I have looked into places good men were never meant to see. I have read the forbidden books —"

"Is that proper for a man of the cloth?" Veilleur said.

"'Know thine enemy' is a wise saying. God may work in the world in many guises, but so does the devil. I have exposed myself to hideous evils and have turned away from them, never having the slightest temptation to release myself to what they offered."

Veilleur appeared to be studying Brother Robert. He nodded respectfully.

"But one cannot tread those coals and emerge unscorched."

"True. The experiences have left me . . . sensitized, as you say. It is as if I've developed an extra sense, something like a sense of smell for the devil's work. And the stench of him is heavy here."

"Not here, exactly," Mr. Veilleur said. "Further to the east."

Brother Robert stared at him. "You, too?"

"As your friend here said —" he nodded toward Martin — "I am not one of you."

"I know that," Brother Robert said. "And yet . . . you are."

"Was. I was, but no longer."

As Mr. Veilleur stood, Grace stepped back. He seemed to tower over the three of them.

"Please tell me," Grace said. "What language was I speaking?"

"The Old Tongue."

"I've never heard of such a thing," Martin said.

"No one has spoken it for thousands of years."

"I don't believe you!" Martin said.

"Hush, Martin," Brother Robert said gently. "I believe him."

Grace looked into Brother Robert's eyes and for the first time sensed the enormity of the events taking shape around them. It made her weak. She turned to Mr. Veilleur. His eyes had a far away look. He spoke, more to himself than to them.

"I don't know where he's been hiding these years, but now it seems he's found a way back."

"Satan has never been away," Brother Robert said. "But now he has taken human form for an all-out assault on humanity."

"Satan?" the man said. "Did I mention Satan?" He shrugged. "Never mind. The fact remains that you're going to need help."

"What kind of help?" Grace said.

"I don't know. Once there was someone, but he's gone. Now . . . "He paused and looked from Grace to Brother Robert to Martin. "Perhaps someone in your group is the key."

"Who?" Brother Robert said. "How can we tell?"

Mr. Veilleur turned and headed for the door. "I haven't the foggiest. But he'll have to be someone special. Someone *very* special."

And then he was gone, leaving Grace staring at Brother Robert and wondering who it might be.

FOURTEEN

Friday
March 8

1.

"What's that song you're whistling, Father?"

Bill looked up and saw Nicky standing on the far side of his desk, all dressed and ready to spend the weekend with the Calders.

"A real oldie called 'It's a Great Day.' "

"What's so great about it?"

"Everything, Nicko. *Everything*. The sun's out, the work week is almost over, spring is less than three weeks away. A great day from morning till night."

He felt almost giddy and had to rein in his feelings before they ran away with him. He couldn't share the details with Nicky just yet, but he had a feeling that come Sunday night, they'd both have reason to celebrate.

Bill reached over his desk and straightened Nicky's tie. It was too red and too narrow to be fashionable, and it hung down below his tightly cinched belt, but it was the cleanest of the three red ties available. The collar of the white shirt was too big for his scrawny neck, and the sleeves of the blue blazer were too short for his gangly arms. The same was true of the gray slacks which showed too much white sock below the cuffs.

All in all, a sight to give a Brooks Brothers salesman a case of the vapors, but it was the best they could do out of that motley collection of hand-me-downs and better quality donated clothing they called the dress-up closet. But then again, Bill didn't want the kids going out on their home visits looking *too* well-dressed. Nicky's attire screamed, *Give this boy a home!* And that was probably all to the good.

He was clean, that was the important thing. His dark hair had been washed and combed up in the front, which was a mixed blessing in a way — although it camouflaged some of the more misshapen aspects of his skull, it exposed more blackheads on his forehead. He had play clothes and some clean underwear in the battered canvas satchel on the floor beside him.

"Nervous?" Bill said.

"Nah. I've been to lots of these."

"No, sweat, ay? Just a cool cat taking off for the weekend."

"Okay." Nicky's smile was slow and shy. "Maybe a little nervous."

"Just be yourself."

His eyes lit. "Really?"

"On second thought . . ."

They both smiled at their private joke.

The intercom buzzed: "The Calders are here," said Sister Miriam's voice from the front office.

"We're on our way."

He took Nicky's satchel and placed an arm on his shoulder as he led him down to the first floor.

"This is it, kid. Strut your best stuff for these people and you'll be in Fat City."

Bill felt Nicky's arm go around his back and hug him.

2.

Bill waved good-bye to Nicky as the Calders drove away with him in the back seat of their new Dodge, then hurried back to his office and pulled the letter from under the desk blotter. It had arrived this morning from the Maryland Provincial and he must have read it and reread it a dozen times since then. Loyola High School in Baltimore had a spot for him! He would have preferred Loyola College, but at least this was a step in the right direction. He could report there June first, and come September he could begin as an instructor in the religion department . . . if he still wished to trade his current post for that of high school teacher.

Wished? He was *dying* to get out of his current post!

And what a great location they were offering him! Just forty-five minutes down the Baltimore-Washington Expressway and he'd be in the capital, right in the heart of the action. There was always something going on in D.C., like the new civil rights bill before the Senate right now.

And it would put him far away from Carol. A few hundred miles would serve to cool his night thoughts. Maybe then he could get some sleep.

He kissed the letter and slipped it back under the blotter.

"Nicky's going to find himself a home and I'm going to rejoin the human race."

He began humming "Everything's Coming Up Roses."

3.

The ground was thawed and the weekend was promising to be a warm one, so Jonah decided to get an early start on the garden. Come Friday afternoon most weeks, he was bushed by the time he got home from the plant. But lately he had been full of life, bursting with energy, and the vegetable garden was as good a place as any to work some of it off. Maybe he'd be able to bring in some lettuce this year.

The first thing he was going to do, though, was set up a decent perimeter fence to keep the rabbits out. He would have loved to set up coils of razor wire to shred the greedy little rodents as they hopped into the garden, but the neighbors would raise a fuss when the same thing happened to their wild little bastards as they took their usual headlong shortcut through his backyard.

So he'd have to settle for chicken wire.

He planned to set up a two-by-four post at each corner of the garden, then string the mesh between it. Three feet would be more than high enough.

He began digging the hole for the first corner post. About eighteen inches would do it. Jonah liked the slicing sound the spade made as he jammed it into the soft earth, loved to feel the countless rootlets part beneath the blade as he drove it deeper into the ground with his foot. There was something delicious in disrupting the delicate balance below. Years of interplay, of give-and-take between the soil, the nutrients, the bacteria, the insects, and the vegetation, all altered forever with the thrust of a shovel.

When he had dug down around a foot, the dirt began to turn red.

Strange. He hadn't known there was any clay around here. And then he saw that it wasn't clay but a red liquid seeping up through the soil. He lowered himself to his hands and knees for a closer look. He sniffed.

Blood.

Jonah's pulse suddenly picked up as a shudder of elation raced through him. This wasn't a hallucination. This was the real thing. Another in a long line of signs he had been gifted with throughout his life.

Breathless, he watched the thick red fluid well up in the hole until it reached the rim, then ooze off into the garden in a thin, slow rivulet. Jonah would have liked to have let it fill the garden, to watch it cool and clot as dusk fell, but there were no secrets in these tiny, crowded backyards around here. It wouldn't do at all to have the neighbors wondering what had happened in the Stevens yard.

Reluctantly, he began shoveling the earth back into the hole, stoppering the crimson flow. When the sod was back in place, he stepped back, reined in his excitement, and stood there thinking.

Blood flowing in his backyard. How else could he interpret that but as a harbinger of death, the death of someone close to his home? It was also a sign that events were gathering speed, and that he should not waste his time tilling the earth.

Fifteen

Saturday
March 9

Bill was reading his daily office in his room when the phone rang, startling him. Only a handful of people had his private number, and when they called it was usually with bad news. So he was especially worried when he recognized Jim's voice.

"Jim! Is something wrong?" he said in a rush, remembering Carol's anxious call on Tuesday and Jim's vaguely hostile reception of his offer of help. *Is Carol all right?*

"No. Everything's fine, Bill. Really fine. I just wanted to apologize for acting so weird when you called me the other day."

"It's okay," Bill said, feeling his muscles uncoil. "We all get uptight now and again."

It was good to hear Jim sounding like his old self.

"Yeah, well, the will, the inheritance, the mansion, everything sort of combined to do a number on my head. Got me all bent out of shape. But I've got everything back in perspective now and I feel a whole lot better."

During the small talk that followed, Bill noticed that Jim danced away from anything that had to do with Hanley or the inheritance or who his mother might be. He gathered from Jim's too-casual air and uncharacteristic use of jargon that he hadn't climbed completely out of the pressure cooker yet. He was dying to ask if he had learned anything about his mother, but remembered how coolly that subject had been received on Tuesday, so he kept mum.

After hanging up, Bill sat by the window thinking how sad and ironic it was that just as he was re-establishing contact with an old friend, he was preparing to move a couple of hundred miles away.

And he *was* moving away. Old friend or not, Bill wasn't going to let anyone keep him here at St. F.'s. *Nothing* was going to delay his departure now that the Provincial had found a teaching spot for him.

He sat a while longer at the window, feeling unaccountably blue. What was wrong? Certainly he wasn't going to miss this place.

Then he realized that this was the time he usually played chess with Nicky. It seemed empty without him here scratching his misshapen head and picking his blackheads. But that was soon to be part of the past. Nicky would be adopted by the Calders and Bill would be on his way to Baltimore.

He was about to return to his breviary when he noticed a late model blue Dodge pull up to the curb in front of St. F.'s. It looked familiar. Just like —

Oh, hell!

Nicky got out of the car and ran up the front steps, disappearing from view. Professor Calder got out of the driver's seat and followed him at a much slower pace. Bill quickly shrugged into his cassock and hurried downstairs.

Professor Calder was already on his way out when Bill arrived.

"What —?"

The professor waved him off. "It's not going to work," he said over his shoulder.

"Why not? What happened?"

"Nothing. He's just not right."

And then he was out the door and gone.

Bill was stunned. He stared at the slowly closing door in mute confusion, then turned to Nicky who was leaning against the far wall, looking at his shoes.

"What did you do this time?"

"Nothing."

"Bull! Let's hear it!"

"I caught him cheating at chess!"

"Oh, come *on*, Nicky! Give me a break!"

"It's true! Everything was going great until we started playing chess. I was winning with that bishop's gambit you showed me. He sent me out to the kitchen for another cup of hot chocolate, and when I came back, he had moved his queen's knight one square to the left."

"And you accused him of cheating?"

"Not right away. I just told him that the knight wasn't where it was when I'd left the room. He got all huffy and said, 'I'm sure you're mistaken, young man.' "

"Then what?"

"*Then* I called him a cheat!"

"Damn it, Nicky!" Bill felt his anger shooting straight to the boiling point, but he kept a lid on it. "Did it ever occur to you that you could be mistaken?"

"You know I don't make mistakes like that!" Nicky said, tears starting in his eyes.

That did it. Bill picked up Nicky's duffel bag and shoved it into the boy's arms. His jaw ached as he spoke through his teeth.

"Get out of the good clothes, put them back in the dress-up closet, then go to your room and stay there. Don't show your face till dinner."

"But he cheated!" Nicky said, his lips quivering.

"So what? Are you so damn perfect you can't overlook that?"

Nicky turned and ran toward the dormitory.

Bill watched him go. Then, for lack of anything better to do, he headed for his office. Once there, he lifted the blotter, pulled out the letter from Loyola High School, and sat there staring at it.

Damn, damn, damn!

He felt like a heel for yelling at Nicky like that. If there was one thing you could say about that kid, it was that he didn't lie. Another thing you could say was that his memory was damn near perfect — eidetic, in fact. He could picture entire pages of a book in his mind and read the text back verbatim. So Bill knew that if Nicky was concentrating on a chess game, he would have the position of every piece etched in his mind.

Which meant that Professor Calder had cheated.

So: The prof was a pompous toad whose ego wouldn't allow him to be defeated in chess by a bright ten-year old kid, Nicky was stupid for not letting the guy have his petty, tainted victory. And Bill had promised to stay on at St. F.'s until Nicky was adopted.

What a screwed-up mess!

In spite of himself, he had to admire Nicky's intellectual honesty in calling the prof out. Maybe he didn't want to be adopted by a phony and a cheat, but for Christ sake, everybody made compromises in life! Nicky could have looked the other way!

His frustration finally reached the overflow point. With an angry growl, Bill balled up the letter from Loyola High and bounced it off the far wall of his office.

I'm never getting out of here!

Which might not be an exaggeration, he realized. If he turned down this post, who knew when he'd get another offer of a teaching job?

There was only one thing to do: Take the job.

He scouted the floor of his office, found the letter, and flattened it out on the desk. He knew he had made a promise to Nicky, but he couldn't be bound by it if Nicky wasn't going to hold up his end. Maybe Nicky didn't want to leave St. F.'s. Okay, that was fine. But Bill Ryan wasn't going to rot here in Queens when there was so much to be done out there in the real world.

He began composing the letters he would have to write.

Sunday
March 10

1.

You walk through the moaning forest outside Targoviste and revel in its beauty. Its splendid trees straddle the road that leads to the south, the road on which the Turks will approach. A young forest, only a few days old, yet numbering twenty thousand trees. When you grip the trunk of one of its saplings, the tips of your thumb and middle finger meet on the far side.

The wind does not sigh through the boughs of this forest. It screams.

Twenty thousand saplings, all freshly planted. Never have you experienced such a concentrated dose of agony. It is making you lightheaded, giddy. You lift your gaze to the upper levels of this forest where dear Vlad's impaled enemies, real and imagined, men and women and children, dead and dying, Romanians, Turks, Germans, Bulgarians, and Hungarians, all await Mohammed II.

It is a still forest, this. Although cries of pain fill the air, there is little or no motion among the boughs. For each victim has learned of the agony beyond bearing that attends the slightest movement. In their subjective time, the nightmare started an eternity ago, when a long, sharp — but not too sharp — stake was driven deep into an anus or a vagina or down a throat, or simply poked through the abdominal wall, after which the hapless man, woman, or child was hoisted into the air upon that stake, which was then planted along the side of this road.

In the fortunate ones, the point of the stake quickly found a vital organ or artery, and death rescued them. You curse their limp, silent, blissful death. But in so many others, the stake moves more slowly, in short hops, remorselessly forging a path of torture through the innards as the weight of the body pulls it relentlessly downward. Sometimes there is a respite of sorts, as when the point lodges against a bone and its progress is halted. Then every movement, even the slightest shudder of pain, must be avoided. And a breeze is the most dreaded thing of all.

You hear soft whimpering from just above your right shoulder. The pain-mad eyes of a young girl look down at you, pleadingly. Evidently the stake within her has run up against something that will not let it pass. The eyes beg for help. You smile. Yes, you will help. You grasp the stake and shake it violently. You are rewarded by hoarse, mindless screeching as her body suddenly slips three inches lower. Blood rushes down the stake and runs over your hand.

You lick your fingers . . .

Carol awoke and ran to the bathroom, retching uncontrollably.

These dreams! Tonight's was the worst, the sickest, the most real of all! What was wrong with her? Please, God! These dreams . . . when were they going to stop?

2.

She was feeling better now, but the lingering memory of the dream had left her queasy. They'd run out of milk so she'd come down here to Stan's Market for a quart, but now the waxed container sweated unnoticed in one hand along with the five-dollar bill and box of Entenmann's doughnuts in the other as she stood at the counter and stared at one of the headlines on the scandal sheet rack. She felt her mouth go dry as she read the words that filled *The Light*'s entire front page.

WORLD RENOWNED
SCIENTIST LEAVES
ESTATE TO SELF!

Oh, my God, it can't be!

She dropped everything onto the counter and snatched up the tabloid, praying it was just an awful coincidence, just another crackpot tale to go along with *The Light*'s usual UFO, eye-injury, and freak-show contents.

"Story on page three," read the small print in the lower right corner. Her hands trembled as she opened the paper.

Please don't let it be!

But her prayer went unanswered. She almost screamed when she saw the byline: "by Gerald Becker."

"Everybody's reading that," said the red-haired, gum-cracking lady behind the counter. "Wished I had twice as many, the way they're selling."

Carol barely heard her. She saw the name "Hanley" in the first line and "clone" in the second, and then she was crushing the paper against her chest as her feet carried her toward the door.

"Hey!" said the woman. "Y'forgot —!"

Carol managed to say, "Keep the change!" and then she was out the door and running for the car. She had to get home, had to get to Jim with this before someone else did!

As she raced through downtown Monroe, one word kept echoing in her head:

How? How had Becker found out? *How?*

After pulling into the driveway, she ran around to the other side of the house and pushed the rhodos aside. The access cover to the crawlspace was still closed. She pulled it open and stared in horror at the sandy emptiness. There was a flattened spot on the sand where she had left the journals, but the journals were gone!

She rushed inside and found Jim sitting in the easy chair. His pale face and stricken expression were like a knife ripping into her chest.

"Somebody left this on the front step," he said, holding up a copy of *The Light*.

"Oh, Jim —!"

"How, Carol?" he said, looking at her with eyes that were so full of hurt she wanted to cry.

"Jim, I didn't!"

"Then how did Becker get hold of this stuff? He's got passages in his article that are practically word-for-word out of Hanley's letter to me. How could that be if the journals were incinerated as you said?"

The phone rang, startling her. It sat at Jim's elbow but he ignored it. As she started toward it, he said, "Leave it. It's just some reporter from one of the New York dailies wanting to know if the story is true."

"Oh." This was awful and getting worse.

"You haven't answered my question, Carol. *How?*"

"Because I didn't really throw them away!"

Jim rose slowly from the chair.

"*What?*"

"I — I only told you that so you wouldn't go looking for them. Actually I hid them in the crawlspace until —"

He took two steps toward her.

"You mean you lied to me about throwing them out?"

"Yes. You see —"

He came closer, his eyes angry now, almost wild. And that damn phone kept ringing and ringing.

"You lied then, but you're telling the truth now?"

"Yes."

His expression had become so fierce it frightened her.

"How do I know you're not lying now?"

"Because I wouldn't!"

"But you already did!" He thrust the headlines of *The Light* to within inches of her nose and shouted, "Will the real Carol Nevins Stevens please stand up and tell me why she did this to me?"

Carol couldn't hold it in any longer. She began to cry.

"But I didn't, Jim! This isn't fair!"

The phone stopped ringing.

"Well, we agree on that, at least," he said in a softer voice. Then: "I know you didn't intend this, but you've got a hell of a lot of explaining to do."

She told him everything — from reading the journals to hiding them in the crawlspace to confronting him the next morning with her fabricated story.

"I wish now they *had* been burned."

"So do I! Oh, you don't know how I wish that! But they were *yours*. It just didn't seem right."

"Yeah. Mine." He sighed. "I think I'll go over to the mansion for a while."

"No!" she cried as he turned and headed for the door. "Don't run away from this. We can handle it together!"

"I'm sure we can. I'm not running away from anything. I've just got to be alone for a while. Just a few hours. I've got to figure out how I'm going to handle this" — he tapped his forehead — "up here. Then we'll face the world together — if you're still with me."

"You know I am."

His face was a tight mask. "Okay. I'll see you later."

And then he was out and moving down the front walk. As she watched him go, Carol felt as if a noose were tightening around her throat.

This was all her fault. God, how had she got them into this? And how were they ever going to get out?

Behind her, the phone began ringing again.

3.

Bill sat in his office and sipped a second cup of coffee while flipping through the Sunday *Times*. This was his favorite part of the week. The boys were all at breakfast and it was quiet. He had said the early Mass at Our Lady of Lourdes and now had some time to himself.

It was especially pleasurable today because *The Week in Review* section was full of news of the coming New Hampshire primary, just two days away, and how McCarthy was gaining on against President Johnson. Not that anyone thought he could actually defeat the incumbent, but if he could make a decent showing, it could possibly influence the rest of the campaign and maybe the Democratic Party's stand on the war when convention time came around.

Bill sighed and stared out the window. More than ever, he wished he could be in New Hampshire for the next seventy-two hours. That wasn't to be. And he wasn't going to get near any of the other primaries if he didn't get on the stick and write those letters to the New York and Maryland Provincials.

He rolled a piece of paper into the old gray Olympia portable his folks had given him as a high school graduation present and began banging away. He was half way through the first letter when he was interrupted by a timid knock on his office door.

"Father Ryan?"

It was Sister Miriam.

"Yes, Sister? Is something wrong?"

"I'm not sure." She held a folded newspaper in her hand and seemed unusually reticent. "Wasn't that friend of yours who was here a few weeks ago — the one who wanted to go through the records — wasn't his name Stevens?"

"Sure. Jim Stevens."

"Isn't he the one who inherited the Hanley estate?"

"That's him. Why do you ask?"

"Now, mind you, Father, I'm not the sort to buy this kind of trash on a regular basis," she said, unfolding the tabloid and extending it toward him, "but this paper has some very strange things to say about your friend and Dr. Hanley."

Bill took the paper and frowned when he saw the logo, *The Light*, and its notorious left ear, "The News That Hides From the Light of Day Can't Escape *The Light*." Sister Miriam was an exemplary member of the Sisters of Charity, but she had an addiction for gossip magazines and scandal sheets. *The Light* was just about the cheesiest member of the latter category.

"Jim Stevens is in *here?*" he said, opening to page three.

"I think that's who they're talking about."

He scanned the first paragraph and saw Jim's name, Roderick Hanley's, and Monroe, Long Island, mentioned. It looked like a long article.

"Can I give this back to you later, Sister?"

"Of course," she said in a conspiratorial tone, no doubt thinking she had won a convert. Then she left him alone with *The Light*.

Fifteen minutes later, Bill had finished the article and was up and pacing his office, feeling rocky.

Bullshit! All bullshit! Has to be!

But the paper had to have a damn near unimpeachable source to dare print something this far out. Otherwise Jim would sue it for every cent it had. And then there was the matter of Carol's call last week, about Jim being so upset as he traced his mother's identity. Of course he would have been upset — if this article was true, it meant he didn't even *have* a mother. Or a father, either, for that matter!

What am I saying?

Of course it wasn't true! How could it be true? This was the stuff of science fiction!

But then again, Jim had been terribly upset on Tuesday.

Good Lord! He wondered if Jim had seen the article yet. Bill didn't want to be the one to tell him about it, but he wanted to be available if Jim needed a friend. And he was going to need a friend or two when the big papers and television got hold of this.

And what about Carol? She was probably hurting as much as Jim.

He dialed Jim's number but the line was busy. After three more futile tries, he knew he had to get out to Monroe. Something told him he was going to be needed there.

4.

The Sunday meeting was late getting started. Brother Robert wasn't here yet, and if he didn't show soon someone would be asked to start it in his place. Grace hoped no one asked her to speak. She wouldn't know what to say.

She glanced around the room at the small, chatting groups. There seemed to be an air of expectation among the Chosen. Martin was paler than usual, and seemed especially tense. She felt it herself and could see it in the eyes of the others. Only that strange Mr. Veilleur seemed immune to it. He was sitting by himself in the last row, in the same spot as Wednesday, staring off into space.

Suddenly Brother Robert burst in, his eyes bright and feverish, his face flushed. He was waving a newspaper.

"This is it!" he cried, waving the tabloid in the air. "The sign we have awaited! It has come!"

He rushed by her to the front. The aura of peace and tranquillity that usually enveloped him was gone. His movements were abrupt as he squared himself behind the lectern. His usually soft brown eyes glinted in the fluorescent light. He radiated nervous energy as he began making the sign of the cross without waiting for the Chosen to be seated.

"In the name of the Father, and of the Son, and of the Holy Spirit, bless this gathering.

"Friends! We've all been touched by the Spirit in a special way. We've been privileged to be made aware of the incarnation of the Evil One, the Father of Lies, the Antichrist who would undo all the work of the Son of God and his followers and his Church, who would plunge the world into eternal darkness. We have sensed his presence but we haven't known in what guise he would come."

Brother Robert held up the front page of the newspaper. Grace recognized *The Light*.

"Now we know!

"The story revealed in these pages is a fantastic one, an incredible one, one I'm sure will be dismissed as deranged confabulation because of the very nature of the story itself, and because of its trashy source. But let me tell you, friends, the story is true!

"How do I know? Because the Spirit was with me this morning as I passed a corner newsstand. The Spirit drew my attention to these headlines, urged me to pick up the paper and read it. And as I read the article inside, I knew that each word was true!"

Brother Robert rolled up the paper into a small baton and began slapping it against his left palm as he went on.

"God works in mysterious ways his wonders to perform. He allowed his Son, Jesus, to be born into the family of a poor carpenter. He allowed a prostitute, Mary Magdalene, to comfort His Son as He carried the cross to his destiny. And he has chosen a humble, much-maligned tabloid to reveal to his Chosen the identity of the Antichrist.

"*The Light* tells the story of a scientist who, with the typical arrogance of all scientists who think man's puny mind capable of unraveling the mysteries of God's nature, decided to play God. This man perverted God's scheme for the reproduction of humankind and, in an arrogant attempt to usurp the power of God, caused a vile abomination to be born. This scientist took a piece of his own flesh and from it grew another human being! He called this thing a 'clone' — an exact replica of himself. Yes! He played God by creating another being in his own earthly image!"

Grace gasped. How could such a thing be possible? She glanced over to where Mr. Veilleur sat. She noticed that for the first time since his arrival he seemed interested in what was being said. *Very* interested. He was leaning forward in his seat, his eyes intent upon Brother Robert.

" 'But what has this to do with the Antichrist?' you say. Let the Spirit flow into your mind as I did and you will see that the creature resulting from this blasphemous experiment is not a man! Oh, he may look like a man, he may act like a man, and he may speak like a man, but he is a hollow thing with no soul! *No soul!* For how can he have a soul? He is not a new human being, born of man and woman, and therefore the possessor of a new soul. No! He is a mere collection of cells donated by a scientist playing God! And as such, he is a perfect vessel for Satan! The Evil One has entered his soulless body and is ready to begin subverting the salvation brought to us by Jesus Christ!"

The Chosen broke out in cries of astonishment and concern. Grace kept to herself. She wrapped her arms around her against the chill that was slowly seeping through her body.

"Consider carefully," Brother Robert went on. "The Spirit has made us aware of the Antichrist during the past month. We have felt its loathsome presence. According to this article, it was four weeks ago today that this scientist died in a plane crash."

A month ago today? In a plane crash? That had a familiar ring to it. Grace's chill deepened.

"When his will was read, it was discovered that the scientist had left his entire fortune — many millions of dollars — to a young stranger who looks exactly like he looked in his younger days. A record of the scientist's blasphemous experiments was found among his papers. They tell the whole hideous story."

Grace was becoming more and more uncomfortable with the scenario Brother Robert was outlining. It sounded too much like . . .

"And doesn't it strike you as strange, and so very convenient for the Heir, for that is what I call him — the Heir to Evil. Wasn't it convenient for the Heir that his creator died just as we were becoming aware of the menace of the Antichrist? Wasn't it convenient that this soulless creature suddenly became wealthy beyond one's wildest dreams? That suddenly he possessed financial power that could soon be parlayed into greater wealth and influence, influence that could be brought to bear on mankind?

"Am I the only one who sees something more than mere chance at work here?"

There was a chorus of Nos from the Chosen. Grace glanced at Mr. Veilleur and found him looking her way. His expression was grave.

"I fear your Brother Robert may be right," he said to Grace in a low voice. "Righter than he knows."

Brother Robert went on. "Who knows what plans the Evil One has to destroy the work of the Son of God and his followers? I'm sure none of our most deranged nightmares can touch the hem of the foulness he has in store for us.

"But there is another hand at work here. One that has singled us out as leaders in the fight against this abomination. Soon the world will know him as the clone of a dead scientist. But we know that he is more, much more. We know him as the Antichrist, and it is our task to stop him!"

"But how?" said Martin from the front row.

"Expose him!" Brother Robert cried, rapping the lectern with the rolled tabloid. "Let the world know who he is! Forewarned is forearmed! The Truth and the power of the Son of God, the True Christ, will be our weapon against him!"

"But how?" another voice said.

"We'll confront him where he lives! We'll put on a demonstration. The Negroes in your country demonstrate for civil rights, the ones called Yippies demonstrate for peace. The Chosen shall demonstrate for Christ. The story in *The Light* will bring him much publicity — perhaps the Antichrist wants that. *We*, however, will guarantee that he gets exactly the type of publicity he does *not* want. Wherever he goes, some of us will be there with signs exposing him as a spawn of blasphemy, a vehicle for Satan. Whenever the TV cameras and newspaper photographers capture him on film, our message — God's message — will be visible in the background."

"Amen!" Martin cried. It was echoed by another, and another. Members of the Chosen began to rise to their feet.

Even Grace could feel herself getting caught up in the fire. The frissons of unease were burned away by the passion of Brother Robert's conviction as he strode back and forth across the front of the room, brandishing his rolled newspaper like a sword.

"Some people will laugh at us, but many more will not. And when the Antichrist tries to exert his influence over the world, our message will be remembered, and a question will linger, even in the hearts of nonbelievers. We can foil his plans, friends! With the help of the Spirit, we can defeat him! We can! And we'll start now! Today!"

They were all on their feet — all except for Mr. Veilleur — and cheering, praising the Lord, many speaking in tongues.

"Where do we find him?" Martin cried when the room began to quiet.

"Not far from here," Brother Robert said. "Which is why I believe we were chosen by the Spirit. He lives a short ways out on Long Island, near Glen Cove. A place called Monroe."

Suddenly all Grace's previous creeping anxieties crashed back in on her with the force of a blow.

Monroe! No, it can't be Monroe!

"What's his name?" Martin called out.

Grace wanted to shut the answer from her ears, did not want to hear the name she already knew.

"James Stevens," Brother Robert said. "A creature who calls himself James Stevens is the Antichrist!"

No! It couldn't be! Not Carol's husband!

The room spun once around Grace, then went black.

5.

Carol had talked to a couple of the reporters who called, the *Times* and the *Post*, specifically. Then she took the phone off the hook. She was now able to paint a pretty clear picture of how the story had leaked out. Both had told her that Gerry Becker had approached their papers, and the *News* as well, with the story. None of them was interested. They'd thought he was a kook and that the journals he claimed belonged to Hanley were fakes.

That weasel Becker had stolen the journals from the crawlspace! That was the only explanation. Carol couldn't imagine how he had found them there, and it really didn't matter now. Eventually she hoped Jim charged him with theft and breaking and entering, but right now all that interested her was Jim's state of mind. He had looked ready to crack this morning — and the worst was yet to come.

Carol wandered through the house, raging at herself. She had made some terrible errors. In fact, most of this awful mess was her fault. If she hadn't been so damn indecisive, none of this would have happened. She simply should have thrown those journals out as she had originally planned. Or better yet, taken them out into the back yard, poured gasoline on them, and set them afire. That would have protected them out of the reach of both Jim *and* Gerry Becker.

If only —

She heard a frantic knocking on the door and hurried to it, praying it was Jim but knowing it wasn't.

It was Emma. Her face was drawn and white. She held a folded newspaper in her hand.

"Where's Jimmy?"

"He's not here. He's —"

"Have you seen this?" she said, her voice cracking and her lips quivering as she held up the paper. "Ann Guthrie showed it to me. How can they say such things? How can they print such lies and get away with it? It's so unfair! Where is he?"

"Over at the mansion."

"Oh, that damn mansion! I wished he'd never inherited it or anything else from that man! I knew it would come to no good! The whole thing makes me nauseous to my stomach!"

Carol was wondering where else you could be nauseated when there was another knock on the door. She was shocked to see Bill Ryan standing on the other side of the glass.

"Carol!" he said as she let him in. "I read that article on Jim. I tried to call but couldn't get through, so I came out. Is there anything I can do?"

Without thinking, Carol threw her arms around him.

"God, am I glad to see you!"

She felt Bill stiffen and quickly released him. His face was scarlet. Had she embarrassed him?

"A priest?" she heard Emma say behind her.

"Hi, Mrs. Stevens," Bill said in a husky voice. He smiled disarmingly as he stepped around Carol and extended his hand. "Remember me? I'm Bill Ryan. Jim and I were friends in high school."

"Oh, yes, *yes*! The fellow who went on to become a priest. How are you?"

"Concerned about Jim and this science fiction that's being printed about him."

"Oh, I know!" Emma said. "Isn't it terrible? Why would they pick on Jim like that? Do you think it's because he inherited that money?"

Carol felt Bill's eyes lock onto hers. "It *is* science fiction, isn't it, Carol?" he said. "*Isn't* it?"

Carol didn't know what to say, couldn't speak. She wanted to tell Bill and Emma. She knew Jim would need their support. But they couldn't help if they didn't know the truth. She tore her eyes away from his.

"My God!" Bill whispered. "It's true!"

Unable to deny it, Carol nodded her head.

Emma's hand was over her mouth. "How can that be? He was a normal boy, just like all the other kids!"

"Of course!" Carol said. "Because that's exactly what he was: a normal boy! And he's now a normal man. He simply has the same genes as Hanley, that's all. He's like Hanley's identical twin! But he won't see it that way. He's over at the mansion now, brooding and probably hitting the Scotch. He thinks he's a freak. He calls himself a 'tumor!' "

Bill expression was grim. "You don't think he'd do anything stupid, do you?"

Carol gathered that by stupid, Bill meant *suicidal*. The idea shocked her. She had never considered the possibility. Still couldn't.

"No, he'd never do that. But that *has* cut him pretty deep."

"Why don't we go over there," Bill said. "I'll drive."

6.

Grace sat in the back seat of Martin's Ford Torino sedan, trying to oganize her jumbled thoughts and emotions as the car headed east on the Long Island Expressway.

Jim Stevens . . . her niece's husband . . . the Antichrist? It seemed too ridiculous even to consider! Despite his atheistic declarations and anti-religious attitudes, Grace had sensed all along that deep down he was a decent man. Perhaps he didn't go to church or even believe in God, but he had always treated Carol well. How could he be the Antichrist?

And yet . . .

What about the sickening dread and terror she had felt the last time he had been to her apartment? And hadn't it been later that very night at choir practice that she had sung about Satan being here when she should have been singing the "Ave Maria?"

Maybe it wasn't so farfetched. Maybe Satan had just been in the process of usurping Jim's soulless body on that day, and she had sensed it somehow.

But why had she been able to sense it while Carol obviously didn't? Was she, as Martin had told her over and over, part of the Lord's plan to combat the Antichrist? Was her participation in the Chosen necessary for her salvation?

She prayed this would bring her the absolution she craved for the terrible sins of her past. That was the only reason she had agreed to accompany the Chosen to Monroe.

She wished Brother Robert had come along with them. She needed his strength of spirit, his support. But Brother Robert had stayed behind in Manhattan. He had not thought it proper for a member of a contemplative order such as his to make a public show of himself, so he had put Martin in charge. Grace respected his wish, but still she missed his presence.

"I believe there's something to this," said Mr. Veilleur at her side in the back seat, tapping the copy of *The Light* in his lap.

Somehow he had finagled his way into Martin's car along with Grace and two others. They were the lead vehicle in a caravan of sorts heading for Monroe. One member had a Volkswagen van and those of the Chosen with the slightest artistic bent were making signs and placards in its rear as they traveled.

"You think it's true?" she said.

"Of course it's true!" Martin said from the driver's seat. "The Spirit is guiding us, pointing us along the Path!"

"I believe the cloning part is true," Mr. Veilleur said to her, ignoring Martin. "As for this Satan-Antichrist business" he shrugged "I've told you what I think of that. But this cloning . . . I've never heard of such a thing, or even dreamed it might be possible. Such a man might well provide a gateway. But why now? What is so special about now, this time, that it should be chosen?"

"I don't know," Grace said.

Mr. Veilleur half turned toward her, his blue eyes intent.

"You say you know this man?"

Grace nodded. "For about ten years, yes."

"When was he born?"

Grace couldn't see how that mattered but she tried to remember. She knew Jim's birthday was in January. Carol always complained that it fell so soon after Christmas when she had already exhausted all her gift ideas, and he was the same age as Carol, so that would make it . . .

"January, 1942. The sixth, I believe."

"The Epiphany!" The car swerved slightly as Martin shouted from the front. "Little Christmas!"

"Is that important?" Grace said.

"I don't know," Martin replied in a softer, more thoughtful voice. "It must be, but I don't know why."

"January sixth." Mr. Veilleur said, frowning. "That would mean that he was conceived — or began incubation, as it were — somewhere in late April or . . . early . . . May of 1941 . . . "

His voice trailed off as his eyes widened briefly, then narrowed.

"Is that date significant?" she asked.

"Someone . . . some*thing* . . . died then. Or so I'd thought."

His face settled into fierce, grim lines.

"What's wrong?"

He shook his head brusquely once. "Nothing." Then once more. "Everything."

Grace glanced out the window and saw the sign for the Glen Cove exit. The dread began to grow in her. Monroe was less than ten miles north of here.

7.

Jim gently pulled Carol aside in the hall just outside the library.

"Why did you bring them here?"

He was annoyed at her for leading Bill and, of all people, Ma, out to the mansion. He knew she meant well, but he didn't feel like seeing anybody today. He didn't know *when* he would ever feel like having company over again.

"It's just a way of showing we love you," she said, running a fingertip along his jawline, sending a chill down his body. "Of saying that none of this matters."

Jim had to admit he was warmed by the thought, but he still felt somehow . . . ashamed. He knew he had done nothing wrong. Being the clone of a Nobel prizewinner was not like having it become public knowledge that you had the syph or the like, yet he could not deny that he felt embarrassed and, yes, *diminished* by the truth.

And a bit paranoid, too. Had Bill's handshake been just a bit less firm than he remembered in the past? Had Ma pulled away just a little too quickly when she had hugged him on arriving today? Or was he just looking for things? Was he expecting everyone else to treat him differently because of how differently he now saw himself?

He watched Carol go off toward the kitchen to make coffee, then he took a deep breath and headed for the library. He couldn't hide forever. Maybe the couple-three belts of Jack Daniels he'd had earlier would help him handle this. As he entered, he heard the conversation between Bill and Ma die out . . .

. . . *Ma* . . . he didn't have a *real* Ma, did he?

Was she looking at him strangely? He felt like telling her that he wasn't about to sprout another head, but that would blow this whole cool, calm, collected, life-is-going-on-as-usual scene. Instead, he put on a smile.

"So," he said, as casually as he could, "what's new?"

8.

"Aren't you coming?" Martin said through the open side window of the car.

"Grace shook her head. "No . . . I can't. She's my niece."

"That may be true," Martin said, "but this is the Lord's war. You've got to stand up and be counted sooner or later."

The authority Brother Martin had given him seemed to have gone to his head.

"I'm with the Lord," she said, "but I can't picket my niece's home. I just can't."

Grace shut her eyes to block out the sight of the placard-carrying Chosen walking toward the little white cottage that had been her brother Henry's home before he and Ellen had been killed. Too many lunches and dinners and afternoon cups of tea with Ellen, plus half a dozen years of living there and making a home for her dear orphaned Carol while she commuted to college at Stony Brook. Too many memories there to allow her to parade in front of it and call Carol's husband the Antichrist, even if it was true.

But looking at that familiar little cottage sitting there in the light of day, she wondered how such a thing could possibly be true.

"Where are the reporters?" Martin said, his eyes flicking up and down the street. "I called all five local TV stations, the big papers, and the local rag . . . .what's it called?"

"The *Express*," Grace said.

"Right. You'd think *someone* would have sent a crew out here to cover this!"

"It's Sunday, after all," Mr. Veilleur said. "You moved pretty fast. You're probably far ahead of them."

"Yes, we did, didn't we?" he said with a note of satisfaction. "But we can't wait forever, and it'll probably be better if we're on line and marching when they arrive. Are you sure, Grace?"

"I can't. Please don't ask me any more."

"How about you?" Martin said, opening the door next to Mr. Veilleur. "Time for you to earn your keep."

Mr. Veilleur smiled. "Don't make me laugh."

Martin's expression turned fierce.

"Listen, you! Either get out and walk that picket line or get out and start walking back to the city. I'm not having any dead weight around here!"

Grace didn't have time to expess her shock at Martin's rudeness. In a blur of motion, Mr. Veilleur's big hand darted out, took hold of Martin's tie, and dragged his head and shoulders into the car.

"I will not be spoken to that way," he said in a low voice.

Grace could not see Mr. Veilleur's eyes, but Martin could. She saw his face blanch.

"Okay, okay," he said quickly. "Have it your way."

Neither Grace nor Mr. Veilleur said anything as they watched Martin hurry over to the cottage. The Chosen were lined up on the walk before the house. She watched Martin pass through them and stride to the front door. He knocked a few times but there was no answer. She saw him try the knob. The door swung open. Grace almost cried out as she saw Martin go inside with a group of the others trailing behind. They shouldn't be in there! Not in Henry's old house!

It took maybe fifteen minutes but seemed like hours before Martin reappeared, hurrying toward the car. His face was flushed, his eyes feverish as he slipped back in behind the wheel.

"No one's home, but I think we found the proof we need!"

"Proof?" Mr. Veilleur said.

"Yes! Books on Satanism, the occult! He's obviously been studying them!"

Mr. Veilleur's smile was wry. "If he's this Antichrist you talk about — the Devil himself or his offspring — one would think he'd already be intimately familiar with all there is to know about Satanism."

Martin only paused for a beat. "Yes, well, whatever . . . it establishes a link between this James Stevens and the Devil."

"Where are the books?" Mr. Veilleur asked.

"I told them to destroy them." He turned to Grace. "Now, do you know how to get to this mansion he inherited?"

"Of course," she said. "It's on the waterfront. Everybody in town knows the Hanley mansion. Why?"

"Because if he's not here, he's probably holed up there."

"Maybe he left town," Grace said hopefully.

"No," Martin said slowly. "He's here. I can *feel* the evil in the air. Can't you?"

Grace had to admit that there was a sense of *wrongness* about Monroe, a vague feeling that some sort of cancer was growing in its heart. But she hated to admit it.

Finally she said, "Yes, I think so."

Martin started the car. "Which way?"

"Down here and to the left until you get to Shore Drive," Grace said, pointing the way.

As the car shifted into gear, Grace glanced out the rear window. The other cars, filled with the Chosen, were falling into line behind them. She looked past them and gasped. Smoke was pouring from one of the cottage windows.

"The house!" she cried. "It's burning!"

Martin glanced in his rearview mirror. "The idiots! I told them to burn the books *out*side!"

"Stop! We've got to put it out!"

"No time for that now! We're going to beard the Devil in his den!"

9.

Carol heard the wail of the siren on the downtown volunteer firehouse. Ever since she had been a little girl, the sound never failed to disturb her. It meant that somewhere, at that very moment, flames were eating someone's home, maybe devouring someone's life. She glanced out the parlor window, southeastward, toward their own little house. She was startled to see a pillar of smoke rising from that direction. It looked as if it were coming from their neighborhood. She wondered with a pang of fear if it was someone they knew, someone who needed their help.

And then she lowered her gaze and saw the cars pulling up outside the mansion's front gate. Her first thought was, *Reporters!* But then she saw the placards and picket signs and knew something else was going on.

"Oh, no!" she said. "Who on earth are they?"

Bill joined her at the window.

"They look like protesters. But what are they protesting?"

Carol strained to read the words on the signs but could make out only the larger ones.

"Something about God and Satan."

"Oh, great!" Bill said. "Just what Jim needs!"

Carol glanced back toward the library where Jim sat with Emma. The presence of people he loved and trusted seemed to have had a bolstering effect. The tension had been oozing out of him since their arrival.

"What can they want?"

"Who knows? Probably a mob of religious nuts who think he's some sort of Frankenstein monster. I'm going out there. Don't say anything to Jim until I get back."

"What can you do?"

"Chase them off, I hope." Bill shrugged and pointed to his cassock and clerical collar. "Maybe this will have some influence on them."

"Be careful," she said.

As she watched him step out the front door, she felt a sudden rush of dread and knew that something awful was going to happen today.

10.

As Bill strode the fifty yards or so to the front gate, he began to make out the messages on the signs. There were quotations from scripture about the Antichrist and Armageddon and the end of the world. Others were original and he found these the most disturbing:

A MAN WITH NO SOUL IS A HOME FOR THE DEVIL!

and

GET THEE OUT, DEMON!

and the worst,

JAMES STEVENS — ANTICHRIST!

Bill would have found them laughable were it not for the fact that they were talking about his friend. He had caught the hunted look in Jim's eyes a while ago, the look of a man who felt like a freak, who wasn't completely sure to whom he could turn or trust. Harassment by a bunch of religious nut cases might push him over the edge.

They were just getting their picket line organized when they spotted him. He heard cries of "Look! There's a priest!" and "A priest! A priest!"

When he reached the open gate, a slim, pale young man stepped forward to meet him.

"What's the meaning of this?" Bill asked, straining to appear calm and concerned.

"Have you been sent here to exorcise him, Father?" the man said.

"What in God's name are you talking about?"

"In God's name, yes, very apt, very apt. I'm Martin Spano. The Spirit has sent us here to expose this abomination for who he is."

"And just who do you think he is?"

"Why, the Antichrist, of course."

He seemed shocked that Bill did not know. Bill felt his control begin to slip.

"That's ridiculous! Where did you get such an idea?"

"He's a clone, father! A group of cells taken from one man and grown into the shape of another in a blasphemous attempt to play God! But he is *not* a man! He is a mere cutting! He is born not of man and woman, and as such he has no soul. He is a tool of Satan, an avenue for the Antichrist to enter into this world!"

Bill was impressed with the force of the man's conviction and momentarily taken aback by the outré logic of his words. If you bought all that Revelations mumbo-jumbo, you could probably be convinced that this fellow was on to something here.

"I assure you," Bill said in his loudest voice, addressing the crowd as well as their young leader, "that you have nothing to fear from Mr. Stevens. I've known him most of my life and he is not — I repeat, *not* — the Antichrist!"

This seemed to slow the crowd, but not as much as Bill would have liked. A couple of them lowered their signs, but the rest stood and waited.

Their leader was taking no chances, however. He turned to them and held up his arms.

"Wait a minute!" he cried. "Just wait!" Then he turned back to Bill. "What is your name, Father?"

"Father William Ryan."

"Of what order, may I ask?"

"The Society of Jesus."

"Ah!" he said, his face lighting as if he had just had a revelation. "A Jesuit! One of the *intellectuals* of the Church! One of those modern priestly rationalists who would put the human mind above faith! A follower of the Black Pope!"

"That's not true at all!" Bill said. "You're making —"

"Obviously the Spirit has bypassed your unreceptive heart and settled in ours! We have been called and it is our mission to spread the word of Truth about this man so that no matter where he goes he will be shunned and cast out by the faithful, and his words of sedition against Jesus Christ and his Church will fall on deaf ears! But the Evil One obviously has your ear already, so we will not listen to you!"

A woman beside Spano suddenly dropped her sign and raised her hands. She began babbling in an alien-sounding tongue that resembled nothing Bill had ever heard before.

"Do you hear?" Spano cried. "Even now the Spirit is with us, telling us not to be swayed by this fallen priest! We stay to spread the warning about the Antichrist within! Let us join hands and pray!"

As they clustered together, grasping hands and saying the Our Father, Bill realized there was no way he could reason with this bunch. Their Pentecostal fervor frightened him. No telling what they would do if they got onto the grounds. So while they were praying, he stepped over to the iron gate and swung it across the driveway. As the gate struck the stop on the brick column to his left, the lock clanked closed automatically.

Spano glared at him as he looked up from their prayer.

"You can't lock out the word of God, Father Ryan!"

"I know," Bill said pointedly. "But I haven't heard any of that here."

Restless and uneasy, he stood and watched the group as it murmured its prayers, remembering someone's comment about the intelligence of a crowd being inversely proportional to its size. He hoped no one did anything stupid. At least the gate barred them from the grounds. That gave him a little comfort. Since reason seemed a useless tool here, Bill turned his back on them and returned to the house.

11.

"So I'm the Antichrist, am I?" Jim said after Bill had related his conversation with the kooks outside. He had spotted the crowd out front and had watched Bill talk to them. When Bill returned, he had met him at the door. "I *love* it!"

"Jim, please!" Said Carol, at his left by the window. "This isn't funny."

"Of course it is! It's a gas!"

He could tell by their expressions that no one agreed with him, least of all Ma. She looked angry and afraid. Jim had to admit to a certain discomfiture himself. He knew he wasn't the Antichrist. Hell, he'd stopped believing in that sort of shit back in his days at Our Lady of Perpetual Motion! That didn't mean he liked *other* people believing he was the devil or whatever.

But that bit about not having a soul . . . that was kind of creepy. It showed some pretty original thinking on the part of those nuts out there. Jim wasn't sure he believed in souls anyway. As far as he could see, you were born, you did your best at what you had to do for as many years as you could, and then you died. That was it. No soul, no Heaven, no Hell, no Limbo,no Purgatory.

But what if there really was such a thing as a soul?

And what if he didn't have one?

Despite all his innate skepticism, despite his contempt for religion and mysticism and spritualism and all the other isms that people used throughout the ages to insulate themselves from the cold hard realities of existence, he knew deep inside that if such a thing as a soul existed, he wanted one.

"I've a good mind to call the cops," his mother said. "Have Sergeant Hall come out and tell them all to get lost! That'll end this fiascal!"

"*Fiasco*, Ma," he said. "But stay put. I'll scare them off."

He was besieged by protests from all sides but he ignored them and hurried out the door. This might be fun.

Behind him, he heard Carol say, "I'm calling the police!"

12.

"Who's this coming now?" said Mr. Veilleur from beside her in the back seat of Martin's car.

Grace gasped as she recognized the figure approaching the gate from within. "That's Jim!"

"The clone? The one they think is this Antichrist?"

"Yes! Walking right up to them!"

"Pretty courageous for someone who's supposed to be the 'spawn of the Devil,' don't you think?"

"I don't know what to think," she said, remembering the smoke rising from Henry's old house, and now this. She felt utterly miserable.

"You're not alone," Mr. Veilleur said in a gentle voice. "Neither does anyone else."

13.

"Hi, folks!" Jim said, strolling up to the gate with his hands in his pockets, looking as casual as he could. "What's up?"

"Who are you?" said the skinny guy who had been talking to Bill earlier. Spano was the name, if Jim correctly remembered what Bill had said.

"Oh, you know me, don't you, pal? I'm Jim Stevens, alias the Antichrist."

There were cries of astonishment from the group. Some of them even scuttled away and hid behind others. It was all Jim could do to keep a straight face. Even their leader took a step back. His voice shook as he spoke.

"You . . . you admit it?"

"Sure. I came into the world to really mess it up for you Christian types. You know, spread sin and fear and war and disease and bring on Armageddon. That sort of stuff. But to tell you the truth, I can't find a place to begin."

"He's mocking us! He's trying to confuse us, trying to make a joke out of this!"

"A joke? Just look back on the last twelve months, Hatchet-face." Jim was surprised how clearly his mind was working despite the drinks he'd had earlier. "We've had a six-day war in the Middle East that upset the whole balance of power there, a military junta in Greece, martial law in Thailand, more fighting in Cyprus, Palestine, and especially Vietnam, thousands upon thousands of homeless, hungry refugees in Somalia and Jordan and good ol' Vietnam. And over in the Soviet Union they're celebrating fifty years of their revolution which has so far cost the Russian and East European populace something in excess of thirty million lives. At home here we've got race riots in East Harlem, Roxbury, Newark, Detroit and lots of other places. The blacks hate the whites, the whites hate the blacks, the shorthairs hate the longhairs, the longhairs hate anybody with a steady job, the Arabs hate the Jews, and the Klan hates everybody. Ever growing numbers of people are spending their lives stoned on grass or else they're nuking their psyches with LSD. And on top of all that, they kicked my dear friend the Reverend Adam Clayton Powell out of Congress! Sheesh! What's left for *me* to do?"

Spano's mouth worked spasmodically. "I . . . I . . ."

"Devil of a predicament, isn't it?" Jim said.

"Do not let yourselves be swayed by the Father of Lies!" Spano cried.

"Right on," Jim said.

He wondered if Hanley had envisioned this sort of scene. Maybe that was why he had kept the whole experiment under wraps. Apparently the scientist's instincts had been on target. Jim had spent days hating Roderick Hanley, but now he was having a slow change of heart.

Besides, I wouldn't be alive without him.

Maybe he hadn't been such a bad guy after all.

"The Antichrist tries to tell us that the evil in the world is not the devil's work!"

Antichrist! There it was again, and Jim was suddenly angry. As his anger grew, the fears and self-doubt of the past week began to melt away. Who was this pasty-faced twerp to tell him who he was? *He* would decide who he was! And he was Jim Stevens. So what if he was genetically the same as Roderick Hanley, Ph.D., and Nobel laureate? It didn't matter. He *wasn't* Roderick Hanley — he was someone else. He was his own man and no one — not these religious nut cases or anyone else — was going to hang a sign on him.

He smiled. Carol had been right all along: Being a clone really didn't matter. As long as Carol stuck by him, he could handle anything. So easy! Why hadn't he seen it himself?

"Pray!" Spano was saying to his followers. "Close your ears to his lies!"

Jim was suddenly tired of the game.

"Get lost," he said. "You're all pretty pathetic. Take off before the cops get here."

"No!" Spano cried. "We *want* the police! We want the world to know your name so that Christians everywhere can be warned of who you really are!"

"Scram!" Jim shouted.

He was really angry now. He pulled on the gate but it was locked. With a sudden burst of energy, he climbed up the iron pickets to the top of the brick gatepost.

14.

"Oh, God! What's he doing!" Carol cried at Bill's shoulder as they watched Jim reach the top of the gatepost column.

Bill had been watching the scene from the front door with Carol and Jim's mother. His palms had grown slick with sweat.

"He's going to get killed!" Emma said.

"Bill!" Carol said, her grip tightening on his arm. "Get him down from there! Please!"

"I'll try."

He hurried down the driveway. This whole affair was getting out of hand. The best thing was to get Jim back inside and let the police handle it. But he sensed that getting Jim to change course once he was on a roll like this was not going to be easy. A nameless fear quickened his pace but he sensed that he was already too late.

15.

Jim sat on the concrete ball atop the column and looked down on the small, uneasy crowd.

"Come on, folks!" he said, making a shooing motion with his hands. "Get packing! This isn't funny any more!"

They recoiled at the sight of his hands.

"Look!" someone cried. "His palms! The Mark of the Beast!"

"It's proof!" Spano shouted. "Proof that Satan dwells within!"

They *oooh*ed and Aaahed and muttered together as they clustered below him. Jim looked at his fuzzy palms.

The Mark of the Beast? What the hell did that mean?

Whatever it was, it seemed to frighten them, and maybe that would scare them off.

"Yes!" he said, rising up, straddling the concrete ball with his ankles, and spreading his hands out in front of him. "The Mark of the Beast! And if you don't leave now, all your future children and grandchildren will be born as frogs and crawly things!"

And then his right foot slipped.

For an awful, gut-wrenching moment, he thought he was going to fall, then his foot found the edge of the capstone again. He thought he was okay, then realized he had lost his balance.

He was falling.

He saw the iron spikes atop the gate rising toward him and thought as clearly as he had ever thought —

I'm going to die!

He tried to twist to the side, but it was too late. He managed to swing his head off to the right but the spikes caught him in the groin, stomach, and chest. There was an instant of blinding agony as the points speared his heart with a tearing, thudding impact, ripping through to his spine and beyond.

Not yet! Oh, please, not yet! I'm not ready to go!

He opened his mouth to scream but he had no air left in his lungs.

Abruptly the pain was gone as his ruptured spinal cord stopped sending impulses to his brain. A strange, ethereal peace enveloped him. He felt strangely detached from the cries of horror rising all around him.

Suddenly Carol's face swam into view, looking up at him with wide, horror-filled eyes. She seemed to be saying his name but he couldn't hear her. Sound had slipped away. He wanted to tell her he loved her and ask her to forgive him for being such a jerk, but then vision slipped away as well, with thought racing close behind.

16.

Carol had seen Jim begin to lose his balance and was already running for the gate when he tilted forward and fell onto the spikes. A voice she barely recognized as her own was screaming,

"*No - no - NOOOO!*"

Time seemed to slow as she saw the black iron spikes drive into his chest and burst from his back in a spray of red, saw him writhe and twitch, then go limp as bright scarlet blood gushed from his mouth.

Her legs wanted to collapse under her and her heart wanted her to follow them to the ground and curl her body up into a ball and hide from what she saw. But she had to reach him, had to get him off there.

Bill was running ahead of her but she passed him and slammed into the gate below Jim, looking up at him, screaming his name over and over in a vain attempt to awaken a spark of life in those glazed, staring blue eyes. She thought she saw his mouth work, trying to say something, then his lips went slack and there was nothing there, nothing at all, and then something warm and wet was on her fingers and she looked and saw his blood running down the fence rail she was gripping and spreading over her hand just like in one of her dreams and her screams became formless wails of horror and loss as Bill dragged her away.

17.

Grace stared in mute shock at Jim's body impaled on the gate above the scattering forms of the Chosen. This couldn't be happening! She felt her gorge rise at the sight of the blood. He was *dead!* Dead in an instant! Poor Jim — no one deserved a death like that!

And Carol! When she saw Carol and heard her screams of anguish, she reached for the door handle. Mr. Veilleur restrained her.

"You can't help him now," he said in a sad, gentle voice.

"But Carol —!"

"Do you want her to find out that you came here with her husband's tormentors?"

She didn't want that — she couldn't bear that!

Suddenly Martin hurled himself into the driver's seat as another of the Chosen slid in on the passenger side. Without a second's hesitation, he started the car and threw it into gear.

"Why are you running?" Mr. Veilleur asked.

"Shut up!" Martin said. "Just shut up! That wasn't our fault! He'd been drinking, you could smell it on him, and he shouldn't have climbed up there! It wasn't our fault, but it could easily be made to look that way, so we've got to get out of here before someone has us arrested!"

As they pulled away from the shoulder, Grace saw a man standing in the bayberry bushes along the side of the road. She recognized Jonah Stevens. She looked back through the rear window and saw him staring at her. His adopted son had just died horribly but he showed no grief, no horror, no anger. All she saw as she looked into his eyes for that instant was worry — surprise and worry. But that couldn't be. It had to be a trick of the light.

"I sense the hand of God here," Martin was saying from the front seat. "The Spirit moved us here to bring this about. The Antichrist is dead. He no longer threatens the work of the Spirit. We didn't know this was going to happen but I believe this was why we were chosen."

"This isn't the work of the God I praise," Grace said defiantly. "And what will Brother Robert say?"

Martin threw her a quick, unsettled glance over his shoulder but said nothing.

Beside her, Mr. Veilleur only shook his head and sighed as he stared out the window.

18.

"It's all my fault!" Brother Robert said, tugging at his beard. His face was drawn and his shoulders slumped inside his woolen habit. "I should have gone with you!"

"I don't think it would have changed anything," Martin said. Martin was subdued, no longer the gung-ho commander.

Grace sat beside him in the barely furnished living room of the brownstone. The rest of the Chosen had gone their separate ways as soon as they had reached the city. The strangely silent Mr. Veilleur had asked to be let off on the Manhattan side of the Queensborough Bridge. Grace had stayed with Martin, hoping to see Brother Robert, hoping to tap into the holy man's reservoir of tranquillity.

What she really wanted was for someone to tell her that this whole day had never happened. But there was no hope of that. And no comfort to be gained from Brother Robert. His tranquillity was gone.

"Don't be so sure of that, Martin," he said, his eyes flashing. "You allowed the people in your charge to become a rabble."

"I'm sorry."

"I know you are," Brother Martin said in a softer voice. "And the final responsibility rests with me. I should have been there. A house is in flames and a man is dead, and it's all my fault."

"A man?" Martin said. "You said he was the Antichrist."

"I believe now I was wrong."

"Please," Grace said. "I don't understand! Why do you think you were wrong?"

"Because it isn't over," Brother Robert said in a flat voice. "If you'll let yourselves feel the sense of *wrongness* that drew you to the Chosen, you'll see that it's not gone. In fact it's stronger now than it was when you left here for Monroe."

Grace sat statue still and opened herself to the feeling.

It's still here!

"God forgive us!" she cried. She buried her face in her hands and began to weep. He was right! Carol's husband was dead and nothing had changed.

It wasn't over!

Seventeen

Wednesday
March 13

Bill stood in Tall Oaks Cemetery and said a silent requiem over Jim's coffin. Carol had insisted on a non-religious ceremony — she'd told him she would have preferred a requiem Mass but said that would have made a mockery of the way Jim felt about religion. Bill had to respect that, but the idea of sending his old friend into the afterlife without a prayer or two was untenable.

So he stood silently in the morning sunlight among the family and friends clustered around the flower-decked grave. Most of the friends were Carol's, from the hospital. Jim had never been a gregarious sort. He did not make friends easily, and it showed here. He had probably never even met half of the people ringing his coffin.

Bill shut out the happy chirping of the birds and the sobs of the mourners and recited the prayers from memory. Then he added a personal coda:

Although he was an unbeliever, Lord, he was a good man. If he was guilty of any sin, it was pride—pride in the supreme ability of the mind You gave him to accomplish anything, to solve all the mysteries of being. As You forgave the doubter, Thomas, who had to put his fingers into Your wounds before he would believe, please so forgive this good and honest man who might have returned to Your fold had he been allowed enough time.

Bill felt his throat constrict. *Enough time* . . . was there ever enough time?

Carol stood on the far side of the grave, flanked by Jonah and Emma Stevens, watching as each mourner stepped up and dropped a flower on the coffin. Bill had nothing but admiration for the way she had handled herself through the nightmare of the past few days. Disturbingly he found himself drawn more strongly to her than ever. He had taken a brief emergency leave from St. F.'s to stay at his folks' place here in Monroe and help out in any way he could. Carol had been staying with her in-laws. Her own place was nothing but a burned-out shell after the fire set by the protesters on Sunday, and she hadn't wanted to stay at the mansion.

She had lost her husband and her home in one afternoon, yet she had been hanging tough through it all. The Stevenses had helped, Bill knew, acting as a buffer between Carol and the world. Jonah was being especially protective. Even Bill had a rough time getting by him to see her. As for reporters, they may as well have been trying to crack Gibraltar with their heads. As a result, the papers had been full of wild speculation about what had happened on Sunday.

Full, that is, until this morning.

The results of yesterday's New Hampshire primary had pushed Jim's death out of the news, thankfully. The headlines and most of the front page of this morning's *Times* were devoted to Senator Eugene McCarthy's stunning upset of President Johnson. It was all anyone on TV could talk about.

It would have been all Bill could talk and think about were it not for Jim's death. Gene McCarthy had succeeded beyond the wildest dreams of his supporters, Bill among them, but it just didn't seem important today. Looking down at Jim's coffin, Bill couldn't imagine what could ever seem important compared to the untimely, senseless death of a friend.

Carol began to sob. She had held up this far, but now, with Jim poised over the hole that was going to hold him for the rest of time, Bill could see that her control was starting to crack. He wanted to go to her, throw his arms around her and cry with her.

But now Emma was doing just that. Jonah merely stood there, his face impassive, his hand gripping Carol's elbow.

Movement off to his right caught Bill's eye. He recognized Carol's Aunt Grace approaching. She had been conspicuous by her absence at the wake the past two days. She stopped at a distance now, lowered her head, and folded her hands in prayer. Her waddling approach and her whole demeanor were so tentative, as if she feared being recognized.

Bill wondered why until he heard Emma's voice shatter the silence.

"There she is!" she cried. "She was with them! She came with the ones who killed my Jimmy! Why, Grace Nevins? Why did you want to hurt my boy?"

The plump little woman raised her face toward Carol and her accuser. She shook her head. Bill bit his lip as he saw the guilt and remorse in her expression. But why should she feel guilty? He had talked to the crowd. He hadn't seen her there. He was sure he would have recognized her.

"She wasn't there —" he began, but Emma cut him off.

"Yes, she was! Jonah saw her in one of the cars!" Her face contorted into a mask of rage as her voice rose to a shrill peak. "You were there! You did this!"

Bill watched Carol's confused, teary eyes flicking back and forth between the two women.

"Please . . ." she said.

But Emma was not to be checked. She pointed a shaking finger at Grace.

"You won't get away with it, Grace Nevins! I'll see you pay for this!" She started toward Grace but Jonah restrained her with his free hand as she screeched, "Now get away from my boy's grave! Get away before I kill you myself here and now!"

Sobbing openly, Grace turned and hurried away.

After a moment of stunned silence, the embarrassed mourners began to offer their final condolences to Carol and the Stevenses, then drifted away.

Bill waited until the end, hoping to have a few private words with Carol, but Jonah and Emma ushered her away before he could reach her. There was something almost possessive about Jonah's protective attitude toward his daughter-in-law, and that disturbed Bill.

EIGHTEEN

Thursday
March 14

1.

Carol closed the front door of the mansion behind her and stood in the cool dimness. She didn't want to be here. Even now she didn't know how she had brought herself to drive past the iron spikes on the front gate. But she had no place else to go. Her own home was a blackened shell, and she couldn't stay with Jonah and Emma any longer. She couldn't stand Emma's constant hovering, her mad swings between rage and grief, and she couldn't bear another evening with Jonah sitting there staring at her. She had thanked them and had left first thing this morning.

She had tried to call Aunt Grace last night to find out if what Emma had said was true. Had she been outside the mansion with those nuts? But Grace wasn't answering her phone.

She had been almost tempted to call Bill and ask if she could stay with his parents but then realized that what she wanted more than anything else was to be *alone*.

The empty mansion echoed hollowly around her.

This is it, Jim, she thought. *You're gone, our house and our bed are gone, all the old photos, all your unsold novels, gone. There's nothing left of you but this old house, and that's not much 'cause you hardly had any time here at all.*

Her eyes filled. She still couldn't believe he was gone, that he wouldn't come bounding down the stairs over there with another of those damn journals in his hand. But he *was* gone, her one and only Jim was gone!

Her throat tightened. *Why'd you have to die, Jim?* She almost hated him for being so stupid . . . climbing up that gatepost! *Why?*

How was she going to do it without him? Jim had pulled her through her parents' deaths when she had thought the world was caving in on her, and he had been her rock, her safe place ever since. But who was going to pull her through *his* death?

She could almost hear his voice:

You're on your own now, Carol. Don't let me down. Don't go to pieces on me. You can do it!

She felt the sobs begin to quake in her chest. She had thought herself all cried out.

She was wrong.

2.

"I'm sorry about your friend, Father Bill."

"Thank you, Nicky," Bill said.

He looked at the boy standing on the far side of his desk. There seemed to be genuine sympathy in his eyes. Bill realized with a pang that most of the boys here at St. F.'s were all too familiar with what it was like to lose someone.

It was Bill's first day back and he had three days' worth of adoption applications, reference checks, and assorted mail piled on his desk, and more coming. Outside it was rainy but warm, more like May than March.

"Aren't you going to be late for class?" he asked the boy.

"I'll make it on time. Was he a good friend?"

"He was an old friend who used to be my best friend. We were just getting to know each other again."

A lump formed in his throat at the thought of Jim. He had walled up the grief since the horrors of Sunday, refusing to shed a tear for his old friend. Jim would mock him out if he knew Bill had cried over him.

And what would Jim say about his dreams of Carol, more carnal than ever, now that she was alone in the world.

"Is it true what the papers said —"

"I'd really rather not discuss it now, Nicky. It's all a little too fresh."

The boy nodded sagely, like someone many times his age, then began his habitual wandering around the office. He stopped at the typewriter.

"So," he said after a moment, "when are you leaving?"

The question startled Bill. He glanced up and saw the half-written letter to the Provincial still in his typewriter. God! The teaching job in Baltimore! He'd forgotten all about it.

"How many times have I told you not to read my mail?"

"I'm sorry! It's just that it was sitting there in plain view. I just looked at it for a second!"

Bill fought the guilt rising within him.

"Look, Nicky, I know we had a deal —"

"That's okay, Father," the boy said quickly with a smile that was heartbreakingly weak. "You'll make a great teacher. Especially down there near Washington. I know you like all that political stuff. And don't worry about me. I like it here. This is home to me. I'm a hopeless case, anyway."

"I've told you not to talk that way about yourself!"

"We've got to face facts, Father. You wait around for me to get adopted and you'll be in a wheelchair from old age! The deal's off. I screwed up my end of it, anyway. Wouldn't be fair to hold you to yours."

Bill stared at the boy as he turned away and continued his casual meander around the office. And as he watched him he heard Jim's voice echoing back from sometime during that night of beer and bad music and near-death in the Village:

We should clean up our own yards and tend to our own neighborhoods first, then *worry about the rest of the world. If we all did that, maybe there wouldn't be so much in the world to worry about.*

Bill suddenly knew what he had to do.

"Give me that letter, will you, Nicky? Right. The one in the typewriter. And the one from the Provincial beside it."

Nicky handed them to him, then said, "I'd better get to school."

"Not so fast."

Bill neatly folded the letters in thirds and then began tearing them up.

Nicky's jaw dropped. "What are you doing?"

"Keeping a promise."

"But I told you —!"

"Not just my promise to you, but one I made to myself a long time ago." *The one that brought me to the seminary in the first place*. "Like it or not, I'm staying."

Bill felt lightheaded, almost giddy. As if a tremendous weight had been lifted from his shoulders. All doubts, all conflicts were gone. *This* was where he belonged. This was where he could make a real day-to-day difference.

"But I'll never get adopted!"

"We'll see about that. But you're not my only concern. I'm here for the duration. I'm not leaving St. Francis until this whole place is empty!"

He saw tears spring into Nicky's eyes and run down his cheeks. Nicky never cried. The sight of those tears tripped something inside him and he felt his own eyes fill. All the grief he had dammed up since Sunday was breaking free. He tried to shore up the barriers but it was too late. He opened his mouth to tell Nicky to run along but only a sob escaped, and then his head was down and cradled in his arms on the desk and he was crying.

"Why'd he have to die like that?" he heard his own voice say between the sobs.

He felt a small hand pat his back, then heard Nicky's teary voice saying, "I'll be your friend, Father Bill. I'm going to be around a long time. I'll be your friend."

3.

The traffic light shifted to red and Jonah Stevens braked to a stop on Park Avenue South at Twenty-third Street. It was late on a weekday night but traffic was still heavy. It never seemed to stop in this city.

For days he had been in a state of anxious depression, fearing that thirty years of fitting himself into the straitjacket life of a regular member of the smugly comfortable community of Monroe had come to naught. The adopted boy — the Vessel — was dead. The suddenness of it had caught him unawares. The Vessel had been Jonah's reponsibility. If the Vessel had died before completing his purpose . . .

But the One still was. He sensed that. And now tonight, a vision . . . a crimson vision.

He was nearing his destination. Carol's aunt's apartment was not far from here. She lived in the area called Gramercy Park. That was where the vision was sending him.

He cupped his hand over his good right eye to see if there was anything perking in the left under the patch.

Nothing.

The vision had come a number of times during the day. He had seen Grace Nevins' head being crushed by a steel ripping bar. He had seen his own hand wielding that bar. The vision was assigning him a task.

Grace Nevins was to die.

And tonight.

Jonah wondered why. Not that he minded a bit. He had as much feeling for that fat biddy as he did for anyone else. He was just curious as to why her specifically.

Revenge? She hadn't had any direct involvement in Jim's death, so that didn't make sense. Why? Did she pose a future threat to the One? That had to be it. And the threat must be in the near future. That would explain the sense of urgency that had accompanied the vision.

He drummed his bony fingers on the steering wheel, waiting for the light to change. He had made good time in from Long Island, but still the sense of urgency plagued him.

Outside the car, the city sang to him. Its daily bumps and bruises, its longterm festering sores of agony and despair were contrapuntal melodies undulating through his head. Around him he heard the harmonies of the filth, the disease, the pain, the anguish, the misery of the people packed together here, humming from the alleys, cooing from the shabby apartments above the stores, shouting from the subway tunnels below the pavement. To his right, Union Square seemed to glow and seethe with the lyrics of a thousand tiny deaths as its drugged denizens destroyed themselves by slow degrees.

He wished he could stop and savor it, but there was work to be done. He reached over and patted the hexagonal shaft of the three-foot curved ripping bar that rested on the seat beside him.

Work.

At last the green. He pressed the accelerator and eased ahead.

4.

Grace stepped into her apartment and flipped the light switch. Nothing happened. She moved it up and down twice more and still no light. The bulb had gone again. Seemed she had just replaced it a couple of weeks ago. Or had it been longer? She couldn't remember. Her mind had been jumbled by the horrors of Sunday. That awful scene with Emma at the funeral yesterday had only made matters worse.

She had been spending most of her free time in church, praying for understanding and guidance. Martin had called her last night, asking her why she had missed the regular Wednesday prayer meeting. She had told him she was through with the Chosen, omitting the fact that it had been very hard to stay away last night.

Something continued to draw her to that group.

She began feeling her way into the darkened apartment. She had only a few minutes to grab a bite to eat and then catch the bus to the hospital for her shift.

Suddenly she froze. Someone else was in her apartment!

Her eyes weren't accustomed to the dark yet. She sensed rather than saw movement — rapid movement — to her right. Instinctively she ducked, and in that instant the front of the étagère imploded above her from the force of the blow aimed her way.

Panic gripped her heart like a cold, mailed fist. A robber! Or worse yet, a rapist! Trying to kill her!

As fragments of shattered glass rained down on her back, she scrabbled away on her hands and knees. Behind her something heavy thudded on the rug with crushing force.

He must have a bat! A heavy bat! To break every bone in her body!

She scurried under the dining room table. Something hit it hard — hard enough to crack the mahogany top. With a burst of fear-fueled strength, Grace reared up under the far edge of the table, taking it with her. She tilted it, then tipped it over toward her attacker.

Then she ran screaming for the door. A hand grabbed at her collar, catching the cord of her scapular and the chain of her Miraculous Medal. She felt them cut into her throat for an instant, then they broke, freeing her to reach the door.

She fumbled with the knob, got it open, and fairly leapt out into the hall, pulling the door closed behind her. She didn't stop screaming then, especially when something thudded heavily against the inside of the door, cracking its outer skin. She continued to howl, stumbling to the other two doors on her floor, pounding on them for help. But when no one answered, Grace ran down the stairs as fast as she dared, almost tripping and falling twice on the way.

She reached the street and ran for the corner phone to dial 911.

5.

"He sure was thorough, Mrs. Nevins," the young patrolman said. "Looks like he smashed almost everything you own."

Grace didn't correct him about the "Mrs." Instead she stared in horror at the shambles of her little apartment. Every inch of floor, every counter and tabletop was littered with debris. All of her statues — the Infants of Prague and the Virgin Marys and all the others — were smashed beyond recognition. Her relics had been ground into dust. Her bibles and other holy books had been torn to shreds. Everything —

She paused. No. That wasn't quite right. Most of her dishes were intact in the china cabinet. The phone had been torn out and smashed, but the screen of her TV was unmarred. And the vase in the corner by the front door was on its side, but intact.

"Not everything," she said to the policeman.

"Ma'am?"

"He only broke my religious articles. Nothing else."

He looked around. "Chee! You're right! Ain't that the weirdest thing?"

Grace could only shudder in fear.

6.

Emma waited in bed. It was early, but Jonah had gone out on another of his unexplained nocturnal jaunts. Now he was back. She heard the garage door slide down, heard him enter through the kitchen. Her excitement grew.

She hoped this would be like that Monday night a couple of weeks ago when he had come in late and had done her again and again through most of the night. She needed a night like that now, needed something to blot out the thoughts of poor Jimmy and his terrible, senseless death. They hadn't seen too much of their adopted son since his marriage, but just knowing that he was down the block and around the corner had been enough. Now he was gone. Forever.

And where was Jonah? What was taking him so long?

Then she heard the refrigerator door open, heard the *ker-shoosh* of a beer can being opened.

Emma bit a trembling lip. Oh, no. The beer meant he wouldn't be excited, wouldn't be in the mood. He'd sit there in the living room in the dark and sip beer for hours.

She turned over and buried her face in her pillow to muffle the sobs she could no longer control.

NINETEEN

Friday
March 15

1.

"Honey, you're not looking well at all," Kay Allen said. "I mean like physically, y'know? Y'eatin'?"

Carol glanced across the desk at her supervisor. There was real concern in Kay's eyes. Hospital social work might have given her a tough skin in regard to patients' problems, but she seemed genuinely worried about Carol.

"I'm feeling worse than I look," Carol told her.

The sickening nightmares kept her in a state of constant nausea. The dreams, combined with the depression and the constant dull ache of loss, had left her without an appetite. She was pale, she knew, and she had lost weight.

She had come here for lack of anyplace better to go. Everywhere but the hospital reminded her of Jim. Everyone she met seemed so uncomfortable. No one made eye contact, and some even crossed the street to avoid her. She knew they felt for her, and knew there were no words to express what they were feeling. Still, it made her wish she could run off to a deserted island somewhere. It wouldn't much increase her present sense of isolation. Aunt Grace was still unreachable. Emma only made her feel worse. She felt completely alone in the world.

"Maybe you should have Doc Alberts check you over."

"I think I need a shrink more."

In an uncharacteristic show of affection, Kay reached across the desk and grasped her hand.

"Oh, honey, I'd need a shrink, too, if I'd been through what you have!"

Carol was touched by Kay's empathy and felt herself fill up. But she was *not* going to cry here.

"So," she said, lightening her voice, "what's new here?"

Kay released her hand.

"Not much. It's still a funny farm. Oh, your old friend Mr. Dodd is back."

"Oh, no. Why?"

"Had a full-blown stroke this time. One of his rusty pipes finally clogged and ruptured all the way. They don't think he's gonna make it."

Wasn't there any good news left in the world?

"Maybe I'll stop up and see him."

"You're still on leave of absence, honey. Besides, he won't know you're there. He's been gorked out since he hit the emergency room four days ago."

"I think I'll just look in on him anyway. A social call."

"Suit yourself, honey."

Carol walked the long route to the elevators. She wasn't in any hurry. The only other place to go was back to the mansion, and she wasn't looking forward to that. In the back of her mind was the idea of coming back to work next week. She certainly didn't need the money — all of Jim's inherited millions passed directly to her — but she needed the distraction, needed to fill the hours. Maybe if she got involved again in patient problems, she could get a better grip on her own.

Mr. Dodd was in a semiprivate on the third floor. Neither he nor his roommate were conscious. The shades were drawn. Despite the warm spell and her sweater and bellbottom jeans, Carol felt a chill in the room.

She stepped toward the bed. In the dim light she could see an IV running into his arm; a green nasal oxygen tube snaked from his upper lip to the tank that stood like a steely sentinel next to his headboard. His eyes were closed, his face was slack and his mouth hung open. He could have been sleeping, but as soon as Carol heard his breathing she knew he was in serious trouble.

His respirations would follow a cycle, starting off shallow, then getting progessively deeper until he seemed to be filling and refilling his lungs to maximum capacity, then gradually becoming shallower and shallower again. Until they stopped. That was the scary part. There would be a period when there was no breathing at all. It never lasted more than thirty seconds but it seemed to take forever before the cycle started all over again.

She'd heard it before. Cheyne-Stokes respiration — that was what one of the internists had told her last year when she had first witnessed it. It was common in comas, especially when brought on by a massive stroke.

Poor Mr. Dodd. Back only a week after his discharge. She hoped his last days were happy and peaceful in Maureen's home. She was sure both daughters were glad now that they had listened to her. Otherwise, if they'd put him in a nursing home only to have this happen, they'd probably never forgive themselves.

She adjusted the covers over him, then gave his hand a gentle squeeze.

That was when it happened.

With no warning, Mr. Dodd reared up in his bed. His eyes were wide. The left side of his face was slack, but the right was a half-mask of horror as he began screaming hoarsely through his toothless, lopsided mouth.

"Get Away! Get Away From Me! Oh, god save me, get away, get away, get awaaaaay!"

Startled and frightened, Carol stumbled away from the bed just as his nurse came charging in.

"What happened? What did you do?"

"N-nothing," Carol said. "I only touched his hand."

Mr. Dodd was now pointing at her. His eyes were still wide but his sightless gaze was directed straight ahead. His trembling finger, however, pointed directly at Carol.

"Get Away! Get Awaaaay!"

"You'd better leave," the nurse said.

Carol needed no persuasion. She turned and fled the room. Mr. Dodd's voice followed her all the way to the elevator.

"GET AWAAAAAAY!"

The elevator doors finally closed off the sound. Unnerved, she stood trembling as the car began its descent.

I only touched his hand.

As she walked out into the sunny employee parking lot, she decided that maybe today she could bring herself to return to Tall Oaks. She had wanted to visit the grave site yesterday but hadn't had the courage to brave it in the rain. Now she felt she *needed* to be near Jim, just to sit by his grave and talk to him, even if he couldn't answer.

Oh, Jim. How am I going to get by without you?

2.

There was an unseasonably warm breeze blowing across the bare knolls of Tall Oaks. They didn't allow gaudy headstones here. Only quiet granite plaques laid flat in the ground. A lot like Arlington National Cemetary, in a way. Carol liked the style. If she didn't look too closely, she could almost convince herself that she was trodding the back lawn of a huge provincial estate.

Jim's grave was easy to find, and would continue to be so until they cleared away the flowers. About twenty yards to the right of his was another flower-decked plot where someone else had been buried the same day as Jim.

Carol paused involuntarily in her approach, then forced herself forward. She had to get used to this, because she intended to come here often. She was not going to forget Jim. If he couldn't live on in this world, she would see to it that he stayed alive in her memory and in her heart.

When she reached the grave, she stared down in shock. What she saw filled her with a creeping terror that sent her running for the car. She wanted to scream but there was no one to hear her.

There was someone she could call, though. She knew of only one person she could turn to about this.

3.

"Look! You see it? It's dead! All of it! Like it's been dead for weeks!"

The afternoon sun was warm on Bill's back as he stared down at Jim's grave. He removed the windbreaker he had thrown over his short-sleeved tunic and collar; he shut out Carol's agitated voice for moment as he tried to think. She had called him in a state of panic this morning about Jim's grave. He hadn't been able to get a really clear story out of her, but had soothed her with the promise that he would come out to Monroe as soon as he could get away from St. F.'s.

The rectangle of grass over Jim's grave was all a dull, dead brown.

Bill resisted an urge to say *So what?* and tried to tune in to Carol's emotions as she huddled behind him, shielding herself from the grave, as if afraid it would bite her.

"Why is it dead, Bill?" she was saying. "Just give me a good, sane reason why it's dead here on this grave and nowhere else and I promise you I'll never bother you again!"

"Maybe they didn't put the sod back right and it dried out," he said.

"Dried out? It *poured* all day yesterday!"

"Well then, maybe they didn't cut it thick enough and killed the roots. There's a special art to cutting sod properly, you know."

"Okay, fine. But do you really think that they cut it all wrong over Jim's grave and all right on that one over there? They were both buried the same day!"

"Maybe —"

"Christ, Bill! Even if they cut the damn grass and sprinkled the clippings over his grave, it would still be green now!"

Bill stared at the dead brown blades curling up from the dirt and had to admit Carol was right. This grass was *dead.* It was as if the life had been sucked right out of it. But how? And why? Why just here in this neat rectangle? Unless someone had poured an herbicide on it. But that didn't make sense. Who would want to do something like that?

And the most disturbing part of the dead patch was the way it didn't quite reach the edges of the replaced sod. The dead grass was confined to a neat narrow rectangle exactly the size of Jim's coffin lying six feet below. Carol hadn't mentioned it. Maybe she hadn't noticed. Bill wasn't about to point it out to her.

He turned and looked at her, saw her tortured, frightened eyes, and wanted desperately to help her. But how?

"Carol, what do you want me to say?"

Her control began to crack. Her face screwed up and tears began to slide down her cheeks.

"I want you to tell me that he wasn't possessed by the devil and that there's a good reason for the grass over his grave to be dead!" She leaned against him and began to sob. "That's all I want! That's not so much, is it?"

Hesitantly, Bill put his arms around her and gently patted her back. It seemed such a wholly inadequate gesture, but it was the best he could do, the most he dared do.

For contact with Carol was sending intensely pleasurable but unwanted sensations racing up and down his body. All those hidden feelings and desires that plagued him in his bed at night were awakening here in the day and beginning to move. He hugged her a moment longer then, with difficulty, put a little space between them.

"No, it's not much at all to ask," he said, giving her a stern look. "But I'm surprised you have to ask it."

"I know, I know," she said, and lowered her eyes. "But after all the things those awful people said on Sunday, and then to come up here and see this, I . . . I just cracked a little."

"It *is* weird," he said, glancing back at the dead grass, "but I'm sure there's a good explanation that doesn't rely on the devil."

"Good. Tell me what it is."

"Let's head back to the car," he said.

He kept a protective arm around her shoulder as he guided her back down the hill toward the drive. He couldn't bring himself to break physical contact with her. Not yet, anyway.

He finally let go when he opened the door for her on the passenger side.

"What do you think?" she said as he started the car.

She was so hungry for an explanation — he wished he had one for her.

"I don't know. I'm not a horticulturist. But surely you of all people know that Jim wasn't possessed by the devil or any of that nonsense. We know he was an atheist, but the idea of Satan was as unacceptable to him as the idea of God."

"But what about the hair on his palms? You heard them out there when they saw it. They called it 'the Mark of the Beast.' They said it's a sign that Satan dwells within."

"Jim was a hairy guy. A hairy palm means he was born with hair follicles in an unusual spot, and that's all it means. Nothing more. Probably genetic. If he was really a clone of that Hanley fellow, then I bet Hanley had hairy palms as well."

"Well," Carol said slowly, "Hanley did look pretty hairy in those old photos."

"What'd I tell you? Really, Carol, all that Satan garbage is just that — garbage."

In the ensuing silence he glanced over and saw her shocked expression.

"Bill!" she said. "You're a priest!"

He sighed. "I know I'm a priest. I've spent the last decade studying theology — studying it intensely — and believe me, Carol, no one in the Catholic intellectual community believes in Satan."

She smiled. Sadly.

"Something wrong?" he asked.

"'Catholic intellectuals,'" she said. "I can hear Jim now."

Bill's throat tightened. "So can I. He'd say, 'That's an oxymoron if I ever heard one.'"

"Oh, God, Bill!" she sobbed. "I miss him so!"

"I know you do, Carol," he said, feeling her pain, sharing a part of it. "So keep him alive inside you: Hold on to those memories."

4.

Carol pulled herself together with an effort.

"But what you said before, about not believing in Satan — you sounded almost like Jim!"

"Well, Jim and I rarely disagreed on ethics or morals, just on their philosophical basis. And we'd both agree that there's no such being as Satan. Frankly I don't know of a single Jesuit who believes in Satan. There's God and there's us. There's no single being who embodies evil skulking through the world trying to get us to commit sins. That's a myth, a folk tale that's useful in helping people grasp the problem of evil. The evil in the world comes from *us*." He jabbed a finger against his breast bone. "From in here."

"And Hell?"

"Hell? Do you think there's a place somewhere, a room or a cavern where all the sinners go to be tormented by demons? Think about it, Carol."

She thought about it, and it did seem kind of farfetched.

"It's all personification," he said. "It's a way of giving people a handle on some complex problems. It's especially useful with children — they have an easier time with theological concepts if we dress them up in myths. When we tell the kids, 'Resist the Devil,' we're really telling them to hold out against the worst that's in them."

"Lots of adults believe in those myths as well — I mean, really *cling* to them."

Bill shrugged. "A lot of adults never grow up when it comes to religion. They could never accept that Satan is just a symbolic externalization of the evil that lurks in all of us."

"But where does that evil in us come from?"

"From the merging of the spirit and the flesh. The spiritual part of us comes from God and wants to return to Him. The physical part of us is like a wild beast that wants what it wants when it wants it and doesn't care who gets hurt in its drive to get it. Life is a process of striking a balance between the two. If the spiritual part prevails, it is allowed to return to God when life is over. If the baser drives and emotions of the physical aspect taint the spirit too deeply, it is not allowed to return to God. *That*, Carol, is hell. Hell is not a fiery place with pitchfork-wielding demons. It's a state of being bereft of God's presence."

5.

Carol was still trying to digest Bill's words when they pulled into the driveway of the mansion.

"I know it sounds pretty radical," he said, "but really it's not. It's just a different perspective. We tend to take what the nuns taught us in school and tuck it away in the backs of our minds and accept it at face value without question for the rest of our lives. But real grown-ups need a grown-up theology."

"I'm working on it," she said.

"And just think about this 'Mark of the Beast' or 'Vessel of Satan' or 'Gateway for Satan' crap. Even if you want to cling to the old mythology, remember that God doesn't move in obvious ways, that's why it's a trial at times to keep one's faith in Him. If Satan existed, don't you think he'd avoid the obvious as well? Because finding proof of the Ultimate Evil — Satan — would make it so much easier for us to believe in the Ultimate Good — God. An' dat wouldn't be to dat ol' debbil Satan's liking, would it now?"

Carol couldn't help laughing — the first time all week.

"You make it sound so simple."

"That's probably because I'm over simplifying. It's not simple. But I hope it helps."

"It does. Oh, believe me, it does."

She felt so much better. She saw the whole idea of Jim being possessed by the devil for the juvenile, superstitious silliness it was. The fear, the uncertainty, all slipped away, to be replaced by a sense of peace.

All thanks to Bill.

But as Bill opened the mansion's front door for her and ushered her inside, the gratitude evaporated in a blast of rage.

You smug, sanctimonious son of a bitch!

She staggered a step. Where had *that* come from?

She didn't feel that way about Bill at all! Why that instant of hatred? He was only trying to soothe her, doing his best to —

— impress her with his pseudointellectual bullshit and make himself look so infinitely superior, so far above the petty fears of the common folk like her. Pompous, self-righteous Jesuit bastard! So fucking aloof! Thinks he's immune to the insecurities and frailties of the flesh! She'd show him!

Carol didn't understand this sudden rage within her. It was a wild, alien emotion, coming out of nowhere, imposing itself on her, enveloping her, making her want to claw at Bill's blue eyes with her nails, making her want to bring him down, degrade him, humiliate him, break him, drag him into a mire of self-loathing and make him wallow in it, rub his face in it, drown him in it.

As soon as he was in the foyer, she closed the door behind her. Passion was suddenly a white-hot flame inside her.

"Kiss me, Bill," she said.

He stared at her incredulously, as if trying to make himself believe that he really hadn't heard her correctly. A small voice deep inside her screamed, *No, I didn't mean that!* But a much stronger voice was overpowering the first, shouting that she did mean just that. And more.

6.

"Carol?" Bill said, watching her. Her face had changed, as if the lighting had shifted to give her a strange, almost malevolent look. "Are you all right?"

"Of course I am. I just want you. Right now. Right here."

"Are you out of your *mind?*"

"I've never been saner," she said, fixing him with her bright, slightly unfocused eyes as she slowly pulled off her sweater.

"Stop that!"

"You say that, but you don't really mean it," she said, smiling. "You've wanted me since high school, haven't you? And I've wanted you. Don't you think we've waited long enough?"

She reached around behind her and began unfastening her bra.

"Carol, please!"

Then the bra came loose and she shrugged free of it, letting it drop to the floor. Bill's mouth went dry as he stared at her bare breasts. They weren't the big bouncy kind he had seen in the men's magazines he had confiscated from the boys over the years, but they were round and firm with pink nipples and they were right within reach.

"Who's going to know, and who's it going to hurt?" she said, in a softly reasoning voice as she drew long strands of her sandy hair over her shoulders, pulling them taut and strumming them back and forth across her breasts until the nipples stood out hard and erect, just as Bill felt himself becoming hard and erect within his trousers. "After all this time, don't you think we owe it to each other? Just this once?"

"Carol —"

"Come on. It's sort of like unfinished business, don't you think?"

Bill closed his eyes. The idea was so appealing. It was almost as if she were echoing thoughts from his own subconscious. In a way, it really was unfinished business, a ghost from his past that would haunt him indefinitely if he didn't do something to exorcise it. Just this once, with Carol, his old love. What could be more perfect? How good to surrender to this delicious warmth spreading from his groin and suffusing his whole being. Just this once and then he could put her behind him and get on with his vocation unencumbered.

When he opened his eyes, he stared in awe. She had slipped out of her jeans and panties and stood completely naked before him. She was beautiful — so beautiful! His eyes were drawn to her light brown pubic hair. He had never seen a completely naked woman before, even in a photo, and this one was naked for him, in the flesh, and she was Carol.

"Come on," she said, smiling and moving closer. She took his hand and placed it against her breast. He could feel the nipple arching against his palm. "Just for old-times' sake."

Just once? In the long run, would it matter if he broke his vow of chastity just once? He tried to reason against that seductive thought but his mind didn't seem to be working too well at the moment.

She released his hand and went down on her knees in front of him.

Just this once. In the long run, in the big picture, what could it matter?

7.

He was weakening. She could feel the arrogant bastard's defenses crumbling as she knelt before him and ran her fingers over the bulge behind his fly. A wave of exultation engulfed her. She felt strong, powerful, as if she could conquer the world. The feeling was better than sex, better than the best orgasm she had ever had.

She reached for the zipper on Bill's pants. If she could get him in her mouth, he'd be hers, she knew it. There'd be no turning back for him then.

She smiled.

So much for keeping the spirit unsullied by the flesh, Mr. Jesuit priest!

Suddenly he backed away two stumbling steps. His face was flushed, tortured. Beads of perspiration dotted his forehead and upper lip.

"No."

The word was spoken softly, in a hoarse, agonized voice, but it was like a red-hot spike driving into her pelvis. Suddenly the powerful feeling was ripped away. The world seemed to teeter, the walls of the mansion leaned toward her, as if about to crash down upon her.

And the pain — the pain inside was like hell.

Bill had turned away. His words were hurried, breathless, spoken to the empty rear section of the front hall.

"Carol, please! I don't know what's gotten into you, but this is no good!"

More pain, but she forced out the words.

"It's love!" she said to his back. "It's sex! What's more natural than that?"

"Yes, but I made vows, Carol! And one of them was chastity. You can argue all you want about the wisdom and utility of that kind of vow, and whether it's productive or counterproductive —and believe me, I've heard *all* the arguments — but the fact remains that I made it freely and I intend to hold to it."

The pain drove Carol to the floor. It felt as if something were slowly ripping apart inside her.

"But you of all people, Carol. I can't understand you," he said, his voice slowly returning to normal. "Even if you think my vows are stupid, you know what they mean to me. Why would you try to get me to break them? Especially now with Jim barely cold in his —"

He turned and saw the agony in her face.

"My God! What's wrong?"

Something felt hot and wet on her thighs. Carol looked down and saw blood gushing from her vagina. The room swam around her. And the pain was so much worse.

"Help me, Bill! I think I'm going to die!"

TWENTY

1.

"Do you really find comfort in all these little statues and knickknacks?"

Grace regarded Mr. Veilleur with a mixture of fondness and wariness as he finished gluing the head of the Archangel Gabriel back onto its body. Brother Robert was at the far end of the living room, sorting the pieces of the large Madonna.

If you had my past, she thought, *you'd take comfort wherever you found it!*

"Comfort," she said. "Yes, that's a good word. They do bring me comfort. Just as the two of you do today."

Brother Robert wasn't listening, but Mr. Veilleur looked up at her with his intense blue eyes. Grace felt an immense attraction for the man. Nothing sordid. Nothing like that. He was perhaps ten years older than she, and talked freely of his wife, to whom he seemed very devoted. There was nothing sexual in the warmth he inspired in her. It was just that his presence gave her such a safe, secure feeling and, Heaven knew, after last night's terror, security had become a precious commodity.

"It must have been a terrible experience for you," he said. "I thought you wouldn't want to be alone."

"I didn't! But how did you know?"

"I called — or tried to — to see how you were faring after Sunday. The phone was out of order. I came by and learned about the break-in from the super."

She hadn't been able to stay here last night. The young patrolman had been kind enough to drive her over to Martin's home. He and Brother Robert had been shocked by her story. They gave her the use of one of the spare bedrooms. But even with the coming of this bright sunny day she had been unable to bring herself to return to the apartment.

Then Mr. Veilleur had shown up at the brownstone this afternoon. He had offered to escort her back. Brother Robert had come along. The super had replaced the lock on the door and went looking for a spare phone to lend her until the phone company could replace the one that had been smashed.

"Why are you helping me fix my things when you no doubt think they're just a silly woman's toys?"

"I doubt that you know very much at all what I think," he said. There was no hostility in the remark. The tone was casual, as if stating a simple fact.

"I'm quite sure that you do not believe as we believe," Grace said, gently challenging him. She wanted to draw him out. He intrigued her so.

"I thought I had made that quite clear."

"Then why do you keep coming back to us — I mean, the Chosen? And why are you here today? I'm enormously grateful for your presence, but surely you have something better to do with a Friday afternoon than help me repair my apartment."

"At the moment, I do not," he said with a quick smile. "And as to why I keep coming back to the self-proclaimed Chosen, I'm not all that sure myself. But this group of yours —"

"It's not mine," she was quick to say, for she did not in any way wish to be held responsible for what had happened to poor Jim. She glanced at the preoccupied monk. "It's Brother Robert's group."

"I meant yours by association. But no matter. This tiny group of Catholics seems to comprise the sum total of everyone who is aware of the return . . ."

His voice trailed off.

"Of the Antichrist?" she offered. "Satan?"

The term seemed to annoy him. "Yes, yes, if you must. But I am drawn to the group. I sense that the one who will finally stand against the threat will be drawn from these Chosen." He looked at her intently. "Perhaps it will be you."

The idea jolted Grace. She almost dropped the broken base of the Infant of Prague she had been holding.

"Oh, Heavens! I hope not!"

"For your sake, so do I." He paused, then said, "But I can't help but wonder if there might be a chance that the attack last night was related to this . . . thing you are involved in."

"You mean," she said, chilled, "someone might have been after *me* — personally?"

"Only idle speculation," he said, waving a hand in dismissal. "I don't mean to alarm you." He held up the repaired Archangel. "There! The glue is set. Where does he go?"

But the idea would not go away. What if it hadn't been a robber? What if the intruder had been lying in wait for the sole purpose of killing her? What if her time of judgment had come and she was to pay for all those lives she had taken in her past? Please, no! It couldn't be! Not yet! She hadn't had time to make full atonement! She didn't want to spend all of eternity in Hell!

Just then there was a heavy pounding on her door and she jumped in fear.

Mr. Veilleur rose to his feet. "I'll get it."

When he opened the door, Martin was there. He looked Mr. Veilleur up and down.

"What are *you* doing here?"

"Just helping out," the older man replied with a slow smile. Martin's roosterish posturings seemed to amuse him.

Martin turned to her. "I've been trying to call here for the past hour!"

Grace pointed to the shattered remnants of her telephone.

"He got that, too. I'm still waiting for a replacement."

Martin looked around, apparently noticing the carnage for the first time.

"Praise God, it looks like the work of the Devil himself!"

"Is a crowbar the devil's truncheon of choice?" Mr. Veilleur said, still looking amused.

Brother Robert stepped forward. "What is it, Martin?"

"I've been having Grace's niece watched," he said in a low voice.

Grace was shocked and annoyed by the news.

Brother Robert appeared surprised as well. His fingers idly twisted a strand of his beard as he spoke.

"Why didn't I know of this, Martin?"

Martin did not meet his gaze.

"Because I was pretty sure you wouldn't approve. But it was you who said that this isn't over yet. I figured she's our closest link to the soulless one, and to that house where I'm sure the heart of this mystery rests!"

Grace said, "But what has that —"

"She was rushed to the hospital this afternoon."

Grace leapt to her feet. "What happened?"

"I don't know. The member of our group who was watching her today called to say that after lunch she met with her priest friend — the Jesuit who tried to send us away from the mansion on Sunday — who accompanied her to the cemetary and then back to the mansion. They both went inside, and then shortly after that an ambulance raced up and took her away on a stretcher. The priest stayed in the ambulance with her all the way to the hospital."

Grace felt her heart pounding. *Poor Carol! And so soon after Jim's death! Good Lord, what can it be?*

"There's something suspicious about that priest," Martin was saying. "He's a little too cozy to this whole situation for me to believe he is completely untainted."

Brother Robert said, "The Jesuits have their own agendas, their own priorities, which don't always coincide with those of the Holy See, but I doubt he's in league with the devil."

"He's an old highschool friend of Carol's!" Grace cried. "Oh, please, God, I hope she's all right!"

"It might be just nervous collapse," Mr. Veilleur said. He had seated himself again and begun arranging the broken pieces of a plaque depicting the Annunciation. "After seeing her husband die like that, I wouldn't be surprised."

"I've got to go see her," she said, starting toward the closet for her coat.

Brother Robert said, "Why not simply call first and find out what the problem is?"

Grace looked at him and guessed from his expression that Brother Robert was just as eager as she to learn the details of Carol's illness.

"Maybe I should."

Grace got the number of Monroe Community Hospital from information and dialed. When she asked to be connected to Carol Stevens' room, there was a pause, and then she was told that the patient was taking no calls.

That upset her. No calls could mean Carol had a serious problem or perhaps had been taken to surgery.

"What's her room number?"

"Two-twelve."

"And who's her attending physician? Dr. Alberts?" She knew he had always been Carol's family doctor.

"No, it's Dr. Gallen."

Suddenly numb, Grace put down the phone without saying good-bye. It took her two tries to set it properly on its cradle.

Brother Robert, Martin, and Mr. Veilleur were all staring at her.

"What's wrong?" Brother Robert said.

"I'm not sure. Maybe nothing."

"Then why do you look as if you've seen a ghost?"

"They said her attending physician is Dr. Gallen."

"So?"

"I've heard of him. He's an obstetrician."

Mr. Veilleur dropped the Annunciation plaque.

2.

"Did I lose the baby?" Carol said, holding on to the hospital bed side rails like an overboard sailor clinging to floating debris.

Dr. Gallen shook his head. He was on the young side — maybe thirty-five — plump and fair, looking sort of like the Pillsbury Dough Boy after a visit to Brooks Brothers. He had yet to develop the imperious air of many of his colleagues. *Give him time*, Carol thought. But right now she was glad he was down to earth and amiable.

"As far as I can tell, no. You came awfully close, but I believe the fetus is still intact."

"But my pregnancy test was negative!"

"Who ordered it?"

"Uh, I did, sort of."

"When did you run it, sort of?"

"The Sunday before last."

"Almost two weeks ago. Too early. You were pregnant but your urinary HCG levels weren't high enough to give you a positive. You got a false negative. Happens all the time. A few days later and it probably would have come out positive." He waggled his finger at her good-naturedly. "That's what happens when nonmedical staff members try to play doctor without going to medical school. Now, if you'd come to me in the first —"

"How far along am I?"

"I figure four to six weeks. Probably closer to four. *If* you're still pregnant."

Carol thought her heart would stop.

" 'If?' "

"Yes. *If*. Although I'm pretty sure you haven't lost it, there's still a possibility you might have. We'll keep you off your feet a couple of days, and keep running pregnancy tests. If they remain positive, everything's go. If not, you'll have to try again."

Reality slammed into Carol with numbing force. She fought the tears.

Try again? How? Jim's dead!

The pain must have shown on her face.

Dr. Gallen said, "Is something wrong?"

"My husband . . . he was killed Sunday."

His eyes widened. "Stevens? Not *that* Stevens! Oh, I'm so sorry. I've been out of town. I'd heard about it but I . . . somehow I never made the connection. I'm really sorry."

"It's okay," she said, but it wasn't. She wondered if anything ever would be okay again.

"All right then, I guess that means we'll just have to see to it that this baby makes it," he said with a determined look in his eyes. "Right?"

She nodded, biting her lip in fear for the child.

"I'll check in on you later," he said. "I'm staying right on top of this. All night if necessary." He gave her a quick wave and then he was gone.

Something about him almost made her believe that they could pull it off.

3.

"It's all beginning to make sense to me now," Mr. Veilleur said as Grace watched him pick up the shards of the plaque.

"Good for you," Martin said sourly. "It has been perfectly clear to us for many weeks now."

"Easy, Martin," Brother Robert said. "A little more tolerance. Remember, faith is a gift."

"Has it really been all that clear to you?" Mr. Veilleur said to Martin. There was no amused smile playing about his lips now. He looked positively grim.

"Of course. The Antichrist is coming and —"

"Can we dispense with the Judeo-Christian mythology for a while? It only muddies the water."

"*Mythology?*" Martin said, huffing and drawing himself up. "You are talking about the Word of God!"

"Let's just use a neutral term, shall we? I can't have a serious discussion if we're going to talk about 'the Antichrist.' How does 'the Presence' sound to you?

"Absolutely not!"

"Oh, come, Martin," Grace said. "That sounds pretty neutral to me. What can it hurt?"

Grace sensed that Martin was as interested as she in what Mr. Veilleur had to say, but that he didn't want to admit it.

Martin glanced at Brother Robert, who nodded.

"It's all right, Martin," he said slowly.

Martin turned to Mr. Veilleur. "Okay. But just remember that —"

"Fine," Mr. Veilleur said. "Now tell me, all of you: When did you get your first inkling of the Presence?"

"I'm not sure," Brother Robert said. "It was all so vague at first. Early February, I'd say."

Martin agreed, nodding vigorously. "Definitely."

"How about the speaking in tongues?"

"Oh, that's been happening since we first began meeting last year. It's common in Pentecostal groups."

"I mean the special tongue, the one Grace used when she spoke to me that night at the meeting."

Grace shivered at the memory. "The one you called the Old Tongue?"

He nodded, but kept his eyes fixed on Martin. "Yes. When did you first hear that?"

"That I can tell you. It was shortly before Brother Robert arrived. I remember it because it was so remarkable. Everyone who spoke in tongues that night spoke in the same language. It was Septuagesima Sunday — February eleventh."

"Interesting," Mr. Veilleur said. "That was the night Dr. Hanley's plane crashed."

"Do you think there's a connection?" Grace asked.

"Think about it," the older man said. "That seems to be the event that set all the other events in motion. Of course, there was another event that might have preceded the crash."

"What?" Grace said simultaneously with Brother Robert and Martin.

"The conception of the Stevens baby."

Grace felt as if all of her blood had drained out in a rush. The words seemed to crystalize an idea in her mind. It was only partially formed now, but it was growing.

"Why would that —?"

"Consider the sequence of events. Hanley's death made James Stevens a rich man. James Stevens' death makes his wife a rich woman, and guarantees that their child will be raised in an atmosphere of financial power, leaving only one person between the child and control of the Hanley millions. Doesn't it all strike you as a little too convenient?"

"The child!" Brother Robert whispered. "Of course! The child is the Antichrist!" His eyes were bright with wonder. "It's so obvious now! Satan used Stevens' soulless body as a conduit through which he could invade this sphere by entering a woman and becoming human flesh! Evil incarnate!"

"You're partly correct," Mr. Veilleur said with a sigh. "But the Presence has been in 'this sphere,' as you put it, much longer than a month."

"How do you know so much?" Martin said.

Really, Grace thought, *he's acting very childish.*

"You wouldn't understand. You wouldn't *want* to understand. Let's leave it at that, shall we?"

"Tell me, please," Brother Robert said. "When do you think the Presence entered the clone's body?"

"In May of 1941, I believe. Shortly after James Stevens was conceived. Perhaps there is something to this business of the soul after all. It's very possible that James Stevens, being a clone, never had one. That being the case, the Presence probably thought he had found the perfect vehicle for himself. But instead, he wound up trapped. And he remained trapped inside James Stevens' body — impotent, ineffectual, raging — for over a quarter-century. Until —"

"Until Carol conceived Jim's child!" Grace blurted.

"Exactly. Whatever powers the Presence possesses were blocked while it inhabited James. It remained viable but . . . disconnected, so to speak. A larva locked in a living chrysalis. But when James Stevens fathered a child, the Presence broke free of him and 'became flesh,' as Martin might say."

"You mean it's taken over Carol's child?" Grace said. The thought horrified her.

"No," Mr. Veilleur said with a slow shake of his head. "It *is* the child. From the moment of conception, its powers have begun to grow. That is the *wrongness* you've sensed in the world for the past month or so. It is the Presence, maturing within Carol Stevens, growing stronger with each passing day."

"This sounds like *Rosemary's Baby,*" Grace said.

Martin said, "God works in subtle and mysterious ways. Perhaps He inspired that author to write such a book; perhaps He made it a best-seller as a warning to us all!"

Grace was dubious. "God works through the *Times* best-seller list?"

"His hand is everywhere!" Martin leapt to his feet. "And even now the Antichrist is growing within the clone's wife. That explains why we sensed no diminution of the evil when the clone died."

"Stop calling him that!" Grace said, her growing resentment of Martin's callousness finally reaching the breaking point. "He was my niece's husband. He had a name. And we are responsible for his death!"

"That was an accident!"

"An accident that proved very convenient for the Presence," Mr. Veilleur said.

Martin looked shocked for a moment. He made no reply.

"I fear Mr. Veilleur may have a point," Brother Robert said. "And speaking of names, don't you have one for this Presence, as you call it?"

"Actually, it's a him, and he has many names, none of which you've ever heard, so they would mean nothing to you."

"How about 'Satan?'" Brother Robert said.

"Satan? Forget Satan! Something evil is coming — you're right about that — but it's not your Satan. Something far worse is on the way, something beyond your worst nightmares. The Antichrist? If only it were! When it gets here, you'll long for your Antichrist. Because prayers won't help you. Neither will guns or bombs."

The utter conviction in Mr. Veilleur's voice drove a shaft of terror through Grace's soul.

"How . . . how do you know so much about him?"

Mr. Veilleur gazed out the window as a stray cloud passed across the sun. "We've met before."

4.

Bill came in, entering her hospital room like an unarmed man entering a gladiator ring.

"Are you okay, Carol?"

Carol's control almost dissolved at the sight of him. She remembered the afternoon — Bill carrying her to the couch, covering her with a blanket, calling the first aid squad, and staying by her side during the ambulance ride.

"Oh, Bill!" she sobbed.

She sat up and lifted her arms, aching to embrace him. Her unaccountable lust of a few hours ago was gone now, gone as if it had never been. This was for friendship, from a deep, simple need for someone solid to hold, to cling to.

But Bill only grasped one of her hands and looked down at her with worried eyes. That had always been his way, it seemed — when she had needed some hands-on support after her parents were killed, he had backed off, just as he was doing now.

But who can blame him for being gun-shy after the show I put on a few hours ago?

She felt her face redden with the memory of it.

"Please, Bill," she said. "I'm so sorry about what I did to you before. I don't know what happened to me. It was like someone else had taken me over."

"It's okay," he said softly, smiling and patting her hand. "We both survived."

"But the baby almost didn't."

His hand tightened on hers. "Baby?"

"Yes! Dr. Gallen says there's every chance the baby's still okay."

"You're pregnant?"

"Four to six weeks along. Maybe that's why I acted so crazy back at the mansion. They say the hormone changes in pregnancy make some women do crazy things."

"I don't know much about that sort of thing," he said, grinning shyly. "But please don't ever do anything like that again. I know they say beware the Ides of March, but you almost gave me a heart attack!" He paused as his smile faded. "A baby . . ."

His voice choked off and she saw tears spring into his eyes as he worked to speak again.

Finally he managed to say, "Carol, that's wonderful!"

She shook her head and then began to cry herself, unable to hold it in any longer.

"Not so wonderful!" she said finally. "Why couldn't this have happened a year ago? It stinks! Jim's child and he'll never see him! He wanted a child so bad and we weren't sure we could ever have one, and now we do but he's gone and the baby will be born without a father! Why does God play such rotten, dirty tricks?"

"I don't know. But maybe it's not so rotten. I mean, in a way, it means that Jim is still alive, doesn't it?"

Struck suddenly by the wonderfulness of the thought, Carol slowly leaned back on the pillow and allowed herself to float on the warmth and comfort it brought.

5.

Grace felt cold all over. She rubbed her hands together as she spoke.

"Then you think we played into the hands of this . . . this Presence when we went out to Monroe. Do you think it was influencing us? Do you think we've been tricked all along?"

"Never!" Martin cried. "How can you say such a thing! The Spirit was with us, guiding us!"

"Wait, Martin," Brother Robert said. "Let us hear Mr. Veilleur's answer. Explain, please."

"Well," Mr. Veilleur said, looking older than when he had arrived here earlier this afternoon, "there *are* two sides to this. I think you've all been touched by the other side, the one that would resist the Presence. The reason isn't clear yet, but I think the one who has been chosen to stand against the Presence will emerge soon."

"The way is clear enough, isn't it?" Martin said. "The baby must never be born!"

"Carol is my niece!" Grace said, a fiercely protective urge rising within her. "Look what happened to Jim! I won't allow her to be harmed! Never!"

"Of course not!" Brother Robert said, glaring at Martin. "The girl is innocent! To harm her is to sink to the level of the evil we wish to oppose!"

"Then what," Martin cried, his expression anguished, "do we do?"

Grace could think of nothing to say. Mr. Veilleur was silent.

Brother Robert turned to Grace. "Do we accept that the Antichrist dwells within your niece?"

Grace turned away. She did not want to accept that, but it explained so much. It explained her own reaction that night a month ago when Carol and Jim visited. Carol must have been pregnant then, and Grace must have sensed the Evil One within her! And later that very night she had unconsciously turned a sacred hymn into blasphemy.

Silently she nodded. Martin, too, nodded. Mr. Veilleur sat motionless.

The monk's voice was soft. "Then we all must also agree that we cannot allow that child to be born."

"Carol is innocent!" Grace cried. "You cannot harm her!"

"I have no wish to. In fact, I forbid it. So we must find a way to strike at this unholy child without harming the woman who carries him. We need a way to cause a miscarriage, or to convince her" — he glanced heavenward — "I never thought I would ever say this — to have an abortion."

Grace felt her blood turn to ice, and then to fire, a holy fire of renewed faith as the slowly growing spark of an earlier idea burst into an epiphany of diamond clear light. Grace was lifted on wings of rapture as she wondered at the glory of God and His intricate ways.

"Oh, glory!" she cried.

"What's wrong?" Martin said, stepping back from her.

"The Chosen One, the one who will strike the fatal blow against the Antichrist. I know who it is."

Slowly, still feeling as if she were floating, Grace turned and walked into her bedroom.

This was the chance she had been praying for all these years. With this one deed she could undo all the sins she had committed in her youth. With this one death, the stains of all the other deaths on her soul would be cleansed.

Awed by the perfect symmetry of it all, she removed the bottom drawer from her dresser and reached into the open space below. Her questing fingertips found the dusty leather box she had placed there so many years ago. She pulled it out. It was as wide and as high as a cigar box but twice as long.

The tools of her salvation.

Ignoring the dust that coated it, she clutched the box to her breast and gazed into the mirror, remembering.

She had started in the mid-thirties when she had been twenty or so. After a few years, all the young girls in trouble had come to call her Amazin' Grace, for she was a trained nurse who was caring and careful with them and knew how to keep them from getting infections after her work was done. Eventually she came to see the sinfulness of what she was doing, and had put it all behind her.

Now she could only wonder if her becoming Amazin' Grace had been part of God's plan all along.

"I'm the Chosen One," she said, beaming at Brother Robert, Martin, and Mr. Veilleur as she returned to the front room.

"Chosen for what?" Martin said.

Grace opened up the box to show the curettes and dilators she had used for so many abortions.

"Chosen to stop the Antichrist."

TWENTY-ONE

Saturday
March 16

"It is too much to bear!" Brother Robert said as he strode back and forth across Martin's living room. Beyond the windows, night had fallen. The hardwood planking was cold against the soles of his bare feet but he ignored the discomfort. "It is out of the question! I cannot allow it!"

"But Brother Robert —" Martin began.

The monk cut him off. "Abortion is a sin! The Lord does not want us to sin! It is blasphemy even to consider such a thing!"

The very idea of abducting this poor young woman, whoever she was, anesthetizing her, invading her most private parts to rip out the dweller in her womb, no matter what its nature . . . it was completely alien to everything he had dedicated his life to, to everything within him. His body shook with revulsion at the mere thought of being party to such a violent act.

"Then why was I guided to the Chosen?"

Brother Robert stopped his pacing and stared at the third person in the room — Grace Nevins. She sat quietly on a chair in the corner with her hands folded on her lap. He had sensed a buried torment in the woman since their first meeting, and yesterday he had learned what it was was. Now that torment seemed to be gone, replaced by an inner peace that shone from her eyes.

"I don't know," Brother Robert told her. "But I cannot conceive that you were brought to us to commit a sin . . . to involve all of us in the sin of abortion."

"But surely this is an exception," Martin said. "Abortion is the taking of a human life. That is wrong. But this is not a human life. We're talking about the Antichrist, Satan himself. A human life would not be ended by this act. The only thing ended would be Satan's threat to Christ's salvation of mankind! To destroy him is not a sin. It is doing God's work!"

The argument was persuasive, but Brother Robert found it too pat, too facile. He was missing something. There was more to this than he had ever imagined. And so confusing. Was his faith being tested? Tested again?

Faith. He had to admit that his had been sorely tested during the past few years by what he had seen and read and heard during his travels. Not that he had ever been in danger of swerving from his lifelong devotion to God, but he could not help but feel that his faith had been sullied during his travels. It had always been like a pristine, diamond-clear liquid, hermetically sealed against contamination. But the secrets he had heard whispered in the darkest, maddest corners of his travels, and culled from the most deranged ramblings in the forbidden texts he had forced himself to read to their vile conclusions, had somehow tainted that fluid, briefly clouded it with doubt. He had persevered, however, and through fasting and prayer had restored the clarity of his faith. But the doubts had remained as an inert sediment. A sediment which had been stirred up by Mr. Veilleur.

Who was that man? What did he know? The things he had said, what he had implied, they echoed what the hidden others had said: that there was no God, no salvation, no Divine Providence, that humanity was but an old franc's worth of booty in an endless war between two amorphous, implacable, incomprehensible powers.

Brother Robert squared his shoulders. Mr. Veilleur was wrong, as were the madmen he had met in Africa and the Orient. Satan was the enemy here, and God the Father, the Son, and the Holy Spirit were guiding them all against him. But guiding them toward an abortion? He could not accept that.

The doorbell rang then. He threw a questioning glance at Martin.

"Are you expecting anyone?"

The younger man shook his head. His expression was annoyed.

"No. It's probably that pest, Veilleur. I'll get rid of him."

He hurried down the hall, but when he returned, he was not alone. Two of the Chosen were with him. Brother Robert recognized them as an especially devout pair — Charles Farmer and his sister, Louise.

"They've come to see you," Martin said, a troubled look on his face. "They say they're supposed to be here."

"We're answering the call," Charles said.

"Call?" Brother Robert said. "But the regular prayer meeting isn't until tomorrow afternoon."

The bell rang again. Martin answered it and returned this time with Mary Sumner.

"I'm here," she said brightly.

Brother Robert turned to Martin. "Did you call anyone?"

Martin shook his head. "No one."

Brother Robert was nonplussed. What was happening here?

The bell rang again. And again. Until ten new arrivals — six men and four women — were gathered in the living room.

"Why . . . why are you here?" Brother Robert asked them.

"We thought we should be," said Christopher Odell, a portly man with florid cheeks.

"But why did you — *do* you — think that?"

He shrugged, looking slightly uncomfortable. "I don't know. I'm just speaking for myself here, but for me it was a feeling . . . an overwhelming feeling, almost like a summons, that I should come here right now."

Brother Robert saw the other new arrivals nod in agreement. Suddenly he was thrilled. Something was happening here. The Spirit was gathering them together — Martin, Grace, these ten especially devout members of the Chosen, and himself — in one place for a reason.

But why?

He decided to reveal to them the moral dilemma with which he and Martin and Grace had been wrestling before their arrival. Perhaps they had been called here to provide him with a solution.

But first he needed Grace's permission. He turned to the corner where she remained seated.

"Grace," he said, "may I share with our brethren what we have learned about the Antichrist, and about you, and about the remedy you have proposed?"

She nodded, then lowered her eyes to gaze at her folded hands.

Brother Robert told them then about Carol Stevens' pregnancy, that she carried the child of Dr. Hanley's soulless clone, and about what they believed to be the true nature of that child. He saw the fear and wonder in their eyes as they listened, then saw it turn to revulsion when he told them what Grace had revealed about herself.

Murmurs of "No!" and "It can't be true!" slipped through the room as they rejected the thought that one of their number could have had such a past.

Grace's voice suddenly cut though the babble.

"It's true!" she said. She had risen from her chair and was now moving toward the center of the room. "I told myself I was helping those girls, saving them from shame and disgrace, saving them from someone else who might butcher them or even kill them with infection. And maybe that was true to some extent. But I was also doing it for the money, and simply for the thrill of *doing* it!"

The ones who had been called here backed away from her, as if mere proximity might taint them. But Brother Robert saw the pain in her face as she poured out the secret she had locked up for so long.

"I didn't think of the consequences to those unborn children, those tiny souls. I simply thought of myself as a courageous problem solver. It never occurred to me how many lives I was destroying. But there came a time when my perspective changed. I became unable to dehumanize them any longer, to reduce them mentally to mere bits of tissue by calling them embryos and fetuses. I saw them as children — and I had murdered them! I returned to the church . . . and I've been atoning for my sins ever since." She sobbed. "Please forgive me!"

"It's not up to us to forgive you," Daniel Ortega said softly. "That's in God's hands."

"But perhaps," Grace said, "I am already in God's hands. Perhaps I am to be his weapon against the Antichrist. That is why he brought me to you. Because I have the skills to prevent his enemy from being born! I can abort the Antichrist while he is small and helpless. And I can do it without harming the innocent woman who harbors him!"

A shocked babble of voices filled the room. Cries of "No!" and "Never!" Louise Farmer turned and started down the hall toward the front door, saying, "I'm not listening to any more of this!"

As Brother Robert raised his hands to quiet them, he felt the hardwood floor ripple under his feet.

And somewhere on the second story of the brownstone a door slammed with a sound like a shotgun blast.

Everyone froze in place and listened in awed silence as, one by one, every door in the brownstone slammed shut.

Brother Robert felt the floorboards ripple again. The others must have noticed it, too, for they all looked down at their feet. Suddenly the air seemed charged with electricity. He felt his face tingle, felt the hairs on his arms and legs stand up. The tension in the room was building quickly, inexorably.

Something was going to happen! Brother Robert didn't know whether to cower or to open his arms and accept it.

And then there was a light. It hovered in midair for a moment in the center of the room over Grace, a flickering tongue of flame, and then it began to expand. And brighten. There came a silent explosion of brightness, filling the room with intolerable, staggering brilliance that spiked into Brother Robert's eyes, making him cry out with the pain.

And as suddenly as it had come, it was gone.

Brother Robert shook his head and tried to blink away the purple splotches swirling and floating before his eyes. Finally he could see the room again. He saw the others squinting and stumbling around the room. Some were crying, some were praying. Brother Robert too felt the urge to pray, for he had just witnessed a miracle . . . but what did it mean?

As he folded his hands together, he noticed they were wet. He looked down. Blood. His hands were slick with it, both palms and backs smeared with red. Shocked, wondering where and how he could have cut himself, he turned to look at the others and felt his foot slip.

More blood. Both his feet were bleeding.

And then he knew. Brother Robert felt the strength go out of him like the air from a ruptured balloon. He dropped to his knees.

He examined his hands closely. There, in the center of each palm, was an oval opening, oozing blood. He touched the right wound with the little finger of his left hand. There was no pain, not even when he probed it. He felt his fingernail slide between the edges of the skin. He pushed farther through the warm, wet flesh within until it emerged on the other side. He stared dumbly at the red, glistening fingertip protruding from the back of his hand.

He snatched his finger free and fought a wave of nausea. Then he pulled aside the scapular and ran his hand over the left side of his chest, not caring that he smeared the fabric of his robe with blood. *Yes!* His skin was wet under there! He had the chest wound as well!

A nail hole in each hand and foot, and a spear wound in the chest! All five of the wounds of the crucified Christ!

The Stigmata!

He struggled to his feet to show the others, and that was when he became aware of the bedlam around him. There were cries and prayers and chaos. And blood. He was shocked to see the blood on all of them. All of them!

Amid the panicked cries and wondering murmurs, Grace Nevins stood straight and still, her rotund figure an eye of calm in the center of the storm. She held out her punctured palms to him as her voice cut through the clamor.

"The Spirit has spoken," she said. "We know what we must do."

Filled with wonder and unable to find another explanation, Brother Robert bowed his head in devotion and accepted the will of the Lord.

TWENTY-TWO

Sunday
March 17

1.

So it is done.

Jonah watched Carol as she sat on the edge of the hospital bed. Morning sunlight streaked the coverlet as Emma fussed over her, adjusting the slim straps of the new sundress she had bought for her daughter-in-law.

He knew now that the first step had been successfully completed. He had sensed it for the past month, but had dared not allow himself to rejoice until he had absolute proof.

The only blot on his mood was his failure to fulfill the vision that had led him to Grace Nevins' apartment. He had so wanted to batter her skull until it was soft as a beachball, but had failed. So he'd unleashed some of his fury upon her belongings.

But none of that mattered.

The One was alive. That was what really mattered.

The One he had awaited all these years had become flesh. The first step had been taken. The next task was to usher the One safely into the world. When that was done, he would guard the One as he grew to maturity. When the One reached the full level of his powers, no further guarding, no further assistance of any kind would be necessary.

Then the world would sink into chaos and Jonah would receive his reward.

He shook off dreams of the future and brought his thoughts to bear on the here and now.

The One had been in mortal danger.

The woman's womb had almost expelled his developing form two days ago. Jonah had been at work at the time. He had sensed the sudden weakness, the impending catastrophe, but had not understood the nature of the threat. Now he knew. The One had been near death then, clinging to physical life by the flimsiest thread.

Now, however, all seemed well. The One's strength was growing again. Jonah could sit here in the same room with the woman and bask in the power seeping through her from the One.

"Doesn't that sundress look wonderful on her, Jonah?" Emma said.

It was long, a blue flowered print, exposing her shoulders. Sunlight outlined her long slim legs through the fabric.

"Very nice," he said.

"She just seems to glow!"

Jonah smiled. "Yes, she does."

"And she's coming home to our place when she's released this afternoon, aren't you, dear."

Carol shook her head. "No. I'm going back to the mansion. It will be months before the house is rebuilt, so I think I'd better get used to the place."

"But you can't! Doctor Gallen told you to rest!"

"I'll be fine," Carol said. "I've put you out enough already. I won't impose on you any more."

"Don't be silly! You —"

"Emma, I've made up my mind."

Jonah was aware of the determination in her eyes. So, apparently was Emma.

"Well, then. If Mohammed can't move the mountain, I suppose I'll just have to keep stopping by that awful old house to keep an eye on you."

Although she said nothing further, Jonah saw Carol roll her eyes toward the ceiling.

It was good to have Emma here. She obviously was thrilled to have a grandchild on the way. She would make an excellent midwife during the journey toward birth, a scrupulous, conscientious guardian who was completely ignorant of what she was guarding.

Just as well.

Besides, it would be good for her, as well. Her spirits had been down so since the death of the Vessel, her Jimmy. But there had been new light in her eyes and new life in her step since she had heard the news of the pregnancy. Jonah wanted Emma to be happy and alert. She was more useful that way. He would need her vigilance.

For the threat to the One was not past. The One was most vulnerable now. There were forces still at large that would oppose the One and try to end his reign before it could begin. Jonah had guarded the Vessel for twenty-six years. Now he must protect the woman and her precious burden.

The priest entered then and Jonah immediately sensed a disturbance in the glow from the One. A ripple of hate and . . . fear.

The reaction was so unexpected, so uncharacteristic. It startled Jonah. And puzzled him.

Why should the One react so to this young priest? He represented nothing that could threaten the One. And yet . . . he had been with the woman when she had begun to miscarry. Had he somehow caused it?

"What do you want?" Jonah said, standing and placing himself between Carol and the priest.

"I'm here to visit Carol, just as you are, Mr. Stevens."

His tone was polite but his expression said, *Back off.*

"Hi, Bill," the woman said from her bed. "They're letting me go today."

"Great." The priest brushed past Jonah and stepped to her bedside. "Need a lift?"

"We'll drive her," Jonah said quickly.

"That's okay, Jonah," she said. "I'd already asked Father Bill."

Jonah doubted that was true, but didn't know what he could do about it. He would have to be watchful. If this priest was a threat to the One, then he was a threat to Jonah as well.

"Very well. Emma will go ahead of you and fix you something for dinner."

"Good idea, Jonah!" Emma said, beaming. "I'll have a nice lunch waiting for you!"

As Carol opened her mouth to protest, the priest said, "I think that's for the best, don't you?"

Jonah wondered at the look that passed between them at that moment.

"Maybe so," Carol said, and looked away.

There's a secret between those two.

What could it be? Did he lust after Carol? Had he attemped to seduce this rich young widow, perhaps even try to rape her?

But no. That would not have weakened the One. It would have strengthened him. He would have glowed brighter from such an encounter. Instead, the One's light had almost been extinguished.

Did the priest know about the One?

That didn't seem to be the case. He showed nothing but warm friendship for Carol. He acted anything but intimate with her. In fact, for such an old friend, he seemed almost afraid to get too close to her.

Yet Jonah could not escape the conviction that this priest had somehow hurt the One. Whether by accident or by design, it marked him as a potential danger. He would have to be watched.

There was danger all around. Now, at least, Jonah had identified one threat. He would watch for others.

Do not worry, he told the One. *I shall protect you.*

He did not intend to be very far from the woman at any time during the next eight months.

2.

During the ride from the hospital, Carol noticed how Bill kept the conversation light. As they listened to the static-charged radio in St. F.'s battered old Ford station wagon, he commented on the music, on the unseasonably warm weather, and told her how it took every bit of his automotive know-how to keep this old crate running. But his face darkened when the newsman told of Bobby Kennedy's announcement that he intended to seek the Democratic presidential nomination.

"That gutless opportunist! What a creep! McCarthy takes all the risks, wounds the dragon, and *then* Kennedy steps in!"

Carol had to smile. She could not remember seeing Bill really angry before. She knew what Jim would say: *That's politics, Bill.*

"Makes me sick!"

They were pulling into the mansion's driveway then, and Carol spotted Emma's car.

"She's already here!"

"I think you could use the help," Bill said as he brought the station wagon to a stop before the front doors. "Don't you?"

Carol shrugged, not wanting to admit that he was right. She was feeling well now — so much better than she had even yesterday — but she was still weak. Dr. Gallen had said she'd lost a fair amount of blood but not enough to make a transfusion absolutely necessary. He'd said he preferred to let her bone marrow make up the deficit. So maybe she did need someone around to lean on now and again. But Emma . . .

"She's sweet," she said, "and her heart's in the right place, but she never stops talking! Sometimes I think I'll go mad from her incessant chatter!"

"Just a nervous habit, I gather. And don't forget — she's lost somebody, too. Maybe she needs to feel needed."

"I guess so," Carol said around the lump in her throat. "But that's another part of the problem: She reminds me of Jim."

Bill sighed. "Yeah, well, she can't help that. Put up with it for a few days. 'Offer it up,' as the nuns used to tell us. It will be good for both of you. And I'll feel better knowing you're not out here alone."

"Thanks for caring," Carol said, meaning it. "It must be hard after that stunt I pulled Friday."

"Already forgotten," he said with a smile.

But the hint of uneasiness in his smile told her that it hadn't been forgotten. How could anyone forget something like that? She had stripped herself naked in front of this old friend of hers, this *priest*, and had thrown herself at him. Had actually been trying to unzip his fly! She shook her head at the memory.

"I still don't know what got into me," she said. "But I swear it will never happen again. You've got to forgive me."

"I do," he said, and there was nothing forced about his smile this time. "I could forgive you for just about anything."

Amid the glow of relief she experienced an intense flash of resentment at his generosity of spirit. It was gone as soon as it came, but it definitely had been there. She wondered about it.

"Listen," he said, hopping out and running around to help her to her feet on her side of the car. "I told my mother you'd be out here by yourself. She's going to check in. And if I know her, she'll be dropping off a pot of stew or a casserole, too."

"She doesn't have to."

"She's dying to. With Jerry off to college this year, she's got an empty nest. She's hunting someone to mother."

Carol remembered the warm, rotund Mrs. Ryan from the days when she had dated Bill in high school. She knew Bill had been staying at his folks' house since Friday and wondered how his parents were doing.

"I'll be fine," she said. "Really I will."

Emma was waiting inside. She ushered Carol to the big wing chair in the library, supporting her arm as if she were an elderly infirm aunt.

"There!" she said. "You just rest easy in that chair and I'll get you some lunch."

"That's really okay, Emma. I can —"

"Nonsense. I made some tuna salad, the kind with the sliced gherkins, just the way you like it."

Carol sighed to herself and smiled. Emma was trying so hard to make her comfortable and look after her. How could she throw it back in her face?

"Where's Jonah?"

"He's home, calling his foreman. He's got some vacation time coming — *lots* of it — and he's going to take a few weeks to stay close by and help you get this place in shape."

Just what I need, she thought. *The two of them around at once!*

But again she was touched by the concern. In all the time she had known him, Jim's father — adoptive father — had been as remote as the moon. Since the funeral, however, his demeanor had changed radically. He was concerned, solicitous, even devoted.

And in all those years she could not remember him ever taking a vacation. Not once.

All this attention was getting to be too much for her.

"Want to stay for lunch, Bill?"

"No, thanks. I really —"

"You've got to eat sometime. And I could use the company."

"All right," he said. "But just for a quick sandwich and then I've got to be getting back to St. Francis."

The sun was so bright and the day so warm that Carol thought it might be nice to eat outside in the gazebo overlooking the Long Island Sound. Emma declined to join them. Bill was already out in the yard dusting off the seats when the phone rang.

"I'll get it!" Carol said, wondering who could be calling her here on a Sunday afternoon. She lifted the receiver.

"Hello?"

"Carol Stevens?" said a muffled voice.

"Yes? Who's this?"

"That is not important. What is important is that you be aware that the child you are carrying is the Antichrist himself."

"What?" Fear gripped her insides and twisted. "Who is this?"

"Satan has transferred himself from the soulless shell of your husband to your womb. You must put Satan out!"

"You're crazy!"

"Will you put Satan out? Will you rip the beast from your womb and cast him back into Hell where he belongs?

"No! Never! And don't ever call here again!"

Her skin crawling, she slammed the heavy receiver down and hurried outside, away from the phone before it could ring again.

3.

Grace unwound the handkerchief from around the mouthpiece of the receiver and stuffed it into her pocket.

That settles that.

She had hated speaking to Carol like that, but she had to know if the poor girl could be frightened into resolving the problem on her own. Obviously she could not. So now Grace's course was set.

She walked back to the front of her apartment where thirteen people waited in her cramped living room. There was Brother Robert, Martin, and the ten members of the Chosen who had been miraculously marked by the Spirit in Martin's apartment last night. They were dressed in sweaters and jackets and slacks and jeans — and all had bandages on their hands. Like Grace's, their wounds had stopped bleeding within an hour of the miracle.

Grace wondered if they had spent the entire night awake like her, staring at her palms, her feet, inspecting the stab wound under her left breast, assuring and reassuring herself that the wounds were real, that she truly had been touched by God.

Mr. Veilleur was there, too. He alone had unbandaged hands. They were all waiting, all staring at her with expectant looks in their eyes.

Without fanfare or ceremony, much of the burden of leadership of the the Chosen had passed to her. Grace felt strong, imbued with holy purpose. She knew what the Lord wanted her to do, and as much as her heart recoiled from what was to come, she was ready to obey. The others, Brother Robert among them, were behind her. The monk had stepped aside — gladly, it seemed — to allow her to decide the next move. Grace was receiving guidance from on high. The Spirit was with her. They all knew that and yielded to it.

Only Mr. Veilleur withheld his allegiance.

"She's home," she said. "At the mansion. It's time for us to act. Our mission today is the reason we were touched by the Spirit. It is the purpose for which we were brought together. The Spirit is with us today. It has made us the instruments of God. Let us go."

They rose as one and began filing out the door.

All except Mr. Veilleur. The sight of him sitting there immobile while everyone else mustered for action triggered a flow of syllables she did not understand. She heard herself speaking in what he had called the Old Tongue.

"Not this time," he said, answering in English. "You've had enough use of me. I'm out of it now. Out of it for good."

"What did I say?" Grace asked, momentarily unsure of herself for the first time since yesterday's miracle.

"It doesn't matter," Mr. Veilleur said.

"You're not coming with us?"

"No. I want no part of this."

"You think we're wrong?"

"What I think doesn't matter. Do what you have to do. I understand. I've been there. Besides, this 'stigmata' you've all incurred has achieved its purpose. All doubt has been cast aside. You're all inflamed with holy purpose."

"Are you saying we're wrong?"

"Absolutely not. I'm merely saying you must go without me."

"What if *I* don't go? What if I do nothing? What if I turn my back to the calling of the Lord and allow the — allow Carol's baby to be born? What will that child do to us, to the world, when he's born?"

"It won't be what he will do to the world so much as what the world will do to itself. He will have little effect at first, although his very presence will cause those living on the knife edge of violence and evil to fall into the abyss. But as he grows older, he will steadily draw strength from the ambient evil and degradation of life around him. And the day will come — as it inevitably must — when he realizes that his power is unopposed. Once he knows that, he will let in all the lunatic darkness stalking the edges of what we call civilization."

"You said something about what the world will do to itself. Will he make us all depraved and evil?"

Mr. Veilleur shook his head. "No. That's not how the game is played."

"*Game?*" Suddenly she was furious with him. Carol's husband was dead and she was going to have to perform an abortion on her niece and he had the nerve — "How can you call this a game?"

"*I* don't think of it as a game, but I have a feeling *they* do."

"They?"

"The powers that are playing with us. I think — I don't know for sure, but after all these years I've come to the conclusion that we're some sort of prize in a contest between two incomprehensibly huge opposing powers. Not the big prize. Maybe just a side bet. Nothing of any great value, just something one side wants simply because the other side seems interested and may find useful some day."

Grace wanted to block her ears against this heresy.

"But God, Satan —"

"Call them whatever you wish. The side we might call Good doesn't really give a damn about us. It merely wishes to oppose the other side. But the other side is truly harmful. It feeds on fear and hate and violence. But it doesn't *cause* them, for forcing you to do evil gains it nothing. The evil must rise from within."

"Because we're evil due to Original Sin."

"I've never understood why people buy that Original Sin business. It's just the Church's way of making you feel guilty from day one. It means it's a sin to be born — patently ridiculous. No, we're not evil. But we have a huge *capacity* for evil."

Grace didn't want to hear, but she couldn't help listening. And as she listened, she sensed the sincerity behind his words.

"And so its agent here — the Presence I mentioned the other day — will strive to make it easier for you to defile yourselves and each other. He will clear the path for all that is base within you to come to the fore, facilitate the actions that destroy the bonds of love and trust and family and simple decency that enrich your lives and feelings for each other. And once each and every one of you is divided from each and every other one, when you all have become mentally, physically, and emotionally brutalized islands of despair, when you have each descended into your own private hell, then he will merge you all into one hell on earth."

"But how bad —?"

"A gentle skim of the history of mankind, even the sanitized accounts preserved in commonly used texts, can give you some idea of man's capacity for what is called 'inhumanity.' That only scratches the surface of what will come. The horrors of daily life will make the Nazi death camps seem like a vacation resort."

Grace closed her eyes in an attempt to envision the future he spoke of, but her imagination failed her. And then suddenly she saw it. The whole apocalyptic vista appeared in her mind — she felt it, touched it, tasted the misery and depravity that lay ahead. She cried out and opened her eyes.

Mr. Veilleur was staring at her, nodding grimly.

"And you won't help us stop him?" she cried.

"No. I'm old. I've had enough of fighting. I have only a few years left; all I want is to live them out in peace. And what can I add to your effort? This is something only you can do. But I wish you luck today. You will need all you can muster."

"I cannot fail. The Lord is with me."

"If that belief gives you strength, then hold on to it. Don't let anything stop you, Grace — no please, no threats of violence, no horrors real or imagined."

"Imagined?"

"You may see things. You may find yourself confronting your worst fears, your deepest guilts. Don't let them deter you. Do what you've been chosen to do. Let nothing stop you. Nothing!"

"How do you know all this?"

"I've been where you are."

He accompanied her down to the street where the Chosen waited by their cars. He shook hands with her, then turned and began walking uptown.

As she got into Martin's car to head for Monroe — with a planned stop at a hardware store along the way — Grace watched the older man's retreating figure and could not shake the feeling that she would never see him again.

4.

Carol had hoped to hide it from him, but it didn't work. Bill looked up from where he had spread a blanket on the lawn and leapt to his feet.

"Carol? What's wrong?"

Sobbing, she told him about the phone call.

"Damn!" he said. "What is wrong with those people?"

"I don't know! They frighten me!"

"You've got to get the police in on this. Have them watch the house."

"I think you're right. I'll call them after lunch." She looked down at the blanket. "I thought we were going to eat in the gazebo."

"It's warmer out here in the sun."

She dropped to her knees on the blanket and stared at the tuna-fish sandwiches. What little appetite she had before the call was completely gone now.

"How'd they learn I was pregnant? *I* found out less than two days ago!"

Bill seated himself across from her. He didn't seem much interested in eating, either.

"It means they've been watching you."

Carol glanced around at the willows, the house, the empty Sound. *Watched!* It gave her the creeps. And it made her suddenly glad that Jonah Stevens would be around.

"Aren't they ever going to leave me alone?"

"Eventually, yes. Once all this publicity dies down, they'll find some other ripe target for their paranoia. Until then, maybe you should reconsider Emma's offer to put you up with them. Or maybe you could stay with my folks. They'd love to have you."

"No. This is the only home I have now. I'm staying here."

She was angry that she should even have to consider hiding from these kooks. But she worried about the baby. Could they really want to hurt her baby?

Jim's baby.

"The voice on the phone — I think it was a woman — said I'm carrying the Antichrist."

Bill stared at her. "And you believe that?"

"Well, no, but —"

"No buts, Carol. Either you believe you're carrying a perfectly normal human baby or you don't. Normal baby or supernatural monster. I don't see much middle ground here."

"But Jim's being a clone —"

"Not that again!"

"Well, it bothers me, what they said. What if they're right? What if a clone really isn't a new human being? I mean, it's really just an outgrowth of cells from an already existing human being. Can it have a soul?"

She watched with dismay as Bill's assured expression faltered.

"How can I answer that, Carol? In the two-thousand-year history of the Church, the question has never arisen."

"Then you don't know!"

"I can tell you this much: Jim was a man, a human, an individual. He had a right to a soul. I believe he had one."

"But you're not sure!"

"Of course I'm not sure," he said gently. "That's what faith is all about. It's *believing* when you can't be sure."

She thought of the awful dreams she had been having, the consummate evil depicted within them. Were those dreams originating in her womb and filtering up to her subconscious? What if they were more than fantasies? What if they were *memories?*

"But what if what you believe is wrong? What if Jim had no soul and Satan used him as a passage into . . . into *me!*"

She was losing it. She could feel all control slipping away. Then Bill reached over and squeezed her hand.

"I told you about Satan. He's a fiction. So is the rest of this mumbo-jumbo. This isn't a horror story, Carol. This is real life. Antichrists get born in works of fiction, not in Monroe, Long Island."

She felt the panic flow out of her. She was acting silly. But right then, surfacing in the midst of the flood of relief, came a fleeting burst of hatred for Bill and for the comfort he had brought her. Why?

Bill smiled and held out the platter of sandwiches to her. She took one. She felt so much better now. Maybe she could get something down.

5.

Time to go.

Lunch, what little they'd eaten, was over. Bill looked at his watch and reluctantly decided that he had better be hitting the road soon. It had been a hectic weekend, a decided change of pace from the routine of St. F.'s. He knew he couldn't survive this kind of stress too often. Who could? But he realized that all the stresses Carol had put him through since his arrival on Friday afternoon were but a sampling of the pressure weighing upon her hour after hour, day after day. Bad enough that Jim had died a week ago today, but then to learn that she was carrying his baby, and now to have some paranoid lamebrain call and tell her she's carrying the Antichrist!

The limitless possibilities for perversity in daily life never failed to astound him.

Time to go.

Bill looked at Carol sitting across the blanket and felt as if he were looking through her sundress. He kept seeing her naked body as she had stood before him on Friday afternoon. Her breasts with their erect nipples, her fuzzy pubic triangle . . .

Time to go.

It was torture being near her like this. And he was ashamed of the regret he felt for not giving into her on Friday. He tried to push it away, walk on and leave it behind, but it kept at his heels, nagging at him, tugging on his sleeve.

To his dismay, he realized he loved her, had always loved her but had submerged the feeling in a well of daily prayer and busywork and ritual.

Now the old feelings had bobbed to the surface and lay floating there like a murdered corpse.

If he didn't get out of here soon . . .

"Time to go," he said.

Carol nodded resignedly. "I guess so. Thanks for staying." She reached out and grasped both his hands, her touch sending an unwelcome thrill through him. "Thanks for everything this weekend. If you hadn't been there Friday, I might have died."

"If I hadn't been there, maybe you wouldn't have —" He stopped, unable to speak of it. "Maybe nothing would have happened."

She released his hands. "Yes. Maybe."

They got up, Carol taking the sandwich platter, he taking the blanket. As he turned to shake it out downwind, he heard her cry out.

"Bill! Look!"

He turned and saw her pointing to a patch of brown grass at her feet.

"What's wrong?"

"That grass! That's where I was sitting! And now it's dead, just like the grass over Jim's grave!"

"Easy, Carol —"

"Bill, something's wrong, I know it! Something's terribly wrong!"

"Come *on*, will you? It's not even spring yet! Some big stray dog probably emptied his bladder there this winter and it hasn't had a chance to turn green again!"

"That's right where I was sitting!" she said. "Did you see it there before you put the blanket down? Did you?"

Seeing the panic in her eyes, he decided to lie.

"Now that you mention it, yes. I do remember seeing a brown patch there."

The relief on her face made the lie worthwhile. Actually, he didn't remember seeing any dead grass there before. But of course he hadn't been looking for it.

"Let's just do a little experiment, shall we?" he said. "Follow me."

Earlier, while waiting for Carol to come out, he had wandered around the backyard and had noticed a row of geraniums blooming in the greenhouse on the south side of the mansion. He led her now to the steamy glass enclosure. The pungent odor of the red-orange blossoms filled the room.

"Here," he said, pointing out a specimen with particularly long stems. "Wrap your fingers around one of those and hold it for a moment without squeezing."

"Why?"

"Because I want to prove to you that neither grass nor flowers nor anything else dies because of you or Jim or your baby."

Glancing at him uncertainly, she knelt and did as he had told her. Bill sent up a silent prayer that this moment would pass free from another example of life's limitless possible perversities.

If it dies, we've got big trouble, he thought lightly.

Carol let the stem go after a good half minute's grip, and leaned away from it as if the blossom might suddenly explode.

"See?" Bill said, hoping his own relief didn't show as the bright flower and its stem remained healthy, green, and unwilted. "You're letting your imagination run away with you. You're buying the paranoid delusions of those demented fanatics."

She smiled brightly and for a moment it looked as if she might hug him, but she didn't.

"You're right! It's all bullshit!" She laughed and slapped a hand over her mouth. "Oops! Sorry, Father!"

"Your penance for that is three Hail Marys and a good Act of Contrition, young lady!" he said in his father-confessor voice, wishing she had hugged him.

Oh, yes. It's way past time to go.

6.

Brother Robert sat stiffly in the front seat of Martin's car. His thoughts churned chaotically as the caravan of three vehicles rolled along the Long Island Expressway.

In a way, he was disappointed. He had taken it for granted that he would be the one to lead the faithful in this divine mandate, that he would carry the fiery sword of the Lord into battle against the Antichrist. But he had been passed over. Grace had been selected.

Still, he had not been passed over completely. Gently rubbing the scabs of the healing Stigmata on his palms, he thanked the Spirit for touching him in such an intimate manner.

To be honest with himself, he had to admit that he was somewhat relieved that the responsibility had been shifted from his shoulders. He was still nominally in charge by reason of his ordination, but it was no longer up to him alone to strike that final blow against Satan. It had been a weighty burden. Now that it had been partially lifted, he felt lightheaded, almost giddy.

What a strange Armageddon this would be. What a motley, ragtag Army of the Lord they made, these everyday people. And their fiery swords: some small surgical instruments!

Where was the majesty, the grandeur of this great battle between good and evil? Who ever would have imagined that the fate of the world would be determined in a small town in this quiet corner of Long Island? It didn't seem right. It was too ordinary, too mundane.

Yet he could deny neither the miracle of the Stigmata nor the message from deep within him: They were about to confront a monstrous evil. If they succeeded in uprooting it before it established itself, the world would be spared enormous pain.

Brother Robert had wanted to do that uprooting. But he did not have the requisite skills for that particular task. Grace did. He consoled himself with the thought that it was for that reason and not for any doubt about the strength of his faith that he had been passed over by the Lord. Personal considerations were of no consequence here. The task was all important.

And soon it would be done. Soon the Antichrist would be sent careening back to hell, and Brother Robert would be headed back to his beloved cell in the Monastery at Aiguebelle.

7.

In the back seat, Grace rested her arm on the leather felt-lined box of surgical steel instruments at her side. She had autoclaved them on her shift last night at Lenox Hill, and now they were perfectly sterile. In her lap she cradled the jar of chloroform she had taken from the hospital. She also had antiseptic solution and supplies of antibiotic capsules and codeine tablets she would give Carol to take after the procedure was completed.

She couldn't help having second thoughts about this. The Stigmata still marked her, the Spirit still filled her, and she would not be turned from her mission . . . but she wished there were some other way. If only Carol had miscarried completely a couple of days ago, none of this would be necessary. Grace knew that for the rest of this earthly life she would pay for what was about to happen here. She just prayed it would be balanced by her reward in the next.

Oh Lord, let this cup passeth from me.

But the cup could not be passed, she knew, because there was no one to pass it to.

Carol . . . her brother's only daughter. In the span between Henry and Ellen's death and Carol's marriage to Jim, the girl had become almost a daughter to Grace. She had sent her off to college in the morning and had stayed up and worried when she was out late on Saturday nights. She had given her away at her wedding.

Nothing was going to happen to Carol, only to the blasphemy she carried. But Carol would never understand, never forgive her, and that was the hardest part. Yet Grace was willing to sacrifice her niece's love for her God, for the safety of humankind.

And sometime after the Antichrist was eliminated, Grace was sure the police would find her and arrest her, as they would most of those with her. None of them cared. They had been marked for glory. They were doing what had to be done. It was the Lord's work, and after it was done, they would put themselves in His hands.

They were filled, all of them, with holy purpose. Eight men and five women, including Grace, all chosen by the Spirit, all ready to die for their God. She needed the men along for their strength in case they had to subdue anyone who might be protecting Carol. And she needed the women to help her with Carol. It would not be right to expose her niece's body to strange men, even if those men were filled with the Spirit. So the women would hold Carol while the men made sure Grace could perform her task undisturbed.

She closed her eyes. This was her salvation. She could feel it. By this one act she would undo all the sins of her previous similar acts. The symmetry of it was perfect.

But of course, why wouldn't it be? Its origin was Divine.

8.

Carol watched Bill drive the old station wagon through the gate and turn out of sight. Suddenly she felt very alone. She walked back in the house to be with Emma — *I must be really desperate!* — and tried to help her clean up the kitchen. But Emma shooed her away, telling her to follow doctor's orders and stay off her feet.

Carol tried. She turned on the TV and spun the dial: old movies, *G.E. College Bowl*, hockey, and pro basketball. She picked up two books and put them down again. She felt restless. She had been cooped up in a tiny hospital room for the past two days. She didn't want just to sit and do nothing, because if she did she'd start thinking of Jim and about what had happened to him and how she would never see him again —

She wandered into the greenhouse to see if she could busy herself with the plants. It was hot and dry under the glass. Almost everything here needed water. *That* was what she could do: Water the plants.

She was searching for a watering can when she spotted the dead geranium.

For a moment she thought she was going to be sick. Then she told herself that it was a mistake — it wasn't the same plant. Couldn't be.

But it was.

As she drew closer she saw the long stems, green and crisp less than an hour ago, now brown and drooping. The orange petals were scattered on the floor. Amid all its vigorous siblings, one dead, desiccated plant — the one she had touched.

Carol stared at it a moment, then turned away. She wasn't going to let this spook her. Holding on to Bill's words about buying into other people's paranoia, she walked straight through the house and out the front door. She had to get away from the mansion, away from Emma, away from everyone.

She walked through the gate without looking up at the spikes and headed toward town.

9.

"That's settled," Jonah said aloud as he hung up the phone. He was alone in his living room.

He had called his foreman, Bill Evers, at home and told him a story about continuing family problems since his adopted son's death and how he would have to use up some of his back vacation for the next couple of weeks. Evers had been sympathetic and had given him the okay.

Jonah smiled. He had never realized how useful a death in the family could be.

The sky suddenly darkened. Curious, he hauled his long body out of the chair and went to the window. Ominous clouds were piling high in the west, obscuring the sun. He remembered the weather forecast on the car radio earlier. Sunny and unseasonably warm all day. But then again, a freak thunderstorm wasn't so out of place in light of the heat wave they'd been having.

Still, something about those clouds gave him a bad feeling.

On impulse he called the Hanley mansion. Emma answered.

"Where's Carol?" he said.

"She's around somewhere. Did they give you the time off?"

"Yes. Can you see her?"

"Carol? No. When are you coming over?"

"Never mind that! Go find her!"

"Really, Jonah. This is a big place and —"

"*Find her!*"

Jonah fumed as he waited while Emma looked for Carol. Emma had her uses, but sometimes she was so thick! Finally she came back on the line, sounding out of breath.

"She's not here. I've called and called but she doesn't answer."

"Damn you, woman!" he shouted. "You were supposed to keep a watch on her!"

"I did! I made her sandwiches, but I can't watch her every minute! She's a grown —!"

Jonah slammed the receiver down and returned to the window. The clouds were bigger, darker, closer, rushing this way. He knew then that this wasn't a simple out-of-season storm.

He ran to the garage and started the car. He had to find her. Even if he had to drive up and down every street in Monroe, he'd find her and get her to safety.

That storm was aimed at her, and at what she carried.

TWENTY-THREE

1.

As she walked along the harborfront, Carol heard the refrain from Otis Redding's "Dock of the Bay" through the open window of a passing car. She remembered how Jim had been so taken with the song when he'd first heard it a couple of weeks ago. Now Jim was dead, just like Otis.

She tried to shake off the morbid associations, but everyplace she went reminded her in some way of Jim. And God, how she needed him now.

The heat and humidity were becoming oppressive. What breeze there was off the harbor was like a big dog panting in her face. She heard a faint rumble of thunder and looked up to see a towering mass of clouds sliding across the sky, smothering the sun. Those thunderheads seemed to be in an awful hurry. Flickers of lightning flashed against their dark underbellies. Before she knew it, the bright afternoon was gone, replaced by the still, heavy gloom that precedes a storm.

Just what I need, she thought.

Carol hated thunderstorms. But Jim had always loved them. She would cringe against him with her hands over her ears and her eyes squeezed tightly shut while he stared out a window in rapt fascination at the lightning. The more ferocious the storm, the better.

But there would be no one to huddle with in this storm, and it looked like it was going to be a whopper. She began to hurry back toward Shore Drive.

Suddenly the storm leapt upon the town. A cold wind beat against the still warm air and drove it off. The lightning narrowed from pale sheets into lancing bolts of crackling blue-white fury, the thunder rose from muttered rumbles to the sound of savage giants wielding monstrous sledgehammers against the tin dome of the sky. Then the rain came. Huge wind-driven drops, scattered at first, left silver-dollar-size splotches on the streets and sidewalks, followed by sheets of icy water that beat the swirling dust into mud and carried it away in eddying rivulets that in no time were running two inches deep along the curbs.

Carol was soaked in an instant. She ran under a tree but remembered how that was supposed to be the worst place to wait out a thunderstorm. Up ahead, half a block away, she saw her old parish church — Our Lady of Perpetual Sorrow. It had to be safer than this tree.

As she dashed for the front door, hail began to pound out of the sky, icy white pellets, mostly marble-size but some as big as golf balls, bouncing off the pavement, pelting her head and shoulders, making a terrific racket on the cars parked along the curb. She ran up the stone steps, praying the front door was unlocked. It yielded to her tug and allowed her into the cool, dry silence of the vestibule.

Abruptly the storm seemed far away.

Church. When was the last time she had been in church? Somebody's wedding? A christening? She couldn't remember. She hadn't been much of a churchgoer since her teens. Looking back, she thought she could blame her falling away on a reaction to her parents' deaths. Her careless attitude toward church had caused some friction with Aunt Grace during her college years, but no big scenes. She never became antireligious like Jim; it was just that after a while there simply didn't seem much point in all that kneeling and praying every Sunday to a God who with each passing year seemed increasingly remote and indifferent. But she remembered times between her parents' death and her falling away when coming to Our Lady alone and just sitting here in the quiet had given her a form of solace.

She looked around the vestibule. To her left was the baptismal font and, to the right, the stairway to the choir loft. During seventh and eighth grades she had sung in the choir every Sunday at the nine a.m. children's Mass.

She shivered. Her hair and bare shoulders still dripped with rain and her wet sundress clung to her like an ill-fitting second skin.

She opened the door and stepped into the nave. As she walked up the center aisle, the rapid-fire lightning flashes from the storm illuminated the stained-glass windows, strobing bright patterns of colored light across the pews and the altar, almost like one of those psychedelic light shows that were so popular with the acid heads.

Thunder shook the building again and again as she walked about two thirds of the way to the altar and slipped into a pew. She knelt and buried her face in her hands to shut out the lightning. Questions kept echoing through her mind: How was she going to do this alone? How was she going to raise this baby without Jim?

You are not!

Her head snapped up. The words startled her. Who . . . ?

She hadn't really heard them. They hadn't been spoken. They had sounded in her mind. Yet she glanced around the church anyway. She was alone. The only other human figures present were the life-size statues of the Virgin Mary standing in the alcove by the pulpit to the left of the altar, her foot crushing the serpent of Satan; over on the right, the crucified Christ.

For a heart-stopping instant, out of the corner of her eye, she thought she saw Christ's thorn-crowned head move, but when she looked again, straight on, it seemed unchanged. Just a trick of the flashing light from the storm.

Suddenly she felt a change in the empty church. The atmosphere had been open and accepting when she had entered; now she sensed an air of burgeoning unwelcomeness, of outright hostility.

And she felt hot. The chill from her rain-soaked sundress was gone, replaced by a growing sensation of heat. Her skin felt scorched, scalded.

A sound like cracking wood startled her. She looked around, but because of the way sound echoed through the wide open nave and across the vaulted ceiling, it seemed to come from all sides. Then the pew shifted under her. Frightened, she stumbled out into the aisle. The cracking sounds began to boom around her, louder than ever. The creaks, the groans, the screams of tortured wood filled the air. She watched the pews begin to shift, to twist, to warp and writhe as if in agony.

Suddenly the pew she had just vacated buckled and split lengthwise along the seat with a sound like a cannon shot. All around her, other pews began to crack in a deafening fusillade. Fighting the trapped, panicky feeling, she clapped her hands over her ears against the roar and staggered in a slow circle. In the flickering, kaleidoscopic light, splinters flew into the air as the pews cracked and pulled loose from the marble floor.

And she was hot! So *hot!* Mist rose before her eyes. She looked at her arms and saw tendrils of smoke curling, twisting, rising from her wet skin. Her whole body was steaming!

The flickering light, the rumble of the thunder, the screams of the tortured wood — it all seemed centered on her. She had to get out of here!

As she turned to run, she saw the head of the crucified Christ moving. Her knees went soft as she realized that this wasn't a trick of the light.

The statue had raised its head and was looking at her.

2.

Curse this rain!

Jonah felt the balding tires slip on the old downtown trolley tracks as he guided his car toward the curb. He couldn't see where he was going. His wipers couldn't keep up with the downpour on the outside and his huffing defogger labored in vain against the mist that blurred the sweating inner surface of his windshield.

He wiped a sleeve across the side window to clear it but that was no help. It was as if he'd driven into a gray, wet limbo. Outside, Monroe's shopping district was completely obscured by the mad torrent of water dropping from the sky. As rain and hail beat a manic tattoo on the roof, Jonah felt the first stirrings of fear. Something was happening. Somewhere nearby the other side was doing something to her. Everything would be ruined if he didn't find her!

Where is she?

In desperation he pressed the heel of his palm over his good right eye, sealing out the light. He lifted the patch over his left.

Darkness. Some drifting afterimages on the right, but on the left, only a formless void.

Well, what did he expect? The visions only came when they damn well pleased. And apparently whatever power he had was keeping to itself today. Today, of all days, when he needed it most! He swiveled his head left and right like a radar dish, hoping something would come, but —

Jonah froze. There, to the right. Uphill, away from the waterfront. He pulled off his right hand and saw only the fogged interior of the car. But when he covered it again . . .

A light.

Not a flashing beacon, not a bright spotlight. Just a pale glow in the sightless black. Jonah felt a burst of hope. It had to mean something! He put the car in gear and began to crawl through the deluge. At the first intersection he turned right and revved the engine uphill against the current. Every so often he would stop and cover his good eye. The glow was growing brighter as he moved. It was now ahead and to the left. He continued to make his way slowly up the slope, turning the car left and then right again, until the glow filled the void in his dead eye.

This is it!

He determined the position of the glow's center, flipped his patch down, and leapt from the car. Through the pelting rain he made out the looming stone and stucco front of the Catholic church.

Jonah froze at the curb. This couldn't be! The Church wasn't involved! It had no power — least of all over the One! What was happening here?

But the girl was inside, and with her, the One. And the One was in danger!

As Jonah started toward the church, the wind and hail doubled in fury, as if to keep him away. But he had to get inside. Something terrible was about to happen in there!

3.

Christ stared — no, *glared* at her from his cross. His eyes glowed with anger.

Carol's heart thudded against her chest wall. Her whole body trembled.

"This isn't happening!" she said aloud into the cacophony of rending wood, hoping the sound of her own voice would reassure her. It didn't. "This is another one of those dreams! It has to be! None of this is real!"

Movement drew her eyes to Christ's right hand. The fingers were flexing, the palm rocking on the spindle of the nail that pierced it. She saw the forearm muscles bulge with effort. But this was a wooden statue! Wooden muscles didn't bulge!

That proves this is a nightmare! Any minute I'll wake up!

For a moment she was transported to a more peaceful place by the thought of waking up next to Jim and finding that all the horrors of the past week had been just part of a dream. Wouldn't that be wonderful?

Blood began dripping from Christ's hand as he worked the nail free. It oozed down his palm in a rivulet and fell to the floor in long, slow, heavy drops.

Carol turned to run down the aisle when she noticed the statue of the Blessed Virgin looking at her. Tears streamed from her eyes. A voice sounded in Carol's head: *Would you undo all He suffered for?*

This was madness! A fever dream! Someone must have slipped some

LSD into her water carafe at the hospital!

Then she noticed movement at the Blessed Mother's feet. The snake was moving, slithering free from beneath her crushing foot.

Would you set the Serpent free?

The snake slid off the pedestal and was out of sight for a moment. Then its thick, brown length appeared again at the chancel rail, coiling up a baluster and then pausing at the top to stare at her with its glittering eyes.

Carol wanted to run but couldn't. The horrid fascination of it had rooted her to the spot. And now the pains began low in her pelvis, just like they had on Friday.

The piercing screech of a nail being ripped from dry wood drew her attention to her right again. Christ's right hand was free of the cross. With the bloody nail still protruding from his palm, he leveled his arm and pointed a finger directly at her eyes.

Would you release the Serpent? Pluck it out! Pluck it OUT!

"It's *my* baby! Jim's and mine!"

Another wave of pain caught her, doubling her over. And as she looked down she saw the snake coiled around her feet. With an undulating motion, it wound itself around her leg and began to climb.

Carol screamed with terror and with the increasing pain ripping through her lower belly. It was happening again! Oh, God, she was going to miscarry! And this time no one was here to help her!

Suddenly a hand gripped her arm and another one pulled the snake off her leg and hurled it toward the altar. She turned and saw Jonah standing close beside her. She gasped at the sight of him. He seemed to be on fire — smoke streamed from his skin and clothes. He appeared to be suffering agonies of his own.

"Got to get you out of here!" he shouted hoarsely.

Carol had never dreamed she'd be glad to see that cold, hard, one-eyed face, but now she fell against him and clung to him, sobbing.

"Oh, Jonah! Help me! So weak! I think I'm going to faint."

He stooped, got one arm behind her knees, the other around her back, and then he was carrying her toward the vestibule.

Safe! She was going to be safe!

Just then the ceiling exploded downward in a blaze of crackling blue-white incandescence. Jonah paused a moment, then dashed for the doors. She looked over his shoulder and saw the iron cross from the church roof hurtling through the opening in the ceiling, driving downward amid the water and debris to smash into the very spot where she had been standing.

It quivered there, spiked into the marble floor on a tilt, glowing and burning with green fire.

And then they were through the vestibule and out the front doors into the rain. The cool water felt good on her burning skin as Jonah carried her down the steps to his car. He helped her into the back seat.

"Lie down," he said. "Didn't the doctor tell you to stay off your feet?"

The barely repressed fury in his face frightened Carol. Beside, he was right. So she laid back and got her feet up as Jonah slid behind the wheel and began to drive.

4.

"The phone line's cut," Martin said, brandishing the wire cutters in his bandaged hand as he sat dripping and shivering beside him in the front seat of the car.

Brother Robert noted the excitement in his eyes and the feverish glow on his cheeks. His rain-plastered hair only added to the effect, giving him a deranged look. He seemed to think he was playing James Bond.

"Good," he said absently.

Martin rolled down the window and looked at the sky. "The rain's letting up," he said.

Brother Robert looked at Grace and saw how pale and tense she was. "What do you think, Grace?"

"I think it's time we began," she said.

Brother Robert nodded. There didn't seem to be a reason to put it off any longer.

"Go ahead," he told Martin. "But be careful."

"Watch out for Jonah Stevens," Grace said. "He's big and strong. He's the only one who'll give you trouble."

Martin nodded and got out of the car. He signaled to the other two vehicles and soon he was surrounded by the other half dozen men from the Chosen. Brother Robert felt a shade unmanly for not going with the men, but he could not risk tainting his vows or his order with even a hint of violence. He would take the women and the cars farther down the road and wait until the men had secured the house, breaking in if necessary, subduing anyone inside who resisted them. They would signal Brother Robert when everything was settled. Two of the men carried axes, and another carried a coil of nylon clothesline. They seemed prepared for everything.

Is this right? he asked himself for the hundredth time since this morning. And each time he had asked, he looked at his punctured hands, as he did now, and the answer was always the same: How could one argue with the Stigmata?

He watched the group approach the open gate. He felt like a missile hurtling through space, nearing its target. It seemed that his entire life had been directed toward this moment.

5.

Emma ran into the front hallway to answer the bell. She hadn't heard a car, so it could only be Carol.

Probably drenched, poor thing!

She reached for the knob but hesitated. A warning sounded somewhere in her brain. Something wasn't right. She peeked through one of the etched sidelights and was startled by the sight of the three men standing there. Where on earth had they come from?

"Who is it?"

"Mrs. Stevens?" said a voice. "We'd like to speak to you a moment."

"About what?"

"About your husband."

About Jonah? Something weird was going on here. Emma peeked again through the sidelight and studied the men more closely. She gasped when she recognized the thin, pale one — he had been outside the gate the day Jimmy died.

"I know who you are!" she shouted. "Get away from here before I call the police!"

But she had no intention of giving them a chance to leave. She was going to call the police right now! Sergeant Hall had said that if any one of those nuts showed his face around Monroe again to call him and he'd pick them up right away.

She lifted the receiver but there was no dial tone. Oh, no! The storm must have —

Just then one of the leaded stained glass windows in the dining room shattered as an ax smashed through it.

6.

Carol was almost hysterical. It took every ounce of restraint Jonah had within him to keep from reaching over the backrest and knocking her senseless. She more than deserved it for endangering the One this way, but he had to keep her confidence. If he was to protect her, she had to trust him, depend on him.

"I'm having Satan's child, aren't I? Isn't that what's happening? Isn't it? What else could explain what happened back there?"

"For the tenth time now, Carol," he said through clenched teeth, "you're havin' *Jim's* baby — my grandson. I don't know where you get this fool Satan idea. Satan's got nothin' to do with that baby."

He hoped the truth of that last statement came through in his voice. Of course, the real truth wouldn't have made her feel any better, maybe even worse, but he had to calm her. Her emotional state was threatening to cause the One to miscarry.

"Then how do you explain the statue of Christ coming alive?" she sobbed. "And Mary — and the *snake!* You'd almost think they were trying to *make* me miscarry!"

And you would be right! Jonah thought.

The other side had come close to succeeding today, playing through Carol's religious superstitions to fill her with guilt and terror. It had failed this time, but it would try again. Jonah would have to be ever vigilant against the next attempt. But right now, for the sake of the One, he had to calm this frantic young woman.

"I didn't see none of that, Carol," he said, lying easily. "The statues looked the same as ever to me."

"But the snake! You pulled it from my leg!"

"I'm sorry, Carol, but I didn't see no snake anywhere in the church. I just happened to stop in to get out of the hail and found you screaming like a banshee in the middle of the aisle."

She pulled herself up to a sitting position and stared at him with haunted eyes over the backrest.

"But it couldn't have been just my imagination! It was too real!"

"You been through some awful times lately, what with what happened to Jim and then the funeral and all, and then near losin' the baby, and all that bleedin'" — he glanced at her over his shoulder to emphasize the next — "and not followin' your doctor's orders to rest and stay off your feet, ain't no wonder you started seeing things! You're lucky that's the worst of it. You could've gone an' lost the baby for sure this time."

Jonah was pleased with the fluidity of his ad-libbed explanations. He could almost believe them himself.

"I know," she said, slumping back to a reclining position on the rear seat. "I was stupid. But I think the baby's okay. I mean, the pain's gone now and there's been no more bleeding."

Lucky for you, he thought. If she lost the One, he would kill her. Slowly.

"But what about that flaming cross almost killing us!" she said. "You can't tell me I imagined that!"

" 'Course not. The church got hit by lightning, the cross got knocked through the roof and ceiling, and that was it. We were lucky."

"But the glow —!"

"St. Elmo's fire. Used to see it out on the farm during storms when I was a boy. Scary, but harmless."

"You and Bill — you've got an explanation for everything!"

"You mean that priest fellow?"

"Yes. He says I should forget all this Satan nonsense and concentrate on having a healthy baby."

Jonah smiled ruefully. He never thought he'd ever find himself on the same side as a priest.

"I couldn't agree more, young lady. We all want that boy to be safe an' strong."

"Boy? Do you think it's going to be a boy?"

"Sure do." *I know it!*

"I have that feeling, too. I think I'll name him James, after his father."

"That'll be nice." *He has no father, but name him anything you want. It won't matter.*

"Thanks for coming when you did, Jonah. You saved my life."

"Think nothing of it."

Because your life means nothing to me without the One.

7.

"Where is she?" said the thin, pale one.

Emma glared up from her chair at the men who surrounded her. The one with the ax had climbed through the smashed window and unlocked the front door for the rest. They wanted Carol but Emma would die before telling them.

"She's gone. Gone for the week. Gone for a rest."

"Really?" said the thin one. "When did she leave?"

"Straight from the hospital."

"She's lying," he said to the others. "We spoke to her here on the phone earlier this afternoon."

Two of the men hurried down from the upper levels.

"No one upstairs."

"Come on, lady," said the thin one. "We have no intention of harming you. We just want to find Carol Stevens."

"What do you want with her?"

"We'll take that up with her."

She didn't like the sound of that. What could —

Suddenly one of the men shouted, "There's a car coming in!"

"Do you feel it?" the thin one said in a hushed voice, his eyes wide and bright with excitement. "Do you *feel* it? It's *her!*"

Emma tried to scream out a warning but a hand clamped over her mouth.

8.

By the time Jonah realized something was wrong, it was too late.

Carol was still shaky when they got back to the mansion, so he got her out of the car and had an arm around her waist as he helped her through the light rain and up to the front door. As soon as he stepped into the foyer, he sensed the danger. He spun Carol around to get her back to the car but suddenly there were four men facing him on the front porch, and more coming from the house.

"Who are you?" Carol said to them.

"We just want to talk to you, Mrs. Stevens," said someone from behind them. Jonah turned and saw a pale, thin man standing inside the foyer. "Come in. Please."

Jonah's mind raced. He knew who they were and sensed why they were here. Inside the mansion, death awaited the One.

I can't let this happen!

"Recognize them?" he said to Carol. "They're the one's who were here last Sunday. They killed Jim."

"Oh, God," she said. He could feel her anger feeding strength into her body as she straightened and stood on her own. He voice gained a sharper edge. "Who are the hell are you and why are you here?"

"My name is Martin," the man said. He motioned the others away from the door. "Please come in. I'll explain everything."

Jonah had calculated their total number at half a dozen or so, but only a few stood between Carol and freedom. If he could keep them occupied . . .

"Let's go in," Jonah said, taking her arm as if to guide her through the door. "Let's hear what they have to say."

As Carol stared at him in disbelief, he watched the strangers. He saw them relax. They thought they had won. That was when Jonah made his move.

Whirling, he shoved Carol toward the porch steps, shouting, "*Run!*"

Continuing the same motion, he grabbed two of the strangers and flung them into the other two. There was an instant of confusion on the porch. He saw Carol stumbling down the steps, looking back with a white, frightened face.

"Lock yourself in the car and *go!*" he shouted.

Then someone leapt onto his back. Then another. And then a third. As he went to his knees under the weight he saw Carol reach the car. Mentally he cheered her on.

Go, girl! Get away from here! Run them down on the way out!

9.

With a scream welling her throat, Carol pulled the car door open and threw herself into the front seat.

Safe!

But as she went to slam the door, someone grabbed the outside handle and yanked it back. The waiting scream broke free!

"Stay away from me! Leave me alone!"

She looked up into the bland face and gentle eyes of someone who could have been an accountant or a hot-dog vendor or a department manager at Macy's. But there was no mistaking the determination as he stood there in the rain and stared down at her.

"We have no wish to harm you, Mrs. Stevens."

"Then let me go!"

"I'm afraid we can't do that. At least not at the moment." He held out his hand to assist her from the car. She noticed that it was bandaged; so was his other hand. He pulled it back as if he had suddenly changed his mind. "Please come with me."

Another man, about ten years older but equally bland-looking, came up beside him and looked down at her. Both his hands were bandaged, too. Despite her fear, she was struck by the strangeness of all those bandages.

"Please don't fear us," the second one said. "We're only here to help you."

Both their expressions showed a strange mixture of serenity and implacable purpose. Here was a pair who had found the answer to all things in life. No further questions were necessary.

The effect was chilling.

She looked past them to the porch where four men were still struggling to subdue Jonah. The first followed her gaze.

"We mean him no harm, either. Come."

Carol fought the hysteria straining against the underside of her diaphragm. They seemed sincere about meaning her no harm, yet something within her screamed in fear at the look in their eyes.

But what choice did she have? She was outnumbered and outflanked. They were out of sight of the road and none of the neighbors were close enough to hear her if she screamed. Her arms and legs felt leaden, too weak to put up a struggle, too heavy to run very far.

And up on the porch, they had Jonah on his feet and were leading him inside.

"All right," she said. "I'll come. Just don't touch me."

That seemed to be the farthest thing from their minds. Both men stepped back out of her way, but she noticed that the first kept a firm grip on the door handle.

They followed her to the porch. The one who had called himself Martin was waiting there. He spoke to the men with her:

"Go signal Brother Robert."

The second one trotted off toward the road.

Carol wondered at the significance of that as Martin preceded her into the front hallway. Then she heard Emma's breathless voice coming from the parlor.

"— tried to warn you, Jonah, but they gagged me and pulled me into the back room!"

Carol followed Martin into the parlor where one of the men was tying Jonah into one of the chairs as two others steadied his arms. In the doorway to the dining room stood Emma, flanked by two more of the men.

And they all had bandages on their hands. What did that *mean?*

"Carol!" she said. "I'm so glad you're all right! I was so worried!"

Carol was suddenly furious at these interlopers. The Hanley mansion didn't really feel like her house, and so she had not reacted as instinctively as she might have had they been in the old family cottage. But with the sight of the smashed leaded window, the shattered glass on the carpet, the axes leaning against the wall, something changed within her. She suddenly felt protective toward this old place. This *was* her house, and it probably had been these people who'd burned her out of her old home. And now they were making themselves right at home here! And tying up her father-in-law!

She stormed into the parlor.

"Get out! All of you get out of my house!"

"We'll be leaving soon," Martin said, unperturbed.

"Not soon! Now! I want you all out of here *now!*" She strode to where they were binding Jonah's wrists to the arms of the chair. "Stop that! Untie him immediately!"

The men glanced up at her, then at Martin, then continued tying their knots.

"All in good time," Martin said. "But there's someone I think you ought to talk to first before you get too upset."

Carol was ready to scream at him when she heard the sound of tires splashing through the puddles on the driveway. She glanced through the front window and saw three cars pulling in. None of them looked familiar. As she watched, the doors opened and a number of women got out — five in all — and a bearded man in monk's robes with the cowl pulled up over his head. As they approached the front porch she recognized the short, portly figure in the lead.

"Aunt Grace!"

"Grace?" Emma shouted from the far side of the room. "Grace Nevins? She's with them? I should have known! She helped them kill my Jimmy!"

Carol barely heard her. Aunt Grace was here! That was good. Emma was just overwrought. There was nothing to fear from Aunt Grace. She had taken her parents' place after they were killed. If she knew these people, she'd straighten everything out!

10.

Grace had sensed the evil within the house as she stepped up onto the porch. But when she entered and saw Carol dash across the front hallway, running toward her with outstretched arms, it slammed against her like a mailed fist.

"Aunt Grace! Help us! We're being held prisoner here!"

Grace willed herself not to to recoil as Carol clung to her. But holding her trembling niece was like embracing a sack of maggots. There could be no doubt now — the Antichrist was within her. Grace was suddenly filled with righteous rage at Satan for doing this to her own niece. How dare he!

"You'll be fine, dear," she said, stroking her niece's long, damp hair.

I will free you from your affliction. I will rip the corruption from within you and return you to your old unsullied self.

She hated herself for being so deceitful. For despite her desire to free Carol from Satan, she dreaded the ugly scene to come and wanted to put off the unpleasantness as long as she could, to compress it and concentrate it into the shortest possible length of time, into a tiny bitter pill that could be downed in a single swallow.

"Aunt Grace, do you know these people?"

"Yes. Yes, I do. I've known them since Ash Wednesday."

"Can you get them out of here?"

"Don't you worry. You know I wouldn't let anything happen to my niece. Just relax. Tomorrow this will all seem like a dream and you'll be fine. In fact, you'll be better than you are right now."

You'll be free of the loathsomeness growing inside you.

She felt Carol relax, but there was still fear in her niece's eyes when she leaned back and looked at her.

"Just get them out of here. *Please?* You should see what they've done to Jonah!"

"Show me."

She followed Carol into the room to the right. She had never seen a house like this, so ornate, so cluttered. She stopped at the threshold, startled by the sight of Jonah Stevens, trussed in a chair and straining at his bonds.

"You!" Jonah shouted when he saw her. His single eye glared at her from a rage-distorted face. "I might have known you'd be involved in this!"

Might have known? What did he mean by that?

But it was Emma who suddenly dominated the scene. She pulled away from the two Chosen guarding her and lunged across the room at Grace, her fingers curved like talons, screaming at the top of her voice.

"It's you! You killed my Jimmy! *Yooouuu!*"

Grace shrank back from the attack, and luckily the other Chosen were able to grab and restrain Emma before she reached her. Emma's words became raving gibberish and she screamed and spit and bit and kicked at her captors as they dragged her to the floor. She was like a madwoman, like a wounded wild animal. Finally, whether from exhaustion or the realization that she was helpless, Grace couldn't say, Emma calmed down and lay there on the flowered carpet, panting and grunting.

Wounded. Yes, she had been wounded, hadn't she? Poor Jim wasn't to blame for being born without a soul. He had been used by Satan to impregnate poor Carol, and then discarded. Her heart went out to poor Emma for her loss, but that did not make Grace fear her rage any less.

Jim used, Carol used. And Carol no doubt destined to be discarded like Jim after she'd served her purpose and the Antichrist was born. It was all so dirty, so treacherous. Well, Grace would put an end to all of that here today.

She watched with relief as they lifted Emma from the floor and prepared to tie her into a chair like her husband. She wailed piteously.

"She killed my Jimmy! She killed my Jimmy and she's got to pay for it!"

"Emma, please!" Carol was saying. "Grace had nothing to do with that!" She turned pleading eyes on her. "Did you, Aunt Grace?"

Grace shook her head.

In a way, she told herself, her denial was true. She had been against that first trip to Monroe, hadn't wanted to come along, and had stayed in the car throughout the whole tragic confrontation.

"She lies!" Jonah cried. "She was there! I saw her in one of the cars!"

Carol stared at her. "That's not true, is it?"

Grace could not bring herself to lie to her niece. "You have to understand, Carol. I —"

"She was there to kill Jim!" Jonah cried. "And now she's here to kill Jim's baby!"

Grace would have given her life then to stop the growing horror she saw in Carol's face.

Carol's voice was a whisper. "No!"

"Carol, dear, you've got to know that the child you're carrying is not really Jim's. It's —"

Carol's hands were over her ears as her voice rose to a scream.

"*NO!*"

11.

Bill had watched the awesome fury of the storm with his parents from the family living room. Now that it had dwindled to a drizzle and distant rumbles, he was on his way. The temperature had dropped a good twenty degrees. Winter was making a last stand against spring. He had the defroster temperature up as high as it would go to keep the windshield clear.

He had to pass Carol and Jim's old house on his way to Glen Cove Road, and he felt an ache in his chest as he drove by the charred ruins at 124 Collier.

That got him thinking about Carol and how she was managing, if she was all right.

But of course she was all right. She was out at the Hanley place with her in-laws.

They why did he have this persistent gnawing feeling that she *wasn't* all right?

He was approaching Glen Cove Road and was about to turn south when he abruptly pulled the car over to the shoulder by a Citgo station and stopped. The feeling was growing stronger.

This is silly, he thought.

He didn't believe in premonitions or clairvoyance or any of that extrasensory nonsense. It not only went against the teachings of the Church, but it went against his personal experience.

Yet he could not escape the feeling that Carol needed him.

He put the car in gear, started toward Glen Cove Road again, then braked and pounded on the steering wheel with his fist.

He could see that he wasn't going to be able to rest easy until he had settled this.

He pulled into the Citgo station, dug the Hanley mansion's phone number out of his pocket, and dropped a dime. No ring. The operator came on and told him the phone was out of order. Lines were down all over northern Nassau County. The storm, you know.

Right. The storm. Maybe the mansion had been hit. Maybe it was ablaze right now.

Damn. He was going to have to take a run out there. Just drive by. He wouldn't stop in. Just make sure everything looked okay, then head for Queens.

He took the direct route through the harbor area but was slowed by the traffic being detoured away from a fire on Tremont Street. He joined the rubberneckers, straining to see what was burning up the hill. Whatever it was, it looked to be near Our Lady. An awful thought struck him — maybe the burning building *was* Our Lady. He had said Mass there only this morning.

He was tempted to park and run uphill to see. If Our Lady was ablaze, maybe he could help Father Rowley. But the sight of the smoke heightened his anxiety about Carol's safety. He gunned the car toward Shore Drive.

He breathed a sigh of relief when he found the street in front of the mansion wall free of fire trucks and no pall of smoke dirtying the air over the roof.

But the driveway inside the gate was loaded with cars.

Something about that didn't sit right with Bill. He did a U-turn down the street and drove by again. Slowly.

A good half dozen cars in the drive — J. Carroll, both the Stevenses', and others he didn't recognize. Curious, he pulled in by the wall and walked around to the gate. Maybe he could knock on the front door and ask if anyone had seen his sunglasses. Nobody had to know that they were sitting on the dashboard of his car.

He was halfway up the drive when he heard Carol scream. He began to run.

12.

Emma was glad to see the pain in that bitch Grace Nevins' face when Carol screamed. That would be the least of her pain if Emma got her hands on her.

She felt her back teeth grind against one another as the two men seated her in a chair next to Jonah and prepared to bind her. She had never felt rage like this before. It bordered on madness. In fact, she was sure that if she ever got free and got within reach of Grace, she would lose completely her present tenuous grip on sanity. The last vestige of civilization would slough away and she would become some sort of raving, slavering animal.

Part of her was frightened by the intensity of the murderous feelings and wanted to hide them away, and yet another part hungered to set the savage free.

She watched Grace as she fumbled with some mealymouthed explanations to Carol. And then there was a commotion at the front door, out of Emma's view, a man calling Carol's name. Suddenly Carol's friend, Father Ryan, burst into the parlor.

"Carol!" he said. "Are you all —?" His voice trailed off as he took in the tableau before him. And everyone, including the monk, stared back, frozen by the sight of the priest's Roman collar.

"Bill, thank God you're here!" Carol cried.

"I'm Father Ryan," he said as Emma watched his astonished eyes take in Jonah, tied into a chair, and her about to be. "What in Heaven's name is going on here?"

"How aptly put, Father Jesuit," said the one called Martin. "Because that's just what this is: in Heaven's name."

"You were here last week!" he said to Martin.

"That is true."

"You're all insane!"

"Please! Please!" said the monk, pushing back his hood as he came forward.

For some reason, the sight of the gleaming scalp of his tonsure startled Emma. She tried to identify his accent as he stepped up to Father Ryan.

"Who are you?" the Jesuit said.

"I am Brother Robert of the Monastery at Aiguebelle," the monk said. "Please, Father, you must leave. You must trust me as a fellow ordained priest that we are here to do God's work."

"Since when does God's work involve binding people to chairs?" the young priest said scornfully. "The game's over. Time to clear out. Get out of here now before I call the police!"

"Man's laws are of no account when doing God's will," Brother Robert said. "Surely you know that, Father."

"We'll see if the police agree."

Emma saw Father Ryan turn and make to leave the parlor, but two of the Chosen blocked his way. The priest pushed them aside. He was strong and they had difficulty holding him. One of Emma's guardians left her to help with the priest, leaving only one standing over her, and he was engrossed in watching the struggle.

And Grace . . . that bitch Grace Nevins had stepped back from the parlor entrance, bringing her closer to Emma.

Without hesitation or even conscious thought, Emma launched herself from the chair and lunged at Grace. The pent-up rage broke free and lent her quickness and power. She felt strong, stronger than she had ever felt in her life.

A high-pitched, feral cry forced itself free as her fingers found the other woman's throat. Grace's shocked, horrified face twisted into view. Her eyes bulged, her mouth worked around a scream but Emma squeezed harder, increasing the driving pressure of her thumbs on Grace's voicebox.

But others could scream, and scream they did. Emma could hear their high-pitched wails of shock and anger faintly through the roaring deep in her ears.

She paid them no mind.

Grace's pudgy hands pawed at her, alternately trying to push her away and pry the constricting fingers free of her throat. Other hands flailed at her, grappled with her, many hands, pulling at her arms, clawing at her face, desperately trying to free Grace from the death grip.

Emma shrugged them off.

So strong. The power surging through her was like nothing she had ever experienced before. No one could stop her now. She watched Grace's red, bulging eyes and slowly purpling face and knew that the end was near. New strength poured into her to finish off the fat bitch.

13.

Carol's mother-in-law was trying to strangle Carol's aunt — the sight held Bill awestruck.

In the back of his mind was a voice urging him to take Carol and run. He knew it was right, but instead of heeding it he stood there and watched the melee in the center of the museum-like Victorian parlor as the ones who called themselves the Chosen converged upon the pair of struggling female figures and tried to separate them.

Carol stood next to him, clutching at his right arm, crying out for the two women to 'Stop it, stop it, stop it'! And the monk, Brother Robert, hovered off to the left, tense and frozen, a statue in a habit.

It would have been like a piece of absurdist theater if it were not apparent to all that Grace was dying in Emma's grasp.

"Get her off of Grace!" shouted the monk at last. "She's killing her!"

Bill was tempted to help, but there were already too many oddly bandaged hands trying to do just that, and accomplishing little more than getting in each other's way.

As Grace's face darkened toward a dusky gray, the cries from the Chosen became more frantic, more terrified. Suddenly one of their number — the thin one named Martin — darted away from the group and hurried past the spot where Jonah Stevens struggled with the bonds that held him in his chair. He went to the corner and retrieved something that had been leaning against the wall over there.

Bill didn't realize it was an ax until the man had raised it in the air over the struggling crowd. After a horrified instant's hesitation, he cried out a warning and leapt forward, reaching for the handle. Brother Robert was beside him. He too was clutching at Martin's arm. But they were too late. Before they could get to it, the blade descended in a blurred arc, burying itself in the top of Emma Stevens' head with a sickening crunch of cracking bone.

Gasps of revulsion, cries of shock and horror mixed with his own, filling the parlor as the crowd fell away like dropped jackstraws. Grace sagged to the floor, gasping and clutching at her throat as Emma reeled and staggered in a circle, her eyes wide, confused, her arms and hands jerking and spasming, the ax blade jutting from her bloodied head, the handle waving in the air over her back like a baton.

Suddenly she stiffened, and for one awful, endless instant, Emma Stevens stood on her toes with her body, arms, and legs steel-rod rigid, her eyes rolled up in their sockets. Then she collapsed. Her body seemed to deflate, sinking to the floor in a flaccid heap, facedown on the carpet.

Bill wanted to be sick. Carol moaned behind him. Many of the Chosen fell to their knees in prayer. Brother Robert rushed to Emma's side and began to administer the Sacrament of Extreme Unction. Martin helped Grace to her feet. She pointed to Emma's body and tried to speak, but no words came.

"I had to do it," Martin said nervously as he patted Grace's arm with a trembling hand. "She was killing you. It was do that or watch you die. I *had* to!"

As Carol clung to him, weeping, Bill glanced over at Jonah Stevens sitting quietly in his chair. His wife had just been murdered before his eyes, yet he showed no more emotion than if someone had swatted a fly.

Martin pointed to Bill.

"Tie him up! Quickly! Before something else goes wrong!"

Bill was too numb with shock to fight off the hands that gripped his arms and pulled him away from Carol. Emma Stevens . . . dead . . . murdered with an ax. He had seen death before, people slipping away in beds after he had administered Extreme Unction, and even the violence in Greenwich Village had occurred in the dark, to strangers. He'd never seen anything like this, never violent bloody murder in the light of day.

By the time he got a grip on the chaotic swirl of his thoughts and feelings, he was in a chair and coils of rope were snug about him. The monk was still ministering to Emma's body.

"Why are you here?" he said to Martin.

"To stop the Antichrist before he is born," Martin said.

Behind Martin he saw the women close in around Carol, and suddenly it was all horribly clear to him.

14.

Brother Robert gave a final blessing to the body of the poor unfortunate woman, then rose to his feet and surveyed the scene.

Father Ryan's shouts of protest mixed with the young woman's screams as she was led out of the parlor and down the hall. Brother Robert wanted to run away, but knew he could not. The young woman — his heart cried in response to her anguish — she was an innocent, unaware of what she carried. But there could be no mistake about the icy core of consummate evil he sensed growing within her. It chilled the room like a blast of arctic air, buffeting him like a gale. They had come to the right place.

He stared at the Jesuit. He had known that forcible restraint might be necessary, but the actual sight of a fellow priest bound to a chair was upsetting. He had a sense that everything was coming apart, that he was losing control of the situation — if indeed he had ever been in control.

He glanced again at the body lying at his feet and felt a gorge rise in his throat.

"What has happened here?" he cried to the Chosen. "We are not a rabble! We are doing the Lord's work! Killing is not the Lord's work!"

"You can't get away with this!" Father Ryan shouted.

"Sure they can," he heard the other man say in a flat, dry voice as he glared across the room at Martin. "They're going to kill us all."

Brother Robert stared at the one-eyed man. Hatred gushed from him. Here too was evil.

"Enough of such talk!" Brother Martin said. His voice had a distant sound in his own ears. "No talk of killing. This has been an awful, tragic mistake, and Martin will answer for it, to earthly authorities, and to God!"

"But I did it *for* God!"

Brother Robert was suddenly furious. "How dare you say that! I cannot accept that! I will *never* accept that!"

Martin looked at him with woeful eyes, then turned and ran from the house. Brother Robert heard a car engine sputter to life and its tires skid on the wet pavement as it roared away.

There was silence for a moment. Peace. Order. Everything was under control. He walked to a window and pulled down one of the heavy curtains. Gently he draped it over the dead woman's still form. Then he motioned the Chosen around him.

"Let us pray that God will guide Grace and give her the strength to do what must be done."

He began the Our Father while the Jesuit and the other man strained at their ropes. But Brother Robert knew the cords were stout, and the chairs were solid Victorian oak. Neither would give an inch.

15.

Carol struggled desperately with the stone-faced women who were dragging her toward the kitchen, but they were as determined to hold her as she was to get free, and there were four of them.

"Please, Aunt Grace!" she cried, sobbing in her helplessness. "*Please!* Don't do this to me!"

Grace wouldn't look at her. She walked ahead, carrying a Gristede's grocery bag. Carol could see swollen purple marks on her neck. Her voice when she spoke sounded hoarse and wheezy.

"It's God's will."

"But it's my baby! Mine and Jim's! It's all I have left of him! Please don't take that from me!"

"God's will," Grace said. "Not mine."

As they entered the kitchen, Grace glanced at the women holding Carol and pointed to the rectangular, pawfooted kitchen table.

"Put her there."

Carol screamed and struggled more violently than ever. For a moment she twisted one hand free and flailed at the women, but they soon trapped it again and subdued her. She used up what little of her strength remained to twist and writhe in their grasp as they each took a limb and lifted her into the air.

Loss of contact with the floor loosed the floodgates of panic and she unashamedly wailed out her fear. She called out to God to save her, to come and tell these maniacs that they weren't doing His will, to strike them dead on the spot for doing this to her.

The women ignored her. They might as well have been deaf. And Grace — Grace stood at the sink, washing her hands and working at something on the counter that was hidden by her bulk.

Then Carol felt the tabletop against her back. She lay pinned and helpless while Grace finished at the counter. When Grace turned, her face was a mask, eyes blood-shot and skin still mottled from the near strangulation. She was holding a wad of gauze in one of her gloved hands.

"Oh, please, Aunt Grace! *Please!*"

Her aunt pressed the gauze over her mouth and nose. It was wet and freezing cold, and the cloyingly sweet smell made her want to gag. The fumes stung her throat. Carol struggled but couldn't shake free for a clean breath.

Gradually, despite her fiercest efforts, a tingling, seductive lethargy crept up her limbs and claimed her.

16.

Grace sobbed as she held the chloroform over Carol's nose and mouth.

I know you'll never forgive me, dear. But someday I hope you'll understand.

Finally Carol's violent struggles eased. In pairs, first the arms, and then the legs, her limbs went slack. When Grace was satisfied that her niece was unconscious, she removed the gauze and watched a moment to make sure she was still breathing regularly. She didn't want to put her too far under. Too much chloroform risked liver damage, and even respiratory arrest. Grace wanted her to have just enough to block the pain and relax the muscles so that she could do what had to be done.

"Carol?" she said, looking for a response. There was none. She brushed her fingertip over her niece's eyelashes but the wink reflex was gone.

Good. She was under.

She smoothed the hair back from Carol's perspiring brow and looked into her eyes between the half-open lids.

"You're going to be all right," she whispered. "You must believe what I am telling you, dear. The Satan-child inside you will be gone, but *you're* going to be all right."

She straightened up and turned to the women.

"Okay," she said. "You can relax now, but don't move out of position."

She didn't want Carol to come to and roll off the table and hurt herself. She watched the women release Carol's limbs and noticed the blue-red marks where they had gripped her during her struggles. Each bruise was a tiny stab through the walls of her heart.

She pointed to the two women by Carol's legs.

"Undress her."

They hesitated a moment, glancing at each other — Grace sensed that they were as uncomfortable with this nightmare as she.

"From the waist down," Grace said, prompting them. "We can leave the dress on." As the two women began lifting the skirt of Carol's sundress,

Grace stepped over to the kitchen door and closed it. It shut out the sound of the prayers being said in the parlor. But that was not the reason she closed it. Although they were all here on a holy mission, she would not expose her niece's nakedness even accidentally to the male Chosen.

The women pulled the hem of the skirt up to Carol's neck and tucked the rest of it under her, then they slipped the beige cotton panties down past her ankles, revealing a tangle of light brown pubic hair. There was a sanitary napkin in place over the vaginal area. This too was removed but showed no trace of blood.

Grace stared wistfully at the unblemished napkin.

If only you'd lost the baby two days ago, none of this would be necessary.

Grace adjusted her surgical gloves and spread the sterile instruments out on their autoclave wrappers. She showed the two women by Carol's lower body how to position her legs — grasp each behind the knee and flex it up and back until the top of the thigh was almost touching the abdomen, then rotate it out to the side a few inches and hold it there.

The lithotomy position.

Grace had to look away from Carol's exposed perineum for a moment. It pained her to see her so helpless and vulnerable. But she steeled herself with the thought that it made the Antichrist vulnerable, too. That was all that —

Something moved on the floor near her feet. Grace looked down and stifled a cry. An infant, a naked nine-month old, was crawling toward her from beneath the table. It gripped her leg and pulled itself to a standing position. She could see now that the baby was a male. He looked up at her with wide, guileless blue eyes.

"Don't do it," the child said in the voice of a five-year-old. *"Please don't kill another helpless baby!"*

Grace bit down on her lower lip to keep from screaming. This must have been what Mr. Veilleur had warned her about. Her worst fear, her deepest guilt. She looked away.

Another infant, a female, was sitting atop Carol's abdomen, staring at Grace, a reproachful look on her chubby face. She spoke in the same voice.

"Haven't you killed enough of us already? Must you add one more innocent life to your long list of victims?"

Grace closed her eyes and felt the room begin to sway.

"You can't hide from us!" the voice continued, rising in volume. *"We are always with you. Everywhere you go, we are there, watching. Open your eyes, Grace Nevins. My friends are all here now. Open your eyes and see what you did to them!"*

Grace had to look. She blinked her eyes open for half a heartbeat and then squeezed them shut again, fighting back the vomit that surged into her throat, clutching the table edge to keep from falling.

Blood. The kitchen was awash with it. And everywhere were torn and mangled infants — ripped limbs, gouged faces, eviscerated torsos. *And they were moving!*

The child's voice never stopped.

"See what your instruments did to them? They'd be whole now, alive, working, loving, having babies of their own — if not for you. Please don't hurt another one of us. Please!"

Grace refused to break down. She straightened her back. This was Satan's work. This wasn't real. The demon wins by deceit and confusion. She would draw on the strength of the Lord to overcome him.

She opened her eyes and forced herself to stare at the bloody carnage. Of course it wasn't real. The other women still stood where she had placed them, oblivious to the charnel house around them.

"Murderess!" screamed the infant on Carol's abdomen, but Grace only smiled at it.

And then the gore and the mangled corpses and the accusatory infants began to fade. In seconds they were gone as if they had never been.

Grace realized she had been holding her breath. She shuddered and let it out, then forced herself back to the task before her. With a trembling hand she rubbed a Betadine-soaked gauze over Carol's pubic area, then dipped a large cotton-tipped applicator in the brown antiseptic and swabbed the inside of the vaginal canal. She felt perverse, as if she were violating her own niece, but it was for Carol's protection, to prevent infection. Only the Satan-child would be harmed.

And it *would* be harmed. Satan would need more than visions to deter her from this holy task.

17.

They were praying! Jonah ground his teeth in rage and frustration as he listened to the lousy bastards. He glared at Emma's covered body where she lay facedown on the carpet. The ax handle raised a tent over her head, but she was covered and apparently that made them feel better. Now they stood around mouthing their worthless Our Fathers and Hail Marys and Acts of Contrition. What fools.

The worst part was knowing that he could break free of this chair if only they'd allow him to move. He could bounce it, rock it, twist it until something broke, and then he'd be on his way to untying himself.

But they wouldn't let him move! Every time he tried to swing the chair or twist himself, hands would clamp onto his shoulders and hold him still.

All the years of waiting, preparing, hoping, planning — most of his life! — all about to be turned to shit by that fat bitch Grace Nevins in the other room. He couldn't stand the thought of it. He wanted to explode and kill them all!

And he *would* kill them all. Jonah memorized their faces. He would spend the rest of his days tracking them down one by one and slowly tearing the life from each of them!

Suddenly he froze.

Something in the room had changed. Something was in the air, gathering, growing. No one could see it, but Jonah could sense it. He forced himself to relax. It might not be too late yet. The One could still be salvaged.

He leaned back and watched. Something was about to happen.

Something *wonderful.*

18.

"You don't deserve to have those prayers on your lips!" Bill shouted to the unheeding room.

Heads bowed, hands folded, they prayed on.

Bill shut out the voices and thought of Carol. Her shrill pleas and piteous wails had cut off abruptly a few moments ago, and then he had heard the kitchen door shut.

My God, my God! What are they doing to her in there?

He knew damn well what they were doing, but his mind shied away from the horror of it, especially since they were doing it in the name of God.

If only they'd listen to him! If only they'd —

The drape that covered Emma moved.

He stared at it, watching for another sign of life, sure that he must have been mistaken. But then he saw it move again. His stomach lurched. This was no random postmortem twitch, if there was such a thing. Emma Stevens' body was rising up under the drapery.

The prayers died in the throats of Brother Robert and the so-called Chosen as they noticed it, too. The room was deathly still as they all stood and stared with gaping mouths at the body beneath the drapery rising to its feet. Bill, too, was transfixed, but he stole a glance at Jonah Stevens and was appalled at the sight of his bright, hungry eyes and flinty grin.

The drape slid to the floor and there stood Emma, the bloody ax still protruding from the back of her cloven skull. Slowly, she turned in an unsteady circle, her eyes wide and blank, her lips pulled back in a grim rictus, dried rivulets of blood streaking her forehead and cheeks.

The tableau suddenly fell apart as all but one of the Chosen males scrambled from the room, crying out and tripping over each other in their mad haste to flee the horror before them. A moment later, Bill heard a car speed away. No doubt some were running back to the safety of their homes and neighborhood churches, but a few remained huddled in the shadows of the hall.

Only Brother Robert stood his ground.

He pulled a long, slim, shiny brass crucifix from within his habit and thrust it before Emma's face.

"Back to Hell, demon!" he cried. "Back to the pit you crawled from!"

She cocked her head to the side and stared at the crucifix. Slowly she reached out and touched it, running a fingertip softly over the figure of Christ.

Then her hand moved quickly, gripping the crucifix and snatching it from Brother Robert's bandaged hand.

"No!" he cried. "You can't have that!"

But he made no move to retrieve it from her. He simply stood there and watched her, as did the other two living occupants of the room.

For a moment Emma held the crucifix up between them, gripping it by the short upper end, her palm wrapped around Christ's head, the crosspiece flush against the body of her hand.

With the light gleaming along the slim length of its long lower end, Brother Robert's crucifix looked like an art deco dagger. That thought was just passing through Bill's mind when Emma's arm straightened in a pistonlike thrust. Still grinning horribly, she drove the lower end of the crucifix deep into the left side of Brother Robert's chest.

With a shout of pain and shock, he staggered back. Blood spurted from the wound, blossoming across the scapular of his habit like a crimson flower opening to the morning. He stared down dully at the crucifix protruding from his chest, a bloodied Christ staring back as it bobbed up and down with the chaotic rhythm of his fibrillating heart. He looked up, looked around the room, his eyes finally coming to rest on Bill's.

Bill flinched from the impact of those frightened, agonized eyes. It took all of his strength not to turn away. Then he saw the life slip from them. Brother Robert's mouth opened but no words came forth, only a trickle of blood, running slowly into his beard. He toppled backward like a felled tree, twitched once, then lay still.

"May God have mercy on your soul," Bill said, and managed to really mean it.

He looked up and saw that Emma seemed to have forgotten her victim. Numbly he watched her step around him and move toward the kitchen, the protruding ax handle bobbing up and down over her back as she walked.

19.

Grace had paused briefly when she heard the cries and commotion from the parlor, but all was quiet now. No doubt Jonah Stevens had tried to break free from his bonds and the men had had to subdue him. It was good that there were so many of them out there. They would assure her of sufficient time to complete the task God had assigned her.

Everything was set, everyone was in position.

Carol's legs were propped in place by two of the women; her vagina and perineum had been prepped with the Betadine; a third woman was standing by her head, ready to administer more chloroform if necessary; the fourth woman was at Grace's side with a flashlight.

Grace lubricated the cold steel speculum and slipped it into Carol's vagina —

No. Not Carol's vagina. *A* vagina. She had to distance herself from this. That was the only way she was going to be able to go through it. This wasn't her niece, this was a doll, a lifelike mannequin.

She inserted the speculum sideways at first, then she rotated it ninety degrees and squeezed the handles. The speculum blades expanded and the corrugated tunnel of the vaginal vault lay open before her. A little adjustment of the angle and the cervix came into view, a pink, quarter-size dome with a deep dimple at its center — the cervical os, the gateway to Carol's uterus —

No! *The* uterus. *Somebody's* uterus. Anyone's but Carol's.

Beyond the cervix, through the os, the Antichrist grew.

She picked up the uterine sound, a slim metal rod with a small knob at the end. With this she would find the depth of Carol's — *someone's* —

uterine cavity. Once she knew that, she could avoid the major complication of an abortion — perforation of the uterus.

After sounding, she would gradually widen the cevical os with a progression of curved steel dilators, until it was open enough to pass the curette.

Then she would begin scraping.

She would clean the inner walls of the uterus until she had torn the embryonic Satan-child from his lair. And then she would take the bloody membranes and bits of tissue and burn them in the fireplace. And then she would scatter the resultant ashes to the wind.

And the world would be safe once more.

20.

Carol slowly became aware that she could see. She found herself looking down the length of her body. It was like looking into a canyon. Her pubes formed the floor and her raised thighs the walls. And framed within the canyon was Grace's head. She tried to move, to call out, but her limbs wouldn't respond.

Was it over? Had they killed her baby?

If only I could move!

Then she heard Grace's voice: "We're ready to begin."

It wasn't over yet! She still had a chance! But she needed help — she couldn't do this herself!

She thought of her parents, dead all these years now, and wished they could rush in and save her. Her Dad could yank Grace away and give his sister pure hell for what she was about to do.

She tried to move again and this time felt her limbs respond a little. But not enough! She had to get away, but she was too weak. Too weak to fight.

If only her Jim were here — he'd wipe the floor with these people and set her free.

But Jim was dead, just like her parents. And Emma, too. All dead. Maybe Bill and Jonah were dead now, as well. There'd be no help from the dead. She'd have to do it herself.

Herself. From now on she'd have to do *everything* herself. Starting now.

The women holding her legs seemed tense and distracted. No one was holding her arms. Carol gathered her strength and turned her body partly on its side. She tried to continue the motion in an effort to roll off the table. She heard Grace's voice shouting in the sudden confusion, felt hands rolling her onto her back again.

That was when she saw Emma's blank-eyed, blood-streaked, grinning face rise in the canyon above Grace's.

21.

As she was slipping the uterine probe toward the os, Grace glanced up and saw Carol staring at her, a look of horror on her face. Her legs began to move. Her pelvis writhed, ejecting the speculum. It clattered to the floor.

"She's coming to!" Grace cried. She looked up at the the woman standing at Carol's head. "Give her more chloroform! Quickly!"

But the woman wasn't paying attention. She too had a look of horror on her face. Grace noticed then that the woman's gaze was actually fixed above and behind her. Suddenly the other women were screaming and moving away from the table.

"What's wrong?" she cried. "Don't let her go!"

And then she felt a cold hand close on the back of her neck in a grip of iron.

22.

The horror of it was slow in coming, for Carol realized in that instant that no one was restraining her any longer. She managed to roll onto her side again, but rolled too far. Suddenly she was falling. She hit the the linoleum hard and lay there a moment, stunned.

She shook off the pain, the dizziness, the nausea, and used the table leg for support to pull herself to a kneeling position, instinctively pulling the skirt down around her legs. Even though she was naked beneath it, the thin fabric gave her a protected feeling.

In the center of the kitchen, Emma and Grace were struggling. Emma was trying to get a lock on Grace's throat but Grace was fighting her off this time, keeping her from getting the death grip she'd had in the parlor. And the ax — Oh, God, the ax was still in Emma's head!

The other women clung to the sides of the room, their backs pressed against the walls like passengers spinning on that amusement park ride, the Round Up.

A couple of the men came in from the front hall, timidly, like mice watching two cats locked in combat. They whispered to each other. Carol wondered where the rest of them were, especially that skinny one — Martin.

Suddenly Grace gave out with a choking cry and Carol saw that Emma was slowly reestablishing her stranglehold on her throat. Still weak and nauseous, Carol fought to make sense of her roiling emotions. She wanted Grace stopped, wanted her put away where she couldn't threaten or hurt her baby ever again, but she didn't want her killed — especially not at the hands of this walking horror that had once been Emma Stevens.

The two men seemed to gather some strength from Grace's peril. They rushed forward and tried to pull Emma away. Two of the women helped. This time they succeeded in freeing Grace by yanking Emma's arms outward and away, one in each direction. As Grace staggered free and gasped for breath, Emma shook off the Chosen and reached behind her head. With no change in her expression, no indication that she felt the slightest discomfort, she levered the ax handle up and down until it came free from her skull with a wet sucking noise.

Carol knew what was going to happen next, as did everyone else in the room, most likely, yet she could not move to prevent it. Neither could any of the Chosen. Neither could Grace.

Still grinning horribly, Emma raised the ax until its red-stained blade almost touched the ceiling. Grace screamed and raised her arms over her head, but to no avail. The ax swung down with blinding speed and crushing force.

Carol screamed and turned away before the blow struck, but she heard the awful splitting impact and heard screams and trampling feet, heard and felt a heavy *thump* on the floor.

Then silence.

Slowly Carol opened her eyes. Her head was down. She could see a limp, outstretched arm and blood on the floor on the far side of the table. Fighting nausea, she raised her head. Emma still stood in the center of the kitchen, stiff, swaying. She looked at Carol, and for an instant there was a spark of something in her dead eyes — maybe a spark of Emma. But if so, it was a miserable, infinitely sad Emma.

She raised her arm and pointed toward the door to the hallway. Shakily, Carol pulled herself to her feet and stumbled toward it, giving wide berth to Emma and averting her eyes from the still form in the pool of blood on the floor. As soon as she was past them, she ran.

As she reached the hall she heard the thud of a second body hitting the kitchen floor but she didn't look back.

When she got to the parlor door and saw Bill, bound in a chair but still alive, she almost lost it. She wanted to cry out his name and throw herself on him, wanted to clutch at him and sob out all the grief, rage, horror, and relief exploding within her. But she couldn't do that. That was what the old Carol would have done. She was now the new Carol.

Besides, even as she stood here, all her emotions seemed to be running out of her. An endless tunnel had opened inside her. All her feelings seemed to be flowing down its black length toward a yawning, bottomless pit, leaving her empty, cool, controlled.

"Carol!" Bill cried. "Thank God you're all right!"

She started toward him, then saw Brother Robert's body with the bloody crucifix jutting from his heart.

I don't know who's to be thanked, she thought, *but I've got a funny feeling it's not God!*

She looked away and darted behind Bill's chair.

"What happened in there?" he said, trying to look at her over his shoulder as her shaking fingers worked at the knots.

Carol experienced another of those sudden surges of hatred for Bill, a blazing rage that urged her to take a length of clothesline and strangle him with it. It frightened her. She shook it off.

"Grace is dead."

"I mean, to you. Are you okay?"

"I'll never be the same," she said, "but I'm okay, and so's the baby."

"Good!"

Oh, I hope it's good!

"What about . . . Emma?" he said.

"Gone. Like Grace. Both gone." A sob built in her throat but she forced it down the tunnel.

Finally the knot at the back came free and she began to unwind the rope from around Bill's chest. As the coils loosened, he managed to pull an arm free.

"I'll get the rest," he said. "See if you can get Jonah started."

Jonah . . . she almost had forgotten about him. He'd been so quiet. She turned toward her father-in-law and hesitated. He was sitting calmly in his chair, smiling at her. She pushed herself forward and knelt beside him to work on the knots.

"You did good!" he whispered.

"I didn't do anything."

"Yes, you did. You kept strong. You kept the baby. That's all that matters."

Carol looked into his eyes. He was right. Her baby — Jim's and hers. That was all that really mattered.

"We've got to get away," he said, still whispering.

"We?"

"Yes. You've got to hide. I can help. I can take you south. To Arkansas."

"Arkansas?"

"Ever been there?"

"No." In fact, Carol couldn't even remember if she had ever said the word before this.

"We'll keep on the move. Never stay in one place long enough for them to gather strength against the baby."

"But why? Why do they want to hurt him?"

She searched Jonah's face for an answer but there was nothing written there.

"You heard them," he said. "They think he's the devil."

"After what just happened, I wonder if they may be right," she muttered.

"Don't say that!" Jonah hissed. "He's your baby! Part of your flesh! It's your bound duty to protect him!"

Carol was stunned by his vehemence. He seemed genuinely concerned for the child. Maybe that was because he and Emma had never had a natural child of their own. But Emma was dead, murdered, and he didn't seem to care. All his concern was focused on the child. Why?

"I'll go to the police," she said.

"How can you be sure some of them won't be involved with these fool Chosen? Or won't join up later?"

The thought was chilling. This was becoming a paranoid nightmare.

"Here," Bill said, dropping to her side. "Let me finish those."

Carol noticed that his hands were shaking, too. She resisted the urge to claw at his face as he worked on Jonah's knots. These irrational bursts of hatred for Bill — she didn't understand them, but she wouldn't let them control her. She would dominate them. She would learn to control everything in her life now.

She stood and walked to the bay window to stare out at the clearing sky. She felt as if she were in the center of a great whirlwind and she desperately wished she knew which way to turn, where to go. The sun was low, shining through a break in the clouds on the horizon. The air was cold again. She clutched her arms across her chest and tried to rub away the chill.

And suddenly felt her blood freeze.

23.

As he loosened the last of the knots that bound Jonah Stevens, Bill heard a low moan, a tragic mixture of shock and pain. He glanced up and saw Carol standing by the bay window. Her back was to him and she was swaying back and forth, as if she were standing on the deck of a ship in a storm.

"Carol? Are you all right?"

He saw her stiffen. She turned to him, her hands thrust stiffly into the pockets of her sundress, her face a deathly white.

"No," she said in a soft, hoarse voice. "I may never be all right again."

She looked as if she were about to keel over any minute. He rushed to her side and took her arm.

"Here. Sit down."

She shook off his hand, then lowered herself to the window seat where she sat with her shoulders hunched, trembling. She looked up at him, her attempt at a smile was awful.

"I'm okay," she said.

Bill didn't believe her, so he went to the phone and lifted the receiver.

"What do you think you're doing?" Jonah said in a low voice.

"Calling the police."

Bill saw a look pass between Carol and Jonah. What had they been whispering about while she was working on his knots?

"I don't think that's such a good idea," Carol said.

Bill didn't want to argue with her. He too was shaking all over, inside and out. He had seen things today he never would be able to explain, had never dreamed possible. He needed the police here to impose some order, some semblance of a sane reality.

He put the receiver to his ear. There was no dial tone.

"Line's dead anyway," Bill said. "But what's wrong with the police?"

"They might be involved."

That was preposterous. "I can't —"

"Bill, will you drive us to the airport?"

"Who?"

"Jonah and me. I've got to hide for now. It's the only way I can be sure of being safe, of saving my baby."

"I can help her disappear," Jonah said.

He glanced at Jonah and saw him nodding. He remembered the complete lack of emotion as his wife was murdered before his eyes. The man was a snake! Bill couldn't let Carol go with him.

"No! It's crazy! This can all be straightened out! The police can round up these nuts and —"

"Jonah can drive me," she said, "or I can drive myself. But I'm going now, and I'd like you to come along. I may never see you again."

Bill stared at Carol. She had changed. Whatever iron had been scattered through her personality in the past had been drawn together and tempered to a solid steely core by what had happened to her today. Her eyes looked out at him with unswayable determination. He felt so damn *helpless!*

Bill forced the words out. "Okay. I'll drive you."

Maybe he could change her mind on the way.

24.

Carol faced Bill at the Eastern Airlines gate.

"Time to go," she said.

She felt scared and alone. Jonah was going to be with her, but that was like being alone. Yet she could see no other way. Head south where things weren't so organized, get lost in between the small towns — that was the plan.

"Will you be all right?" Bill said, his eyes searching her face.

She hid her real feelings from him. He had been trying to talk her out of this since they had left Monroe, but she had no choice. She had to go.

"I think so. We'll buy a car once we reach Atlanta, then we'll drive off. I suppose we can be easily traced as far as Atlanta. After that, Jonah promises we'll be almost impossible to find."

And that was just what she wanted right now. She was going to have her baby and raise him in peace and quiet. And no one was going to stop her.

She watched Bill glance over to where Jonah was standing by the ramp, waiting to board with her. When Bill looked back at her, his expression was stricken, his eyes full of foreboding.

"I don't trust him, Carol," he said in a low voice. "He's hiding something. Don't go with him."

"I have to, Bill." She didn't particularly trust Jonah herself, but knew he would protect her and the baby.

"Does he know what he's doing?"

"I think so. I hope so."

She saw Bill's hands curl into fists of frustration as he said, "God, I wish there was something I could do!"

They stood in silence for a moment, then Bill spoke in an even lower voice. He seemed to fumble for the words.

"Carol . . . what happened back at the Hanley place?"

She did her best to keep her expression neutral, blocking out the horrors of the afternoon. She'd work them out later.

"You know," she said. "You were there."

"Emma was dead, Carol. As dead as can be. I know. I sat there looking at her unblinking eyes and her motionless chest before they covered her up. Yet she got up and killed two people."

"Then I guess she wasn't dead."

She knew how cold that sounded, but she couldn't help it. This was the only way she could deal with any of what had happened and what might yet come.

"She was *dead*, Carol. But she got up and saved you and your baby from your aunt. That wasn't Emma in Emma's body. It was someone else — some*thing* else. What's going *on* here?"

Something wants to kill my baby and something else is trying to protect it!

This was the first time she had allowed the idea to put itself into words, and the bald truth of it terrified her. But the truth was there, staring at her, and she had to face it.

And she had to choose sides.

There was a monstrous struggle going on, and she seemed to be at the heart of it. She dreaded the thought of which side of that struggle might be protecting her child. But no matter what the nature of her ally, there was no question with which side she would align herself.

She would chose for her baby, now and forever.

"I don't know what's going on, Bill. All I know is that my baby was threatened and now he's been saved. That's all I care about at the moment."

"I care about that, too," he said. "But I've got to know more." Another glance over his shoulder at Jonah. "I bet he knows more than he's saying."

"Maybe he does. Maybe he'll tell me." Although she wasn't sure she wanted to know.

"We're being used," Bill said suddenly.

Carol didn't let him see that she instantly knew exactly what he meant.

She said, "I don't understand."

"Jim, you, me, Grace, Emma, that monk, even Jonah over there — I don't *know* it but I *feel* it: we've all been used like pawns in some sort of game. And the game's not over yet."

"No," she said with leaden certainty. "It's not."

Suddenly she felt another of those inexplicable bursts of rage at him. *Run out of facile rationalizations, smart ass?* The words very nearly escaped her before she bit them back.

The loudspeaker announced the last call for passengers to board the Eastern flight to Atlanta.

"Gotta go," she said quickly, forcing good feelings for Bill to the surface. "Tell the police whatever you know, or as much as you dare."

"I guess this is good-bye, then," Bill said. "Let me hear from you once in a while, to know that you're safe."

He reached for her hand but she embraced him instead, kissing him on the cheek.

"I'll be in touch."

And she would. She fully intended to return to New York sporadically for brief periods to answer any police questions about the three corpses in the mansion and to settle any problems regarding the estate. Once the baby was born, she was going to use Jim's inherited fortune to insulate their child from any and all outside threats. She would make the money grow, and one day it would all go to him.

Turning, she hurried to join Jonah where he waited by the boarding ramp.

TWENTY-FOUR

1.

The setting sun had gained some borrowed time up here, miles in the air. It shone redly through the oval window at her shoulder. Jonah sat on her left, head back, eyes closed, hands folded in his lap. He could have been either dozing or praying. Carol doubted it was either.

She allowed herself to relax just a little. She let her shoulders sag to ease the tension in them, but kept her hands balled into fists. The Chosen were below and behind her. She and the baby were up here, out of their reach. Things were under control for the moment.

Suddenly she felt a chill. A frozen, crystalline locus was expanding deep within her, sucking the heat from her tissues. Quickly it grew, taking her over, radiating icy malevolence. It coursed through her limbs. Sheer viciousness shot from her, streaking outward and down, bathing the globe below.

2.

Below and to the south, in Memphis, a burly white man watches Martin Luther King speaking on the news. He doesn't listen to the words. He doesn't have to. Always the same damn thing. He hates these uppity niggers making trouble everywhere, especially here in the South, hates all of them, but most of all he hates this one with his Nobel Peace prize and his ability to get his face on the TV screen and into everybody's home whenever he wants.

And now, in this instant, the man decides that he's had all he can take. He ain't gonna sit back and grouse any more like some piss-ant wimp. He's gonna *do* something about it.

He goes to the closet, pulls out his rifle, and begins to clean it.

3.

Far to the east, in Bengal, a one-armed man who is far older than he looks suddenly dreams of the burned-out ruins of an ancient temple and decides, despite his many numerous futile attempts in the past, to search once more for a large mottled egg that may lie hidden there.

4.

To the west, in Los Angeles, a Jordanian student watches once more the news footage of Robert F. Kennedy announcing his intention to seek the presidential nomination of the Democratic Party. He has searched the channels all day, watching the footage over and over. It seems amazing and somehow sinful to him that a man would seek the same post as his assassinated brother. A half-formed plan abruptly coalesces into firm determination.

He forms his hand into the shape of a gun and points the finger-barrel at RFK's toothy grin. His voice is barely a whisper.

"Bangbang!"

5.

Farther to the west, in Indochina, an ancient primordial force, known to the locals as *Dat-tay-vao*, begins a slow, meandering journey that will bring it halfway around the world to the United States.

INTERLUDE ON CENTRAL PARK WEST - III

Mr. Veilleur stares out his apartment window at the growing darkness, thinking.

The Chosen have failed. He doesn't need to call anyone to know that. He has sensed the burgeoning strength of his ancient enemy, and that is enough. The enemy is leaving for now and the woman carrying him is alerted and will be on guard. He will be born, and with no one to oppose him, his power will grow. With luck, he will not realize that he is unopposed, so he will remain cautious. The world will be safe until he grows to manhood.

Mr. Veilleur turns and glances at his wife, busy setting the table for Sunday dinner.

And then he'll come for us — but mostly for me.

For himself, he doesn't care much. He has lived long enough. But what of the world? What of the horrors the enemy will bring about when he comes of age?

Ah, well. That will be someone else's problem. And it will be a couple of decades hence. Maybe he and the wife will be lucky.

Maybe they'll be dead by then.

EPILOGUE

As suddenly as it had begun, the dark radiance diminished, shrinking to a cold, tight, hard little knot, and then it was gone. Carol shuddered.

Oh God, what's happening to me?

She looked at Jonah. She found him staring at her, smiling and nodding, his eyes aglow.

"I . . . I have to go to the bathroom," she said. She was feeling weak and nauseous. She didn't want to be sick on the floor.

He hopped out of his seat and stood in the aisle to let her by. As she rose, the cabin seemed to spin around her. A passing stewardess reached for her outstretched hand to steady her, but Carol pulled away and clenched it into a fist between her breasts. She wasn't letting anyone touch her hands until she'd had a chance to shave off the fine litle hairs she had found sprouting from her palms a few hours ago.